DOWN DEEP

KIMBERLY KINCAID

Get down!

♡ Kim Kincaid

KIMBERLY KINCAID ROMANCE

DOWN DEEP

This book is a work of fiction. Any resemblance to persons, living or dead, or places, events or locations is purely coincidental. The characters are all productions of the author's imagination.

❀ Created with Vellum

DEDICATION

This book is dedicated to Cat Parisi,
without whom I would be a scattered mess.
XO

ACKNOWLEDGMENTS

So many people offer help, support, and all-out love (by way of everything from hugs to writing advice to wine) when it comes to putting together a book. I knew going in to DOWN DEEP that I was going to need all three when it came to getting Gamble and Kennedy just right on the page. This book simply wouldn't exist without the following people.

Reggie Deanching of R Plus M Photography, BT Urruela, Cara Gadero, and Jaycee DeLorenzo, you were all instrumental in getting the cover perfect (*perfect*!) for this book. I am so grateful. Nicole Bailey, as always, you keep me and my dropped commas and wonky hyphens in line. KP Simmon and the "team of awesome" at Ink Slinger, you are the very best dream team a girl could ask for.

Rachel Hamilton and Cat Parisi, I would not get through half a day without you on either side of me, holding my hands! I cannot even describe in words how much I adore you both.

Amanda E. Fletcher, my avid Facebook reader, who came up with Chaz McCory's name for this book. Thank you for following and being so darned smart!

To the lovely Geoff Symon, who tells me things like whether or not fire destroys fingerprints, and the equally lovely Dana Carroll, who uses her super-nurse skills to tell me where to wound my characters, you both keep my facts straight, and I am so very grateful for your giant brains and good hearts.

Avery Flynn and Robin Covington, I simply don't have enough words to say what I feel for our friendship and how much it fuels my writing, my heart, and my sanity. I love you both.

And oh, the girls and Mr. K. After twenty-five books, you still put up with me and all my writerly quirks. Your belief in my journey humbles me, and I am able to write true, deep love, because I know it every day. You are my everything.

1

Ian Gamble was going to get good and fucking drunk. A solid bender wasn't usually in his repertoire, what with the whole twenty-four hours on, forty-eight hours off thing he did at the fire house. By the time he caught up on his sleep and his workouts, there wasn't usually much time to get shit-faced and recover, especially if he was going to abide by Remington Fire Department's eight-hours-from-bottle-to-throttle rule. Being Station Seventeen's engine lieutenant and a former Marine, Gamble was big on regs. Order. Control.

But tonight was an exception. One he made every August. One he'd continue to make until the day he went into the ground.

Because he was the only person left from his recon unit who could.

"Hey, boss! Who died?"

The words, spoken by Gamble's engine-mate and resident smartass, Shae McCullough, ripped into the old scars he kept hidden, turning them fresh and raw. "What?"

She traded a tiny bit of the sparkle in her stare for

concern, sliding into the space next to him at The Crooked Angel's bar. There was no way McCullough could know how spot-on her words had been, namely because Gamble had never told another living soul all the gory details (okay, fine...or any details) of his past as a Marine, aside from his CO and the headshrinker they'd made him see after he'd come home from Afghanistan. But he had to give his friend credit. She wasn't an idiot. In fact, right now, she was looking at him shrewdly enough to make his heart pump out a potent cocktail of defenses and dread.

"That's a mighty serious look you're wearing," McCullough said, and yeah, it was time to lock this shit up, no matter how tight the two of them were.

"All good. Just having a drink since we're not on shift tomorrow." Gamble picked up his beer for a nice, long draw as proof, rolling his shoulders beneath his T-shirt and leather jacket combo. "What about you?"

The gruff redirect worked, just as he'd known it would. "I'm watching DC lose her shirt to Faurier," McCullough said brightly.

Shit. "Please tell me that's not literal."

Without waiting for a response, he turned from his spot at the bar to laser a stare at the pool table by The Crooked Angel's side door. Lucy de Costa, who had been nicknamed "DC" by both McCullough and their other engine-mate, Kellan Walker, on her first day in-house a couple of months ago, was standing among the other firefighters from Seventeen and a few cops from the Thirty-Third district, wearing an epic frown and—thankfully—her damned shirt.

McCullough threw her head back and laughed. "Please. Girlfriend might be a rookie, but she's not making *that* rookie mistake. Especially not with a horndog like Faurier."

Gamble exhaled in relief. Not that it was technically any

of his business who de Costa got down and dirty with. But she was brand-spanking-new to the RFD, and it was his job to look out for her. Plus, if she decided to ride the bone train with their rescue squad's second-in-command—or any other firefighter at Seventeen, for that matter—it would likely make Gamble's universe a fuck-ton more complicated in terms of getting her *and* her bed-buddy to focus. Especially when shit started burning down.

"I assume you're talking about Lucy," said McCullough's live-in boyfriend and tech brainiac for the police department's elite intelligence unit, James Capelli, as he walked up to stand beside her. Gamble wasn't shocked to see the guy, mostly because he and McCullough were far enough gone for each other to be attached at the hip most of the time, but also because Gamble's head was on a permanent swivel. He'd seen Capelli approaching from fifteen paces out. Not to mention where he, and nearly everyone else in the bar, had been in the room for the last fifteen minutes on top of that. Score one for the highest state of awareness. Not that Gamble could turn that shit off even if he wanted to.

Which he didn't.

"Oh, hey, babe!" McCullough's run-of-the-mill smile became something altogether deeper in less than the span of a heartbeat at the sight of Capelli. "Yeah. She's scrappy, and she talks a good game, but Faurier's kicking her ass pretty good at eight-ball."

"That's definitely accurate on all counts," Capelli agreed. "But as far as her getting too personal with him, I don't think you have anything to worry about. I just overheard her telling Quinn she'd rather be skinned alive with kitchen shears than date a fellow firefighter."

Gamble's brows lifted to match the *huh* winging through his veins, and he slid another glance at the spot where de

Costa now stood talking to Station Seventeen's lead paramedic. "I'm assuming that's a direct quote," he said.

Capelli sent an ultra-serious look past his thickly framed glasses. "I have an eidetic memory, Lieutenant. Not to put too fine a point on it, but yes, any time I quote someone, it's exact."

McCullough laughed, clearly used to and enamored with the guy's quirks. "Looks like DC's virtue is safe. Even if her pride isn't," she added. Spinning her gaze back to Gamble, she said, "You coming over for a game? I'm not nearly as bad at eight-ball as de Costa. Bet I could take you."

"Nah. Not tonight."

"You sure?" Surprise mixed with the slight hint of worry on her face. "You've been sitting here by yourself for almost an hour."

Ah, hell. He'd nearly gone to a shitty dive bar instead of their regular hangout for this very reason. Firefighters were a perceptive bunch, their lives depending on it and all. He probably shouldn't be shocked that McCullough had noticed the personal-space bubble he'd created around himself. The two of them were fairly tight, with her having the most tenure on engine besides him. On any other night, he would've taken her up on her challenge, then had to keep every last one of his wits about him to try and beat her. But tonight wasn't any other night. It was the only night out of the year when his fire house family wasn't enough to dull his memories.

Five had gone out. One had come back. The only thing that could dull the anniversary of that came in a shot glass and clocked in at eighty proof.

"Yeah. I'm sure," Gamble said. "I've got something to take care of over here."

Whether McCullough believed him or had decided to

let him off the hook, he couldn't be sure, but either way, she simply shrugged. "Suit yourself, chicken."

"That's Lieutenant Chicken to you," Gamble reminded her.

"Oooh, I kind of like the sound of that." When he skewered her with the most "don't you dare" stare he could work up, she grinned and—smartly—reconsidered. "But maybe I'll stick with good, old-fashioned Gamble, just for the sake of tradition...and not being assigned to scrub the fire house toilets with a toothbrush during next shift."

"You're in love with a smart woman," Gamble told Capelli, who finally allowed a smile to sneak a half-path over his mouth.

"I'm well aware of her aptitude."

"Aw, flattery will get you everywhere, baby," McCullough said with a laugh. She took a step back, letting Capelli thread his arm around her shoulders before turning back to give Gamble one last smile. "You know where we'll be if you change your mind."

Gamble lifted his chin in acknowledgment. "Copy that."

Watching the two of them head back toward the pool table, he couldn't help but shake his head a little at the idea of a relationship that deep. Sexual attraction, he got. A couple of hot-sex hookups here and there to satisfy said attraction? He got those, too. But the sort of no-holds-barred love that McCullough and Capelli and a few other members of Seventeen had tumbled into lately seemed as alien to him as little green men, complete with flying saucers and moon dust.

People swore they saw that shit; hell, they believed it in their bones. But as far as he was concerned, they were all fucking crazy.

"Well, well. Lieutenant Gamble. Aren't you a sight for sore eyes?"

The throaty, feminine voice hit Gamble point-blank from the business end of the bar, and God *damn* it, he must have more of a beer buzz than he'd thought. He was almost always hyper-aware of his surroundings—especially when they involved someone as sexy as Kennedy Matthews. Yet, here she was in front of him, wearing a form-fitting red top and a brash, brows-up stare, and for a fleeting second, he wondered if her smile tasted as tart as it looked.

"If you say so," he told her, while snuffing out the unbidden thought. Not that he hadn't entertained it dozens of times before, or thought about tasting Kennedy in places other than her mouth. But as the manager and head bartender of their regular hangout, she was almost as much a part of his inner circle as his fellow firefighters, and—like his rookie—Gamble knew far better than to muddy that water with a good, fast fuck. "Can I get another beer, please?"

Kennedy's darkly lined eyes widened for just a heartbeat before narrowing over the frost-covered bottle in his hand, the piercing in her eyebrow glinting in the soft overhead light of the bar.

"That one is nearly full."

"Not for long." He was already on his way to a decent beer buzz, courtesy of the bartender who had been working this section of the bar before Kennedy had come out of the back. He'd stick to beer for now to keep a low profile. Once everyone from Seventeen started heading home in a little while, he'd kick his night into high gear.

Kennedy paused. She was tougher than she looked, which was saying something since she had as much ink and even more hardware than Gamble did, with a watercolor tattoo that spanned from the middle of her bicep to her shoulder and the top of her chest, and tiny silver studs and hoops marching all the way up her left ear to match the piercing in her eyebrow. But he returned her calculating stare with one of his own, until she lifted one sleekly muscled shoulder and let it drop.

"It's your liver, tough guy."

She reached into the cooler built in beneath the bar, popping the cap off the beer she'd unearthed and placing it over a napkin on the glossy wood in front of him before turning to saunter off. Gamble watched her go, his eyes lingering on the way her ass filled out her jeans like a fuckable version of an upside-down heart. He couldn't deny being tempted. Shit, he'd have to be pulseless not to be. But even if he *did* decide to break his personal protocol and see if Kennedy was up for blowing off a little steam between the sheets, it wouldn't be tonight.

Tonight wasn't about anything other than him, a bottle of Patrón Platinum, and the ghosts he'd never shake.

As far as Kennedy Matthews was concerned, tequila made men dangerous. So, when the most dangerous man she could think of upgraded from the beers he'd been drinking for the last two hours to two shots of Patrón Platinum, it definitely sent her red flags waving in the wind.

She could handle a guy like Lieutenant Gamble sober, no problem. Drunk?

Christ, it was going to be a long night.

There was a plus side, she thought, as she poured the two shots of high-end tequila he'd just ordered. She'd never had to kick him out of her bar before; in fact, Gamble had always been essentially respectful, albeit in a dark and deadly, I-could-eat-you-alive-I-just-choose-not-to sort of way. They weren't friends, at least, not like she and Shae and Quinn and Kellan's fiancée, Isabella, were. They definitely weren't close, like she and her co-bartender, January, were. But January also ran all of the admin at Station Seventeen, and The Crooked Angel had been the go-to hangout for both the firefighters and the detectives down at the Thirty-Third for years now. Gamble might've given Kennedy a covert up-and-down look that had made her skin heat and her mind wander every now and then, but he knew better than to sling shit in her bar.

Probably.

Fucking tequila.

Kennedy straightened her shoulders and placed the two shot glasses on a small serving tray. She'd have to keep an eye on him, for sure, but she'd handled far worse than a drunk firefighter, even one who was sexy as sin and built like a German tank. The last time Gamble had gotten chemically inconvenienced in here—God, it had to have been a year since she'd last seen him order shots of tequila—he'd done so thoroughly but without fanfare. As long as he remained well-behaved and didn't try to drive, they'd be all set.

"You're drinking off the top shelf tonight, huh, Lieutenant?" she asked after taking the handful of steps needed to get back to his spot at the bar. Like clockwork, he'd chosen the seat at the very end of the wood. It was a vantage point thing, Kennedy guessed. Like most of the other cops and firefighters who frequented The Crooked Angel, Gamble never seemed to like his back to face anything other than a wall. Hell if she didn't know the feeling.

He arched a brow over his black-coffee stare. "You worried I'm not good for it?"

At that, she had to laugh. "If I was, you wouldn't still be sitting here." Kennedy tapped one glossy, dark red fingernail against the shot glass in her hand. "All I meant was, overindulging isn't really your style. You haven't gone hard-core with your liquor in about a year."

"You're perceptive," he said, the slightest hint of surprise coloring his tone.

"Don't sound so shocked." Kennedy put the shot glass on the bar in front of his thickly corded, very inked forearm, following it with the second shot of tequila before continuing. "I'm a bartender. It's my job to be perceptive."

"Hmm." He threw back one of the shots without so much as a wince or a shudder. Placing the empty glass on the bar between them, he asked, "Can I get two more of these?"

Confusion prickled a path up her spine. "You haven't done the other one."

"There you go, being all perceptive again."

Gamble followed the remark with enough of a dark smile to sand the edges off his words. For a hot second, Kennedy considered flirting back with him. God knew the orgasm train hadn't rolled through her station in longer than she cared to admit. But just as top-dollar tequila made men dangerous, guys like Gamble made *her* dangerous, and she'd stayed out of trouble for far too long to fuck up her track record now.

No matter how hot that wicked smile of his had just made her.

Still, an odd memory surfaced from the back hallways of her brain, keeping her feet rooted to the bar mats when she'd been about to turn away. He'd done this last year, too, ordering two shots for each one he'd taken, and something in his stare made her say, "You know, in addition to having a flair for serving up copious amounts of liquor, I also happen to be a kickass listener."

"Do you."

Gamble didn't elaborate, simply shifting his huge frame against the ladder back of the bar stool where he'd slung his leather jacket, and God, she should've known he'd make her work for it.

"Sure." Kennedy shrugged, studying him through the low light of the bar. "People come in here all the time, getting all lubricated and needing an ear to bend. Listening goes with the territory. In case you feel like unloading whatever's on your mind."

"Who says I've got anything on my mind? Maybe I'm just here to get all lubricated," he said, and she let him know he wasn't the only one with a dark smile by allowing one corner of her mouth to kick upward.

"You talk a good game, but I have eyes. A guy comes into my bar and orders expensive tequila, then only drinks half of what's in front of him, there's no way there isn't a story there. I'm just wondering if you need to tell it."

A muscle tightened beneath the heavy stubble on Gamble's jaw, just the slightest pull and release before his expression went blank again. "Thanks for the offer, but the only thing I need right now is another two shots of tequila."

"Suit yourself," Kennedy said. At least she'd tried. "But if I pour it, it goes on your tab."

He followed her stare to the untouched shot of tequila that looked like it was going to stay that way, pulling out a twenty along with his credit card and placing both in front of her. "I told you, I'm good for it."

Sliding the card and the cash off the bar, she headed to

the alcove housing both the register and whatever extra barware they could fit on the shelves built into the open space. She carefully stored Gamble's card and the tip in their designated spaces before turning to fill his order for liquid crazy, but she'd barely made it three steps from the alcove before a voice stopped her in her tracks.

"Hey. Hey, sweetheart!" A guy wearing a meticulously pressed button-down shirt, a dark gray vest, and a pair of glasses that all but screamed "world's biggest hipster" snapped his fingers twice in rapid succession. "What does a guy have to do to get a little service around here?"

Kennedy's heart skipped faster in her chest, although she made certain not to let it show as she turned toward the guy, who—judging by his glassy eyes and balls the size of Canada—had clearly gotten a head start drinking at a different bar. He hadn't been there thirty seconds ago. She was sure of it. She made it a point to do regular head counts on her patrons and their locations after midnight, when the crowd was thinner but also potentially stickier. Although the finger-snapping thing made her want to tell him to kiss her sugar-sweet ass, guys like Hipster Dude were mostly harmless. Definitely not worth the effort it took to tell them off, or the flak she'd take for the bad service. Even if this douche canoe deserved it.

"Welcome to The Crooked Angel," she said with a perfectly cordial smile she knew didn't come within a nautical mile of her eyes. "What can I get you?"

"What craft beers have you got?" Hipster Dude asked, and Kennedy listed off a few before he chose the cheapest one.

"Did you want to pay as you go, or start a tab?" she asked, praying he'd go for door number one. She'd already sprung their cook, Marco, and her fellow bartender, Javier, for the night since they were within an hour of last call, plus, she still had to keep an eye on tall, dark, and tequila over there in the corner.

"The view in this place doesn't suck," the guy said, giving Kennedy a leering once-over that made her reconsider telling him to kiss her ass. "I'll start a tab."

"Great." She bit her tongue to keep from punctuating the sentence with "kill me now". She filled Hipster Dude's order, then Gamble's, then got started on the various breakdown tasks she could do while the bar was still open. Track by track, songs filtered down from the overhead speakers, measuring the passing time in bass lines and catchy lyrics. Kennedy divided her attention between her work and her remaining customers, serving up a couple more crappy beers to Hipster Dude and cashing out three of the seven people still lingering over one last game of darts. Gamble ordered two more pairs of shots, doing only one of each and leaving a total of four completely untouched on the bar, and the whole thing sparked her curiosity more than it should. But he was a quiet drunk—if he even *was* drunk, because, God, it was impossible to tell—so Kennedy let him be.

She lifted a tray of clean pint glasses to the shelf beside the alcove, her shoulders and back both squalling in protest despite the fact that her body was well-used to the rigors of running a bar and grill. But between the five hours she'd burned in the office on paperwork, the four more she'd already spent in the front of the house with one more to go, and the last two dozen nights she'd spent in the exact same way, her muscles were a tight, tangled mess. Kennedy didn't mind the work; hell, she'd busted her ass for the privilege of an honest living. She *did* take exception to the reminder that she had physical limits, though. She hadn't clawed her way out of one of North Point's shittiest neighborhoods by being weak.

Why the hell had Gamble ordered eight shots of tequila and only done four?

Kennedy's chin hiked at the utterly random thought, and, okay, she officially needed to toughen up. Yeah, she'd put in a ton of hours lately, and more yeah, Gamble's drinking habits had leaned toward the bizarre tonight. But she couldn't blow what little energy she had left worrying over either. She had a bar to manage, and she took her job at The Crooked Angel as serious as a sledgehammer.

And that meant nothing was going to stand in the way of her closing down her bar for the night, nice and quiet.

Business as usual.

2

"**O**kay, everybody, last call! Drink 'em or dump 'em, because it's time to go home."

Kennedy's voice echoed through the bar, working its way under Gamble's skin. She had the sort of voice that was caught between velvet and gravel, kind of like a muscle car at a low idle. You never knew if it would purr or scream, but no matter what, you could count on it being sexy as fuck.

Christ. With a thought like that, he *must* be drunk.

Grabbing his jacket, Gamble pushed off from the bar and turned toward the bathroom. He'd had the good sense to walk the four miles from his apartment to the bar. Humping it had never hurt a guy, and he'd responded to way too many drunk driving accidents not to know what an epically stupid move that was. The trip home would still take long enough to make things uncomfortable if he didn't hit the head before he left, though, so he made his way past the pool table and down the narrow corridor by the side door. The bar was eerily quiet without the overhead music on, although the chatter and footsteps of the half-dozen stragglers Kennedy was herding toward the front door kept things from total silence. An ache knifed through Gamble's chest as he thought of the four shots of tequila still sitting on the bar, and he let it settle between his ribs, nice and hard.

Five had gone out. One had come back.

Funny how a seven-year-old wound could still bleed.

He shook his head and tamped down the memory. He'd have plenty of time to let his ghosts have their way with him once he got back to his apartment. For now, he needed to pay his bar tab and get gone. Being vulnerable in public, in any sense of the word, wasn't part of his game plan. He might've taken strides toward getting obliterated tonight, but he wasn't all the way there yet. He'd save the most hardcore part of this little ritual for when no one would be around to see it.

Including Kennedy, who was far more perceptive—not to mention far more provocative—than anyone should be. At least, as far as tonight was concerned.

Gamble finished up in the bathroom and made his way back down the long stretch of the hallway. This section of The Crooked Angel was the only part of the place he hated, mainly because the hallway led to a section of the game room with limited visibility to the rest of the main dining room. He had six strides to go before he'd reach the corner that would give him eyes on the bar, and he'd only covered three before his senses tripped into red alert.

"Okay, buddy." Kennedy's voice sounded off from around the blind corner. "You're all cashed out and you're the last person in here. It's time to go."

"I have a better idea," came a male voice Gamble instantly recognized as belonging to the dickhead with the vest and the over-styled hair who had been a couple stools down from him at the bar, and his fingers knotted into fists at his sides. "Why don't you bring that fine ass of yours just a little bit closer so we can have some real fun?"

Gamble froze, a fresh burst of adrenaline sharpening the blurry edges of his buzz. As badly as he wanted to barrel around the corner to pummel the shit out of this guy (and oh, he really. Really. Wanted to), he forced himself to take a split-second for a more tactical approach. Letting his impulses dare him into a situation he couldn't see was dangerous on so many levels.

Wasn't *that* just something he knew by heart?

He snuffed out his inner voice, silently stealthing forward until both Kennedy and the dickhead came into view. Her back was to Gamble, and—his gut sank—she must have been putting up stools on the customer side of the bar, because she was within arm's length of the guy. Even though the dickhead stood with his back to the bar, he was too focused on Kennedy to notice anything else, and Gamble measured no less than a dozen variables with light-ning-fast speed as she gave up an icy reply.

"As tempting as that offer is, I'm going to pass. Door's that way." She gestured with a firm lift of her chin. "Don't let it hit you on the ass on your way out."

"Come on," the guy said, making a noise of disgust. "Don't be so uptight. I've got something that'll loosen you right up. Here, let me show you."

He reached out to grab her shoulder, and Gamble stepped forward without even realizing he'd moved. Not, it turned out, that Kennedy needed him to. The guy had no sooner made contact with her body than she'd swung her arm under and around his, pivoting to guide him face-first into the bar and capture his upper body in one of the fastest and most solid hammerlock holds Gamble had ever seen.

"You're touching something that doesn't belong to you," she said, the heel of her left hand pressing hard against the back of his shoulder and her right fingers curled around the wrist of the limb she'd wrenched behind his back. "If you want to keep this arm in one piece"—she tightened her grip and lifted until the guy let out a corresponding yelp—"then I suggest you take it, and the rest of yourself, out of my bar. Right now."

"Get your hands off me, you frigid bitch!" The guy struggled, then quickly stilled once he discovered how well that was going to work out for him. "I was trying to do you a favor."

Again, Gamble went to move, but again, Kennedy proved she needed zero assistance.

"What was that?" she asked, applying another hint of pressure to the back of his shoulder, and the guy made a noise suspiciously close to a whimper.

"Fine. Whatever," he spat in concession. "I'm out of here. This place sucks, anyway."

Kennedy released her grip, but only enough to turn him away from the bar and maneuver him toward the door with a pointed shove. The guy opened the door with his free hand, and only then did Kennedy fully release his arm so he could stumble through it, pushing the heavy mahogany closed directly after him and flipping the deadbolt in precise, purposeful movements.

"And don't come back, asshole," she muttered. Placing both hands on the door, she let out an audible exhale. Only then did her shoulders, which had been coiled tight and perfectly unyielding, release in a noticeable sag.

An odd sensation Gamble didn't recognize expanded behind his sternum, pushing words on a fast path past his lips. "Are you okay?"

Tension yanked Kennedy's spine into a rigid line, as if she'd been spring-loaded, and she wheeled around to face him, both fists up.

"Whoa," Gamble said, holding out his hands even though she stood halfway across the bar from him. Damn it, he knew better than to take her by surprise, especially when her adrenal gland had probably just tapped the fuck out. "It's cool. It's just me."

"Jesus!" she bit out, tacking on another, less ladylike swear that he'd fully earned. "You scared the shit out of me."

He examined her closely, his own adrenaline making his pulse pound against his eardrums. "Sorry. But, seriously, that guy was a dick. Are you alright?"

"Of course."

Her answer came out too fast to be anything other than a default. Although he was tempted to throw the bullshit flag, one look at Kennedy's hands made him pause.

A person could master a game face or talk smack all day long. But hands never lied.

And hers were shaking.

"I'm going to go behind the bar and get some water," Gamble said, kicking his boots into motion before she could protest. Of course, he should've known she'd do it once she recovered her wits two seconds later.

"You don't need to do that. I'm really fine." She put her hands on her hips and watched him with all the attention and accuracy of a sniper as she followed him briskly behind the bar, and, huh, he hadn't pegged her as quite so territorial. Still, all the tenacity on the planet couldn't save her from her own physiology, so he was going to have to spin this just right in order to get her to breathe.

"Who said the water was for you?"

Ah, that got her. She stopped short on the bar mats. "What?"

"I'm thirsty," he said, taking two of the oversized cups they used for sodas and filling them first with ice, then water, before handing one over to her. "Might not be terrible for you to throw back a little water, either. It helps with the adrenaline letdown."

Kennedy sighed. "You're not going to let it go unless I do, are you?"

"Probably not. You might as well go on and humor me."

"Fine." She lifted the cup to her mouth for a sip. "Good?"

"Better," Gamble corrected. "The way you handled that guy was pretty impressive." Not to mention ridiculously hot, but he'd keep that little nugget to himself.

Her brows disappeared beneath the heavy fringe of her bangs. "You saw the whole thing?"

"It was a little tough to miss," he said, and she shrugged in concession.

"A pretty standard curb-toss. They're an occupational hazard from time to time." Her words were perfectly steady, even though her hands still weren't—a fact that she must have noticed, because she busied them with another sip of water. "I'm surprised you didn't jump in and try to help."

Gamble let himself smile, but only for a split second. "You didn't need me to. Still, if it's all the same to you, I'm going to stick around to walk you to your car." When Kennedy pinned him with a high-level frown, he added, "Not that I don't think you can handle yourself. Clearly, you can. But you're not fucking bulletproof, and you pretty much put a wrecking ball to that guy's ego. On the off chance he decides to wait in the shadows to give you a hard time, there's safety in numbers."

She paused, but then surprised him with, "Fine. But I'm

only agreeing because I'm too tired to argue with you. And if you stick around, you're helping me put the rest of these bar stools up."

"Deal. Let's get started."

∼

KENNEDY EXHALED for the first time in ten minutes. When faced with fight or flight, she'd go with fight every single time and twice on Sundays. That still didn't change the fact that the adrenaline was a bitch to manage. Add to it that she hadn't needed to forcibly boot anyone from The Crooked Angel in over a year—even then, Javier had done the actual handiwork—and she was definitely out of practice with the defenses that had once been daily survival skills.

You sure you're not going to get soft on me if you move out of the neighborhood, sis?

Setting her shoulders despite the ache that was making a comeback now that her nervous system was (sort of) returning to business as usual, Kennedy spun toward the pass-through at the far end of the bar. Gamble followed her to the customer side, taking a decent-sized draw from his water before putting it out of the way, shrugging out of his leather jacket, and grabbing the nearest bar stool. She had to admit, having him stick around and walk her to her car *was* smart from a strategic standpoint, and his quiet, steadfast presence calmed her down.

Even if the way he'd trusted her to handle herself had revved her way up.

"So," Gamble said, yanking her back from crazytown as he turned the stool in his grasp upside-down and put it on top of the bar. "How did a woman like you end up managing a place like The Crooked Angel, anyway?"

"A woman like me," Kennedy repeated, treating the stool in front of her to an expert flip.

If Gamble had caught the steel in her tone, he didn't show it by backing down. "Yeah. Something tells me they don't teach hammerlocks like that at Remington University."

She released her bar stool to cross her arms over her chest. "Are you saying I don't look smart enough to have a college degree?"

"I'm saying you look like you have a story," he qualified, and her muscles burned with a fresh shot of fatigue.

"Yeah, well, I'm not about to tuck you into bed with a glass of warm milk and tell it to you."

Gamble flipped another bar stool over, the ink on his left arm dancing with the flex and release of his ridiculously well-defined biceps. "Why not? We've got a little time to kill while we finish up in here, right?"

"We do," Kennedy said slowly, moving another stool to its proper place. They'd reached the end of the bar, where one last stool remained in front of four shots of tequila. Gamble's eyes met hers, glinting briefly, and God, she wasn't the only one with a story. But since she knew he wasn't about to get all loose-lipped, and he *was* right about them having some time to kill while she finished closing the bar down, she figured what the hell. Her background wasn't exactly top secret information, and it was less awkward than shooting the shit about something mundane, like the weather.

"I guess I ended up here the way most people end up where they work. I applied for the job and got it."

Bypassing the shots of tequila and the last bar stool—at least, for now—Kennedy moved back to the pass-through at the other end of the bar with Gamble right behind her.

"Did you always want to manage a bar and grill?" he

asked, mirroring her movements as she began restocking clean wine glasses in the racks behind the bar.

"Not always. When I was a kid, I wanted to be Wonder Woman."

He rumbled out a laugh. "Not a bad pick, but something tells me there's not a lot of availability for a position like that."

Kennedy bit back the urge to tell him there had probably been an equal likelihood of her honestly working her way out of North Point as there had been of her becoming a superhero. "Exactly. And while office jobs work out great for a lot of people, they're not really my jam, so I decided the restaurant industry was a good way to go."

"Yeah, I'm not a nine-to-fiver, either," Gamble said. "Not that I don't respect those kinds of jobs. I just wouldn't last more than two minutes doing one."

Curiosity flickered in her mind, and she put it to words. "So, what did *you* want to be when you were a kid?"

"Race car driver," he said, taking the last wine glass from the tray in front of them and putting it carefully in place. "But I decided it'd be safer to run into burning buildings instead, so here I am."

Kennedy laughed. "I guess that makes sense."

"The Crooked Angel is a cool place to land a full-time gig." Gamble followed her to the kitchen cart she'd brought from the back of the house earlier, hefting up one of the last remaining trays of glassware while she grabbed the other.

"The owner is a decent guy, but he's got a lot of restaurants and bars all over the U.S., so he's not too hands-on. He made it pretty clear from the get that he wanted a manager who would be in charge of all the operations."

It had worked out great, actually, since that was exactly what she'd been starving for. She'd never needed help. A micromanaging, breathe-down-her-neck kind of supervisor? Even less.

"Miles is a good boss, but I'll admit, we don't talk much other than through occasional calls and emails. I think the last time I actually saw him was seven, maybe eight months ago. He doesn't even live in Remington. He sticks mostly to New York and Napa."

The edges of Gamble's mouth tugged downward in the slightest suggestion of a frown. "And you're cool with just running the place on your own like that?"

"Of course, I'm cool with it." Kennedy shrugged. "Working here was a huge step up from the jobs I'd had before he offered me the spot, and I knew how things would be when he hired me. Miles has never been a Big Brother type. He likes the money he makes on his investments, and I like running the place without the hassle of someone watching every move over my shoulder or the high-dollar price tag attached to owning it."

The fact that her boss not only paid her well enough to live in an apartment in one of the nicest parts of downtown Remington, but also to take a nice chunk out of her student loans *and* send her mother some money every month was a perk Kennedy kept to herself. She'd set aside money for her brother in the beginning, too, but, God, she hadn't seen Xander face-to-face in nearly eight months now. Not that it had been for lack of effort on her part.

A pang unfolded in her gut, growing stronger as she realized Gamble was staring at her, unmoving. "Anyway." She lowered her tray of glassware to the counter in front of her, forcing her movements to remain steady even though she had to work for it. "I like being able to make decisions on my own and take care of everything the way I see fit, so it all works out."

"I get that," Gamble replied, and didn't *that* just make the Top Ten list of things she hadn't expected him to say.

"You do?"

"Sure." He lifted a massive shoulder and let it drop. "I'm an engine lieutenant for the same reason, really. I like being in control of as much as I can."

They fell into a comfortable rhythm of putting away the rest of the glassware, then completing a few more small tasks behind the bar. The accompanying silence might've felt awkward if Kennedy had been there with anyone else. But Gamble had always struck her as the sort of guy who watched and listened five times as much as he spoke, and she found herself relaxing despite her endlessly long night and her rattled nerves from tossing Hipster Dude out of the bar.

She collected the empty trays and stacked them on the kitchen cart, nodding in thanks as Gamble helped her maneuver the thing past the swinging door leading to the back of the house.

"I just have to grab a case of cocktail napkins from the dry storage room in the back, but once those are restocked, the rest can wait until tomorrow," she said. In truth, she'd planned to do half a dozen other things in addition to that before heading out, but he'd stuck around when he'd certainly had no obligation to, and it was well past one a.m. now. God knew he probably wanted to be at home in bed like any normal person. She could always come back in the morning to catch up.

"Okay." Gamble followed her to the dry storage pantry, which was little more than a glorified walk-in closet at the back of the kitchen. Having created their inventory system from the shelves up, Kennedy knew the layout by heart, and her boots thumped softly against the dark gray kitchen tiles as she made a beeline for the cocktail napkins. There was no sense in taking the time to hit the light switch—the door was propped open, as it normally was during prep and breakdown times, and enough light filtered in from the kitchen for her to find what she was looking for. She scanned the shelves, her gaze quickly landing on the over-sized boxes of cocktail napkins stacked neatly toward the back of the L-shaped space.

"Gotcha," she murmured, pressing up on her toes to liberate one of the cases from the shelf overhead. But Kennedy hadn't even gotten her arms halfway through the upward reach before her shoulder muscles clamped down, locking her into place mid-move.

"Ah, *ow*." She swore through her teeth, dropping both arms and rolling her shoulders in an effort to find some relief from the shooting pain. Gamble had had the good sense to give her two strides' worth of personal space, but now he closed half of it, eyes narrowed in concern.

"Are you hurt?"

"No," Kennedy said, and he tagged her with such a look of bullshit that she had no choice but to backtrack before he verbalized it. "My shoulders are a little sore, that's all. It's just been a long night." *Or year. Maybe two.*

Gamble tilted his head, his disbelief turning to a look of deeper thought. "On either side of your spine, right? Here?"

He reached back and touched the group of muscles bracketing his massive shoulders, and damn, how had she never noticed exactly how much graceful power he seemed to have hidden beneath all that bulk?

"Yeah. It's no big deal, though."

She turned to suck it up, grab the napkins, and go, but Gamble surprised her with, "There are a couple of pressure points you can work that will relieve some of the tension. They're not hard to find."

"How do you know that?" Kennedy asked. It seemed like such a strange thing to have in his wheelhouse.

"I get the same sort of pain every now and then, mostly if I work back-to-back shifts. Quinn showed me a few tricks when she was studying for her last paramedic certification." He paused. "Plus, I have some training in that area, too."

Right. Keeping her surprise under wraps was a total no-go. "On pressure points?" It wasn't exactly Firefighting 101, and it sure as hell wasn't common knowledge.

"Yeah."

He didn't elaborate, nor did he look like anything she could say would make him do so, so she put a pin in that little tidbit, reserving it for later. "I'll be fine. I usually just take some ibuprofen to knock the edge off the ache."

One dark brow went up. "Does it work?"

"Not really," Kennedy admitted. "But it's better than nothing, I guess."

"I've got something that's better than both ibuprofen and nothing." Gamble's gaze flicked over her shoulders, and he paused. "I'm going to have to touch you. As long as that's okay."

She huffed out a laugh, thinking of Hipster Dude. "I'm not going to throw a punch at you, if that's what you mean."

The reply, like a lot of things she said, had come out with no small amount of tartness attached, but he didn't give in to her sarcasm or her smile.

"It's not. What I meant was, is it okay if I touch you?"

"Oh." An odd sensation moved through her, gone before it really registered. "I guess. Yeah, sure."

"Turn around."

Kennedy paused. She wasn't in the habit of being bossed

around; hell, she wasn't even really in the habit of accepting help, mostly because she never needed it. But her shoulders really did hurt like a sonofabitch, and anyway, this would only take a couple of seconds. How hard could it be?

She turned to face the shelving unit, pulling her hair over one shoulder. Gamble stepped in behind her, his hands finding the middle of her back a second later. His touch was surprisingly soft, so unlike his work-hardened body and dark stare and gruff demeanor, and Kennedy relaxed against the contact without meaning to.

"I usually do this with a tennis ball," he said, his fingers traveling over either side of her spine as if he were trying to read her through the cotton of her shirt. "You just put it against a wall, press your back against it to keep it from falling, then roll it around a little to get it in the right place."

"Sounds easy enough." He slid his fingers higher, resting them just above her shoulder blades, and *ah*, her muscles squeezed in a burst of pleasure/pain.

"The trick is finding exactly the right spot and applying enough pressure to get everything to let go," Gamble said. His hands kept moving, seeming to take stock of everything they touched, and with each pass of his fingers, Kennedy felt the tension in her body unwind. Her frazzled nerves, her fatigue, all of it fell away, and the pure goodness left in its wake made her mouth act independently from her brain.

"For the record, I do have a college degree."

"Sorry?" His voice rumbled from behind her, and she turned her chin toward her shoulder to look at him—at least, as much as she could—as she answered.

"Before, you said"—his fingers found a spot, deep in her musculature, that made her pause for an exhale—"that you didn't think they taught hammerlocks like that at

Remington University. But I do have a degree. In business management."

"Ah." He rubbed slow circles over her shoulders, his hands wide and strong on her back until they zeroed in on a bundle of muscles at the juncture of her shoulder blade and spine. He applied just enough pressure to make the last of her tension release in a rush, and Kennedy swallowed the moan drifting up from her chest.

"Good to know," Gamble said. He'd shifted toward her, just enough to return the half-look she'd sent over her shoulder, and enough for her to catch the scent of him on her inhale. He smelled clean—not like soap or laundry detergent, and definitely not like cologne, but of something sexy and intoxicating all the same, and, suddenly, the pantry seemed to have all the square footage of a postage stamp.

Kennedy's heart slammed in her rib cage, her nipples going traitorously tight beneath her bra. This was impulsive at best, and insane at worst, but right now, she didn't care.

Right now, she wanted him.

She lifted her chin to look up at Gamble through the shadows. At five foot ten, she didn't usually feel small around people, but between the seven inches he had on her in height and the wide expanse of his well-muscled chest so close behind her, he came as close to eclipsing her as anyone ever had. His hands were still on her shoulders, and although it was the only place their bodies touched, she felt the heat of him everywhere.

"Kennedy." The glint in his already-dangerous stare told her he wanted exactly what she did. Kennedy nodded, just the briefest signal of consent, and in less than a breath, he moved. Skimming his hands to the tops of her arms, Gamble cupped her shoulders to turn her around. His fingers pressed against her bare skin below the cap sleeves of her top, and her sex clenched with greedy want.

But then he froze, every part of him going still except for his heart, which she felt beating swiftly against her chest. "Do you smell that?"

She blinked, trying—and failing—to make sense of the question. "I...what?"

He took a step back, his entire body coiling as he sent a calculating gaze over the pantry, then the kitchen beyond. "Your cook turned off all the ovens and the flat-top grill before he left, right?"

"Of course." Marco had never once skipped such an important step in breaking down his station. "Why?"

Gamble paused, but only long enough to grab her hand before he said, "Because your bar is on fire."

3

Of all the things Gamble had been in the mood for when he'd followed Kennedy into the dry storage pantry, fielding a goddamn fire hadn't been one of them. But he'd have to table his dirty thoughts and raging hard-on, at least for a little while, because if they didn't make getting the fuck out of there a priority, he and Kennedy were definitely going to be sorry.

The Crooked Angel might not be burning down around their ears—yet—but the smoke he'd nosed out would make that inevitable if whatever was causing it went left unattended.

As if she'd been on a five-second delay, Kennedy's eyes widened. "What are you talking about? I don't smell—" She sucked in a breath, and yep, there it was. "Shit!"

Gamble's heartbeat worked quickly in his chest, but he forced himself to focus. Unlike every other fire he'd ever been in the middle of, he wasn't booted and suited. He might have a crap-load of experience knocking down fires, but without gear and *with* a civilian, tempting fate wasn't really on his agenda.

"We need to get out of here and call nine-one-one," he told her, leading the way toward the pantry door. The sharp bite of smoke hit him harder as they crossed the threshold into the kitchen, and he took a lightning-fast visual tour of the space. A definite haze hung in the air, gray and thick in the fluorescent light trying to slant down from overhead, and his throat tightened involuntarily.

"Whoa," Kennedy managed, starting to cough, and Gamble snatched an apron hanging on a nearby hook.

"Wrap this over your nose and mouth like a scarf and crouch down low. Got it?"

She nodded and quickly complied. But before he could say or do anything else, the smoke detectors in the kitchen began to wail full-bore. Kennedy flinched but didn't freeze, turning toward the side of the kitchen leading away from the front of the building.

"The back door is this way," she half-yelled, her voice carrying over the steady shriek of the smoke detectors. Gamble didn't have eyes on any active flames in either direction, although that didn't thrill him the way it might anyone else. He knew from experience that the only thing more dangerous than fire you could see was fire you couldn't. Still, with no obvious hazard keeping them from the closest exit, that was definitely the direction they needed to head, so he ducked down lower and followed Kennedy deeper into the kitchen.

A dozen more steps had him pulling up short, though. The smoke had changed in both intensity and color, turning just thick enough to make the hair on the back of Gamble's neck stand at attention and his gut to crank down in warning.

"Kennedy, *wait*," he barked, just as they reached the heavy, industrial door marked *Deliveries Only, Do Not Block*.

Too late.

She shoved the door open, immediately jerking her hand back from the door handle with a sharp cry. But the door swung wide to reveal a wall of flames in the alley, orange and angry and close enough to make Gamble's heart slam urgently in his chest. Kennedy sucked in a startled gasp at the sight of the rapidly burning fire and stumbled back as a wall of smoke and heat surged toward them. Before his neurons had finished firing off the command to his body to move, Gamble hooked an arm around her waist, spinning her in a rough one-eighty toward the kitchen, then making sure the door fell shut behind them with a bang. His conscience warred with his survival instincts over whether or not to stop to see if she was alright—Christ knew she had to have burned her hand on the metal door handle, and she was coughing loudly enough for him to clearly hear her over the blare of the fire alarm. But whatever was burning back there was doing it insanely fucking fast, and now that he knew which way not to go, he needed another escape route. *Now*.

He pulled up the mental schematic of the bar that he'd memorized after his second visit, ages ago. "Side door by the game room," he told Kennedy. "Go."

She gave up a broken nod, but turned to quickly retrace her steps back through the kitchen. The smoke made his eyes burn along with his lungs as he followed close behind, scanning their surroundings and their exit path for any hidden danger or signs of more fire, but thankfully, the rest of the kitchen looked clear. Kennedy paused, only long enough to shoot a glance at him over her shoulder when she reached the swinging door leading to the dining room, and he shifted to look through the glass and palm the wood to test its temperature.

Clear and cool. Gamble metered his breathing to accommodate his exhale of relief. "Go," he said, gesturing her forward while he fell back in behind her. He'd kept his attention split on what lay ahead as well as what might creep up from the part of the path they'd already crossed—you could take a guy out of the Marines and all—but the fire seemed contained to the back alley. Given how fast and how hot things were cooking up out there, that wouldn't last for long, though. They needed to get the hell out of the building and get the fire department here, ASAP.

Kennedy moved quickly through the dining room, her boots slapping against the floorboards as she dodged the handful of tall bistro tables dotted around the game room, then the pool table beyond. She had to stop to turn the deadbolt on the side door, but a second later, they were spilling onto the sidewalk, the cool night air prickling against Gamble's face and bare arms.

"Keep moving," he told her, squinting hard from both the smoke he'd been exposed to and the distinct lack of light out here on the side street. He pulled her to a stop at the corner, his eyes burning and watering and his lungs threatening to go on a complete labor strike.

"Are you okay? How badly did you get burned on the door handle?" Gamble resisted the urge—barely—to run his hands over her in a rapid trauma assessment, settling for a fast but thorough visual.

"I'm fine. It's nothing," Kennedy said, although the coughing fit that followed did damn little to reassure him. She'd taken a faceful of smoke, and, depending on what had been burning, the consequences could range from hey-that-sucks to hospital-here-we-come. Plus, he wasn't convinced that hand she was now cradling was as fine as she'd claimed.

Airway first. "Take slow breaths. Count to five on each one," he said. As tempting as it was, gulping down air was the best way to guarantee hyperventilating, or worse. He pulled his cell phone out of the back pocket of his jeans, tapping the emergency icon at the bottom and watching her carefully to be sure she remained upright.

"Nine-one-one, what's your emergency?"

"This is Lieutenant Ian Gamble with the Remington Fire Department, Station Seventeen. I'd like to report an active fire on the Charlie side of fourteen seventy-six Marshall Avenue, no entrapment, one civilian on-scene at the corner of Marshall and"—he looked up at the overhead street sign —"Spring Hill Street."

Gamble gave up a few more particulars before replacing his phone in his pocket and turning his attention back to Kennedy. She was still coughing, albeit a little more inter-mittently now, and he took a step toward her to check her vitals and look at her hand, just to be on the safe side.

But he was so lasered in on her that he didn't see the car approaching from the side street until it had sped past them and screeched around the corner, whipping off into the dead of night.

"Holy *shit*." He jumped reflexively, blinking twice in an effort to process any details his eyes might've grabbed up independently from his brain. The car's headlights couldn't have been on—he'd have definitely noticed it approaching a hell of a lot sooner if they had. His back had been to the side street, which was strike two in the useful-details depart-ment, since it meant he hadn't seen the car until it was already skidding around the corner, and Kennedy had been coughing hard enough that his concern for her had taken precedence over taking in the scene around them until it was too late. There hadn't been anything out of the ordinary about the vehicle, just a standard-issue sedan, white, or maybe silver—but maybe not. Gamble could've sworn the right brake light had been out, but he'd only caught the briefest glimpse before the car had disappeared up Marshall Avenue. He couldn't even be certain which direction it had headed since the next major intersection was over a hill.

In short, as far as anything definitive was concerned, he'd seen precisely dick.

But nobody tore away from the scene of a fire at Mach 2 with no headlights on unless they were up to no goddamned good, and fires like this didn't just erupt out of thin air, which meant whoever was in that car had likely started the blaze. Kennedy had been facing the side street when the car had approached, and the intersection was decently lit. She had to have seen more than he had. She had the perfect vantage point to put eyes on the driver, or at the very least, the vehicle.

Gamble turned toward her, stepping closer as her expression registered in his brain. Her pretty face was drawn and pale, even in the low light afforded by the nearby street lamp and the bar behind them, and she was still staring, wide-eyed and startled, at the far end of Marshall Avenue, even though the street was now totally empty. Her lips were parted, her body still, and it struck him that in all the time he'd known her, he'd never once seen a look like this on her face.

Kennedy was scared.

"Did you get a good look at that car?" Gamble asked. She didn't speak, didn't move, not even to take a breath, and no, no, he couldn't let her go into shock.

"Kennedy." He kept his voice low but firm, stepping into her field of vision. The sight of him seemed to deliver her back to the here-and-now, and she gave up a few rapid blinks before coughing and knotting her arms around her rib cage.

"What?" she asked, and yeah, first thing's first.

"Are you sure you're okay?"

"Yes."

The word came out too softly to be accurate, and he tried again. "Why don't you let me take a look at that hand?"

"I told you, I'm fine." She punctuated the affirmation with a don't-fuck-with-me lift of her chin, but, funny, Gamble had never been the sort of guy to heed most warnings. Especially when his instincts were thrumming with warnings of their own.

"Great. Go on and prove it."

He held out his hand. She must have realized that backing down was nowhere in his vocabulary, because after a beat, she extended her hand, palm up.

"It's no worse than I'd get helping Marco in the kitchen. Seriously."

After a quick look by the light of his cell phone, he discovered Kennedy was telling the truth. At least, about her hand. "Did you see that car before it passed us and took off?"

She wrestled with another cough. "No. I didn't see anything."

His gut tightened. This was a woman who had the awareness to put a guy into a fucking hammerlock in less time than it took most people to fully exhale. How could she have seen *nothing*?

"Details are the most accurate directly after an event has been witnessed, and I'd bet whoever was in that car had something to do with this fire. If you saw the driver—"

"I said I didn't," Kennedy snapped, sending his brows sky-high and his hackles to high alert.

But somehow, he managed to trade the unease in his gut for caution. "Okay. I know this is a lot to process. Did you maybe see the make of the car, or what color it was?" At least they might get somewhere with more general details.

"No."

Her answer arrived just a heartbeat too quickly, making Gamble warily ask, "Are you sure?"

She speared him with an icy look. "That's the second time you've asked me that question in the span of less than a minute. I might've had a hell of a night, but I'm not fragile, and I'm damned sure not an idiot. If I say I'm sure of something, it means I'm fucking sure."

For a sharp second, he was tempted to give back as good as he'd just gotten. After all, he didn't even take shit from seasoned firefighters or hardened Marines. But then he caught the flash of emotion stuffed beneath Kennedy's tough-girl stare, and ah, hell. She really had been through the wringer tonight. Expecting her to see details the way he'd see them as a former Force Recon Marine and active firefighter wasn't really fair, no matter how street-savvy she was. He was trained for this sort of thing, to the point that it was sewn into every last fabric of his instincts. Of course, his version of normal was *far* from normal for things like this.

Even if those instincts were still telling him something wasn't quite on the level here.

Turning her back on Marshall Avenue, Kennedy returned her stare to the side street and the entrance to the alley leading to the back door of The Crooked Angel, her expression turning to pure worry at the sight of the orange glow and the heavy curtain of smoke churning from the narrow space. "The fire department is coming as fast as they can, right? Like, they know my bar is definitely on fire?"

Her voice wavered over the last word with just the slightest hint of softness, followed by another chesty cough. Some foreign sensation twisted behind Gamble's breastbone, but he managed to snuff it out and jerk his chin in an approximation of a nod. He didn't want to let go of the topic of the car, but he wanted to push Kennedy even less. Especially when she had a look like *that* on her face. "Yeah. They know. They're coming as fast as they can."

"Good," she whispered, her eyes not moving from the smoke and fire-glow pouring out from the mouth of the alley. Sirens sounded, in the distance at first, then growing quickly louder as the minutes ticked by. Red and white flashes ricocheted off the darkened buildings from down the block, announcing the arrival of both the engine and the truck from Station Forty-Two. They barreled up Marshall Avenue in a diesel-fueled roar that was as familiar to Gamble as his own heartbeat, followed by an ambulance and a department-issued Suburban that matched the one Gamble's captain drove on calls.

The Suburban came to an abrupt halt not far from where he and Kennedy stood on the corner, Station Forty-Two's captain wearing a definite look of surprise as he slid out of the driver's seat. "Gamble. Can't say I expected to see you here."

He gave up a clipped nod in reply. They'd have time for pleasantries later, after things like buildings were no longer on fire. "Captain Wilder. You've got flames showing in the alley on the Charlie side of the building. No entrapment. We were the only ones inside."

"Copy that. Any idea what's burning up back there?"

Gamble looked at Kennedy, whose stare was glued to the

firefighters jumping down from the engine and prepping water lines. "What? Oh." She shook her head, her expression toughening up. "I couldn't see, exactly, but there's a dumpster in the alley that we share with the other two businesses on the block, and it's pretty close to the back door. It's the only thing I can think of that's big enough to burn like this."

"Got it," Captain Wilder said, firing off a few commands to his engine lieutenant on the radio on his shoulder before returning his attention back to Gamble and Kennedy. "You the owner?"

"Manager," she said hoarsely, and Wilder nodded.

"I'll keep you posted." He shifted his stare to Gamble, even though he was already on the move toward his firefighters. "You know the drill."

Gamble read between the lines easily enough. But no matter how territorial firefighters were, he wasn't brainless enough to jump into the fray with no gear and a squad that wasn't his own.

If Walker and McCullough and de Costa were here? He'd jump into the fray buck fucking naked if the circumstances called for it.

"Come on," he said to Kennedy, jerking his chin toward the ambo, which had parked on Marshall Avenue, away from the immediate danger of the fire.

"What? No." She frowned, digging her boots in over the pavement as soon as she saw the ambulance and connected the dots. "I already told you—*twice*, actually—that I'm fine."

Gamble ground his molars together and stood firm. "Yep. I heard you say that. But you ate a decent amount of smoke in that alley, and we don't know exactly what's burning. You should still let the paramedics give you a once-over to be sure."

"No." She turned back toward the firefighters, who were shouting commands back and forth and hauling lines into the alley, and Christ, had she always been this big of a pain in the ass?

"Kennedy—"

"I don't need to get checked out," she rasped, but he was in her dance space in the span of a heartbeat.

"You also don't need to watch your bar burn when there's nothing you can do about it. The place is in good hands, and, quite frankly, you sound like shit. You can't manage the place if you keel over from smoke inhalation, so would you do me a goddamn favor and just let the paramedics check your vitals?"

A second slid off the clock, then another, both of them drenched in tension. Just when Gamble was certain she'd tell him to fuck straight off, though, Kennedy shocked him by giving up the tiniest nod.

"Fine. If it'll get you off my back," she grumbled. Not wanting to give her a chance to recant, he turned toward the ambulance, letting her lead the way. The paramedics were thankfully swift about their ABCs, taking her pulse and listening to her lungs and doing a bunch of other things she looked like she thoroughly hated.

"Your hand looks okay. Just a small first-degree burn," the blond paramedic, whose nametag read "Chelsea", said. "Keep it wrapped in clean dressing for a couple of days, and apply an over-the-counter burn ointment to the affected area twice a day. Your pulse ox is ninety-two, which is on the low side. Your lungs sound pretty clear, but I'd still like to put you on some oxygen for a few minutes, just to cover all the bases."

Kennedy's dark red lips parted in what was sure to be a

protest, but Gamble sent a high-octane frown in her direction, and she huffed out a slightly wheezy breath.

"Fine. Whatever will get me out of here fastest."

"Your goals are my goals," Chelsea said with a smile. She settled Kennedy on the gurney in the back of the ambo, sliding the pulse ox clip over the forefinger on her non-bandaged hand and hooking a portable O2 tank to some tubing and a mask. After a couple of quick adjustments, she slid the clear plastic mask over Kennedy's nose and mouth and tucked the tank on the gurney beside the rails.

"The oxygen is flowing through the tank. You won't feel it blowing on your face or anything, but I promise, it's doing its thing. Just take regular breaths and try not to talk too much."

Kennedy nodded, and Chelsea looked across the ambo to the bench seat where Gamble sat beside the gurney. "You good to keep an eye on her, Lieutenant?"

"Yes, ma'am."

Chelsea's brows winged up, and—damn it—so did Kennedy's, so Gamble covered his slip-up with a scowl.

At least it worked on Chelsea. "Oooookay. I'll be in the front of the rig with my partner, filling out the paperwork. Holler if you need anything, especially if she starts feeling dizzy."

Chelsea hopped down from the back of the ambulance, leaving both doors open to the cool nighttime air. The view was of Marshall Avenue, which—other than the eerie glare of the lights from the throng of emergency vehicles around the corner on the side street—didn't show any signs of the fire unfolding nearby. Under any other circumstances, Gamble would've hated the lack of a visual. But he'd meant what he said to Kennedy. There wasn't anything either of them could do right now.

Except try and figure out who had set the fire so the little bastard could pay for putting people's lives at risk. No way was a blaze like that a pure accident. At the very least, someone had been negligent.

At worst? It was flat-out arson.

Gamble looked at the pulse ox monitor, his gut squeezing at the sight of the bright red ninety-two still flashing in the corner. He shifted his gaze to the gurney where Kennedy lay, staring up at the roof of the ambo. Her black hair was tangled a bit beneath the elastic holding the mask in place, and her shoulders were tight and tense against the sheet-covered gurney cushion. A spray of goose bumps dotted her bare arms, and even though he was tempted to bring up the car that had sped past them (along with how she'd sped past it as a topic of conversation), he shrugged out of his jacket, draping it over Kennedy's torso like a blanket instead.

"You don't have to do that," she said. "You've got to be cold, too."

She went to tug the leather from her body, but he shook his head. "I'm solid." So she wouldn't argue—because, of course, she looked like she was going to—Gamble added, "If it makes you feel better, I'll shut the doors to keep the chill out."

He levered up from the bench seat. Before he could get more than halfway to his intended destination, though, a uniformed police officer poked his head into the back of the ambulance from around the corner.

"Hi. I'm Officer Lynch, and this is my partner, Officer Boldin." He gestured to the woman next to him, and Gamble exhaled in relief. This fire might not be more than negligence or a prank that had gotten out of hand, but he and Kennedy could've still been seriously hurt, or worse, as could any of the responding firefighters or anyone else who happened to be passing by. At least the brass was taking it seriously.

"Ian Gamble, RFD, and Kennedy Matthews," he said, so she could save some of her breath. "She runs the place."

Both officers nodded in greeting. Boldin said, "We've got a couple of questions, if you're up for them."

Gamble nodded and Kennedy followed suit, albeit less enthusiastically, and Boldin continued, "You two witnessed the fire, is that correct?"

"Yes," Gamble said, at the same time Kennedy replied, "No."

Lynch's brows went up, and yeah, Gamble was right there with the guy. "I'm sorry," Lynch said. "Dispatch told us the fire was called in by someone claiming he was with a witness to the fire. Weren't you here when the blaze started?"

"Well, yes," Kennedy said, making a face at the oxygen mask muffling her words. She tugged it away from her mouth and nose, and seriously, Gamble knew she was tough, but how had he never noticed how freaking hard-headed she was? "We were here, but I don't think we *witnessed* anything, really."

She began coughing again, and Lynch shook his head in concern. "It's okay. You don't have to do all the talking right now. Why don't you take a second to catch your breath"—he shifted his gaze from Kennedy to Gamble, brows lifted —"and you can just tell me everything you remember first. No big deal."

"Copy that," Gamble said. After Kennedy put her mask back in place and got a deep breath or two past her unrelenting frown, he launched into a methodical retelling of the night's events, starting when Kennedy closed the bar. He left out their near-kiss—not that it was forgettable by any goddamn stretch, but it also wasn't pertinent to the fire—and by the time he got to the part where Forty-Two had arrived on-scene, Lynch had scribbled off a full page of notes.

"So, this guy Kennedy tossed," Boldin said, her tone clearly substituting the word "dickhead" for "guy". "Have either of you ever seen him before?"

When they both shook their heads, she followed up with, "Did you happen to catch his name?"

Gamble went for a repeat with his head shake, but Kennedy slipped her mask aside to say, "He ordered a couple of craft beers so obscure, we only serve a handful of them a week, and he paid with a credit card. I can pull the receipt, no problem, but..."

"But?" Lynch asked, and she replied with a tight shrug.

"I don't know. Do you really think this fire wasn't just an accident? Some dumbass throwing a lit cigarette into the dumpster, or something? That guy was a jerk, but he hardly seemed the type to try and hurt me, let alone vandalize the bar."

She had a point on both counts, Gamble had to admit. Plus, the dude would've needed wings on his feet and gallons of accelerant in his back pocket to have started a fire like that in the time between when Kennedy had booted him and when they'd smelled the smoke.

Still, Boldin split a glance between Gamble and Kennedy, finally keeping her eyes on Kennedy as she answered. "That's possible, sure. But you kind of kicked this guy's pride in the balls when you threw him out. Not that he didn't deserve it"—she nodded—"but you'd be shocked at what some people are capable of when they're knocked down a peg like that. He might've just wanted to scare you, or he might've been pissed enough to want to torch your bar. Maybe he wasn't involved at all, like you said, but either way, we have to find out."

"Right. Of course," Kennedy said. "I can pull the receipt as soon as I can get back inside."

"That would be really helpful." Lynch looked at his notes again. "And, just to confirm, neither one of you got a look at this car that went speeding around the corner, other than it was light in color and possibly had a malfunctioning right brake light."

"No." Frustration heated Gamble's veins, doubling up when Kennedy shook her head to echo the sentiment.

"I didn't see anything. I'm sorry."

The officers finished up with a few more questions, then handed over their cards in case he and Kennedy remembered anything pertinent. Chelsea gave Kennedy the all-clear a few minutes later—that oxygen had done the trick, just as she'd said it would—and Kennedy signed the medical release form with a quick scrawl.

"If that's all you need, I'd like to go see about my bar," she said, her titanium-reinforced demeanor perfectly back in place.

"Of course," Lynch said, gesturing to the card he'd given her. "Just do me a favor and give us a call if you remember anything. Even if it's something small."

"I will, Officer."

But as Gamble watched Kennedy jump down from the back of the ambulance and disappear around the corner and into the night, he knew she'd just lied through her teeth about not seeing that car.

And he was going to find out why.

4

Most people would probably call Randall McGee crazy. Generally speaking, he supposed they were right; at least, by their own narrow definition of the word. He was admittedly conscience-free—although, fuck, you couldn't miss what you'd never had—and if someone so much as lit a cigarette within a fifty-foot radius of him, his dick would get harder than advanced algebra. Fire was his best friend, his boss, his lover. The more he started, the more he *wanted* to start, until the flames and heat and smoke consumed everything.

So, yeah. Most people would probably call him crazy.

But most people lacked vision.

"What the *actual* fuck, Rusty?" A distressed huff sounded off from the passenger seat of the freshly boosted POS Camry Rusty was currently driving through downtown Remington, and oh, Christ, here they went. "You said this was just practice to see if the remote ignition device worked. You never said the fire would be that big, and you definitely didn't tell me there would be anyone inside that place!"

"Don't be such a pussy, Xander," Rusty said, his tone

dangerously close to boredom. Seriously, this was the problem with breaking people in to the higher levels of the game. They got so goddamned squeamish when the rubber met the road. Or, in this case, when the flames met the two days' worth of trash that had been sitting in that dumpster. "This *was* practice to see if the device worked, which it obviously does. And did you honestly think there wouldn't be any fire when we were testing a remote ignition device? God, that's so cute."

The shot at Xander's lack of toughness made him scowl and straighten, just as Rusty had known it would. "No. You just...you didn't say exactly where we were going to test the stupid thing, or that there would be people there. That's all."

Irritation sliced through Rusty's chest, tightening his knuckles over the steering wheel. "First of all, that device is going to make you a lot of money, so watch your fucking mouth. Second of all, what do you care about a trendy bar in the middle of downtown?"

Xander shrugged and looked out the passenger window. "I don't. Those people who live downtown are so damned entitled. They don't even know how good they have it. Most of them wouldn't make it ten minutes in North Point without pissing their pants."

"Exactly," Rusty said, although, with all this wah-wah there-were-people-there sniveling, he wasn't quite convinced that Xander's societal disdain had stamped out enough of the guy's conscience to get him to the next phase of the plan without balking. "So, there were a couple of people in that stupid bar after-hours. So, what? They were too busy choking on their own lungs to see us."

The thought sent a smile over Rusty's face, his scar pulling taut from his lip all the way to his right ear. He knew all too well what the burn felt like in his lungs, filling his chest and covering the delicate tissue of his respiratory system in dirty, bitter ash. Fire was such a nasty mistress when she really got going.

"I'm not so sure about that," Xander said quietly, then shrugged. "I mean, what if they did see us when we drove by? I don't want to get busted for this."

"Please." A snort rose from the back of Rusty's throat. Xander was such a goddamned amateur. It was a good thing he had other skills—and also that Rusty had him by the balls, although, right about now, those balls seemed to be the size of marbles. "I'm too smart to get busted, especially on something like a trial run. This car isn't ours, and the plates are stolen, anyway. There's no street cam in existence advanced enough to pull facial recognition at this time of night—not with how fast we were going. Even if those two morons on the street corner did catch a glimpse of us, which I highly doubt, it wasn't enough for an ID. And do you know how many silver Camrys there are in Remington?"

"Lots," Xander said. The guy had probably stolen enough of them to know. Shit, he'd stolen *this* one just a couple hours ago. Rusty had the photographic evidence to back it up.

"Thousands," he corrected. "And this one isn't going to be recognizable as a car, much less a silver Camry that may or may not have been spotted at the scene of a dumpster fire, in a day or so." Torching the thing was going to be his reward for the remote ignition device working so flawlessly. He could barely wait the twenty-four hours he needed as a precaution, just to be extra-sure the cops didn't string the dots together. He'd promised The Money he'd be extra careful, and even though that guy was a self-righteous pain in the dick, Rusty didn't want to jeopardize the whole project. Not when he'd get to torch half the city while the other half watched, and make a shitload of cash on top of it.

He turned toward Xander. "Seriously. Nobody died, and nobody saw us. Just fucking relax, would you?"

The raw truth was, Rusty had been glad there had been people in that bar. Not because his goal was to hurt anyone, although, hey, sometimes shit happened. But if setting fires was what made his cock hard, then having an audience for those fires was what made him blow his load. He loved the thrill of watching things burn, yes. But he was addicted to the voyeurism of other people watching him do it, and knowing exactly what he was capable of.

That was the pain in the ass of testing these devices before they'd been perfected. He had to be stealthy about it. As much as he hated it, city cams and surveillance videos were fucking real. Not that Rusty didn't know ways to get around them—tonight's little getaway was case in point— but the job in front of him was all about stepping up his game and getting a *real* spotlight. He'd had to climb under the sheets with some sleazy-ass people in order to set it into motion, but in the end, he was going to get the great, big moment of glory he'd always craved. Which meant he'd needed to test the device where The Money had wanted him to. He'd needed *that* dumpster, behind *that* bar on Marshall Avenue, no matter who had been inside.

The Money had been clear about the location, and Rusty would've been game if the guy had told him to smoke the place up during the halftime show on Super Bowl Sunday.

They were a match made in heaven. Or, no.

Probably, it was more like hell. Either way, Rusty was going to get what he'd always wanted.

Xander's silence drop-kicked him back down to the

right-here, right-now of the Camry. "What's up your ass?" Rusty asked, making sure to stick the words with enough venom to sting.

"Nothing," Xander said, looking out the passenger window again. Jesus, the guy was like a bad ex-girlfriend, with all the freaking mood swings. "It's just that you said no one would get hurt on this job."

Rusty pushed an impatient exhale through his teeth— not an easy task with all the scar tissue on his jaw, but he was pissed enough to do it anyway. "No, I said that wasn't the goal. Bodies will make this job harder to do, and the last thing any of us wants are the cops nosing around if someone gets cooked before we get to the good stuff."

At Xander's obvious grimace, Rusty said, "You're not having second thoughts, are you?"

"No."

The reply was far from convincing, and Rusty pulled over to the side of the deserted street they were on, right on the fringes of North Point. "Listen to me, Xander, and make sure you do it good. You said you were in, so you're in. There is no backing out of this job."

"I get it," Xander said, his light green eyes flashing through the shadows in a display of the street punk tough-ness Rusty had recruited him for, and he'd give him this. The guy wasn't a total limp-dick. "I don't want to back out. Not with this much money on the line."

"Good." Rusty measured him with a long glance, and screw it. A good insurance policy never hurt. Plus, he loved a good bedtime story. "Do you ever wonder what happened to Billy Creed?"

Shock moved over Xander's features. "Billy? I heard he took off. Got tired of the shit life in North Point and went back to Tampa, or wherever he was from."

Rusty laughed. That was the lamest of the rumors that had floated around about the guy who had been in the same position as Xander eight months ago. "That's not what happened to Billy."

"Okay," Xander said with obvious confusion. "So, what did?"

"A gas can and a match," Rusty said, the words making his blood heat with excitement as it moved faster through his veins. "See, Billy was a lot like you, Xander. He came at me for the small stuff, the amateur shit where no one got hurt and it was no big deal—Molotov cocktail in a lowlife wife-beater's parked car, fake explosive devices to scare rival gang members off a job. You know the beat."

Xander nodded. The poor guy had tried to blank the fear from his face, but oh, it was there in his eyes, giving him away as the weakling that he was.

Rusty continued, "But then, I got a line on a big job. One of my clients needed a real device placed under a fire engine. High profile, lots of people around. Enough C-4 to put a crater in Washington Boulevard and turn everyone within a thousand feet into finger paint. Serious shit. Serious enough that Billy tried to back out, and dealing with him cost me the time I needed to make sure the device was foolproof."

"I'm not—"

"I'm not *done*," Rusty snapped. He needed to keep Xander in line, and that meant keeping him scared. He wasn't about to let the job of a lifetime go pear-shaped over a fucking disciplinary issue. Bad enough that Billy's freak out had cost Rusty precious time in making that bomb, and that he'd left a loophole the goddamn bomb squad had taken advantage of to keep the thing from detonating like it was supposed to. That explosion would have made the national news. Hell, it would have made him a god.

Rusty's pulse flared along with his anger. "What Billy didn't realize, even though that bomb never went off, is that he didn't get to back out. He'd done so many things—illegal things, *bad* things—that I could have had him busted for. See, I kept proof of all the vandalism he'd done, all the times he'd gone to the hardware store for things that could be used as accelerant. Did you know even pool supply stores keep track of frequent flyers who buy a lot of chlorine?"

"No." Xander paled, likely thinking of the last four times Rusty had sent him out for chlorine, and how they'd all been this month, and Rusty laughed.

"Of course you didn't. But even though all the evidence for those crimes pointed to Billy, I didn't want to turn him in to the cops for all the terrible things he'd done."

Xander asked, "Why not? It would've gotten you off the hook if he went down for stuff you did, right?"

Off the hook. Rusty's smile disappeared in less than a breath. Circumstances would have to be pretty goddamn grave for him to let a fuckwad like Billy Creed take credit for the fires he'd started. Those fires had been his. The credit, *his*. No way would he let the media tell the world Billy had set those. Not unless he'd had no choice.

And, oh, he'd made sure he'd had the best choice. "Because I wanted to watch Billy burn instead. Just because bodies make things complicated doesn't mean I don't know how to hide one from time to time, and it's a hell of a lot easier to do when I'm just spreading ashes."

He turned toward Xander, nailing him with a stare through the shadows of the car. "Billy screwed with me, Xander, but what he didn't know was that I owned him from the first time he flicked a Bic. And, like Billy, I own you, too.

So don't get any ideas about doing anything other than exactly what I tell you, or talking to *anyone* about this deal. Because I mean it."

His heartbeat accelerated, his smile returning with a vengeance. "A gas can and a match. I won't hesitate to find out if you scream louder than he did when he died."

KENNEDY WAS one hundred percent certain her chest was going to explode. Never mind that her lungs felt like someone had beaten them with a rust-encrusted tire iron. It was the nasty combination of guilt and dread that had parked itself on her sternum like a utility truck when she'd seen that car go screeching around the corner that was making her feel like her rib cage was T-minus three seconds from detonating.

She hadn't lied to Officers Lynch and Boldin last night when she'd said she hadn't seen the driver of that car. There had been too much adrenaline and not enough time for that, given her vantage point. But the lights from the bar and the positioning of the vehicle had afforded her just enough of a glimpse inside to see the passenger. Kennedy didn't know if she'd have been able to pick him out of a lineup if she wasn't already wildly familiar with his dark hair, his green eyes, and his clean-shaven face.

But since he was the baby brother she'd practically raised while their mother had held down three jobs in the worst part of the city, yeah, she'd recognized him, alright. Just like she recognized the fact that she was going to give him a gigantic raft of shit as soon as she got her hands on him.

God, Xander. What have you gotten yourself mixed up in?

Taking a deep breath even though it burned like a sonofabitch, Kennedy slung her black leather messenger bag over one shoulder and squinted through the Saturday morning sunlight. She'd planned to sleep in—Lord knew her body was tired enough to hit snooze for a bloody month. Her brain had had other ideas, though; namely, ones that involved the recurring nightmare that had been popping into her sleep schedule since she'd been twelve. In the dream, she'd lost her brother in a department store. It was, of course, the way Kennedy had known it *was* a dream that first time, since the only time she'd ever seen the inside of a department store at that point in her life had been in the movies. But she'd been in one in her nightmare, and she'd lost Xander somewhere among the racks of clothes. Every time she'd shove the hangers aside to try and find him, more clothes would pop up in their place, until she'd search so frantically that she'd wake in a cold sweat and a complete panic.

Which was exactly how she'd flown into consciousness this morning, three and a half hours after she'd fallen asleep.

"Just as well," she grumbled to herself, slipping her oversized sunglasses over her face and heading toward The Crooked Angel, which stood a block away. Although her assistant manager, Sadie, was scheduled to open the bar and grill, she had a ton of cleanup to coordinate. The fire marshal might have green-lighted them to open today, but Kennedy still had to schedule someone to come in to assess whether or not there was any permanent smoke damage to the back of the kitchen, not to mention figure out how they'd handle deliveries and trash removal with the alley roped off until the fire department had concluded their investigation and the owner of the building had completed repairs and cleanup on his end.

More importantly, she needed to figure out exactly how she was going to pin her brother down to determine what the hell was going on with the stunt it looked like he'd taken part in last night.

Kennedy tugged the keys to The Crooked Angel from the side pocket of her bag, firming her shoulders and tacking her resolve into place despite her throbbing hand and worn-out lungs. She had an hour before Sadie arrived. She'd already texted her an hour ago, along with January, Javier, and Marco, to tell them what had happened, and she'd spent a solid thirty minutes on the phone with Miles last night, convincing him not to fly out from Sonoma. So, first thing was first. She needed to get down to business and focus on her bar.

Getting past the front door and through the dining room, Kennedy stowed her stuff in the office before putting on a pot of coffee behind the bar and taking a visual of the back of the house. The dumpster was far enough away from The Crooked Angel's back door that no water had breached the threshold when the firefighters had put out the blaze, but close enough that she could definitely smell the bitter-burnt stench in the air from fifteen paces away.

Ugh. Lovely. At least most of the space affected by the smell was taken up by her office and the walk-in freezer, which had —thank *God*—been blocked off from the smoke getting in by the air lock system that kept the cold air in and the air from the kitchen out. Their fridge was equipped with the same system, and the pantry, liquor, and dry goods were far enough away to be safe, so Kennedy headed back to the bar. The four shots of tequila that she hadn't cleaned up last night still sat in front of the very last seat, lined up like soldiers, and her gut panged involuntarily at the sight of them. Heat spread out in her belly, heading quickly lower to settle between her legs at the memory of how Gamble's hands had felt on her, how his voice had sounded when he'd asked her permission to put them there. How badly she'd wanted him to put them everywhere. How if he hadn't smelled the smoke from the fire, they'd have...

"Stop."

Kennedy picked up the shot glasses one by one and put them on a bar tray before carrying them to the sink for a good wash. She'd had an uncharacteristic moment of weakness last night, letting Gamble stick around to help her close down the bar, but she wouldn't make it again.

With the way he'd looked at her in that ambulance, as if he could see right freaking through her, and the fact that her brother might now be involved in whatever prank had started that fire, she *couldn't*.

A firm knock echoed through the dining room from the front door, snuffing out the thought and sending her brows up, just slightly. It was a little early for Sadie to arrive, although she and Marco were married, and sometimes he liked to come in early to make breakfast for whoever was scheduled to open. They'd both been worried when they'd gotten her text about the fire. Chances were, they just wanted to make sure the bar was good to go.

Kennedy flipped the lock on the heavy mahogany door and pulled it open. "You guys, you didn't have to..."

The rest of her words log-jammed in her throat at the sight of Gamble standing in front of her.

"Hey," he said, and for Chrissake, did he have to fill the *entire* doorframe with those ridiculous shoulders of his?

"What are you doing here?" Kennedy blurted, quickly

gathering the game face she hadn't realized she'd need. *Damn it.* "We don't open until eleven."

"I'm not here to eat. How's your hand?"

Kennedy slipped her bandaged hand behind her back. "Good as new." Of course, the stupid thing pulsed in disagreement, but whatever. She'd put more ointment on it after she sent Gamble on his merry way. "If you came by to check on me, you wasted a trip. I'm fine."

He studied her, his dark brown eyes narrowing. "Actually, I didn't."

He followed the words with nothing but silence, and finally, she caved. "Okay. Why did you come, then?"

"I want to know why you lied to the police last night about that car."

Kennedy's heart beat fast enough to rattle her ribs, but she forced her expression to remain entirely blank. "I don't know what you're talking about."

But rather than retreating at her icy reply, Gamble stepped forward, close enough for her to catch the scent of leather and soap, and see the sheer determination in his dangerously sexy stare as he said, "I think you do. And I'm not leaving until you convince me otherwise."

5

F or the love of all things sacred and holy, Gamble was a righteous pain in the ass. But since he was a pain in the ass who had refused to budge from Kennedy's threshold unless she let him cross it, and she could think of no less than a thousand things she'd rather do than argue with the big ox in front of God and everybody on Marshall Avenue, she stepped back with a frown.

"Fine. Come in. But if you want my time, you're going to have to take it while I work. I have a bar to run."

"Fair enough," he said, giving Kennedy one less reason to throw him out. Not that she needed a reason—perks of running the place, and all—but still. No point in calling attention to the fact that she didn't want to talk to him about last night when she could dodge him in a less obvious way.

She anchored her armor into place, watching Gamble carefully as he crossed the threshold into the bar. He was shockingly lithe for such a big guy, as if every ounce of his bulk had a precise purpose, and she swallowed past her suddenly Sahara-like throat.

"Don't you have a shift at the fire house, or something?"

she asked, pivoting on her boot heels to walk back to the bar.

Gamble shrugged out of his leather jacket to reveal a black T-shirt that surrendered to his muscles and showcased the ink running down his left arm all the way to his wrist as he followed her to the back of the dining room. "Not until tomorrow at oh-seven-hundred. And nice try, going for a subject change."

"No point in trying to change a subject that's closed." Kennedy shrugged for good measure. "Like I already told the police, I didn't see who was driving that car."

"You saw *something*," Gamble said, and her heart tapped faster at the accuracy of the statement. But she'd taken care of Xander ever since they'd been little—for Pete's sake, she'd been the one to drop him off for his first day of kindergarten on her way to her fifth grade classroom. She might not have seen her brother for far too long, but she knew he was a good person, just like she knew people like cops and judges and pretty much anyone *not* from her neighborhood never saw it that way when they clapped eyes on a Northie. The vandalism of torching a dumpster had been epically stupid. Kennedy couldn't—and wouldn't—try to justify it, brother or not. Still, she couldn't throw Xander under the bus without at least knowing what the hell was going on first, and she really *hadn't* seen anything other than his face.

"Everything happened really fast," Kennedy said, sticking to the truth she could tell. "Coffee?"

Gamble tilted his head from the customer side of the bar, his gaze not budging from hers even though she'd held up the carafe in an effort to distract him. "You like to change the subject, don't you?"

Damn. "Is that a no?"

"No, thank you."

Kennedy's curiosity bubbled despite her defenses warning her that she should remain uninterested. Gamble had come out to her bar at eight thirty on a Saturday morning to try and bully her into spilling her guts about what she'd seen, yet he was all manners when she asked him if he wanted a cup of coffee? He'd called that paramedic "ma'am" last night, too. Who even did that anymore?

Her brain gave up the sharp reminder that she couldn't care, and this time, it stuck. "Suit yourself," she said, pouring herself a cup and hitting it with a heavy splash of the half and half they kept in the fridge built in beneath the service station.

"You want some coffee with that cream?"

Kennedy looked up, a brassy retort ready to roll right off her tongue. But then she caught the way one corner of Gamble's mouth had lifted just enough to form a devastatingly hot half-smile, and her comeback coalesced into a breathy exhale.

"Don't hate on my coffee," she managed to say a second later when she'd found her voice. "You probably drink yours black and strong enough to stop a charging rhino."

"I drink mine any way I can get it." His smile stuck around, but now, Kennedy was prepared for it.

"Unless I'm pouring?" she asked, gesturing to the empty spot in front of him at the bar.

Just like that, his expression hardened, his lips pressing into a firm line amidst a solid three days' worth of dark stubble. "I told you, that's not what I came here for. Look, is somebody bothering you here at the bar? Maybe trying to scare you?"

Surprise filled Kennedy's chest. "What, like that jackass from last night?" Fenton Ames, according to the credit card receipt she'd pulled for the police after the fire marshal had let her back inside to do so last night.

"You and I both know that guy doesn't have one tenth of the balls to do something like set that fire," Gamble said with a snort. "So, what? Is someone trying to shake you down?"

"God, no," Kennedy said. "I would never let that happen." She'd worked far too hard to make The Crooked Angel a successful bar and grill to let anyone intimidate her. Plus, aside from a handful of aggressive offers from a cheesy local real estate developer to buy the place, and the occasional stupid review on Yelp—both of which were more cause for eye-rolling than actual concern—no one had been anywhere near enough to disgruntled to mess with the bar.

And yet, Gamble persisted. "What about your boss? Is he in debt, or in some kind of trouble, maybe?"

Kennedy's laugh lasted for a full second before she realized he was serious. "Are you kidding? Miles is as straight as an axe." She'd never caught so much as a whiff of trouble on the financial end of things. The rent on the building, the utilities, the bills for food and liquor deliveries, the payroll —everything was paid in full and on time.

"That doesn't mean he didn't get in over his head with a bad investment or a big loan," Gamble said.

"Miles has been a successful restaurateur for over twenty years, and The Crooked Angel is one of seven places he currently owns. He made his way up from the bottom of the food chain in the restaurant business. He's not dumb enough to make a bad investment *that* big, and even if he did get jammed up, he's independently wealthy. I'm telling you, this fire was probably just a prank."

Gamble crossed his arms over his chest. "And I'm telling you, I think you're hiding something." Instead of pushing harder, he shocked the hell out of her by softening both his expression and his voice as he added, "Look, if someone is trying to intimidate you, I can help."

Just for an instant, Kennedy froze. For all his serrated edges and terse demeanor, it was obvious that not only did he mean what he'd said, but that he was genuinely concerned for her. A strange sensation—one she didn't recognize—arrowed through her, tempting her to tell the truth. But she'd never needed help in all of her twenty-eight years, and anyway, Gamble's version of "help" would be to go straight to the cops if she told him about Xander. Cops who wouldn't think twice about slapping a Northie with a laundry list of charges that would send him directly to jail, do not pass GO, do not collect two hundred dollars.

And she couldn't let that happen until she could at least figure out what was going on with him first.

She planted her hands over the hips of her jeans, working up her most and-I-mean-it expression. "No one is trying to intimidate me, and I can assure you, I don't need any help."

His frown was all menace, his dark brown stare glinting in the daylight spilling in from the windows on the far wall. But before he could deliver the argument he was very clearly working up, the front door opened, and her brother walked into The Crooked Angel for the first time in his life.

GAMBLE TURNED TOWARD THE DOOR, his fingers becoming fists out of ingrained instinct. Kennedy must have forgotten to lock it after she'd let him in—a move he'd bet his left nut was uncharacteristic as fuck, especially given the soft swear he'd just heard her utter under her breath. The guy who had slipped over the threshold didn't look familiar in a way that made Gamble think he'd ever seen him before, but something about his dark hair and wary stance tickled at the back of Gamble's awareness, like an itch he couldn't quite reach.

"Hey, Ken. It's, uh, good to see you," the guy said, jamming his hands into the pockets of his threadbare gray hoodie. Kennedy stood perfectly still behind the bar, wearing the same shell-shocked expression that had crossed her face last night as that car had whipped past, but only for a fraction of a second before she replaced it with something far less readable.

"Hey, Xander. It's good to see you, too."

He spun a gaze around the dining room, taking in the high-backed booths and trendy yet comfortable décor. "Wow. This place looks"—he paused as if pulling a human auto-correct—"really great."

"Thanks," Kennedy said softly. "Why don't you come on in? Coffee's fresh, and it's on me."

The guy—Xander—eyed Gamble with a not-small amount of distrust. "I don't want to interrupt."

"You're not interrupting," Kennedy insisted, pouring a cup of coffee and putting it down at the opposite end of the bar from Gamble. Subtle, she wasn't. "This is a friend of mine, but he was just leaving."

Gamble telegraphed every ounce of I-don't-think-so that he possibly could into his stare without pissing her off outright or spooking Xander—whoever he was—into bolting. He opened his mouth to say something to that effect, but Xander's chin snapped up before he could launch so much as a syllable.

"What happened to your hand?" Xander stared at Kennedy's bandaged palm. He looked weirdly stricken, his light green eyes round and wide, and God, how did Gamble *know* him?

Kennedy closed her eyes for just a beat too long to be a blink before dropping her hand back behind the bar. "Nothing. It's fine."

"She burned it. There was a fire here at the bar last night," Gamble said. He knew he'd earn a death glare from Kennedy in response, and if the heat on the back of his neck was any indication, she was already delivering in spades. But what he'd *wanted* to know was how Xander would react to the particulars of Kennedy's injury, so he didn't take his eyes off the younger man as the words sank in.

"You were hurt last night?" Distress hung heavily in Xander's voice, which didn't surprise Gamble all too much since he and Kennedy seemed to be friends. The guilt that accompanied it? Now that was interesting as hell, and not at all what he'd been expecting. How the fuck did these two know each other, and what, if anything, did it have to do with the fire that Xander was looking increasingly agitated about?

"Barely," Kennedy said, emphatic. "It's no big deal."

"Good. I'm...really glad you're okay." Xander took a step back, turning toward the door. "Well, sorry I busted in on you like this without calling. I know you're really busy here, so—"

"No, wait." Despair clung to her tone, sparking Gamble's interest yet again, but she quickly cleared her throat to smooth it out. "It's just been a while since the last time I saw you. I was hoping we could catch up."

Xander shook his head, his expression suddenly tough and unyielding. "Yeah, you know what, I forgot I have a thing. An appointment I have to get to. I just, uh, wanted to stop by to say hey. I'll catch you some other time."

"Xander, wait—"

Anything else Kennedy meant to say was cut short by the heavy thump of the front door closing in Xander's wake, and damn, the kid was fast.

"Thanks a lot," she hissed, skewering Gamble with a stare that said she wasn't done with him by a long shot. Which was fine by him, because that made them dead fucking even.

"Kennedy," he started. But the word went unanswered as she strode out from behind the bar and through the dining room, headed toward the door. Gamble followed her— Christ, she was just as fast as Xander, moving in the same wily, street-smart manner—nearly crashing into her when she stopped short on the sun-brightened sidewalk in front of The Crooked Angel.

"Shit," Kennedy muttered, twisting a stare up and down Marshall Avenue, which was dotted with a handful of pedestrians, but none of them were Xander.

"He must've gone down the side alley," Gamble said, gesturing to the small cut-through in the city block two storefronts down. Either that, or he'd parked incredibly close by.

As soon as the thought delivered itself into Gamble's brain, a silver sedan pulled away from the curb from five spots down, tires spinning over the pavement just enough to catch both his and Kennedy's notice. His heart tripped, slapping against his rib cage as he took in the make, model, and —holy *shit*—the busted rear brake light. He watched the car speed down Marshall Avenue, memorizing what he could see of the license plate before turning toward Kennedy.

"That's the same car from last night." Gamble lifted a hand to stifle any argument she might try to work up. "There might be a shitload of silver Camrys in Remington, but not ones with busted brake lights and drivers who show up at the scene of a crime the morning after, acting suspicious and looking guilty as hell. So, start talking. Give me one good reason why I shouldn't go straight to the RPD with this, Kennedy."

"Fine." She exhaled, pressing her lips into a dark red line before looking him directly in the eye to say, "That was my baby brother."

6

Of all the things Gamble had expected Kennedy to pop off with, Xander being her brother had pretty much been dead last on the list. Even now, fifteen minutes later, the revelation still sent ripples of surprise through his mind. Of course, *that* was why Xander had looked familiar. There wasn't enough family resemblance to smack a person in the face with the fact that they were siblings—Kennedy's mouth was fuller, her eyes a much darker green and her skin far more fair than her brother's darker, almost olive complexion. But now that Gamble knew, he was kicking himself in the ass for not picking up on the similarities sooner.

After all, not a whole lot of people wore a shit-ton of armor and carried themselves with the sort of awareness that had been earned rather than taught.

Kennedy pushed past her office door with a bump of one hip, reminding Gamble that a) she had really sexy hips, and b) he was here for a reason that had nothing to do with her body parts, no matter how hot she looked wrapped up in all that dark, low-slung denim.

"Sorry for the wait," she said, placing the cup of coffee in her left hand on the desk in front of him while cradling the cup in her right hand carefully to protect her bandaged palm. "I really appreciate you letting me get my staff updated and ready to prep for the shift in front of us before you and I talk."

Gamble waited for her to shut the door behind her before answering. "You've got a business to run, and I'm sure they're a little rattled about the fire." Annnnnd cue up the segue. "But you still haven't given me a good reason not to go to the police."

Irritation flickered over her face, but she banked it quickly—not an unwise move since he had the upper hand.

"Let me guess," Kennedy said, arching a brow. "You're an only child."

The words slipped under his skin with a sharp sting he wasn't prepared for, and his shoulders knotted as he drew back to stare at her. "I'm not sure how that signifies."

She surprised him by softening, even if only by a degree. "I just meant you'd understand my reason for not saying anything last night if you had a sibling you were close with. Or used to be close with, I guess."

Her gaze lowered to the cup of ridiculously over-creamed coffee in front of her. She remained quiet for a heartbeat, then another, and *God*, his inclination was to push. Someone—her brother, from the look of things—had started a fire that had grown big enough to potentially hurt bystanders and the firefighters who had responded to the scene, not to mention cause a truckload of property damage. Gamble was through waiting for explanations. But he knew from experience that sometimes the best way to get the information you wanted was to simply wait for it, just as he knew that if he pushed before she was ready, the only thing he was likely to get was push*back*, so he metered his breath to a steady inhale/exhale and stayed quiet, until, finally, Kennedy spoke.

"Look, first, I need you to know that I didn't lie to the police about not seeing the driver of that car, or anything else about it, really, other than my brother in the passenger seat, and if I thought for one second that he'd done something seriously malicious, I wouldn't hesitate to come forward."

"People could've been hurt by that fire," Gamble said by way of argument. "Bystanders, firefighters. Fuck, Kennedy. You *were* hurt."

The pang that had spread out in his gut grew stronger as she nodded in agreement. "I know. I get it. I *really* do. But this isn't what it looks like."

Time to get all the cards on the table, patience be damned. "Really?" Gamble asked. "Because what it looks like is your brother was involved in vandalism and arson. Christ, he and whoever he was with could've been purposely trying to burn down the entire block for all we know. If that's not seriously malicious, I don't know what is."

Emotion flashed, dark green in Kennedy's eyes, and she shook her head, adamant. "Xander wouldn't be a party to trying to burn down a building. Not willingly, and definitely not here, when he knows this is my bar. You don't understand."

A noise of irritation rose in Gamble's throat. "Then explain it to me. Because all I see right now is a guy who, in all likelihood, committed a crime, and his sister, who's lying to cover for him."

"Of course, that's all you see," she said. But rather than snapping at him, her voice went uncharacteristically soft. "That's all the police would see, too. But I'm telling you, now that I've seen him and the look that was on his face, I know there's something else going on here. Something that isn't right. I don't just love my brother, Ian. I *raised* him."

The use of his first name pinned Gamble into place. He hadn't had a clue she'd even known it, that was how frequently anyone ever addressed him as "Ian". What's more, her brutally fierce certainty was a complete one-eighty from the guarded nothing-to-see-here attitude she'd given up before.

His gut was rarely wrong, and right now, despite the warning pumping down from his brain, it was telling him to hear her out.

Crossing his arms, he sat back in the chair across from her desk. Just because he was giving her a chance didn't mean he trusted her. Fire still burned, whether you meant to set it or not. "Start from the beginning, and don't hold back on the details."

"There aren't that many," she said, caution returning to her expression. "Xander and I grew up in Hillside Bay."

Gamble's well-shit meter inched up a notch. Hillside Bay, or just The Hill to Remington locals, was the most notoriously dangerous section of North Point, which was already a pretty crummy part of the city to begin with. No wonder she and Xander both carried themselves with such toughness. Christ, even your battle scars had battle scars growing up in a neighborhood like that.

Kennedy continued, "Our mom meant well, but she grew up in The Hill, too, and nothing out that way is a walk in the park. Xander and I have different fathers. Not that either one of them was ever close to being in the picture." She paused for a shrug that was all fact. "But it didn't make life easy. Our mom juggled three jobs to keep a roof over our heads and food in our mouths."

"Three?" Gamble asked, unable to cage his surprise. He didn't make a king's ransom working for the RFD, but it was definitely enough to live on, and pretty decently, at that.

As if she could read his mind, Kennedy nodded. "There aren't exactly a whole lot of legit job opportunities for a Northie with her GED and a limited skill set, so yeah, my mom took what she could get, even when her employers offered her less than minimum wage. But that left me to look after Xander."

"That's a lot of responsibility for a kid," Gamble said slowly.

"Maybe," she agreed, "but it was far better than going into the foster care system, where we'd get separated, for sure. Plus, at least if we stayed with our mom, we knew we'd eat most of the time and that no one would knock us around. Or worse."

The thought sent a spear of something hot and dark through Gamble's chest, but he tamped it down. *Stay focused.* "So, you weren't exaggerating when you said you raised your brother."

"Did you really think I'd make something like that up?" The question came out mostly tenacious, but there was enough of a bittersweet edge to make Gamble pause. He understood that brand of loyalty—certainly not from anything he'd experienced growing up, but he wasn't going to think about that now, or, hey, ever would be cool, too. Still, he knew exactly what it was like to devote himself to a family, even if his had been chosen rather than blood.

He'd have done anything for the Marines in his recon unit, just like he'd do anything, including lay down his life if he had to, for the firefighters and paramedics at Seventeen.

Which meant the chances of getting Kennedy to see reason here were slim to fucking none.

"No. I guess I didn't. But your relationship with your brother still doesn't change the fact that he sped away from the scene of a fire last night."

"I know it looks bad," Kennedy said, her spine straightening against the back of her desk chair. "That's exactly why I didn't say anything to those officers. But Xander wouldn't have come here today unless something was seriously wrong, and he damn sure wouldn't have done anything like intentionally set that fire. There's something else happening, here."

Gamble frowned. "Like what?"

Well, *that* took the wind out of her sails. "I don't know yet, but I'm going to find out." A handful of emotions flickered through her olive-green stare, each lasting for the briefest second before turning into pure resolve. "Listen, Gamble. I may have a lot of loyalty to my brother, but I'm also not an idiot. A crime was committed, and I understand how serious it is that it looks like Xander was involved. If he genuinely committed arson, I'll haul his ass to the Thirty-Third precinct myself. But I truly don't think that's what happened. All I'm asking is that you hold off on saying anything until I talk to him and figure out what's really going on."

"How do you know he won't lie to you?" Gamble asked, and if Kennedy was offended by the question, she didn't show it.

"Because he's my brother, and I trust him," she said simply. "I also think he's in trouble. All I want to do is get to the truth."

Indecision wasn't something Gamble felt often, and right now, he remembered how much it sucked. Still, he had to examine every angle in order to figure out the best plan to proceed. "Xander could be headed out of town right now."

Kennedy's laugh held not one trace of happiness. "To go where, exactly? He's never been outside of Remington in his life, and he still lives in North Point. I doubt he even has enough gas money to get all the way home, much less skip town."

"So, you know where he lives, then?"

She paused, and wait, was that guilt on her face? "Not for sure, no, but things in The Hill don't change. I know where he works and where he hangs out; plus, I know how to get intel in the neighborhood. I can find him without a problem."

Gamble connected the dots, his gut ratcheting in a twist of oh-hell-no. "You're not going into North Point by yourself."

"You're kidding me, right?" Kennedy said on a huff. "I lived there for over twenty *years*. I'm pretty sure I can handle a run to my old block."

"Oh, I know you can." This next part was going to sting, but he was far past giving a shit. The fact that he was even considering not calling Isabella or Capelli or any number of the other cops he knew from the intelligence unit was crazy enough. "But here it is. While you might trust your brother, I don't, so you've got two options. You can either take me with you into North Point when you go talk to him, and let me listen to every part of every conversation the two of you have, or I can call the police right this second and let them do the dance with him. Your choice."

Kennedy opened her mouth to reply, and judging by the way she'd just lowered her mug to her desk hard enough to send a splash of coffee over the stack of invoices piled there, she wasn't going to wish him a happy birthday. Which didn't hurt Gamble's feelings any—hell, he'd just as soon call the cops and let them wade through the particulars of who was really responsible for this fire. He might understand loyalty, but family ties, the kind you shared with your flesh and blood?

They never amounted to a hill of shit as far as he was concerned.

But then, Kennedy paused. Closed her lips. Pursed them in the mother of all scowls and said, "Fine. You can come with me. But you're going to have to let me do all the talking"—she held up a hand to press back the protest that must have been obvious on his face—"unless you want Xander to clam up, or worse yet, run again before we get any answers."

Although he didn't like it, Gamble nodded once in terse agreement. "Okay, but if things even hint at becoming a cluster fuck, or if he cops to setting the fire on purpose—"

"He won't, because he didn't," Kennedy insisted.

But oh, Gamble had just as much tenacity as she did, and he was equally happy to sling it around. "*If* he does, or if we run into any trouble otherwise, you can bet I won't keep quiet. Understood?"

"Has anyone ever told you that you're a pain in the ass?" she grumbled, meeting his unamused stare with a, "Fine, yes. I understand."

"I have one other condition," Gamble said, sending Kennedy's scowl on a comeback tour.

"I already told you, we have to do this my way. You're not in any place to be making demands."

"And you're not in any condition to go running around North Point without some sleep and a decent meal," he pointed out. The shadows beneath her eyes didn't lie. He'd deal with the way they'd sent a funny feeling to the pit of his belly later. "We won't get any answers if I have to worry about you falling over from exhaustion the whole time."

Kennedy scoffed, but at least she didn't push back. "I can take care of myself. I'll be well-rested and ready to go by dinnertime. You just worry about you."

"Not a problem," Gamble said. "But I mean it, Kennedy. Make sure you're solid, because I *am* getting answers tonight. Even if I have to dig them up myself."

Slowly, she stood. Gamble's heart pumped faster, the air growing thick with the sort of energy he'd call tension, except it left him far too fucking aroused. Placing her hands on the desk in front of her, Kennedy leaned forward, just enough to heat his blood with a subtle flash of the ink trailing toward the black lace bra beneath her snug, low-cut T-shirt.

"Let's get something straight right now, Lieutenant. I'm *always* solid. Be here tonight at six. If you're so much as a minute late, I'm going without you."

KENNEDY STOOD behind The Crooked Angel's bar and cursed under her breath for the eight-hundredth time in the last eight hours. Although it had righteously chapped her ass to do so, she'd taken Gamble's advice-slash-order, power napping for three solid hours on the couch in her office and eating a Cuban sandwich that she'd barely tasted, despite the fact that the dish was not only one of their most popular menu items, but her favorite, to boot. She hadn't really expected that sleeping or eating would make her feel any better, but seriously, not even a two-week vacation sipping umbrella drinks in Maui would put a dent in her stress levels right now.

Her brother hated coming into downtown Remington as much as he hated that it was now her home. At least, she suspected that he hated her change of address. He'd never quite copped to it out loud, but she'd heard him bitch far too many times about the spoiled "other half" who never knew what tough times were like because they lived in a different zip code. The chip on his shoulder had been thorny enough that he'd made it a point to never set foot in her bar before today, despite the dozen and a half invites she'd extended over the past couple of years. That he'd not only broken his unspoken standoff, but spooked so thoroughly at the mention of last night's fire told Kennedy all she needed to know.

Xander was in trouble. And she needed to find him before it got worse.

Desperate for a distraction, Kennedy grabbed the remote for the TV over the bar and punched the volume button. It was just after five o'clock, and while they were open, the dinner rush wouldn't start in earnest for another two hours. There were only a small handful of folks in the game room, enjoying an early beer, and the wait staff had them covered. She didn't feel too bad about losing herself in whatever happened to be on the ol' tube right now.

"...and in local news, the Remington Fire Department was called to battle a considerable blaze outside The Crooked Angel Bar and Grill, on the fourteen-hundred block of Marshall Avenue in the early hours of this morning."

Kennedy's stomach dipped as the camera cut from the perky blond reporter to a grainy video image of the dumpster behind her bar, engulfed in angry orange flames.

"The fire, which was quickly contained, is the latest in a string of dangerous happenings on Marshall Avenue in downtown Remington. While the cause of the fire is yet unknown, it appears that there's very little evidence, if any, for investigators to go on, and the police have confirmed that no arrests have been made in connection to the incident. The fire is just one of several recent acts of vandalism and burglary in the trendy downtown area, and some residents are growing concerned. Local real estate developer, Chaz McCory, is one such individual."

Just when Kennedy had been certain her day couldn't get any worse, a highly manscaped face, complete with Botox-smooth forehead and teeth too perfect to be anything but veneers, flashed over the screen above the bar.

"I have to tell you, Amanda, as someone who is personally invested in the safety of this city, this fire *is* troubling."

Chaz paused for a flawlessly timed grave nod, and Kennedy barely resisted the twin urges to scream and fastball the remote at the TV. This guy might have the public fooled into thinking he was on their side, but she'd been to enough community meetings and zoning board hearings to know a flashy, cheesebag opportunist when she saw one. The only side Chaz McCory cared about was his own.

"I've taken serious measures to up the security around all McCory properties to ensure their safety. If it's got the McCory name on it, you can bet it'll be protected. Now, I know the RPD will find whoever is responsible for these crimes and bring them to justice. But it's truly a shame that such a promising part of Remington is becoming so riddled with danger that people can't even feel safe going out for a burger or—"

Okay, yeah, that was enough. Kennedy stabbed her thumb over the remote to shut Chaz up, mumbling her eight hundred and first curse of the evening.

"Dear God, thank you," said her closest friend and fellow bartender, January Sinclair, as she slid in next to

Kennedy behind the bar. "This bar is perfectly freaking safe, and that guy is a colossal ass-clown."

"Mmm hmm." Damn it. On top of all the other crap she had to worry about, now Kennedy would have to call Miles to let him know about the potentially bad press. But better he hear it from her than from Chaz Fucking McCory. She made a mental note to contact the TV station to tell them The Crooked Angel was safe and sound and open for business as usual, and that they weren't experiencing any setbacks as a result of the fire, first. Miles expected her to take care of business, so that's exactly what she'd do. Then she'd get this mess with Xander sorted, even if it drained the last of her already questionably thin energy.

Kennedy realized just a beat too late that January had zeroed in on her with a calculating stare. "Are you okay?" her friend asked, her dark blond ponytail swinging over one shoulder as she leaned in to squeeze Kennedy's forearm. "I hate to give that idiot, Chaz McCory, any due, but this fire was pretty scary, and the Korean barbecue place and the coffee shop up the street *were* both vandalized last month. It looks like the whole thing has you kind of...I don't know, worn out. I'm worried about you."

Well, *shit*. Of course, January would notice that Kennedy was off. Friendship aside, January's father ran the Remington Police Department's intelligence unit, which was the most elite group of cops in the city. She was as observant as any of her old man's detectives, and just as shrewd when it came to protecting her own.

As much as Kennedy appreciated the sentiment, she didn't need protecting. "I'm fine," she said, shifting to make triple-sure the bar was stocked before the Saturday night crowd started getting busy.

But January didn't let go. "Sorry, girlfriend, but I'm not

buying it. You've been totally distracted all day. Is the cleanup from the fire running you ragged?"

"Not really," Kennedy said, grateful as hell that she could fork over some pure truth. "Other than waiting for the RFD to be done with their investigation, we're pretty much right side up on all of that."

The insurance inspector had come out today to assess any minor damages, and Kennedy had scheduled a smoke cleanup crew to scour the kitchen first thing Monday morning, per his just-in-case recommendation. They'd gotten incredibly lucky. Even though the dumpster had been completely fried, the building itself had ended up essentially unscathed.

Curiosity pushed January's brows upward, and after a pause, she said, "Sadie mentioned that Gamble was here last night. And again this morning."

Ah, hell. Kennedy's heart beat faster without her consent, but she'd be damned if she'd let it show. "Are you asking me a question?"

"Well, that depends," January said with a smirk, and, ugh, Kennedy should've known better than to think she'd back down. "Is there anything to be asking about?"

"All that fantastic sex you're having is making you see things," Kennedy said, rolling her eyes enough to poke fun, but not so hard as to be rude. January had reconnected with her former best friend and current boyfriend, Finn Donnelly, a couple of months ago. Kennedy couldn't begrudge January's happiness, nor could she deny that the sexy professional hockey player was perfect for her sweet yet feisty friend. The dreamy look that had just crossed January's face was case in point.

"Mmm. Finn and I *are* having fantastic sex," she mused, biting her lip and mouthing *sorry* a second later at

Kennedy's hi-I'm-in-a-sex-drought frown. "But that doesn't mean I'm seeing things. Not things that aren't there, anyway. I mean this as impartially as possible since I'm off the market and I work with the guy at the fire house, but Lieutenant Gamble is pretty hot in a strong, silent, badass kind of way. He doesn't usually hang around 'til closing. Are you two...?"

January made a swirling motion with her index finger to cap the sentence, but Kennedy shook her head emphatically. Near-kiss or not, she had to nip this in the bud right now. She couldn't be distracted by thoughts of Gamble's brooding, black-coffee stare or his statue-sculpted body. Especially since he'd muscled his way into going with her into North Point tonight.

"Sorry to disappoint you, but there's nothing going on between me and the Jolly Green Giant," she said evenly. "He was here until closing last night and offered to help me clean up, so he was also here when the fire broke out. He just stopped by this morning to see if I was okay. That's it."

Fine, so she'd twisted the truth on that last part. But it did the trick. "Okay," January said, her smile turning soft. "I'm sorry. I didn't mean to push."

"It's all good." Kennedy gathered up a smile of her own, hoping it would make the words stick. "I promise, I'm really fine."

Or, at least, she would be. Once she found her brother and figured out why the hell he'd been in that car, she'd be right as rain.

7

Kennedy leaned against the brick façade of the bakery two doors down from The Crooked Angel and eyeballed her surroundings. The bakery had been closed for nearly two hours, so she had the luxury of taking her sweet time to hone her awareness, watching people window shop while others jogged by, running shorts on and earbuds firmly in place. Occasionally, a couple would pass her, hand-in-hand, bright smiles on their faces as they chattered about where they'd go for dinner, or, hey, let's go look at that new furniture place to see if we can find end tables that'll go with the new sofa.

Talk about a far cry from the three weeks she and her mother and Xander had lived in their ancient Oldsmobile because their shifty-ass landlord had decided to double the rent with no warning. Yet, this was Kennedy's life now, her not-so-new normal, the one she'd craved ever since she could remember.

The one she'd wanted badly enough to leave her brother behind.

Rubbing a hand over the ache that had just dug in

behind her sternum, Kennedy scanned the street again. Her sunglasses made it easy to observe the foot traffic on Marshall Avenue without being obvious—only one of several reasons she'd chosen the earlier hour to go looking for Xander. The summer-evening sunlight would hang around for another couple of hours, making her sunglasses seem normal and necessary the whole time she searched. But she hadn't been to The Hill in ages, and even though she'd made a point of keeping every last one of her street-smarts intact after she'd left the neighborhood, she knew she'd need all the help she could get to stay sharp tonight.

She spotted Gamble from half a block away, and chalk up reason number two for wanting good cover. He looked imposing as hell, striding down Marshall Avenue in the same dark jeans and black T-shirt he'd worn this morning, his muscles and ink and attitude on full display. A pair of aviator sunglasses hid his eyes from view—*well played, Lieutenant*—and the dark stubble on his wickedly handsome face was in danger of becoming a full-fledged beard at any second.

Kennedy clamped down on the Ode to Joy coming from her highly neglected lady bits, the bricks of the bakery scraping her shoulders just slightly through her black and gray baseball-style T-shirt as she pushed away from the building to greet him.

"You're early," she said. She knew it was ten before six, because she'd made it a point to come out here early, herself, along with keeping track of the time as she'd people-watched.

"And yet, here you are," Gamble replied, cocking his head and giving up just a trace of a smile.

God, she needed to get laid. Preferably soon and extremely well, and definitely not by the man standing in front of her in all his moody, broody, distracting-as-shit glory.

"I like to see everything coming," she said. Pulling her keys from the back pocket of her jeans, she gestured farther up the block, to the spot where her car was parked. "If you're ready to go, I'll drive."

"Okay."

A tiny part of her had expected him to balk at her tenacity. An even bigger, definitely darker part of her felt the deep pulse of a thrill when he didn't, and oh, this was going to be a long-ass trip.

Kennedy led the way up Marshall Avenue. Gamble walked next to her, but remained a half-step behind as if to protect her back, silently taking in every step of their surroundings, and when they finally reached her nine-year-old Nissan, she stopped to plant her boots into the sidewalk.

"You don't have to do that, you know."

"Do what?" he asked, but she met his mostly-hidden stare with one of her own.

"Watch my back. I'm perfectly capable of looking out for myself."

Gamble said, "I know you are." When Kennedy lifted her brows in a nonverbal "oh, really?" he let out a breath and added, "Look, I'm not bullshitting you, Kennedy. I really do know you can take care of yourself. I watched you do it last night. But I'm a firefighter, and before that, I was a Marine. Asking me not to keep my head on a swivel is like asking me not to breathe, and when we're together, especially when we're headed to a place like North Point, that swivel involves watching your back along with mine. You don't have to like it, but you *are* stuck with it."

Kennedy did her damnedest to keep a neutral expression while she processed the multiple shockers in his statement. His military background made so much sense—God, how had that not occurred to her before now? But she didn't have time to parse through everything now, so she took a deep breath and dealt with what was in front of her.

"Fine," she said. "Just don't go all commando on me once we get to The Hill, okay? Chances are high we'll see a whole lot of things that aren't above-board, but unless any of them are an immediate threat, all I want is to find Xander."

"Understood."

Again, he didn't push when she'd expected him to, and again, it sent a shot of something warm and strange right to her belly. "Great."

She hit the button on her key fob to unlock the Nissan and slid into the driver's seat. It took Gamble a full minute to get the passenger seat as far back as it would go, and even then, he had to pull a bit of creative maneuvering before he looked even close to comfortable.

"Sorry," Kennedy said, checking her mirrors before pulling out into the flow of traffic and heading away from the bar. "I guess my car isn't made for guys your size."

Gamble lifted a shoulder halfway before letting it drop. "I'm used to it. Anyway, I've been in a lot worse places."

Her curiosity flickered like a dare. "When you were in the Marines, you mean?"

A noise that could've passed for agreement rose from the back of his throat. He followed it with a whole lot of two-ton silence before finally settling on, "How long has it been since you've seen Xander, anyway?"

"Way to boomerang the subject," Kennedy said, partly as a deflection and partly because it was true. Gamble looked at her, his expression so unyielding even through his sunglasses that she found herself proceeding with care. "So, what? Your past is off-limits, but mine is fair game?"

"We're not chasing my past into The Hill because it's connected to a crime."

"Allegedly connected," she said, although, *shit*, she couldn't deny he had a point. She sighed. "Fine. It's been a while since I've seen Xander."

"A while," Gamble repeated, and guilt peppered Kennedy's gut with tiny, white-hot pinpricks.

"It's kind of a long story."

She hung just enough toughness in her tone to hope he'd get the message and drop the topic. Which, of course, he didn't.

"We've got a solid twenty-minute ride in front of us. Thirty, if there's traffic," he said, pointing to the line of brake lights in front of them. "And as it turns out, I'm a great listener."

Fucking spectacular. Kennedy slowed the Nissan to keep pace with Saturday evening city traffic, cherry-picking the truth for the bare minimum to get the story told. "Not a whole lot of people want to live in North Point, but the reality is, not a lot of people who *do* live there ever get the chance to leave. I decided early on that I was going to be the exception to the rule."

"That's admirable." The way Gamble's voice had gone quiet, yet not soft, told her he meant what he'd said. Still, Kennedy lifted a shoulder in reply.

"It was necessity. I watched my mother try to scrape by in crappy jobs with just her GED, and I knew I'd never have any sort of security if I did the same. I wanted better, *more*, for me and for Xander. For my mom, too. So, I buckled down in high school and got really good grades. I had to wait tables and eat Ramen Noodles for a year after I graduated to save enough money, and apply for a massive amount of financial aid on top of that, but I got a deferred acceptance to Remington University."

God, she could still remember the day that letter had arrived. She must have read it six thousand times to be sure it hadn't been a mistake, or, worse yet, a joke. Then she'd panicked at the thought of the logistics—Xander had been just about to start high school, there had been no way she'd be able to afford things like books and gas money and campus parking without keeping her waitressing job, and she'd need to maintain a 3.0 GPA to keep her financial aid. Funny, it had been Xander himself who had talked her off the ledge. Only after he'd promised her he'd be fine, then reminded her how hard she'd already worked to get accepted to the school in the first place, had she allowed herself to think just *maybe*, they'd make it out of North Point.

Kennedy's hands began to ache, and she realized—too late—that she'd gripped the steering wheel in front of her tightly enough to make the muscles in her forearms pull taut from the exertion. She could feel Gamble's eyes on her even through the dark lenses of his sunglasses, but he kept true to his word as a good listener, not pushing her to continue before she was ready or giving her some pep-rally line about how awesome it was that she'd pulled herself up by her bootstraps.

And didn't that just make it even easier to let more of the story escape. "I focused on getting my degree in business, and started working my way through better restaurant jobs as I studied. The jobs were closer to school than home, but they paid a hell of a lot better. Plus, I was making great connections."

"Sounds like a win-win," Gamble finally said as she paused.

"Yes, and no."

She released a breath from her tightening lungs. But she couldn't change what had happened, no matter how badly she wanted to now. Might as well get the retelling over-with.

"Halfway through my senior year—Xander's, too, only he was in high school—our mom met a guy who worked for a snack food distributor. She'd been working the late shift at a Mini-Mart at the time. Larry would come into town every couple of weeks from Tampa to make deliveries, and they hit it off. It wasn't long before he asked her to move to Florida with him."

Gamble's brows arched over the frames of his sunglasses, and despite the gravity of the conversation, Kennedy had to give up at least part of a smile. "I know, right? It surprised the hell out of us, too. But my mom was just so tired of living a hard life. I was about to graduate college, Xander had just turned eighteen and was about to do the same from high school. She'd done her best, but she'd never really parented either of us."

Gamble flinched visibly against the passenger seat, making Kennedy's heart speed up. "I don't mean that in a bad way, necessarily. She did more for us than a lot of other kids in The Hill got, and even though her life was tough, unlike most everyone else in our neighborhood, she lived clean. But Xander and I weren't close with her like we are"—she swallowed—"were with each other."

"So, your mother left you and went to Florida," Gamble said flatly.

"Of course she did." No sane Northie wouldn't have. Kennedy couldn't be angry about her mother's choice; hell, she'd wanted out of The Hill her whole life, too. That she genuinely cared for Larry and he cared for her in return made the whole thing even easier to reconcile. "I'd just landed a full-time gig as an assistant manager at a popular place over by the university, and the hours were brutal. Xander got a job doing manual labor down at the pier for some shipping company. I wasn't crazy about the location or the lack of opportunity for advancement, but at least he was gainfully employed."

Gamble nodded in slow agreement. "Yeah, I know what you mean about the area. We get called to that part of the city from time to time. Mostly as backup for Quinn and Luke on the ambo, though. Lots of drug overdoses and shootings."

"That sounds accurate for the pier," Kennedy said. She reached the split in the main thoroughfare, where most folks branched off to head toward the suburbs, and at least they'd shake this traffic by taking the road no one wanted to travel. "Anyway, I was finally making enough money at that point to move out of The Hill permanently, and my job was downtown, so it made sense for me to move there. I asked Xander to come with me." Begged had been more like it—not that she'd admit that to Gamble. "But he said no."

"Really?" Gamble asked, and oh, look, here they were at the part of the story Kennedy hated most.

Her chest ached, and she doubled up on her defenses to cover the sensation. Showing weakness now, when she was headed into North Point to look for her brother? No fucking thank you. "He had his reasons, and for the first year or so, everything was fine."

Gamble looked at her, quietly waiting her out like he had before. Only this time, she refused to budge, and damn it, why had she opened her stupid mouth in the first place?

Of course, Gamble wasn't about to let her off that easy. "And then?"

"And then, over time, Xander and I started drifting apart."

It was one hell of a summary for the way she'd worked too many hours to even have the energy to shower on some days, let alone check in with her brother, or how her heart would squeeze every time that—when she finally *was* able to try to connect—he'd make her work so hard for any kind of meaningful conversation, most of the time she'd just given up. The rift had grown so gradually that she hadn't really noticed it happening, until one day, she'd realized it had been nearly a year since they'd seen each other face-to-face. But even when Kennedy had made an effort to reach out to Xander after that (okay, fine. Hundreds of efforts), he'd dodged most of her calls and texts.

The same way he had last week. And today, when she'd sent him one simple line that had gone delivered yet unanswered.

Are you okay?

She straightened in her seat, the harsh glare of overhead sunlight showcasing the increasingly shabby city blocks and anchoring her resolve. "But that doesn't matter. Xander and I might have grown apart recently, but I still know him. He would never try to burn anything down."

Gamble's expression broadcast his wariness loud and clear, but thankfully, he didn't verbalize it. "You said this morning was the first time you'd seen him in a while. Are we talking weeks, a month or two? What?"

At her exasperated exhale, he tugged off his sunglasses, leveling her with the full strength of his nearly black stare. "Look, Kennedy, I get that you two were close, but you can't ignore the facts, here. Xander was at the bar last night when that fire broke out, and he came in again today, looking guilty as sin. So, you can either throw me a freaking bone and be completely straight with me, or I can call the cops and let them shake this out. What's it going to be?"

God, she hated the big oaf right now. Even if he *was* right to challenge her. "Okay," she bit out. "We've texted here and there, but it's been eight months since I've seen him. Nothing seemed out of the ordinary then, but—like you—he's not exactly a Chatty Cathy."

A smile flashed over Gamble's face, as fast as it was devastating, and even though he'd gone right back to that stern look he wore like a badge of honor, the back of Kennedy's neck still heated in response to his original gesture.

Focus. Right now, she commanded herself as she turned onto a side street she knew as well as her own signature. She navigated a few more in silence before continuing. "Xander and I always meet up on neutral ground, usually at a diner on the outskirts of downtown. He's never been to my place in the city, and I've never been to his. He knows where I work, but this morning was the first time he's ever set foot in The Crooked Angel, and it was the first time he's ever done anything like run from me. I'm telling you, this is something other than a textbook case of vandalism."

Gamble paused. "What if it isn't?"

Kennedy's pulse knocked at her throat. As much as she believed her brother would never intentionally set a fire, she also wasn't a dolt. Of course, she'd considered all the possibilities—even the ones she fucking hated. But he was her brother. The same guy who would feed the neighborhood strays on his way to middle school even if it meant he'd go hungry. The same guy who had helped their across-the-hall neighbor, Mrs. Abromowitz, with her groceries every Tuesday despite the fact that the nasty old crone hated everyone with a pulse.

Xander wasn't a saint, either—he'd also done his fair share of cutting classes and drinking too much and, in one unfortunate instance Kennedy had found out about after the fact, gotten arrested for participating in a bar fight. Still, in the end, he was far better than worse, and he was her brother. She owed it to him to at least give him the benefit of the doubt until he proved he didn't deserve it.

"If I'm wrong, and Xander knowingly did something that stupid, then I'll call Officer Boldin to come get him myself. But I'm telling you, that's not what's going on, here."

"You really believe he's innocent, don't you?" Gamble asked, and she pulled over to park between a laundromat and a pawn shop before turning to look him directly in his handsome, unreadable face.

"Yes. I really do. And I'm going to find him to prove it."

8

As soon as Gamble saw the determination on Kennedy's face, he knew he was screwed, and not even in a way that would leave him satiated and smiling. He knew, damn it, he *knew* that not only was it a complete dumbshit move to withhold information about a crime from the cops, but it was illegal to boot. But every time he'd been tempted to reach for his phone and do the right thing by making the goddamned call, he'd run into the same roadblock.

Kennedy kept swearing her brother would never do anything truly shady, and fuckall if Gamble wasn't starting to believe her.

"Okay," he said, surveying the city block on either side of them from beneath his aviator glasses. They'd have answers either way tonight. He wasn't going to wait any longer, not when someone was out there, playing with matches in very public parts of the city. "Where do you want to start?"

She drew back as if surprised, and ah hell, he couldn't help but let one corner of his mouth drift up into a half-smile. "What? You thought I didn't hear you when you said we were going to do this your way?"

"I didn't think you'd listen," Kennedy corrected. Whether it was the assumption she'd made that he'd strong-arm her into having his way or the fact that she'd doubted his honesty, Gamble couldn't be sure, but something made him lean toward her, cutting the space between them in half.

"Before we do this, let's get one thing straight. I'm a man of my word. I told you we'd do this your way, and so we will. But I also told you that if anything goes sideways, or seems dangerous in the least, you can bet I'm not keeping quiet. All of those things still apply. Got it?"

Kennedy's lips parted. Her exhale slipped out, fanning over his cheek in a warm puff of air, and Gamble was hit hard by the unexpected urge to destroy the space between them and cover her mouth with his.

But then she pulled back, leaving him to mentally bitch slap himself for thinking so impulsively. "Got it," she said. "I texted Xander earlier to ask if he's okay. After this morning, I'm sure he knows *I* know something's going on."

"Makes sense that he would," Gamble agreed, his brain kicking into go mode. "Did he answer you?"

Kennedy shook her head and looked out the driver's side window, her gaze focused on the stretch of run-down row homes across the narrow city street. "No, but I wasn't expecting him to. Just like he's not expecting for me to come down here looking for him."

The fact that she and her brother always met on neutral ground had grabbed at Gamble's curiosity, for sure. But he'd have to put a pin in those questions for now. "You don't think he'll feel blindsided once we find him and start asking a bunch of questions about last night?"

"He might," Kennedy allowed. "But you're not the only one who wants answers. Blindsided or not, I'm not letting Xander run from me twice."

Christ, her determination shouldn't have been so hot, yet there it was, giving Gamble a bigger hard-on than if she'd lifted her shirt and flashed him her tits.

He swallowed roughly, then did it again for grins before blocking all thoughts of her determination—and her flawlessly pretty tits—from his mind. "So, what's your play, then?"

"I'm not one hundred percent sure where Xander's living right now," Kennedy said, frowning as if the fact bothered her more than a little bit. "He told me he'd left his apartment last year after the landlord refused to call an exterminator, but all he said was that he was crashing with friends in a row home on Collins Street."

"Okay, but this is Franklin." Gamble jutted his chin at the faded green and white street sign gracing the post at the intersection a half a block up. Damn, what he wouldn't give for Shae's freakishly accurate mental map of the city right now. After (wo)manning the wheel of Engine Seventeen for the past three years of her nearly six as a firefighter, she knew every street, side street, and alley in Remington.

Kennedy, it seemed, didn't need the same assist. "Collins Street isn't far from here. But it's Saturday evening, and chances are, Xander won't be home, anyway."

"I take it you have an idea of where to find him, then."

"I have some guesses, but they might be a little dated. Since neither you nor I feel the urge to waste time trying a bunch of maybes until we get lucky, we're going to cut through the chase to narrow down the list." She turned to face Gamble more fully, her expression heart-attack serious.

"You're going to have to follow my lead, though. No matter what."

"You're not the only one who can take care of herself, you know." He'd gotten out of more shit-box situations than he could count, for Chrissake. Not that he'd ever brag about them, but still.

A huff of frustration rose from Kennedy's throat. "I don't doubt *that*. For God's sake, you're like a wrecking ball with legs. But it's bad enough that I've been gone from this neighborhood for five years. You're a complete stranger to these people, and let's just say that around here, goodwill doesn't grow on trees. If we want to find Xander, you're going to have to let me do the talking. All of it."

"Fine," Gamble said. She had a point. Hostile territory was way easier to navigate when you had intel from a local. "Where do you want to start?"

"With the person who's our best shot at getting good answers. Come on."

Kennedy got out of the car and walked around to the curb, and he met her on the crumbling sidewalk. A wall of summer air greeted them like a smack in the face, but between his day job and his multiple deployments to the Middle East, a little North Carolina humidity wasn't even enough to make him blink. He fell into step beside Kennedy, assessing their surroundings with a quick yet meticulous visual sweep, and even though he couldn't see her eyes past those oversized sunglasses of hers, her body language told him she was doing the same.

They walked in silence for a minute, passing first the laundromat and pawn shop they'd parked in front of, then a convenience store and a handful of row homes in various states of disrepair. A handful of people dotted the sidewalk, and a handful more sat on the steps leading up to a couple of the homes. He and Kennedy drew a few stares as they passed, him probably for his size, and her, more for her looks. But Gamble had to give her credit. If she noticed the lifted brows and turned heads—and he couldn't imagine she didn't—she didn't show it. In fact, she carried herself with an inherent toughness that said she was perfectly at home on an urban street, in a neighborhood with a worse reputation than most professional cage fighters, yet her fortitude wasn't aggressive or showy.

And here he'd just gotten rid of that goddamned hard-on.

"Okay, here we go," Kennedy murmured, slowing her pace as they neared the street corner. A woman with bright orange hair—who appeared to be at least fifty, although the heavy layers of makeup spackled to her face, coupled with the leathery skin of someone who had spent far too much time in the sun made it tough to gauge—strutted over from the spot where she'd been loitering close to the curb, squinting her eyes at Gamble and Kennedy as they approached.

"Kennedy fucking Matthews! Is that you?"

Kennedy's smile was genuine, arrowing into all sorts of places Gamble didn't want to contemplate. "Hey, Darlene. How's it going?"

"This is The Hill, baby. Same shit, different day." Darlene's gaze slid over Gamble, her darkly penciled brows shooting sky high. "See *you've* been busy. Damn, girl."

Kennedy didn't confirm or deny, or so much as flush at the obvious innuendo, although she did keep that easy smile of hers hooked firmly over her lips. "Busy isn't a bad thing. You know what they say about idle hands. You still with Tommy DeLorenzo?"

Darlene let go of a snort, pulling a small, bright purple

vape from the back pocket of her jeans, which were as painted on as her eyebrows. "Mmm hmm. Ain't no other game in town for a lady of a certain age." She took a drag from her vape, exhaling in a thick, cotton candy-scented cloud before shrugging. "Plus, Tommy treats me pretty good. Doesn't make me work as hard as some of the other girls. Just lets me stick to my regulars, mostly, and he even paid my bills at the clinic when I had pneumonia last winter."

Kennedy's smile lost its luster by half, and damn it, Gamble hated putting two and two together to come up with a sum of what Darlene probably did for a living. "I'm glad to hear I don't have to knock his teeth in, then," Kennedy said.

"No doubt that you could if you set your head to it, although I doubt he'd fight back. It ain't Tommy's speed to throw a lady a beating. Bruises don't sell nothin'," Darlene said with a raspy laugh. "Anyway, it's been a long-ass time since we seen you in this neighborhood, baby. What are you doin' all the way down here on my street corner?"

"Quick visit for old times' sake," Kennedy said, and Darlene's laugh grew louder.

"Girl, please. You ain't never been the type to come slumming." Her stare traveled over Gamble again as if to say *see?* "You got out. Which means you must have a hell of a reason for comin' back."

Kennedy lifted her hands in concession. "Okay, okay. I'm actually looking for Xander. Nothing major," she added with a demi-shrug and a roll of her eyes that was obvious even with her sunglasses in place. "Just a family thing. I'd have called him, but his phone got turned off. You know how it goes."

The lie slid out of Kennedy's mouth without even the

tiniest hitch. Granted, it wasn't exactly a whopper, but still. Her game face was a thing of beauty. And something to keep a goddamned eye on.

Darlene nodded. "Had mine turned off twice this summer. Greedy bastards charge an arm and a leg for those damned plans. Anyway, Xander hasn't been around lately, at least not in this part of the neighborhood. Last time I saw him was at Houlihan's, down on the pier. Maybe a week ago?"

As luck would have it, Darlene's poker face was a lot less bulletproof than Kennedy's. The older woman winced, shifting her weight from one patent leather stiletto to the other as she continued, "Yeah, it was last Friday. I remember, because I was working that whole stretch on the south end of the docks, and I went into Houlihan's to use the ladies' room and cool off a little. Xander was in a booth, with some shifty-looking dude with red hair. You know who I'm talking about?"

"Patrick O'Doul?"

"Nah." Darlene shook her head. "Paddy's a hoodlum, but he's harmless. This guy is...different. He's only been in Remington for like, a year. Maybe two? I don't know his name, but Xander's been hanging with him lately. He's got some kind of scar on his face."

Kennedy stilled, and yeah, that made two of them. "What kind of scar?" she asked. "Like he was cut, or something?"

"No. He keeps it kind of hidden, but it's not like he had stitches. It's almost shiny."

"Like a burn."

Both women turned toward Gamble as he spoke, and after a beat, Darlene replied. "Yeah, I guess. Yeah. Anyway, I don't know the guy, but I can't say I wanna."

Fuck. *Fuck.* Every last one of Gamble's senses tripped to high alert. He knew he'd promised Kennedy he'd let her take the lead here, but come on. The whole shady-guy, burn-scar, brother-at-the-scene-of-a-fire thing couldn't possibly be a coincidence.

Screw it. Gamble opened his mouth to start launching all the questions flying around in his head. But then Kennedy's fingers were on his forearm, the soft brush far more plea than protest, and his interrogation faded in his throat.

"Hey, Darlene, you got your cell on you?" she asked.

"Mmm hmm," the woman said, fishing it out of her purse.

Kennedy reached for the thing with an unspoken *may I?* and Darlene passed it over. "Here's my number," Kennedy said, her dark red nails clacking softly over the phone screen as she thumb-typed. "If you put eyes on Xander, can you text me?"

"Sure. You want me to tell him you're looking for him if I see him?"

Kennedy's slight pause was her only tell, one Darlene probably hadn't caught, but Gamble definitely had. "Nah. Just hit me up when he comes around, yeah?"

"You got it." Darlene replaced her phone in her purse, pressing her shellacked lips together. "Hey, between us, that redheaded guy gives me the creeps. I hope Xander's not jammed up with him, you know?"

"Yeah," Kennedy said softly. "I know."

～

RUSTY FLICKED the lighter in his hand, letting the flame grow hot enough to sting his thumb and forefinger before releasing the tiny red button with a grin. His smile was fueled by several things—not just the dance of the orange flame against the dead-dark of the midnight shadows around him, although there was no denying the thrill that sent through his blood. But not only had his remote incendiary device worked just as efficiently as the design had promised, but he and Xander had officially slipped the notice of both the RFD and the RPD while testing it in that dumpster—thank you, Tiffany Chase from KLN News, for that little nugget—which meant the bigger plan was going to go forward exactly as scheduled.

But first, he got to treat himself by lighting up something a whole lot bigger than a campfire.

Flicking the Bic back to life again, Rusty peered at the Camry through the dim light of the single flame. He scanned the gravel lot where he stood, then the rest of the industrial park stretching beyond the reach of the soft fire-light, taking in the inky black water of the river and the far-off lights of the pier beyond. From a tactical standpoint, torching things at night was smarter. Yeah, there was always the chance someone would see the flames and call nine-one-one, but he ran that risk no matter when he started a blaze. At least at night, the smoke was harder to spot from a distance, and with how far this industrial park was from civilization, let alone anyone who would give a shit enough to call in a crime, the Camry would likely be halfway back to room temperature before any upstanding individual set eyes on it.

Plus—he let go of the button on the lighter, but only long enough to repeat the ignition process, the soft *tsch* like a symphony in his head—fire at night was a masterpiece. The way the flames snapped and danced and licked and moved, taking control over everything they touched until there was nothing left but dead, gray ash—fuck, it made Rusty's adrenaline skip harder in his veins just thinking about it.

But he wasn't going to hold back like a pussy and *just* think about it. He didn't have to control himself like usual, or hold back on what he wanted. What he needed. Craved.

Tonight, he was going to set a fire and watch it burn.

And he'd have an audience from start to finish.

"Are you sure that's such a good idea with all this accelerant around?" Xander asked, his eyes fixed on the open flame of the lighter. Even in the nighttime shadows, the wariness on his face was as clear as a beacon, and for fuck's sake, it wasn't as if this was the kid's first rodeo. Seriously, hadn't Xander learned anything in the last few months?

Rusty would just have to keep schooling the guy. "Why are you so worried? I'm about to set the damned thing on fire, anyway," he pointed out.

"Well, yeah. But I don't want to go up in smoke with it," Xander said.

Rusty snuffed out the flame with an abrupt jerk of his wrist, irritation flaring in his chest. "Do you really think I'm dumb enough to let that happen?"

"No, dude." Xander's answer came swiftly enough to mark it as genuine. "All I'm saying is, accidents happen. This shit's really flammable, you know?"

He turned, his silhouette barely visible in the ambient light provided by the overhead streetlamp positioned at the front of the lot, and gestured toward the pair of plastic gas cans he'd filled at the Gas 'n Go on the way here. Rusty hadn't been brainless enough to fill them himself. With all the surveillance cams at gas stations—even the shitty places had them now—he wasn't about to take the risk. That Xander had been naïve enough to do it for him, and without a baseball hat on or anything, God, it was like shooting fish in a barrel.

Or, better yet, setting them on fire.

"That's the point," Rusty said, giving in to the slow grin pulling at the unscarred corner of his mouth and forcing the other one to go along for the ride. "It's really flammable because it's made to burn."

"Okay, but we're supposed to be setting stuff on fire, not people," Xander said, and *Christ*, the guy was turning into such a fucking whiner.

Rusty snorted. "Lose your skirt, would you? I already told you, you'll be fine."

"That's not what I meant."

Huh. This pushback thing was a new development, and not one Rusty was sure he liked. "Okay. Then what are you talking about?"

Xander shrugged, but the tension in the outline of his shoulders canceled out any casualness the move might normally carry. "You said no one would get hurt, and that we'd be setting fires in vacant buildings."

"Are you seriously *still* hung up on those two idiots at that bar last night?" Rusty asked. "For fuck's sake, no one died, and I already told you, sometimes shit happens."

"And I already told you, I'm not down with that. I want the money, not a murder rap."

Although Xander's words held a little more mettle than when he'd protested last night, that fear that had made Rusty zero in on him for this job in the first place was still there, lurking in his voice, and okay, it was time to remind Xander who was calling the shots here, once and for all.

"Do you think I was kidding when I said I own you?" he asked, his boots crunching over the gravel beneath them as he took a step, then another, in Xander's direction.

The line of Xander's shoulders tightened further. "I get it, Rusty, but—"

"I don't think you do."

In less than the span of a breath, he'd reached out, grabbing Xander's arm in an unforgiving grip and twisting it around. The guy struggled—Rusty had to give him points for spirit—but this wasn't Rusty's first, or even tenth, spin on this particular dance floor.

There was nothing quite like making someone watch while their own skin burned.

"Jesus, Rusty! Fine! I'll forget about those people. I fucking hear you, okay?" Xander hissed. Rusty torqued his hold on Xander's arm until he grunted in pain, making absolutely certain Xander got the message that the only thing trying to run would get him was a dislocated shoulder.

"You're about to hear me more clearly," he said, flicking the lighter to life with his free hand. "See, you're not special. I did you just like I did Billy Creed."

At the sight of the flame, Xander renewed his effort at struggling, although, damn, it had to hurt. "What are you talking about?"

"Who went and bought all the supplies for these devices, hmm?" Rusty held the lighter steady so he could see Xander's face, and—more importantly—Xander could see his.

"I paid cash for all that stuff," Xander said slowly. "Just like you told me to. It can't be traced back to either of us."

Oh, to be so naïve. "It can when the receipts end up in your apartment with your fingerprints all over them, and, oh, by the way, you've been pretty active online, too. Seems you've been researching how to make remote incendiary devices and buying even more goodies from that new laptop you bought online."

"What are you talking about?" Xander's eyes narrowed in the scant firelight. "I barely have the cabbage for my rent. I sure as shit didn't buy a laptop."

"Sure you do. You snapped it up two months ago with that new credit card of yours. For the record, you probably could have gotten a better interest rate."

Xander's muscles went rigid beneath Rusty's grip. "Are you kidding me? You're setting me up?"

"I'm buying an insurance policy," Rusty corrected. The idea of letting a dipshit like Xander take the credit for his magnum opus rankled, and not a little. But Xander was weak. In the end, Rusty wouldn't need to play this card, just as he hadn't played it with Billy. He'd kill Xander first—hell, he might kill him anyway, when this beautiful, brilliant job was said, done, and burned to the ground. Until then, Rusty would use Xander's fear as leverage to get him to do whatever he was told from now until Rusty no longer needed his sorry, sniveling ass.

Speaking of which... "Buying all that stuff and researching how to commit arson isn't nearly the worst thing you've done, though, is it?" Rusty asked. "I mean, you stole this car"—he sent his glance to the Camry, but only for a split second before returning it to Xander—"and unfortunately for you, there *are* pictures of that going down. And then there's the surveillance video from the gas station where you filled these cans up, and video of you arriving here, where this car is going to burn, just as the sun was going down. It all looks really bad. But here's the thing. All of that can go up in smoke."

He laughed at his own joke, but Xander, the freaking killjoy, wasn't nearly as amused. "Listen, Rusty, I—"

"Stop *interrupting*," Rusty bit out, yanking up on Xander's arm as a fresh shot of anger burst through his veins. Xander grunted, reminding Rusty just how weak he was, and yeah, it was time to get to the good part of this lesson. "Let me spell it out for you, since you seem to have missed this last night. This plan is set. There is no backing out, not even if someone dies. You'll do what you're told, and you'll do it without complaint or question from now on. Am I clear?"

Xander's breath emerged on a strained huff, sweat forming a sheen on his forehead. "Yeah, man. Fine. We're cool."

"Good. Then let me give you a little reminder. A souvenir, if you will, just in case you ever think of changing your mind."

Rusty brought the flame closer to the thin skin on the underside of Xander's forearm, his pulse jumping in wild anticipation.

Xander's eyes widened. "You...you don't need to do that, dude. I mean it. The dead body thing just freaked me out for a second, but I'm solid now, just like I was before."

Too little, too late. "You won't struggle. You won't close your eyes, and you won't look away," Rusty told him, making sure Xander knew he fucking meant every syllable of what he said. "You'll watch every second, or I'll keep burning you until there's nothing left. Do you understand?"

"Rusty—"

Rage surged up from his chest, making him crank Xander's arm up so high that the bastard hit his knees. "Do. You. Understand?"

Xander gave a shallow nod. "Y-yeah."

"Good. Eyes up, then. Oh," he added nonchalantly. "Don't worry about the smell. You get used to it."

Without waiting, he moved the flame over Xander's skin, his smile growing wider with every scream.

9

Gamble squinted through the Sunday afternoon sunlight, watching as his rookie stood in front of the fire house and beat the shit out of a tractor tire with a sledgehammer.

"Easy. Pace yourself," he warned with a frown, hoping like hell that de Costa took his advice before she pulled something vital. There were worse things to be than gung-ho, he supposed, and she'd been trying to prove her worth since day one—being the daughter of one of the city's most respected battalion chiefs was a helluva rap to have to navigate. But given that Gamble's current mood could only be labeled piss-poor and de Costa wouldn't learn how to swing a sledge properly if she puked or passed out on the cement, her enthusiasm wasn't about to deliver him to his happy place.

"Like this?" she asked, slowing down a fraction. Her gray RFD T-shirt was already darkened with sweat around the neck and both shoulders, where the bright red suspenders attached to her bunker pants slid against the fabric with every swing. Her brows creased, forming a deep V of concentration over her medium brown skin, and Gamble huffed in frustration.

"Only if you want to turn your rotator cuff into Silly Putty."

"Oh." de Costa stopped, her frown growing stronger. "But you said to swing with purpose and hit hard. Isn't that what I'm doing?"

Ah, hell. That was the thing with rookies. They made rookie mistakes. And as tempted as he was to snap at her for going so hard when he'd told her a hundred times before today that it would burn her the hell out, it wasn't her fault he was tired and distracted.

Chalk *that* up to a long night spent outside of a shitty dive bar, looking for a guy who didn't want to be found.

Taking a deep breath, Gamble looked at de Costa and gestured for the sledge, which she passed over. "You need to widen your grip a little bit more, like this." He wrapped both hands around the sledge handle, one close to the head, the other much farther down. "The movement's not just coming from your arms, so set your feet and tighten up through your core." Because he was a practice-what-he-preached kind of guy, he firmed his muscles, turning to face the tire head-on. "When you swing, let your right hand really slide through so you can use that energy and control your aim with the left. Like this."

Gamble went through the motion, the steel head of the sledge bouncing off the tire with a precise, satisfying *thump*. Although it was way more muscle memory than conscious effort, his body still sang from the small coil-and-release, to the point that he went for three more rounds before handing the sledge back to de Costa.

"And for the love of God, slow down," he said. "It's ninety-two degrees out here with a billion percent humidity.

I'm not too interested in having to get Luke or Quinn to come start an IV to rehydrate you because you worked yourself into too much of a damned lather. You copy?"

"Yes, sir." She grasped the sledgehammer and put his advice to work, popping off a couple of awkward swings before finally connecting with one that didn't look like it would destroy her shoulder.

"Good," Gamble said. He stepped back to keep an eye on her, quickly getting lost in the (thankfully slower) repetition of the thump-thump-thump against the tractor tire. His thoughts drifted back to his trip into North Point, to the silent yet tender-hearted way Kennedy had slipped Darlene some cash before they'd left, so far on the down low that if Gamble hadn't been watching her every move, he'd have missed it, then to Kennedy's somber silence as they'd headed to that rat-hole bar, Houlihan's, to try to find Xander at the pier. After four hours of loitering in a bunch of places that smelled even worse than they looked, he and Kennedy had finally given up and gone home, empty-handed.

Her brother was a ghost.

"Damn, it's hotter than hell's hinges out here."

Gamble's pulse escalated at the unexpected voice sounding off from behind him, and *damn it*, he needed to lose this distraction, and fast.

"A burning building is hotter," Gamble pointed out, tilting his head at his fellow engine-mate, Kellan Walker, as the guy strolled the rest of the way across the front walkway toward the spot where he stood a few paces away from de Costa.

"That, my friend, is a fact. Just wanted to let you know, Shae and I finished checking all the equipment and we're good to go after this morning's call."

It was SOP—not to mention, just plain smart—for them

to check all of their equipment after going on a call that required they use it. This morning's minivan fire on the freeway had been pretty standard-issue, as far as calls went. But since their masks had come out and their SCBAs had been kicked on while they'd taken care of business, Gamble had dialed up a full equipment check when they'd returned.

"Copy that." Gamble paused to eyeball de Costa, whose swings looked considerably better than when she'd started. "Okay, DC. Now, switch sides and do it again."

The look on her face was pure confusion. "You want me to hit the other side of the tire?"

"No. I want you to do the entire drill again. Left-handed."

Her chin snapped up, one black corkscrew curl escaping from the ponytail where she'd tethered the others. "But I'm not left-handed."

"A fact of which I've been aware since the first day you set foot in this fire house," Gamble said. "But you never know when you'll be stuck in a situation where the only way you'll be able to swing is left-handed, so go ahead and give me fifty on your other side."

"Are you trying to kill me?" de Costa asked, and the fact that she'd raised the question with nothing but pure honesty was the only reason Gamble didn't turn the fifty into a hundred.

"I'm trying to make you a firefighter," he said, sending a pointed stare at the sledge in her hands. "You'll either get there, or you won't."

Kellan chuffed out a soft laugh. "Don't complain, Lucy, or he'll have you go at these in full turnouts. Coat, hood, helmet. The whole nine."

The rookie's amber-colored eyes widened, and she scrambled to start the drill, left-handed and all. Gamble lifted a brow at Kellan in a silent *really?* and the guy returned it with a shrug.

"What?" Kellan murmured, his easygoing smile still front and center. "You can't tell me you weren't thinking it."

Gamble couldn't argue because, of course, it was exactly what he'd been thinking. Instead, he shrugged by way of reply, his shoulder muscles vise-gripping his bones in a reminder of all the tension he'd been accumulating that he couldn't seem to shake.

"So," Kellan said, watching de Costa struggle through her first few left-handed swings before continuing. "At the risk of you telling me to fuck straight off, I've got to ask. Are you okay?"

Gamble continued his silence, simply looking at Kellan with one brow arched up. But Kellan had balls, and what's more, the same sort of loyalty to his fellow firefighters that Gamble did.

"I'm not trying to get in your shit or anything," he continued, metering his voice low enough to keep their conversation from de Costa's rookie ears. "It's just that you seemed a little...I don't know, off the other night at The Crooked Angel. Then there was that fire and everything, so I just want to be sure you're straight."

The question didn't surprise Gamble as much as it should've. Kellan had spent years as an active-duty Army Ranger before becoming a firefighter. He was as likely to miss details—even subtle ones—as he was to stick himself with pins just for fun.

Gamble nodded. "Yeah, man. I'm solid."

Fuck, he hated to lie. But since the truth involved either talking about the four fallen recon squad-mates he hadn't properly honored the other night, or a fire that may or may not have been started by the long-lost brother Kennedy seemed hell-bent on protecting no matter the cost, coming out with the truth wasn't really an option.

Kellan ran a hand over the front of his uniform shirt, looking for all the world like he was going to argue. But then an all-too-familiar car pulled up in front of the fire house, with an all-too-familiar brunette behind the wheel, and damn, it looked like Gamble was about to do a swan dive from the frying pan right into the fire.

"Keep an eye on de Costa for me," he murmured, noting and ignoring the curiosity splashed all over Kellan's face. Kicking his boots into motion, he covered the small patch of grass in front of Station Seventeen in short order, stopping when he reached the aging Nissan Kennedy was now standing next to. She was wearing a pair of skin-tight black pants with knee-high boots to match, and even though her sleeveless white top was doing this flowy thing that made the fabric hide her curves and cover her ass for the most part, the sight of her did absolutely zero in terms of helping Gamble focus.

"Sorry to bug you here at work," she said, shooting a glance over his shoulder toward the spot where Kellan and DC stood, hopefully not staring. "But I didn't want to do this over the phone, and I don't have your number, anyway."

"That's okay." Gamble looked at her more closely, trying to take her temperature a little, but between her sunglasses and her game face, he came up with a whole lot of nothing. "What's up? Did you hear from Xander?"

"Not yet," she said with a sigh. "But Officers Boldin and Lynch stopped by the bar earlier to let me know that guy, Fenton—you know, the jackass?"

A bitter taste formed in Gamble's mouth at the mental image of the guy Kennedy had tossed from The Crooked Angel. "Yeah, I remember him."

Kennedy nodded, her expression suggesting she had about as much love lost for the guy as Gamble did. "Well, the cops caught up with him yesterday afternoon. It looks like after I threw him out of the bar, he went to the 24-hour convenience store two blocks over. Their security footage shows him buying cigarettes at 1:07 a.m., then, the outdoor camera shows him standing in front of the place, smoking, until he got into a car six minutes later. Fenton claimed it was an Uber, and the company confirmed the car was one of theirs. The driver dropped him off at his apartment in Grant Park."

"That's fifteen minutes from The Crooked Angel," Gamble said after a quick mental measure.

"Yep. With that sort of distance and timeframe, there's no way he could've started the fire. So he alibi's out."

In truth, the fact that the douche truck had an alibi was just a formality as far as Gamble was concerned—not only did Fenton not have the stones to do something like set that fire, but Kennedy had seen Xander, not Fenton, speeding away from the bar. As far as the RPD went, though, the alibi was a relief. Fenton might be an ass, but he didn't deserve to get tabbed for a crime he didn't commit.

Which brought them right back to the matter at hand. "So, how do you want to play this, Kennedy? With Fenton ruled out as a suspect, that means the RPD's investigation is going to dead-end unless they come up with a lead. I get that it was 'only' a dumpster fire"—he made sure his tone carried the air quotes—"but that shit is still serious, and if your brother is tangled up in it, guilty or not, we need to tell the cops."

Kennedy surprised him with a nod. "I know. And I know it looks bad, but I'm telling you..." Her voice wavered, tiny hints of emotion slipping through the cracks in her tough façade for only a breath before she went chin up, armor on. "Xander wouldn't do something that would hurt people. He *wouldn't*."

Gamble could strong-arm her, he knew, and at this point, he probably fucking should. They'd waited too long to talk to the cops as it was. But forcing her hand meant she'd clam up, and then the cops wouldn't get anywhere regardless. They both wanted the same thing, which was to find her brother, albeit for different reasons.

"Okay," Gamble said. "Then let me help you find him so we can get this sorted out."

Her shock quickly fell prey to her fortitude. "I don't need—"

"I don't care," he bit out, because on this, he wasn't budging. "Look, I get that you're tough, and I get that you're used to flying solo, but this is bigger than me and you. I want to help you, Kennedy, but for Chrissake, if you want to help your brother, you're going to have to *let* me."

For a heartbeat, then a handful more, the only sound that passed between them was the muted thump of the sledgehammer hitting the tire from across the yard. Then, finally, Kennedy's lips parted to accommodate her slow exhale.

"Fine. I know a way I can get him to meet me. It's going to take a little time"—she held up a hand and kept talking before he could loosen the protest rising from the back of his throat—"I'm talking a couple of hours, okay? But it'll work, and then we'll know once and for all what we're dealing with, here. I swear."

Gamble hoped for all of their sakes that she was right.

10

K ennedy pulled her Nissan to a stop at the bottom of a dead-end street she hadn't seen in half a decade. The scene looked mostly unchanged, although she couldn't admit to being shocked to find it that way. After all, the city wasn't going to sink the money into fixing up a park in the middle of the lowest-rent part of North Point only to have said park become a more scenic place for drug deals to go down. The residents who lived in the crowded row homes surrounding the stretch of scraggly grass either didn't care about the view or didn't have the means to try to refresh the place on their own, so over time, the playground equipment had faded and cracked, and the picnic tables and benches had been covered with so much graffiti, they were probably more spray paint than actual metal and wood.

Yet this had been Kennedy's refuge, her very safest place, and didn't *that* just put the first twenty-three years of her life into sharp perspective.

Especially since she'd left it firmly in her rearview, and Xander was still here.

She dusted away the thought—*one mess at a time, girl*—and turned toward Gamble, who had once again origamied himself into her life and her passenger seat. "You didn't have to bring dinner, you know," she said, since she'd already told him a half a dozen times that he hadn't needed to cover the rest of his shift at the fire house to accompany her back into North Point, all to no avail. Despite her arguments, here he was, cozied up next to her in all his dark and broody glory.

"Sure I did," he said. "I'm hungry." Despite the claim, he passed her the foil-wrapped sandwich he'd taken out of the bag in his lap, waiting until she pulled back the wrapping to reveal a pastrami on rye that made her taste buds suddenly and unexpectedly giddy before digging back in for his own sandwich. "Plus, Hawkins is like a mother hen when it comes to feeding all of us. He wouldn't let me leave the fire house without them."

"Lieutenant Hawkins made these?" Talk about a *whoa*. Kennedy had known Station Seventeen's rescue squad lieutenant ever since she'd taken over the helm at The Crooked Angel—the guy had been in the RFD far longer than her three-year tenure as the bar's manager, and the men and women from Seventeen had been hanging out there since the dawn of time. Like the rest of them, Gabe Hawkins had come with the territory. His quick smile and Southern charm made him easy to like, although he carried a quiet edge that told Kennedy he was probably fierce as hell when it came to being a firefighter. Still... "I never pegged him as the Martha Stewart type."

Gamble laughed, the deep, rich sound arrowing right to Kennedy's belly. "He'd probably stroke out if he heard you say that, but yeah, I suppose it's accurate. Hawk has some pretty mad skills in the kitchen."

He unwrapped his sandwich, his smile still firmly in

place, and God, Kennedy couldn't look away for all the world.

A fact that Gamble noticed in short order. "What?" he asked instead of starting to eat, and her cheeks heated. It was well into the evening, now bordering on dusk, so she couldn't quite pass off her sunglasses as necessary, but clearly didn't have the cover of the early nighttime shadows at her advantage just yet.

"No, nothing." She took a bite of her sandwich—good *Lord* it was delicious—but Gamble simply lifted a brow at her.

"Are we seriously not past the bullshit phase by now?"

He'd stuck just enough humor to both his tone and his stare to pull a soft laugh past her lips. "Okay, fair enough. It's just...you don't laugh very often, and it's, I don't know. Nice, I guess."

"Is that a compliment?" he asked, the humor on his face traveling up toward his eyes, and damn it, Kennedy laughed, too.

"Take it as you will. Just don't let it go to your head."

He took a bite of his sandwich, chewing for a minute before saying, "You're a tough audience, you know that?"

"As a matter of fact, I do."

They ate in silence, although it wasn't some awkward gap in the conversation Kennedy felt she had to fill. She'd been hungrier than she realized, polishing off not only her sandwich, but also the snack bag of chips and half the bottle of water Gamble had also unearthed from the bag. He gathered the trash from their meal, carefully putting it back in the bag before tilting his head to look at her.

"So, I've gotta ask. What makes you so sure Xander will turn up now when he hasn't returned any of your texts and we haven't been able to put eyes on him anywhere else in the city? Because from where I sit, it looks like he really doesn't want to be found."

Kennedy's pulse picked up the pace even though the question was totally legit. "Me texting him to ask if he's okay is one thing. But telling him to meet me here is kind of like our bat signal."

"Your bat signal," Gamble echoed.

"Yeah, you know, when the people of Gotham City needed Batman, they'd flash that big ol' beacon up in the night sky? The bat signal."

"I know what it is," he said, although not unkindly. "I'm just not following how this park is yours."

Kennedy paused. She knew she could shrug it off or balk —God knew he was probably expecting her to do one or the other, possibly both. But he already knew most of the score between her and Xander. Letting go of this part of the story wouldn't make her vulnerable or otherwise hurt anything, and anyway, as pushy as he'd been about coming with her, he *had* given her the benefit of the doubt, choosing to give her one last shot at finding Xander and hearing him out instead of simply going to the cops. She owed him at least this much.

"When I was thirteen and Xander was eight, we lived in a row home not too far from here. The park is nothing special"—she paused to gesture through the windshield at the decrepit playground equipment and crumbling black-top, and God, time wasn't kind to anything in The Hill —"but it was what we had."

Here, Kennedy's stomach squeezed, but she was already in for a penny. How much worse could the pound really be? "Xander was tough, but he was still a kid. Although he'd never admit it out loud, he loved the swings. So, when things got really bad, if we were hungry or we didn't have power because our mom couldn't afford to pay the electric bill on time, Xander and I would come here. I'd push him on the swings and we'd play the lottery game."

"The lottery game?" Gamble asked, squinting at her through the deepening post-sunset shadows.

She squinted back. "Yeah. 'What would you do if you won the lottery?' Didn't you ever play that game with anyone when you were a kid?"

"No, I...no."

"Oh." She bit her lip. She'd thought pretty much everyone had given in to the imagination-fueled game with a sibling or a friend or a classmate at some point, but maybe it was just a poor-kid's game. "Well, the sky was the limit in our version of the lottery game. We'd conjure up houses with ice cream parlors in them and bowling alleys in the basement, trips to Africa where we'd ride on elephants— you name it, and we probably turned it into a what-if."

"So how does that make this your bat signal?" Gamble asked, and even though answering made her chest ache, she did it anyway.

"Because. When the world got shitty and we really needed each other, this was where we came. Even when we got older and I stopped pushing him on the swings, even after our mom moved us to a new place farther away, Xander and I still came back here when things got really tough. If either of us asked the other to meet up at the park, it was our way of sending up the bat signal. It meant things were serious, and whoever was asking needed the other one. And even though we're not"—*do not waver. Do. Not. Waver* —"close like we used to be, I have to believe that if I ask my brother to meet me here, at this park, he'll understand that I really need him, and he'll show up."

Gamble looked at her, his dark stare making her feel

unexpectedly naked. "When was the last time he met you out here?"

Damn it, she should've never opened her big, fat mouth. "It's been a...while."

"How long?" Gamble pressed, and she exhaled slowly.

"Five years. But that doesn't matter. He'll come."

A noise of doubt huffed past Gamble's lips. "You know he's probably guilty of a crime here, don't you?"

"No," she said, her blood beginning to move faster in her veins. "I don't *know* that."

"Kennedy—"

"I'm not an idiot," she interrupted, her sharp tongue getting the better of her clam-up defenses. "I know Xander is probably mixed up in something he shouldn't be. But that doesn't make him guilty until proven innocent, and it sure as *hell* doesn't make him a bad person."

"The Xander you knew might not have been a bad person," Gamble argued, low and gruff. "But you haven't seen him for a long time, and he's not living an easy life. Family isn't always what it seems, and people change."

Her chest constricted, the interior of the car feeling suddenly hot even though the engine was idling and the air conditioning was going full blast. "Not Xander. Not like that."

Gamble shook his head, his expression hardening. "I just don't get this blind loyalty you have for your brother."

"Oh, yes, you do."

The words vaulted from her mouth before she could bite them back, but now that she'd let them loose, she had no choice but to back them up, no matter how much it might piss him off.

"You ordered tequila shots the other night for someone who never came to drink them." Although she spoke the words softly, he flinched nonetheless, and the flash in his eyes and the titanium set of his jawline told Kennedy she wasn't wrong about what he'd been doing. Between the admission that he'd been in the military and the undiluted emotion that had been in his stare as he'd ordered those drinks and then left half of them untouched, it hadn't taken much to connect the dots.

She'd worked in a bar long enough to know when people were celebrating anniversaries. Good *and* bad.

And the look in his eyes right now told her with one hundred percent certainty that whatever had happened to Gamble hadn't been anywhere close to good.

"Those shots I ordered the other night don't have anything to do with this," he said, his voice sandpaper-rough.

Kennedy's heart twisted before picking up speed in her rib cage. "They do, Ian. You say you don't get why I have Xander's back no matter what, but you understand that brand of loyalty just fine. The only difference is that you have a brotherhood, and I have a brother. That's all."

"I don't..." He broke off, and for a split second, the emotion churning in his stare was enough to pin her breath to her lungs. He blanked it in less than the span of a heartbeat, but she still felt the effects as he continued to stare at her through the growing shadows. There was no denying that Gamble had been an integral part of the Station Seventeen crew ever since she'd known him, but he'd always been reserved, too, as if he stood on the cautious edge of the deeper inner circle. Kennedy had always thought it was because maybe he had secrets.

Now, she realized they were ghosts.

~

GAMBLE NEEDED a goddamned tourniquet for his mouth. He should have tied this conversation off as soon as Kennedy had brought up those tequila shots. The relationships he'd had with his recon teammates, much like the relationships he had now with everyone at Seventeen, had never been about blind faith. Those loyalties had been hard-earned, mostly because it had taken Gamble years to trust that he could even *have* them for anyone other than himself. He sure as shit wasn't going to go yapping about what had happened to him in the Marines, no matter how big Kennedy's pretty green eyes got. But there she sat, staring at him from the driver's seat, expecting him to say *something*, and even though his brain commanded him to put a kill switch to this entire conversation, he couldn't deny the raw reality filling his chest.

He trusted her, and it was starting to become a habit.

"You were right when you guessed that I'm an only child," he said slowly. A good thing, probably, although, growing up he'd always wished it had been different. "I don't have any siblings, and I've always been pretty much a loner."

"I could see that," Kennedy said. "I mean, obviously you're tight with everyone at Seventeen and the cops from the Thirty-Third, but you're kind of quiet about it. Like you're maybe a half-step outside the circle."

She turned toward him as she spoke, and Gamble shifted a little, too, even though the passenger seat didn't give him a hell of a lot of room to do so.

He nodded. "When I tell you I don't understand blood ties, I really do mean that. I'm not trying to be a prick. They don't mean anything to me."

Kennedy's lips parted as she, no doubt, imagined all sorts of horrible things about his family life. Funny how horrible didn't always look like people expected it to. "You weren't close with your parents at all?" she asked, and ah, at least this was an easy question to answer.

"More like, they weren't close with me."

"I'm sorry." Her forehead creased, a delicate little V forming right in the center. "I'm not following."

"My parents weren't very interested in being parents." Gamble had never said this out loud to anyone even though he'd known it well for over twenty-five years, not even the head shrinker the Marines had forced him to go see after he'd come back from the nightmare that had ended his military career. The words didn't feel awkward in his mouth, though—probably because they were true. "My mother and father were both really career-focused. High profile Ivy League professors with doctorates, her in biochemistry, him in molecular biology. She actually won a Nobel Prize when I was in high school," he added, giving up a small smile at Kennedy's whispered "whoa" in response.

"Sorry," she said sheepishly. "I just didn't expect that."

Gamble shook his head. "My parents didn't, either. I think the last thing they thought they'd end up with was a son with no interest in academia. While they were trying to force-feed me Mozart and Molière, I was begging to play Pop Warner football and join the wrestling team. It didn't help that I've always been kind of big."

Kennedy laughed, the throaty, surprisingly sweet sound wiping out some of the tension in his shoulders. "Gamble, please. Linebackers are 'kind of big'. You're..."

She trailed off, wiggling her fingers at him in an up-and-down motion that made him laugh right along with her.

"I'm what?"

"Gigantic?" she asked, and okay, he was six foot five and weighed in at about two fifty-five. She wasn't exactly wrong.

He nodded in concession. "Well, as you can imagine,

once it became clear that I wasn't going to follow in their scholarly footsteps, my parents had no fucking clue what to do with me. So, they decided to go with full-on ignorance is bliss."

"What do you mean?" Kennedy asked.

Gamble shrugged. He knew this story should bother him, but he hadn't been raised as much as he'd simply grown up with his parents as distant bystanders doing their due diligence. Yeah, he'd lived in their house and eaten their food and slept under their roof, but he'd never really known them, and they sure as shit had never known him. His anger had turned to indifference a long time ago—not coincidentally, around the same time he'd joined the Marines and discovered what real bonds looked like. "My parents were both full-time professors on various academic boards. They also sponsored a small theater company and were active in the local arts community. It became clear pretty quickly that hands-on parenting wasn't on their agenda."

"So, what?" Kennedy asked, her eyes round and wide. "They just left you to fend for yourself because you weren't who they wanted you to be?"

"Not at first, obviously. I went to child care after school until I was old enough to stay home alone."

By then, he'd fully gotten the message, though. There were only so many times a kid could be the last person at the ball field, waiting to be picked up by a parent who had not only skipped the game, but been too wrapped up in his —or her—own universe to remember carpool duty altogether. And Gamble's parents had been nothing if not equal opportunity about forgetting him.

Still, he'd seen enough terrible shit and heard even more terrible-shit stories to think a childhood's worth of benign neglect was the worst thing that could happen to a person. "I'm not really complaining. It wasn't necessarily a bad life. I was provided for—lived in a big house, and I was never hungry or cold or sick. I didn't really want for anything."

Kennedy made a sound that was equal parts disbelief, sadness, and anger, yet was strangely devoid of the poor-sad-you sympathy Gamble had always expected if he ever decided to trot this story out. "Except for parents who gave a crap about you and loved you for who you are instead of ignoring your existence, you mean?"

"I guess," he said. "In the beginning, I wished my parents would care, or at least try, but I realized pretty quickly that it wasn't going to happen. So, after a while, I stopped expecting it and just did my own thing."

"Is that why you joined the Marines? To find a place to belong?"

Kennedy's question was innocuous on the surface, one that made perfect sense given the conversation they were having. But it punched Gamble in the throat regardless, and while he might be cool telling her about his deadbeat parents, there was no fucking way he was going to talk about the time he'd spent in the Marines. Not with her. Not now. Not ever.

Time to wrap up this little share-fest, the sooner, the better. "I joined the Marines for lots of reasons. But I never had any siblings—my parents pretty much learned the error of their ways after I came along—so this faith you have in Xander, just because he's your blood? I really *don't* understand it. It's not even close to my wheelhouse."

"Actually, it's not as far as you think." For a couple of heartbeats, then a couple more, she didn't elaborate. Then, finally, she said, "You trust Kellan, right? And Shae and Hawkins and Dempsey and everyone else on squad?"

Hello, no-brainer. "We're firefighters. I wouldn't work with them if I didn't trust them," Gamble said.

"And if you hadn't seen Kellan, for, say, five years, would you still trust him?"

"Yes." The answer was automatic, out before Gamble even realized he'd voiced it, and Kennedy nodded.

"That's how I feel about my brother. I might not have seen him in a long time, and he might be jammed up in something bad, but I still trust that he'll show up and at least talk to me. You say you don't get that, but I think you do. Otherwise, you'd have called the cops already."

Gamble took a long breath. Held it for a second. Then slowly let it go. "I really hope he shows, Kennedy."

"I'm telling you, he will." She paused, examining him closely through the dusky shadows beginning to settle in around them. "You've never told anyone at Seventeen about your parents, have you?"

His pulse flared. "No."

"Then why did you tell me now?"

"Truth?" he asked, and he nearly laughed when she responded with a brows-up look that read *like I want anything but.* "I'm not really sure, except that I figured with how your mom wasn't around much either, you'd get it."

Kennedy reached out, her fingers resting lightly on his forearm by his wrist. "My circumstances might be different than yours, but I do get it. And for what it's worth, I'm really sorry for how your parents treated you."

Gamble met her apology with a shake of his head. "Don't be sorry for something you had no hand in."

"Your parents could've been there for you, but they weren't. Just because I didn't have a hand in that doesn't mean I can't hate it for you," she pointed out, but again, he protested.

"It's not worth the energy. Really."

He saw her brow go up just a second too late to guard himself against her all-too-sexy candor. "Jeez. Who's a tough audience now?" she asked, just teasingly enough to make him smile, and damn, her laugh in reply made him feel far better than it should.

"Guess we're one hell of a pair, huh?"

He dropped his gaze to his forearm, where her fingers still pressed gently over his skin, and her eyes went round as she followed his downward stare.

"*Oh*. I shouldn't...I mean, I didn't...ugh, sorry," she breathed, shifting to pull her hand away. But instinct collided with the desire already pumping through his veins, and he covered her fingers with his free hand, not hard enough to keep her from moving if she wanted to, but with enough intention to let her know he didn't mind her touch.

In fact, he wanted it. *Badly*.

"I don't want you to be sorry," Gamble said, his heart beating faster as—instead of pulling away—Kennedy leaned in even closer.

Her fingers tightened, her pupils darkening her stare. "Then what do you want?" she whispered.

"This."

He erased the space between them in one swift movement. But she'd moved, too, pressing forward to meet him at the same time he'd leaned in to slant his mouth over hers. Her lips were soft, yet full of purpose, quickly parting to give him better access, and fuck yeah, he took it. Sliding his tongue along the seam of her lips, Gamble tasted her once, then twice, before deepening the kiss. Kennedy was far from a passive participant—and didn't *that* just make his cock stand up and pay all sorts of attention—angling herself closer despite the constraints of the Nissan's front seat. A low sound rose up from her throat as he swept his tongue further into her mouth to let it tangle with hers. Her moan prompted him to drop the hand that had been covering hers in favor of reaching out to cup the back of her neck, hauling her closer for another hot, deep taste.

Christ, she gave even better than she got, and before Gamble could process the movement, she'd curled her fingers around the front of his T-shirt to grip the cotton by his shoulders and hold his body in place against her chest. His heart slammed against his sternum, each beat sounding off in his ears and daring him to kiss her harder, touch more of her, to not stop until she begged him for unspeakable things with that sharp, sultry mouth. Kennedy edged her teeth over the sensitive skin on the inside of his bottom lip, applying just enough pressure to send a bolt of dark, dirty want all the way through him, and the last of his already shaky common sense snapped.

"Be careful," Gamble ground out against her mouth, his cock throbbing behind the fly of his jeans. "I bite back."

But before she could loosen the sexy retort her expression said she'd worked up in her head, the streetlights clicked on with a snap. The flash of light illuminated not only the end of the street that stood about ten feet in front of them, but the handful of benches surrounding the blacktop in the park.

Where a lone male figure sat, slumped low in his hoodie. Waiting.

Kennedy was an idiot. No, check that. She was a *selfish* idiot. How the hell could she have let herself get distracted from her purpose—from her brother, who needed her, maybe now more than ever?

The answer to that question sat next to her, his mouth smudged with her lipstick and his face as unreadable as ever, and God, even though it made her a terrible person, she still wanted him.

A lot.

No. She'd already failed Xander once. She wouldn't do it again.

"Here," she said, reaching for the glove box and pulling a napkin from its depths, passing it over to Gamble without actually touching him. "For the lipstick on your face."

"Kennedy," he started, but she cut him off with a firm shake of her head. She couldn't focus on anything that wasn't Xander right now. Especially since he'd been sitting there for who knew how long.

"No, we're good. Come on."

Without waiting, Kennedy grabbed her leather moto

jacket from the back seat and got out of the car. The weather wasn't particularly chilly; hell, it had been in the nineties a mere eight hours ago. But the jacket would provide a buffer for some of her more involuntary body language, and anyway, down here in The Hill, any armor was good armor.

Probably why Xander's hoodie was zipped up to his chin.

Gamble shut the passenger door quietly and rounded the front of the car to fall into step with her. Her body was still pulsing with a whole lot of please-fuck-me endorphins —damn, physiology was such a bitch sometimes—and having his huge frame and hard muscles so close to her didn't help matters.

"This is the same as last night," Kennedy murmured quietly, pulling her shoulder blades tight to her spine and making herself as tall as possible. "Neither of us is interested in having to find my brother again, so let me do the talking."

"Copy that," Gamble said, almost under his breath. "If he stays cool, I stay cool."

Great. She couldn't argue now, not when they'd reach the bench where Xander sat in less than a minute, but she still shot Gamble a look that telegraphed her displeasure. Xander had already caught sight of her, the shift in his stance broadcasting his wariness as he found his feet, and damn, she had her work cut out for her with a hacksaw.

"Hey," Kennedy said, giving him a couple of strides' worth of space even though her instincts screamed at her to hug him. God, even with the hoodie hiding much of his frame, he looked so much thinner than when she'd seen him eight months ago. His face was drawn, the shadows beneath his eyes suggesting a definite lack of sleep, and her gut twisted into a triple-knot before dropping low between her hips.

"Hey. I thought you'd be alone." Xander stared pointedly at Gamble, who—thank God—took the disdain on her brother's face pretty well.

"Yeah," she agreed, wanting to acknowledge the mistrust in Xander's eyes before she tried to sway him. "This is my friend, Gamble. He's okay."

"Your friend." Xander's lip curled up in doubt, but Kennedy stood firm.

"Yep."

Xander shrugged, one thin shoulder lifting halfway before dropping haphazardly. "If you have a friend, what do you need me for?"

The words sailed directly into her sternum, which had probably been their intended target, but that sure as hell didn't take the sting out of things. Gamble stiffened noticeably on the blacktop beside her, and Christ, she was on one hell of a high wire, here.

Time to cut through the crap. "I think you know why I asked you to meet me here."

Xander looked at the toes of his worn-out Converse All-Stars. "I'm sure I don't."

"Then let me spell it out for you," she said, because two could play at the attitude game, and she'd gold medaled in dauntlessness before she'd even graduated from middle school. "I want to know why you were at my bar when it caught on fire the other night."

"I'm not sure what you're talking about," Xander said, but there was a zero percent chance she was going to dick around now that he was right here in front of her.

Especially since her bullshit detector had just exploded.

"Do me a favor and let's skip those pleasantries, okay? You were at The Crooked Angel on Friday night when the dumpster behind it caught fire"—her hand lifted to quell his protest before he could even work it up—"I saw you, so don't even try. Then you came all the way downtown to see me after months, if not years, of dodging my texts, only to bolt five minutes later. So, do you want to tell me what the hell is going on, here? Because I don't think you need me to point out that it looks like you're into something you shouldn't be."

"It's not that simple," Xander said, huffing out an exhale. "Anyway, even if I *was* going to talk about anything, I'm not airing out my shit in front of an audience."

"I was there," Gamble said, and even though his voice was quiet, the dead-seriousness in his tone still sent goose bumps over Kennedy's skin. "I'm not just some random guy trying to get in your business. I was in that bar with your sister on Friday night, so as far as I'm concerned, you don't just owe her an explanation. You owe me one, too."

The toughness in Xander's expression slipped, just a little, but it was enough. "Nobody was supposed to be there."

Oh, God. "So, you set that fire in the dumpster on purpose?"

"No," Xander said, and at Gamble's lifted brows, he added, "I mean, *I* didn't set a fire at all. Look, I can't talk about this, okay?"

"Oh, you're going to talk about this," Kennedy said, her disbelief quickly spilling into anger. Bar fights were one thing. Hanging around with someone who intentionally set fires, *while* they set them? God, it was spectacularly stupid.

Not to mention, arson.

Xander shook his head, adamant. "You don't understand. I can't."

Taking a deep breath, she tried a different tack. "Look, if you're jammed up, I can help you."

"Right." His sneer was as unexpected as it was mean. "Xander the fuck-up needs bailing out by his perfect older sister, yet again. I'm all good, thanks."

Another direct hit, and this one left her momentarily speechless. Gamble, however? Wasn't having that problem.

"Hey," he bit out. "Your sister is just trying to help you." He'd taken a step forward, but Xander stood his ground.

"I don't need any help. From her or from you or from anybody else." He swung his gaze around the park, hunching down lower into his hoodie. "I shouldn't even be here. This was a mistake."

Kennedy saw his instincts turn from fight to flight in a blink, and no, no, no. She couldn't let him run. "Xander, this is serious," she said, positioning herself closer, but keeping her frustration far from her tone and her expression so he wouldn't be tempted to bolt. "If that fire was set intentionally, it's arson. That's a felony."

"Believe me, I know."

The words came out almost inaudibly, as if he hadn't meant to speak them, and the way his mouth had just pressed into a thin, rigid line confirmed it. "Listen, I'm sorry about your bar, and I'm glad you're okay. But you can't help me, here."

"I can help you," Kennedy argued softly, her heart locked in her throat. "No matter what you've done or what you're mixed up in, you're still my brother. I know you're a good person."

Xander's laugh held only bitterness. "You're wrong, Ken. I'm not the person you knew anymore, and I'm definitely not good."

"Bullshit."

Her reply seemed to startle both Xander and Gamble, because they stared at her, slack-jawed, but she wasn't about to wait for Xander to recover and slap his guard back into place.

"Don't try to tell me you're not a good person. You're here, aren't you?" she asked. "I told you I needed you, and you came. You're exactly the person you've always been, only right now, you're just caught up in something. Now, would you please tell me what the hell is going on? Because I'm really worried about you, and I meant what I said. I can help."

For a minute that felt more like a millennium, Xander stood there on the blacktop and said nothing. Although Gamble didn't move, Kennedy could feel him beside her, watching and waiting, and finally, Xander let out a breath.

"That dumpster fire was the tip of the iceberg, and the guy who set it...he's dangerous, okay?"

"Dangerous how?" Gamble asked.

"He's crazy. Like, not just fearless or stupid, or whatever, but really *crazy*." Xander paused as if he were caught up in one last, long internal debate. The look on Kennedy's face must have told him not to even bother holding back now, because then he added, "He's got this big plan to burn down a bunch of condos and storefronts that are under construction downtown."

Confusion outmuscled the holy-shit shock filling Kennedy's chest. "What? Why?"

"Normally, he wouldn't need a reason. He likes fire, and he's a complete wingnut. But this time, it's for money."

"What, like some kind of insurance fraud?" Kennedy asked, and oh God, how had she gone from slinging drinks and balancing payroll to a this-is-your-life episode of *Law & Order* with her brother as the special guest star?

"I didn't ask a lot of questions, and this guy is pretty tight with the details, so I'm not really sure," Xander said. "I wouldn't put much past him, but insurance fraud doesn't seem like his thing. Plus, he doesn't own the buildings, anyway. They belong to a bunch of highbrow real estate assholes. I guess he could be doing the wet work for a cut, but..."

"Arson is notoriously hard to prove unless it's done impulsively or by an idiot," Gamble said slowly. "But when big policies are taken out on properties, especially commercial properties, the fire marshal and the arson investigation unit take a really close look at the scene, along with all potential causes for the fire. The investigations are pretty extensive. Overall, using arson to commit insurance fraud is actually a lot less common than you'd think."

At Xander's bewildered expression, Kennedy said, "Gamble's a firefighter at Station Seventeen."

"Great," Xander muttered. "Anyway, the dumpster was just a test run for the device he wants to use to trigger the bigger fires he's going to set later. This guy said all the nearby businesses would be empty since it was so late, but I didn't even know until we got downtown that we'd be anywhere close to your bar."

At that, Kennedy's anger surged. "But you *were*, and I was inside. Any one of my staff could have been closing that bar instead of me. They could've been seriously hurt!"

"Do you think I don't get that?" Xander snapped, jamming a hand through his hair. "Jesus, Ken, it's been killing me, okay? None of this is what I signed on for!"

"What *did* you sign on for?"

Gamble's voice was low and shockingly soft, and Xander blinked in the harsh fluorescent light spilling down from overhead before answering.

"Like I said, it's a job. There's money in it. Among other things. But this guy told me no one would get hurt, either last night or when we set the bigger fires. He said it was going to look like negligence and there would only be property damage, and that all I had to do was help him set things up. Only now, that's not how it's turning out."

"Does this guy have a name?" Gamble asked, but Xander shook his head almost immediately.

"I'm not talking names. Believe me, you don't want to know him."

Although Kennedy's mind spun in no less than six different directions, one thing stood out as wildly clear. "We might not, but the police sure will. You need to tell them about this, Xander. Before whoever this guy is does damage to something far bigger than a dumpster."

"Are you out of your mind?" Xander asked, the look on his face suggesting the question was rhetorical. "I can't go to the cops with any of this."

"Of course you can. They might offer you a deal. Or—"

"No." He stepped back to stare at her, his hands jammed over his hips. "First of all, this guy is one fry short of a fucking Happy Meal, and secondly, he's cagey as shit. I don't know any details like the whens and wheres, and I don't have access to anything that would count as hard physical evidence, like the materials or the ignition devices or the plans. He makes all that stuff somewhere other than his apartment."

Kennedy's brows winged up. "Then how do you know what to do and where to go?"

"He gives me the plan verbally from a burner phone, and only when things are about to go down. I'd have nothing concrete to give the cops, even if I *wanted* to go to them—which I don't. Plus..."

"What?" Kennedy asked. Seriously, how much worse could this get?

Xander's shoulders slumped. "He's got enough on me to make it look like I'm the one who started the dumpster fire and is planning everything else. I'm not," he emphasized. "But I'm not a choir boy, either, okay? He sent me to buy a lot of the stuff he's using to make the remote ignition devices, and he set up fake accounts on the Internet using my name to buy even more. He's even got surveillance footage of me buying the gasoline he used to torch the Camry last night, which—oh, by the way, I stole."

Oh, my God, she was going to kill him. "You *stole* a car?"

"I told you, not a choir boy," he said with a frown. "It's not like I can just waltz right in to some precinct and start pointing fingers. You know how far the word of a career Northie goes with downtown cops. They're gonna trust me about as far as they can shotput a baby grand. If I go to them now, I might as well be signing my own death warrant."

Kennedy opened her mouth to argue, but God *damn* it, she couldn't. If this guy, whoever he was, had evidence that pointed to Xander starting the dumpster fire and burning up that stolen car, as soon as the cops picked him up on a knock and talk, he'd throw Xander under the bus.

Still... "Okay, I know it looks bad—"

"Bad? Shit, Kennedy. You really have been downtown for a long time. A D&D outside of Houlihan's looks bad. This? Looks like prison, straight-up."

"So, what?" she asked, her frustration seeping into her shoulders and her voice. "You're just going to go along with it and burn down some freaking buildings in the middle of the city and hope no one gets hurt?"

"I don't have any other *choice*," Xander snapped, taking a step back from her and Gamble. "I was stupid to come here. I've got to go."

He turned on the heels of his sneakers, but Kennedy had

anticipated the movement, reaching out to grab his arm at the same time he pulled away.

"Xander, wait, just—"

His entire body went bowstring tight as her fingers tightened around his forearm, and he yanked back from her with a pained grunt. Her adrenaline, which had already started chugging away when he'd turned to run, sent her heart surging halfway up her windpipe.

"*Ah.*" The sound slipped through Xander's teeth, and he staggered, cradling his arm with his opposite hand. For a split second, Kennedy's fear froze her to her spot, but then Gamble was there, moving in seamlessly to steady her brother's feet.

"It's all good, dude. I've got you. I'm going to roll up your sleeve and take a look at your arm."

His tone brooked no argument, although Xander still looked like he wanted to cough one up. In a move that was shockingly gentle despite how huge his hands were, Gamble lifted the loose cotton to Xander's elbow, revealing a flimsy, bloodstained bandage that had torn away from a horrific three-inch burn mark on the underside of his forearm.

Kennedy's pulse lunged for her breastbone. "Oh, my God," she spat. "Did he do this to you? This *guy*?" She was going to rip this asshole limb from fucking limb.

"I told you," Xander said shakily, a sheen of sweat covering his forehead. "You don't know who you're dealing with. He's a complete psycho."

"I don't care! He needs to go down for this!" she cried, her hands cranking into fists. Steeling herself, she dropped her stare to his arm again, trying not to shudder. "We need to get you to urgent care, or maybe even Remington Memorial."

Xander shook his head. "It's fine."

"I'm not kidding." Her gut panged hard before twisting into knots. "That already looks infected, and—"

"I said it's *fine*. Jesus, I'm not a goddamn kid anymore, Kennedy. Anyway, urgent care costs money. In case you forgot that little nugget."

"Okay, you two," Gamble ground out, splitting a glance between the two of them. "Let's focus on what's right in front of us, first. Kennedy, do you have a first aid kit in your car?"

She blinked until her brain caught up to the question. "I—yes."

"Good. Go grab it."

By the time she'd done what Gamble had asked and returned, he'd walked Xander back to the bench and tossed the ratty old bandage that had slipped off the burn. He popped the first aid kit open, taking out some antibiotic ointment along with some tape and gauze.

"This is a really nasty second-degree burn," Gamble said, rubbing some antibacterial hand gel onto his fingers before slipping the pair of nitrile gloves from the first aid kit and tugging them over his hands. "I can put some of this ointment on it and bandage it back up, but your sister is right. You really need for a doc to debride the wound and assess the extent of the tissue damage, otherwise it's going to get infected. If it isn't already."

"Oh, so now you're a medic, too?" Xander asked, and Gamble's jaw clenched.

"I don't have to do this, you know."

Xander dipped his chin to his chest and slumped back against the bench. "Yeah, I know. Sorry."

Kennedy watched carefully as Gamble tended to her brother's wound. She couldn't help but flinch a couple of times when Xander was clearly in pain, but finally, the clean gauze and tape were in place.

"Thanks," he mumbled, and Kennedy sat down next to him as Gamble stood to ditch the gloves and trash in a nearby garbage can.

"Look, Xander, I'm not trying to baby you or bail you out," she said. "But this situation is clearly dangerous in a lot of ways." She would not let her voice hitch. She *would* be strong, here. "But you can't just sit back while this guy sets fires all over downtown Remington."

"No, you really can't," Gamble said, holding up his cell phone as he walked back over to the bench. "I just got a message from a buddy of mine over at the fire marshal's office. They recovered enough of the ignition device from the dumpster fire to know that this is arson, and they're opening an active investigation. So, either you go to the cops, or chances are, they'll come to you. Which one is it gonna be?"

12

Gamble never thought he'd feel uncomfortable in the Thirty-Third District's police headquarters. He was certainly tight with enough of the cops in the intelligence unit to know they'd welcome him with a friendly hey-how-are-ya and a smile every time he walked into the place. Yet, as he signed the top spot on the Monday morning visitor's log and went through the metal detectors at the desk sergeant's station, his stomach filled with dread.

He and Kennedy had withheld information from officers during an active investigation into a fire, a fire that was now officially listed as an arson and being investigated by the RFD. The punishment, he could handle; hell, he'd earned whatever the department decided to throw at him, fair and fucking square.

But having Sergeant Sam Sinclair of the intelligence unit chew his ass out wasn't going to be a picnic. Especially since Gamble's captain, Tanner Bridges, would be next in line once Sinclair was done.

And yet, Kennedy had been right. Not only had her brother shown up at that park, but he was in way over his head with an arsonist who had plans to burn down half the damned city.

"Hey," came a throaty, familiar voice from beside him, and Jesus, this woman could put his composure through a shredder. Last night's kiss had been case in point.

Hot. Reckless. Needy. And not at all smart considering where they'd been and what they'd gone there to do. Still, he'd still wanted nothing more in that moment than to strip her bare and kiss a whole lot more than her mouth, right there in the front seat of her car, and wasn't *that* just all the more reason he needed to get his shit together, ASAP.

Losing focus was dangerous. But giving in to impulse, and one that strong, to boot?

That was downright deadly.

Gamble snuffed out all thoughts of the kiss, blanking his expression and lifting his chin at Kennedy in greeting. "Hey." His gut tilted as he looked beside her and came up with nothing but empty space. "Where's Xander?"

"Over there," she said, hooking her thumb at a small cluster of chairs about a dozen paces away, where her brother clearly sat, stock-still. "He said he needed a second. I think he's nervous."

Gamble nodded. "Understandable. How was last night?"

He'd been hesitant to wait the twelve hours to come in, at first, and even more hesitant to agree to let Xander go with Kennedy to her place for the night with only the guy's word that he'd come to the precinct this morning, as planned. But Xander had sworn no fires, practice or otherwise, were going down last night, so Kennedy had suggested they get a decent night's sleep and meet here this morning. Under any other circumstances, Gamble might've balked. But she'd been unable to mask the concern on her face for her brother's well-being, and to be honest, the kid had looked like he'd been through the wringer—twice. Gamble had trusted her this far, and she'd been clear from the get that if Xander was involved in something sketchy and didn't cooperate, she'd be the first to turn him in. So Gamble had gone with his gut and trusted her again.

Which would be nine kinds of fucked up, except it felt too right in his gut to be wrong.

And, hey, wasn't *that* just nine kinds of fucked up, all on its own?

Kennedy blew out a breath, and the soft sound dropped Gamble right back to reality. "Last night was awkward and tense, but at least Xander didn't backpedal or try to bolt. Not even when I texted Isabella and told her I needed to stop by first thing this morning for a talk."

"So, he didn't tell you anything else about this arsonist?" Gamble asked.

She shook her head, her dark hair brushing the shoulders of her T-shirt. "No, but I didn't really think he would. I took him to urgent care and got that burn taken care of. He told the doc it was a bonfire accident." She paused to wince, and after having seen the wound up-close and personal last night, Gamble didn't blame her. "After that, we went to The Fork in the Road for something to eat, and then back to my place to crash. Xander wasn't happy about not going home, or about calling in sick to work today, but at least he's got a note from the doctor at urgent care to back it up. And I knew he was safe, so..."

"It was smart that he stayed with you and got a good meal and some sleep."

At that, Kennedy's stare slid to the linoleum beneath her boots. "Yeah, well. I guess we should do this, huh? I told Isabella we'd be here at nine."

"I'm ready when you are," Gamble said. Kennedy sent

one last fleeting look at Xander before walking over to murmur in his ear. Although he didn't look thrilled, he stood, following her back over to the spot where Gamble waited.

"Hey," Xander said, lifting his chin in greeting. "So, uh, before we do this, I just wanted to say...thanks...for looking at my arm last night."

Surprise rippled a path through Gamble's chest, and Kennedy's eyebrows lifted to match the sentiment as Xander continued.

"You were right about the wound needing to be cleaned out. The doc said if I hadn't come in, it would've definitely gotten infected and made me really sick, so, you know. That was cool."

"Don't worry about it, man," Gamble said, meeting Xander's light green stare for a nod before shifting to look at Kennedy. "You ready to do this?"

"Yeah."

She locked her shoulders around her spine, turning toward the door leading to the intelligence office. Gamble knew she must have no less than a hundred emotions winging around in her system right now—dread and fear being the two headliners—yet, still, she walked through that door without hesitation, and a strange sensation unfolded in his gut. On the surface, it felt like attraction.

Under the surface, he didn't want to contemplate how much better it felt than run-of-the-mill want.

Gamble tamped down the thought, following Kennedy and Xander into the intelligence office. Rather than being boxed off into a bunch of isolated cubicles, the room was open, with the detectives' desks clustered to form several work stations within the larger space. Windows lined the wall to the left, taking away any air of stuffiness or sterility.

The opposite wall was mostly covered in a half-dozen computer monitors that formed an array, the kind that could make either one large digital image or several different ones all at once. Capelli sat at the oversized desk in front of that work area—not exactly a shocker considering his status as the intelligence unit's tech guru—clacking rapidly on his keyboard with one hand and eating an apple with the other. Isabella sat at a paper-strewn desk in the center of the room, cradling a cup of tea and laughing at something her partner, Detective Liam Hollister, had said from the work station next to hers. Detective Matteo Garza, the intelligence unit's newest member and a recent transfer from the RPD's gang unit, sat nearby and joined in on the laughter. Isabella straightened as she caught sight of Gamble, Kennedy, and Xander, although her smile didn't slip.

"Hey, you two made it in." She stood, and despite her cheerful greeting and slender frame, she gave off a definite air of someone not to be messed with—one that the Glock on her belt and the badge around her neck had nothing to do with.

"Yeah." Kennedy leaned in to return the hug Isabella had offered, pulling back a second later to add, "Isabella, Liam, Matteo. This is my brother, Xander Matthews. Xander, these are detectives Moreno, Hollister, and Garza."

All three detectives wore matching expressions of shock at the whole brother-revelation thing, even Garza, who had only been part of the fold for a couple of months.

Hollister recovered first. "Xander, it's great to meet you." He leaned forward to extend his hand, which Xander took with not a little hesitation.

"Thanks," he mumbled, nodding a hello at Isabella and Matteo. Isabella's brows tugged downward. She was perceptive as hell—took one to know one, and all that—but she kept her questions to herself as she turned toward Gamble with another smile.

"Hey, Lieutenant. You keeping my fiancé in line over there at the fire house?"

"Always," Gamble said, and Isabella nodded.

"Well, as nice as it is to see you two, something tells me this isn't a social call."

Kennedy shook her head and exhaled slowly. "No, it's... definitely not. We need to, um, talk to you guys about something. It's important."

In an instant, Isabella's demeanor changed, and she exchanged a loaded glance with Hollister. "Why don't you three come on back this way? We can get comfortable in one of the private rooms. Garza, you good out here?"

"Sure," he replied. Gamble's heart tapped a little faster behind his T-shirt as he followed the two detectives, Kennedy, and Xander to the back of the room. They moved down a narrow hallway and into a much smaller space, where the only option was to sit at the rectangular table in the center of the room. Instinctively, Gamble angled his chair so his back was to the far wall and he could see not only the exit, but everyone in the room regardless of where they chose to sit or stand, and it didn't escape his notice that Kennedy did the same.

"I know this isn't intelligence's area of expertise," Kennedy started, opting to cut through all the pleasantries and just dive right in. "But I didn't know where else to turn."

Isabella shook her head, the concern in her eyes genuine. "We've got your back, girlfriend, and you can always come to us. You know that. So, what's up?"

Kennedy flashed Gamble one quick look before beginning to recount everything that had happened from the night of the fire forward. He remained mostly quiet, only adding details when Isabella or Hollister asked for them. Both detectives tried to keep their expressions passive, although neither one of them looked particularly thrilled (or, okay, even remotely close to happy) when Kennedy admitted they'd kept Xander's identity and possible involvement under wraps. After the first run-through of the story, Isabella excused herself and came back with Sinclair, who listened silently as Kennedy ran through the whole chain of events again.

"So, let me get this straight," Sinclair said, sitting back in his chair to pin first Kennedy, then Gamble, then Xander with a set of frost-covered stares. "The dumpster fire at The Crooked Angel the other night was a test-run done by a serial arsonist to make sure his design for a remote incendiary device worked before he uses the device to set fires in multiple, potentially well-populated locations around the city. A plan which you"—he pointed at Xander—"are privy to, and you two"—Gamble's chest tightened as the sergeant sent the same gesture at him and Kennedy—"looked into on your own instead of calling officers Boldin and Lynch like you should've."

"Yes, sir," Gamble said. "That's accurate."

Sinclair's exhale telegraphed his displeasure, his gray-blond brows lifting up toward his crew cut. "And you didn't think it would be wise to let the RPD help you find your brother and investigate this by the book instead of potentially putting yourselves in harm's way?"

Kennedy's eyes glinted in the fluorescent office lights, and damn it, nothing good was going to come of whatever she was about to say. "With all due respect, Sergeant, Gamble and I took a couple of trips to my old neighborhood, which is hardly dangerous. Yes, I know we—*I*—

should've come to you sooner. Gamble wanted to, and I convinced him not to. But I didn't know about this psycho or that the fire was definitely arson until last night, and I was worried about my brother. People from North Point don't always get the benefit of the doubt."

Sinclair looked like he wanted to argue with her on several points, but instead, he turned to Xander. "Okay. I've heard your sister's version of this story. Now, it's time for yours."

"I'm not sure there's much to tell," Xander said sullenly, and Isabella leaned forward with both forearms on the table.

"Why don't you start at the beginning? Who is this guy, and how did you meet him?"

Talk about something Gamble wanted to know, and Kennedy, too, if her expression was anything to go by.

Xander let out a breath, closing his eyes for a heartbeat before opening them again to reply. "He goes by Rusty, but I don't know his real name or his last name. He's about five ten, not huge but not scrawny. He's got red hair and a burn scar on his face."

"He's not from North Point?" Hollister asked.

"He's not born and bred, no. The first time I remember seeing him around was maybe a year and a half or two years ago. I'm not sure where he's from, but he came up hard. You can tell."

None of the cops in the room needed the "how" of that spelled out for them. "So, you met him in the neighborhood," Sinclair prompted, and Kennedy flinched slightly at Xander's nod.

"Yeah. For a long time, I'd just see him around here and there. He mostly kept to himself. But then, six months ago, we were both kicking back at the bar at Houlihan's when

Brandy O'Donnell came in, all crying about how Mickey Fletcher had thrown her a beating for spending their last thirty bucks on groceries when he wanted it for blow. Mickey's a dick"—Xander paused, an apology in his eyes as he looked at both detectives and Sinclair, none of whom looked fazed in the least—"I mean, he's really a jerk. So, I said he really needed to pick on someone his own size. That was when Rusty leaned in and asked me if I wanted to do somethin' about it. I figured we'd just go find Mickey and tune him up a little, you know? Teach him not to smack girls around."

"But that's not what happened," Isabella said, and even though there was no question in sight, Xander shook his head.

"No. Rusty torched Mickey's car, right in front of the dude's house. Just tossed a Molotov cocktail right through the back window, easy as breathing, then stood there and laughed while the damned thing burned. I was surprised, but…"

Xander broke off, looking at his hands, and ah hell, Gamble knew that look on his face. He knew what the kid was going to say before he quietly continued with, "Mickey deserved it, and the karma felt good. After that, Rusty and I started hanging out. Nothing major. Every once in a while we'd do something like that, set a small fire or a fake bomb or something, just to scare somebody, but it wasn't a lot, especially at first. Mostly, we'd just drink beer and bitch about work and all the rich people who have it so easy living downtown and stuff."

"So, that escalated when?" Sinclair asked, his stare unflinching from across the table.

"About four weeks ago," Xander said. "Rusty came to me and said he had this job opportunity and that there was a lot of cash in it, was I interested. Before you ask"—he swung a look at Kennedy, who had made a soft noise of frustration from between him and Gamble—"yes, I knew it sounded sketchy. But money is money, and I live in The Hill. It's not like I have a lot of the stuff. Plus, he said the only people who would lose out would be rich, snobby developers who had too much cash to know what to do with, anyway. It wasn't like we'd be ripping off anyone honest. So I told him I was listening."

Kennedy's frown was practically a living, snapping thing, and even though Isabella couldn't possibly have missed it, she stayed focused on Xander instead.

"Okay. We're not passing judgment," she said, and either she was the world's best liar, or the honesty on her face was entirely genuine. "We just want to know what this guy Rusty is up to."

Xander sat back, his shoulders tight against the back of his chair. "He said he needed help setting up a couple of really big fires in vacant buildings that are under construction—some crappy, older places that had been bought up by a bunch of slick developers so they could turn them into a bunch of upscale condos and restaurants and shops. Rusty swore he could make it look like an accident with the new electrical going in, and that we'd set the fires at night so no workers would be inside. It was the only reason I didn't stop listening right then and there."

"So, this has to be some kind of insurance scam, then," Hollister said. "Buy a couple of run-down buildings on the cheap and torch them before renovations get too far underway to keep the loss at a minimum. Then cash in on the easier money once the policies pay out."

Gamble had to admit, it made sense. At least, until you looked past the surface. "I don't know. In order to get an insurance payout, he'd have to actually own the buildings. Rusty clearly doesn't have the kind of assets to let him snap up a couple of investment properties downtown—not even at a steal. And with really high-dollar payouts, insurance companies send out privately contracted teams to do independent investigations on top of everything the RFD and the fire marshal's office conducts. There's a metric ton of red tape. It could be years before anyone saw any money, even if the fire *is* ruled accidental."

"Rusty definitely doesn't own the buildings," Xander said with a shake of his head. "Not that he wouldn't buy a couple of places and torch them just for grins, if he could. But with the kind of money it would take to buy a building and the amount of cash he promised me for helping him, someone else is bankrolling this."

Sinclair raised his brows and sent a look at Isabella and Hollister that was loaded with all kinds of nonverbal shorthand Gamble couldn't decipher. "He mentioned any names?"

"Nothing other than 'The Money'."

"The Money?" Isabella echoed, and Xander nodded.

"Yeah, you know. 'The Money wants this', 'I met with The Money last night', that sort of thing. Someone else is definitely pulling the strings. Plus, Rusty's done plenty of stuff for hire. He brags about it all the time, going on and on about how he nearly blew up a fire house for some gang guy a couple months ago."

Gamble froze, pinned into place by his own slamming heartbeat. "What did you say?"

"What, about the fire house?" Xander asked, although Gamble barely heard him past the white-noise rush of blood whooshing in his ears. That bomb, which had been commissioned by Remington's most ruthless gang leader after Seventeen's paramedics, Quinn Copeland and Luke Slater, had gotten tangled up with him on a call a few months ago, had not only nearly killed Gamble and everyone else in the fire house, but it had been one of the most sophisticated devices he had ever seen—and definitely the most well-made one he'd ever disarmed.

"Yes," Isabella bit out, and Christ, who could blame her? Kellan had been front and center in that bomb scare, too. "The fire house. Rusty planted that bomb?"

Seeming to get the gravity of the situation, Xander didn't wait to fork over any intel. "That's what he says. He never told me who hired him to do it, but he did say the job was really high profile, and that the device was the real deal. Said it would've gone off without a hitch if the guy who was helping him hadn't tried to back out and cost him extra time. He also told me..."

Here, Xander's words crashed to a halt, his gaze whipping toward Kennedy's.

"What?" she asked. As badly as Gamble wanted the answer to the question, his gut panged in warning, his unease spreading like a low, hot flame at Xander's exhale.

"Rusty told me he killed the guy and burned his body, and that he'd do the same to me if I tried to back out of this job."

13

Kennedy was going to vomit. The room in the back of the intelligence office, which had been decently comfortable until a few minutes ago, had suddenly shrunk to the size of a shoebox and heated by about fifty degrees.

Her brother's life was being threatened by a deranged serial arsonist-slash-bomber, and the maniac had made it clear he wouldn't hesitate to take Xander piece by piece if he had to.

No. *No.* She couldn't let anything else happen to him. She'd already let things get this bad.

She had to keep her brother safe.

"That's not going to happen," Kennedy told him, steeling her voice to keep it from sounding as small and scared as she felt. "Do you hear me? I'm not going to let that happen."

"None of us are going to let that happen," Isabella said, and Hollister and Sinclair nodded in quick agreement. "But in order to get there, we're going to have to catch this guy with enough evidence to arrest him. And whoever he's working with."

Kennedy scraped for a breath, and okay, yeah. Arresting this fucking psycho sounded good. For starters. "So, how do we do that?"

"First thing's first," Sinclair said. "We open a case. Hollister, see if Hale and Maxwell are in yet and grab Garza so we can bring everyone up to speed. Also, tell Capelli to start running preliminary searches on the nickname Rusty to see if anything pops. Moreno, get arson investigation on the phone. We're going to need to loop them in on this and find out everything they can tell us about that device from the dumpster."

"Copy that," came the chorus from both detectives as they pushed to their feet and moved toward the door.

Sinclair surprised Kennedy by refocusing his attention not on Xander, but on the spot where Gamble sat silently next to her at the table. "I'm going to need to know everything you remember about the bomb that was planted under your fire engine so arson investigation can run it against the device from the dumpster. If this guy's got a signature, a unique method for putting these things together, or specific materials he likes to use—*anything* we can potentially track or trace—I want to know it."

"I'm happy to tell you everything I know about that bomb," Gamble said, his voice low and quiet. "But I'm not sure the information will do you any good."

Sinclair started, "Sometimes even small details can help build a profile or break a case..." but Gamble cut him off with a shake of his head.

"I meant with the investigators, not the facts. Frank Wisniewski, the head of the department for a couple of decades? He just retired from arson two months ago. Moved down to Florida. Natalie Delacourt took over as the lead investigator. She's not bad at her job," Gamble added, likely in an attempt to quell the panic that had probably just made the trip from Kennedy's chest to her face, or maybe to reassure Sinclair, who looked less than happy at the news, as well. "But she's only led three investigations since Wisniewski left, and none of them were ruled arson in the end, so she doesn't have a whole lot of experience. Especially with cases as tangled up as this one. That's all."

"I see." Sinclair shifted forward without breaking eye contact with Gamble. "And what about you?"

Gamble's shoulders hit the back of his chair with a hefty *thump*. "What about me?"

"You disarmed the bomb under the fire engine, right?"

Oh, God. "You did that?" Kennedy blurted, her lips falling open in shock. She'd heard the nuts and bolts of the story, of course, since some of her best friends had been targeted in the attempted bombing, but everyone involved had been pretty tight-lipped with the details. She'd assumed it had been because none of them had wanted to relive something so terrifying, but now…

"Yeah," Gamble said, his gaze flickering to hers. "We didn't disclose it to the media since the investigation into the gang leader who had been after Quinn and Luke was still ongoing at the time, and Kellan, Luke, Shae, and I all worked with the bomb squad as a team once we found the device and knew we couldn't evacuate. But I have"—he paused—"experience disarming IEDs, so I did the hands-on part and disarmed the bomb."

"And you have firsthand knowledge of what this guy Rusty's work looks like, in addition to your familiarity with explosives and incendiary devices. Like what was found in the dumpster," Sinclair pressed.

"I do, but I'm not sure how that signifies."

Determination sharpened the sergeant's already-hard

features, turning his stare ice-blue and immoveable. "I want you on this case."

"What?" Gamble and Kennedy both asked at the same time, and even Xander, who had been taking everything in without comment, lifted his dark brows in shock.

"You want me to work on this case?" Gamble reiterated after a second.

Sinclair nodded. "As long as you're willing and Captain Bridges is okay with it. But you're the closest thing we've got to an expert right now, and you're definitely the only person who's had a close-up look at Rusty's handiwork. I could use your eyes on the device that was pulled from the dumpster. Along with anything else Delacourt and her people have pulled from the scene."

"This bastard put the lives of my entire team at risk and now he wants to start fires in the middle of the city," Gamble growled. "I'm good for whatever you need to gutter-spike his ass to the nearest wall."

"Excellent. Now that we've got that out of the way..."

Sinclair turned toward Xander, but before he could continue or Kennedy could work up one of the two hundred questions she had about how they'd keep Xander safe while they went after Rusty, her brother beat them both to the punch.

"So, this is where you arrest me, right? For stealing the car and buying all that stuff for Rusty and being with him at The Crooked Angel when he started the fire in the dumpster."

Kennedy was so shocked that, for a heartbeat, she could only listen, pinned to her chair, as Sinclair said, "Actually, that's not up to me, although, technically, it *is* an option."

"*What*?" Kennedy half-barked, half-choked out as she found her voice with startling speed. "You're going to arrest him and call the ADA? He came here willingly and he answered every single question you asked him!"

"Your brother did come here willingly," Sinclair agreed. "But he also admitted to committing at least one felony, not to mention being a willing participant in this arson scheme."

"But—"

"Kennedy, stop."

Xander straightened, and God, he looked like he'd aged ten years in the last two. "It's cool. I told you this was how it was going to go. With all the shit I've done, I wouldn't trust me if I was on the other side of this table, either. At least this way, I got to say my piece, and maybe now Rusty will get caught."

He went to push to his feet—God *damn* it, she'd trusted Sinclair to give Xander a fair shake!—but the sergeant stopped him, mid-shift.

"You didn't want to hear the other option, then?"

"Sorry?" Xander asked, clearly confused, and okay, that made two of them.

Sinclair tilted his head, the slightest of smiles ghosting over his mouth. "I said arresting you is an option, but I never said I was going to do it. Your sister is right. You did come in to tell us about Rusty's plan, and you didn't lawyer up or use the intel just to get a deal."

"Maybe he should have," Kennedy muttered. Gamble arched a brow at her in a nonverbal *shush*, but oh, no. No way was she going to just let Sinclair haul her brother off without a fight. Especially when his life was on the line.

Sinclair continued. "You could have taken your chances with the arson investigation, or even run, but you didn't. You came here instead. That tells me you must really want Rusty behind bars."

"He's got my ass in a sling." Xander shrugged, but the movement was just stiff enough to file the edge off the nonchalance he'd surely meant to accompany it. "I don't do what he tells me to, he kills me. I come to you, and he makes it look like the whole scheme is my idea. I can't really win, either way."

"That would be true, except for one small thing," Sinclair said.

"And that is?"

"I believe you."

The words knocked Kennedy's breath from her lungs. Xander looked equally stunned, although his expression quickly morphed into doubt.

"What's the catch?"

Sinclair's hesitation was Kennedy's first clue that she wasn't going to like what he had to say. When he leaned forward over the desk to be sure he had Xander's full attention? That was when her gut did a full-on nosedive.

"I told you, you have options. We could arrest you and keep you incarcerated while this plays out. We could also hold you in protective custody while we investigate the case. But that could take weeks, and if you disappear, chances are pretty high Rusty will figure out that you came to us, and he'll cover his tracks or change his plans. Either way, it'll make him hard to catch. We can't arrest him without concrete evidence of a serious crime, and if the case against him doesn't stick..."

"You spring me from protective custody and I'm kindling as soon as he gets his hands on me," Xander finished.

Kennedy revisited the urge to throw up. "I told you, that's not going to happen. Anyway, protective custody isn't necessarily a bad option. At least there, you'd be safe."

"Only until the case falls apart," Xander argued. "Then I'd be dead."

"Will you stop *saying* that? Look, I know protective custody isn't ideal, but—"

"There is a third option," Sinclair interrupted, effectively snagging both her and Xander's attention. But that look in his eyes was back, the one that told her she was going to hate the next thing he said with the burning passion of ten thousand white-hot suns, and she had to give it to the guy. He didn't fucking disappoint.

"You could sign on as a CI, and we could spring you now. You'd have to agree to let us track you, and you'd also have to check in on a regular basis," Sinclair added, sending the point home with a lift of his index finger. "But we'd have you under surveillance, which would keep you safe, not to mention giving us a lot of evidence to build a solid case against Rusty and whoever he's working with."

Sweet baby Jesus, Sinclair was out of his mind. "You want to let Xander go *back* to this lunatic so you can build a case against him?"

"I do. I think we can all agree that Rusty's a threat, and this is the best chance we have to catch him before he hurts somebody."

"By putting Xander at risk," Kennedy cried. "Absolutely not. You need to find another way."

Funny, neither Gamble nor Xander seemed ready to jump on the oh-hell-no bandwagon. "So, let me make sure I've got this straight," Xander said slowly. "You want me to wear a wire and snitch on Rusty, and that's how you're going to put him away?"

Sinclair nodded. "It's our best shot at getting the evidence we'll need to hook him for these fires, and hopefully the attempted bombing at Station Seventeen, too. This unit has got some of the best surveillance equipment available, thanks to Capelli. But, to answer your question, yes. You might need to wear a wire. Grab downloads of whatever you can off Rusty's laptop. Take photographs and relay a list of materials and plans to the team. All of that would be fair game."

"And in exchange, I'd be able to go home tonight. Go back to work tomorrow. Go through my life, business as usual," Xander said, and no, no. No, no, no, he couldn't possibly be thinking about agreeing to this.

"Xander, are you crazy?" Kennedy hissed. "Rusty held a lighter to your arm and *burned* you to keep you quiet." She swung toward Sinclair, whose expression had just flickered with surprise, and nailed him with a glare. "Xander left that little tidbit out. But if you want to know how crazy this guy is, feel free to check out the second-degree burn on my brother's right forearm. You can take your time with that, though, since he'll have a scar for the rest of his life."

Sinclair sat straighter in his chair, dividing his stare between her and Xander. "Believe me, I understand Rusty's a threat. That's exactly why I want him off the streets, and I think this is the best way to make that happen."

"No," Kennedy said. "Sending him back in is way too dangerous. Rusty's clearly not stable *or* predictable. You'll have to find another way."

She knotted her arms over the front of her T-shirt, partly to punctuate the refusal, partly to keep her heart from clattering right past her rib cage and onto the linoleum. Protective custody wouldn't be great for the case, she knew. But intelligence worked hard cases all the time. Sinclair and Isabella and the rest of the team would figure something out. At least Xander would be safe if they put him in protective custody.

And he had to stay safe. He was all the family she had, and it was her job to take care of him.

"There is no other way, Kennedy. We need Xander on the inside."

Kennedy had expected the protest from Sinclair. But since it had been Gamble, not the sergeant, who had delivered it, and that he'd done so with such certainty, she was thrown off-kilter, enough to make her argument stick in her windpipe. Xander and Sinclair both looked at him, but his dark, dead-serious gaze was locked in on one place.

Hers.

"If I'm going to have any prayer of making the physical evidence line up, I need your brother's eyes and ears, and Sinclair is right. If Xander ghosts because we pull him into protective custody, Rusty will know something is up. Xander will be more at risk than ever, and the case will fall apart. We won't even be back at square one—we'll be so far in the hole that Rusty could burn down half the city, and Xander along with it, without any warning. We'd never see him coming. We need your brother on the inside, Kennedy. It's the only way to catch Rusty."

Kennedy's throat threatened to close off, but she managed to choke out, "No. You saw that burn on his arm. You disarmed that *bomb*, for God's sake! You know what Rusty is capable of."

"I do," Gamble agreed, his nearly black stare piercing right through her. "And we need to stop him. Xander is the key to that. If we're going to catch Rusty, we need Xander on the inside. Nothing else will work."

"I'll do it," Xander said, kicking the air from her lungs with those three simple words. She wanted to tell him no— hell, she wanted to scream it as loud as humanly possible— but she was terribly, desperately out numbered.

Gamble had made sure of that.

"I want immunity from prosecution. I'll do retribution for the car I stole," Xander added, nodding at Sinclair. "Whatever it takes to pay the owner back for any losses. But if I'm going to put my life on the line, then I want a clean slate. These fires weren't my idea, no matter what Rusty says. I'm not going down for them."

"I can talk to the ADA," Sinclair said. "But considering the circumstances, I don't think that'll be a problem. We'll have to get you set up in the system, and after that, we'll put our heads together and come up with a plan to get you started. But after all of that shakes out, you should be able to go about your business at home and at work."

Kennedy's temples pounded, her heart doing its best to show them how the job was *really* done. "Xander, please. Think about this. It's"—*dangerous. Crazy. Highly possible you could be killed slowly and horribly by a complete psychopath* —"not a good idea."

Her brother shook his head. "Gamble's right. It's the only way to catch Rusty."

Seriously, she was going to throttle that firefighter. Later. After she'd convinced her brother that this was a spectacular fail of an idea. "It's not. If you'd just listen to reason—"

"This *is* reason, Ken." Xander turned toward her. But rather than giving her a mountain of attitude, or, worse yet, blowing off her fears, he simply said, "I know you're scared, and I'm not gonna bullshit you. You have good reason to be. But I can't do this halfway and hope for the best, and you can't protect me forever."

Her brother blew out a breath, making her heart corkscrew against her ribs. "I know, but—"

"No," Xander interrupted, and even though his voice was quiet, the words hit Kennedy with all the force of a Mack truck on a steep downhill grade. "I screwed up, Ken. I got myself into this, fair and square. Now, I need to get myself out."

He looked at Gamble, then Sinclair, and, oh God, this couldn't be happening. "If you need me to become an informant in order to catch Rusty, I'll do it."

"Great," Sinclair said, pushing up from his chair. "I'll go ahead and write up the paperwork and call ADA Kingston so we can get started as soon as possible. We've got an arsonist to catch."

14

Gamble had endured all sorts of hellish conditions in his life. The Crucible at boot camp. The heat and stench and danger of more third-world countries than he could count. Buildings that had burned down over his head as he'd desperately searched for the civilians trapped inside their own literal version of hell.

But none of that held a candle to the anger that had vibrated out of Kennedy the second her brother had agreed to sign on as a CI this morning, and had continued to fill the space between them as Xander's paperwork had been processed and Gamble had been officially signed on to the case.

Other than a few glares he'd bet good money she hadn't been able to help, Kennedy hadn't spared him so much as an extra glance for the rest of the time they'd spent at the Thirty-Third, and she damn sure hadn't said goodbye to him when they'd parted ways outside of the intelligence office eight hours ago. Not that, at least on the surface, he didn't get it. His brain reminded him she'd practically raised her brother, and that she just wanted him safe. Gamble didn't want the guy in harm's way, either—Rusty definitely seemed like a diabolical SOB, and they'd barely scratched the surface of the investigation. Gamble had a feeling things would get a fuckload more dangerous before they got better, so yeah, Kennedy hadn't been wrong when she'd said-slash-yelled that there were a whole lot of chances for things to go tits up with her brother signing on as an informant.

Even if Xander had been right to say yes, and Gamble had meant every syllable of what he'd said.

He needed Xander's eyes and ears if they were going to make the case. And there was a negative thirty-seven percent chance that Gamble wasn't going to do every single thing within his power to take down the bastard who had threatened his fire house.

After all, he had a family, too. They just weren't related by blood.

Letting go of a slow breath, Gamble used the towel around his neck to get his shower-wet hair somewhere in the vicinity of damp. He skinned into a pair of black boxer briefs, then the jeans he'd grabbed from his bedroom, not bothering with a shirt because, well, it was August, he lived alone, and really, what was the frigging point? Not much formality in the fact that he was about to eat leftover Thai food for dinner and read through the case notes he'd picked up from the office of arson investigation on his way home from the gym. Not much personal connection, either, but at least he'd learned to live without *that* a long time ago.

Even though he hadn't stopped wanting it since the second Kennedy had put her mouth on his.

Right. The same mouth she probably used to curse your name all afternoon, Gamble reminded himself before shaking off the unexpected thought and even more unexpected shiver it had sent down his spine. Hanging up his towel, he hit the bathroom light switch with the flat of his palm and heel-toed it into his bedroom, his sights set firmly on the case. Somewhere out there, closer than any of them would like, was a nasty arsonist with plans to set fire to a whole lot of city real estate. He really needed to focus on the shit he could control and get over the stupid pang he felt every time he thought of Kennedy goddamn Matthews, once and for all.

He was halfway down the hall when the banging on his front door stopped him dead in his tracks. His pulse went through the ozone layer at the same millisecond his gray matter sorted and discarded all the viable possibilities, from a misguided delivery guy to overzealous Girl Scouts trying to offload that last case of Thin Mints. Gamble had chosen this apartment building for its solid reputation and even more solid security systems. Everyone who didn't have a keycard had to get buzzed in by a resident. Period. Hard stop.

So who the fuck was going all Muhammad Ali on his front door?

The banging went for round two, and okay, yeah, he'd had enough of this shit. His Glock 19M was in his bedside table drawer—one of the perks of being highly trained and living alone—but he sincerely doubted that anyone who was aiming for bodily harm would knock, even aggressively, so he left it behind. Gamble was all for personal safety, but wasting precious seconds to grab a sidearm he might not need, or worse yet, recklessly drawing a deadly weapon without knowing all the facts of a situation, weren't on his great, big list of hell yes.

Especially since he could strip the last breath from an intruder with nothing more than his goddamned thumbs if the occasion called for it.

Cranking his shoulders into a firm line around his spine, Gamble kicked his bare feet into motion and headed toward the source of the racket. Taking care to keep his center mass away from the middle of the door, he angled a lightning-fast look through the peep hole until the person on the other side of the wood and steel registered. The burst of relief in his chest only lasted long enough for him to pop the slide bolt and swing open the door, though, because as soon as both actions were in the past tense, a very fiery, very familiar brunette had invaded every last inch of his personal space.

"I've spent the last eight hours telling myself I wouldn't come over here and do this, but screw that. I'm too mad at you to keep quiet," Kennedy said in a rush, and Gamble's brain was so inside-out at the sight of her that he replied with the first thought that popped into the stupid thing.

"How did you even find out where I live?"

Without so much as a blink of her blazing green eyes, she said, "I told Isabella you left your phone at the precinct today and that I wanted to come drop it off."

"You could have just asked me," Gamble told her. They'd exchanged numbers last night, and at least it would've spared his adrenal gland the unnecessary workout.

Another not-happening on the blink. "I could have, but I'm too mad to do anything other than yell at you." She pressed forward, her palms planted firmly over the low-slung denim hugging her hips. "After everything I told you about my brother and how he and I grew up, how could you do this to him? To *me*?"

Gamble's brain engaged in an epic battle with his baser instincts as he tried like fuck to balance the question against the fact that Kennedy now stood so close to him that her breasts had just brushed over his bare chest and her mouth was close enough to claim with a simple shift of his weight.

"Do what?" he asked, pausing just long enough to make sure the door had swung shut behind her the way it was supposed to before returning his focus to the matter at hand.

Or make that, *in* his hands, because Kennedy hadn't budged one bit from his front nine. "Are you kidding me? How could you have encouraged Sinclair to turn my brother into an informant like that when you know how dangerous Rusty is?"

"Your brother didn't have a hell of a lot of choices, Kennedy." Anger pulsed, quick and hot in Gamble's veins, but she met it with emotion of her own.

"He had *plenty* of choices. He could've gone into protective custody. Or taken some sort of deal from the ADA. Or, God, anything other than flip on this lunatic, who—news flash—already has zero qualms about killing him."

Gamble dug way down deep for composure he wasn't sure he had, especially when it came to the woman currently standing toe to toe with him. "Chances are, Xander would go to prison that way." A fact Sinclair likely hadn't come out with only because he hadn't needed the leverage.

And one that, from the look of things, wouldn't have swayed Kennedy even if he had. "His being in prison is better than him being dead!"

"Not if Rusty walks," Gamble ground out. "You think guys like that have no reach in prison? Jesus, Kennedy, where do you think the gang leader is who hired Rusty to make that bomb in the first place?"

Well, *that* got her attention. For a heartbeat, anyway. "Xander would still be safer that way."

Gamble shook his head. He might not like the truth,

here, but that didn't make it any less real. "No, he wouldn't, and you know it."

"What I know is that Xander is out there, sitting in his shitty apartment in The Hill, probably hungry, definitely in pain, and one hundred percent in danger because you and Sinclair will use whatever means necessary to get what you want."

Just like that, Kennedy's chin hiked right back into fuck-you territory, and the control Gamble had been white-knuckling slipped a notch.

"Nobody strong-armed Xander into becoming an informant, and it's not as if Sinclair and I are looking to use him for personal gain. We're talking about putting a serial arsonist behind bars."

"At what cost?" Kennedy asked, her voice pitching higher with rising emotion. "You're talking about his *safety*."

The waver that had accompanied her words took the razor-wire route directly under Gamble's skin, and he inhaled on a three-count before answering with, "And that's something that was made very clear to your brother before he willingly signed on for this."

"He's only twenty-three. He has no idea what he willingly signed on for," she snapped. "You don't understand. He can't do this. He *can't*."

The tension that had been simmering in the depths of Gamble's chest ever since Xander had told them that bomb at the fire house was Rusty's handiwork surged upward, moving Gamble forward without his brain's permission. Heart slamming in his throat, his ears—fuck, *everywhere*—he shifted forward until his face was only inches away from Kennedy's, close enough that he could hear the catch in her breath.

Yet, still, he didn't stop. "Do you know what that bomb

would've done if it had detonated, Kennedy? I'm not just talking about the deaths or the damage," he added in a pre-emptive strike against the obvious answer. "I mean, do you know what happens? Can you even conceptualize what it does to a human body? Or that these fires could do the same thing if someone gets trapped inside these buildings Rusty is trying to burn down?"

The three weeks of flashbacks and unspeakable nightmares Gamble had endured after he'd disarmed that bomb came crashing back, and he didn't think. Just spoke.

"People don't always die right away. Not even when they lose limbs in bombings. Not even when their injuries are bad enough that they should, or"—he pulled in a breath that was quicksand in his lungs—"when they do later, anyway. People die because guys like Rusty decide they care more about what they want than they do about human lives. So, yeah. I'll do whatever it takes to stop him, and I'll do it without apology. I get that Xander means a lot to you."

Again, Gamble broke off, but damn it, he couldn't stop the rest from pouring out. "I get it, because I've been there, too. I've lost people who meant...a lot. But we can't nail Rusty without Xander's help. Just because I pushed for that doesn't mean I don't get it, Kennedy. I *really* fucking do. No one wants Xander hurt. We're all on the same side, you know?"

A soft sound crossed her lips, torn halfway between irony and pure despair. "Of course, I know! But he's my brother. If something happens to him, it might be Sinclair's responsibility, or yours, or the RPD's. But it'll be my *fault*. If he gets hurt, if Rusty figures out what he's doing, if..."

Kennedy paused, her voice turning to an emotion-filled whisper that seemed to stick in her throat before finally emerging. "A long time ago, I promised my brother I'd take care of him, and that I would have his back no matter what. If Xander dies, that's on me, Ian. *Me.*"

In that moment, as her bright green eyes filled with tears, Gamble's gut panged with realization that stole the breath right out of his lungs.

She wasn't throwing around her bravado to be tough, and she wasn't angry.

She was terrified.

15

S tanding there, in the middle of Gamble's foyer with her hands on her hips and her heart in her windpipe, Kennedy hated herself.

The fact that not only was she about to do something as idiotic as *cry* in front of him, but that she wanted nothing more than for him to wrap those big, bruiser arms of his around her and hold her while she did it?

Yep. She was a serious contender for self-loathing right now.

"Is that really what you think? That this is your fault?" Gamble asked. His voice had grown quiet, although no less intense than a minute ago, and damn it, *damn it*, she needed to eighty-six the hot, stupid tears that had gathered in her eyes, fast.

But then, Gamble reached up to cup her face with one massive palm, and instead, she broke in two.

"It is," Kennedy said, a ripple of mortification moving through her as a choked sob escaped from her throat. "Maybe not directly, but I shouldn't have left him behind in the first place. I should have made him come with me when I left North Point."

Gamble's dark brows gathered over his stare. "But you tried. You told me you asked, and Xander said no."

"He was eighteen." She made a noise of frustration, sharp and quick. "He didn't know anything other than The Hill even existed outside of his wildest dreams. But I did. I knew better, and I didn't *do* better. Don't you see?" Her tears spilled down her face steadily now, but God, she was so scared and angry and just plain raw that she couldn't make herself try to be tough. "It was my job to keep him safe, and I let this monster get at him. If Rusty hurts him, if anything happens, it's on me."

"No."

The word split the scant space between them with no measure of leeway or apology. It stunned Kennedy into stillness, her pulse knocking so hard against her throat that all she could do was stand there and listen as Gamble continued, his gravelly voice pinning her into place.

"None of this is your fault. I know he's your brother, and I get that you're scared right now. But Xander is an adult, who made his own decisions." Gamble paused to swipe his thumb over the tears streaming across her cheekbone, his hand warm and soft despite its sheer size, and God, when was the last time she'd felt something so purely good?

As if he sensed her need for him to just keep touching her, to hold her steady in this moment, he continued. "Yes, your brother made bad choices, and yes, you can help him get his shit together, but nothing that's happened to him is on you."

"My brain knows that," Kennedy said, because, while she might have a dump truck full of loyalty to her brother, she also wasn't a moron. "Logically, of course I realize that he's an adult with his own life. But I raised him, far more than our mother did. It's so hard for me to be okay with a choice that I know puts him in danger. Even if that choice is for the greater good."

"I know, but it really is the best shot we have at getting Rusty off the streets, which is also the best way to be sure he never gets to Xander."

Just like that, all the fight seeped out of her, leaving behind only the fear that had fueled it. "I'm sorry I came over here and yelled at you like a raving lunatic. I'm just really scared."

"You're not a raving lunatic." Gamble huffed out a small breath that likely meant to be a laugh. Sliding his hand lower over her face, he hooked his index finger beneath her chin to lift it far enough to catch her gaze. "Do you think it was easy for me to tell Xander I need him on this case when I knew it could put him in harm's way? When I knew it would upset you?"

The words registered on a delay, her mouth parting on a gasp. "You cared about upsetting me?"

"I care about not hurting you," he said. "I care...about a lot of things."

"Oh."

It was precisely that moment when Kennedy realized she must have barged in on him moments after he'd gotten out of the shower. He was shirtless—she swallowed thickly—and his hair was just the slightest bit damp where it curled over his forehead. He smelled like soap, nothing fancy or overdone, just simple and clean, but also masculine. Their bodies were close enough to touch, his hips near her belly, her shoulders by the hard, flat wall of his chest. His finger still rested under her chin, mere inches from the pulse point that was fluttering madly beneath the hinge of her jaw, and oh God, oh God, oh God.

Kennedy didn't just want him. Right now, she fucking *craved* him.

A fact that must have clearly shown on her face, because Gamble's pupils flared, turning his stare dark and dangerous. "Kennedy," he started. But he didn't continue, so she tilted her head until her mouth was less than a breath from his.

"Hmmm?" she murmured, a decadent thrill shooting through her body as he exhaled in a hot burst.

"You know this is probably a bad idea."

She lifted one shoulder, her T-shirt shushing against his skin. "Unless it's a great idea."

Still, Gamble didn't budge. "A lot has gone down in the last few days."

"You're not really going to give me the whole let's-not-do-this-on-impulse line, are you?" Kennedy asked. She pulled back, but only far enough to arch a brow before adding, "Look, I'll grant that today has been emotional, and that the foreseeable future isn't going to be a skip through the park. But I don't make decisions I can't live with, and I don't think you do, either."

"I don't," he said, his glittering stare backing the claim one hundred percent. "But I still need the words."

Heat rushed through her blood, making her even bolder than usual. "What is it you want to hear me say? That I want you to kiss me?"

Gamble's body tightened, so close to Kennedy's that she felt the tension vibrating through him like a low, powerful hum, and oh, she fed off of it.

"You want me to tell you, out loud, how badly I want you to take off all my clothes so you can touch me? Wherever you want." She paused to let one corner of her mouth kick up in suggestion. "However you want."

A muscle flexed over his jawline, his gaze dropping to her naughty smile for just a heartbeat before he demanded, "Keep talking."

"You need me to say that I've been aching for you to fuck me ever since you put your hands on me in the supply closet the other night? That everything you want to give me, I want to give back even more?"

"Kennedy."

It was a warning. Or maybe a benediction. Either way, she said, "Because I do. I want all of that. I want you to kiss me, and I want to let you touch me. I want your cock inside my body, so hot and dirty and deep, I can't tell where you end and I begin. I want you to make me come so hard that I forget my name, then I want you to do it again, to be sure I remember yours. And I want it. Right. Now."

She hadn't even stopped speaking before Gamble moved, closing the space between them in a rush. Their bodies slammed together—sweet Jesus, he was perfect, all hard muscles and harder grip on her shoulders—and Kennedy let him guide her roughly backward until she found purchase against the nearest wall.

"Ah," she gasped against his mouth, trying fiercely to ground herself amid all the wildly intense sensations pumping through her brain and body.

Gamble showed her no mercy. Parting her lips with a sweep of his tongue, his demand for her mouth quickly became a claiming. He held her in place, palms wide over her shoulders, his huge frame as unyielding as the wall at her back, and kissed her deeply. Kennedy returned the kiss with matching intensity at first, but all too soon, she realized Gamble wasn't about to let go of the control he wore like a shadow. She arched into his touch, letting him take what he needed from their kiss, letting him give her what *she* needed, and every movement, every press and slide and lick, made her own desire coil tighter between her thighs.

"So soft. Your mouth is so..." Gamble trailed off in favor of tasting her lips with another brush of his tongue. For a hot second, she surrendered to the glide, but *God*, Kennedy wanted more, and she tightened her fingers around the top of his jeans to haul him even closer.

"Are we doing this here?" she asked, her voice so husky with need that she almost didn't recognize it as belonging to her.

Gamble's smile pressed against the tender spot where her jaw met her neck, making her nipples tighten. "Are you asking if I want to fuck you standing up in my front hallway?"

If he was trying to turn her on with his directness, it was totally working out in his favor. Not that she wasn't going to go for turnabout as fair play.

Kennedy released her hold on the denim around his hips, creating just enough space to deliver a brash-as-hell stare as she looked at him. "It's a yes or no question, Lieutenant."

He didn't look away. Didn't hesitate, or even blink. Just reached down and pulled her shirt over her head in one seamless yank.

"Does that answer your yes or no question, Ms. Matthews?" he asked, tossing the cotton to the floorboards.

Unwilling to trust her throat to do anything other than loosen a moan, Kennedy nodded, but of course, Gamble wasn't done. His fingers found the button and zipper on her jeans, freeing them both and pulling the denim just low enough to expose the tissue-thin fabric of her thong before he hooked his hands beneath her arms and lifted her off her feet.

Looked like her traitorous throat was going to have its way with that moan, after all. "Ohhh," Kennedy breathed, wrapping her arms around his shoulders and her legs around his waist out of pure instinct. He guided her back against the wall for leverage, using his hands—which were now splayed wide over her ass—and the strong, corded frame of his hips to balance out the rest of her body weight.

"That's more like it," he said, a bolt of provocative want blooming deep between her legs as the hard length of his cock notched over her pussy. Gamble's words scraped between them as if every syllable had been coated in gravel, the rough edges a perfect fit for the uncut intensity on his face. The overhead light in the foyer was the only one that appeared to be on in the main living space, and it illuminated the evening shadows spilling in from the eighth-floor windows she could see, just barely, in the main room over his shoulder. His muscles bunched and released as he held her in place against the wall, his skin surprisingly soft despite the bulk of the body it covered.

He pressed his mouth to her neck, both of them now perfectly in line. Kennedy turned her head to the side to grant him easier access, and every inch of her body begged for the touch of his insanely wicked mouth.

"Please," she murmured, and although she didn't have the breath or the brain cells to elaborate on exactly what she wanted, Gamble gave in to her plea, regardless. Trailing a path of suggestive, open-mouthed kisses up the column of her neck, he made his way toward the hinge of her jaw. His movements slowed without losing any of their intensity as he ran his tongue over her earlobe, tugging the studded flesh between his lips before moving higher, to the sensitive piercings around the top outer edge of her ear.

Heat unfolded in Kennedy's belly, settling low and heavy between her legs. The piercings—which had hurt like a sonofabitch when she'd received them—made her hyper-aware of sensation in a way she hadn't been before, to the point that even light contact with them could set off sparks of pleasure/pain. But this? With Gamble's mouth applying just the right amount of pressure on her over-sensitive skin?

Holy hell, she could come from the feel of that alone.

She tightened her grip on Gamble's shoulders, and he got the message, loud and goddamned clear. He worked the shell of her ear with masterful swirls and flicks of his tongue, pausing to linger in every spot that made her breath hitch in her chest. Wetness gathered behind her thong, quickly turning the thin satin damp where it clung to her body, and her clit pulsed from both the feel of his mouth and the slide of the fabric below.

More. *More.* She needed more.

She needed him.

"Okay, baby. I've got you," Gamble said, and Kennedy realized, too late, that she must've made the demand out loud. He shifted his mouth from her ear, and she mourned the loss of the sexy contact...right up until he gave her a glittering stare more palpable, more intense, than any touch.

He meant what he said. It might just be for tonight, but he *had* her.

And in this moment, right here and now, despite all the toughness of her usual armor, she wanted nothing more than to let him.

Loosening one hand from his shoulder, she reached between them, sliding the strap of her bra lower, until the black, satiny ribbon draped over the tattoo covering her bicep. The ink traveled upward toward her shoulder, the swirling watercolor design drifting over her collarbone and the back of her shoulder, and Gamble traced it with his eyes.

"You are beautiful," he murmured. Reflexively, she wanted to tell him he didn't need to sweet-talk her—she'd meant what she'd said about being certain of her consent, and she didn't want to pretend tonight meant something that it didn't. But his honesty flashed in his stare, stripping down the pleasantries to leave behind only the truth. He took her in slowly, as if time not only didn't matter, but it wasn't even a thing, as if he wasn't holding her up against a wall in the middle of his hallway and his rock-hard cock wasn't throbbing against the hottest, most needy part of her. He dipped his chin, the rasp of his beard making Kennedy shudder as he kissed everything he'd just learned with his eyes—her shoulder, her collarbone, the indent beneath her throat. He paused over the tiny silver anchor pendant resting there before moving to the flat of her upper chest. Her heart slammed so hard and so fast that he had to be able to see it moving beneath her skin, but God, she didn't care. Gamble rounded his shoulders, using the leverage of his hands and his hips to lift her slightly higher at the same time she bowed up to meet his mouth.

"*Ah.*"

The sound ripped from her throat, more desire than actual word. Gamble parted his lips over her nipple, pulling the fabric-covered tip into the heat of his mouth just once before releasing her to edge past her already-loosened bra with a tilt of his chin. Kennedy strained upward, desperate for his touch. But he was right there, closing his lips around her without the barrier of her bra in the way, and her pussy clenched as her breath shot out in a gasp.

"There you are," Gamble said. His mouth hovered over

her nipple, so close that his exhale sent a shiver laddering up her spine. He closed the space a second later, turning slow, firm circles with his tongue until she was sure she'd fly out of her skin. Her body felt too tight for the sensations coursing through it, and she let go of Gamble's shoulder again in favor of cupping her breast while he sucked and kissed and licked. The nails on her opposite hand curved into his other shoulder, hard enough that Kennedy fleetingly wondered if he was bothered by the sting. But he worked her nipple even harder in reply, moving his lips and tongue in a steady rhythm, and when his hips joined in? All thoughts of anything other than her bright, desperate need to shatter were lost.

"Show me," Gamble ground out, moving his hips against hers in a punishing thrust. "Fucking show me how pretty you are when you come undone. I'll be right here to help put you back together."

Kennedy tried to hold on, she really did. But the friction from his mouth on her nipple and his jeans on the want-soaked satin now pressed hard between her legs left her too full of dark, greedy need that she gave in. Her climax exploded from deep between her hips, so many sensations crashing through her that, for a second—or a minute or a month or a year, for all she knew—she was unable to do anything other than simply let them have their way with her. Finally, when the last wave subsided, she realized that, while Gamble had slowed his movements and dialed back on the intensity of his touch, his hold on her was still steady and unyielding.

A good thing, since she was pretty much a no-go in the able-to-use-her-limbs department.

The shift in her body weight a second later brought her synapses back online, lickety-split. "Whoa," she murmured, her eyelids fluttering in a trio of rapid-fire blinks as her senses scrambled to adjust to the fact that Gamble had pulled her away from the wall and was carrying her further into his apartment.

"Where are we going?" Kennedy asked, a smile hanging in her voice as her post-orgasm endorphins kicked in, good and hard.

Gamble didn't break stride as he answered, "My bed."

Her endorphins were strong enough to lead her smile into a full-blown laugh. "I thought you liked the idea of fucking me standing up in your front hallway."

He crossed the threshold into a tidy bedroom, carrying her to the foot of the perfectly made king-sized bed before lowering her to her feet. "That was before I watched you come. Now, I'm going to do so much more than take you quick and dirty. Now"—he raked a stare over her in the dusky shadows of his bedroom—"I want you to come for me like that all fucking night."

Kennedy pressed up to kiss him in reply. His hands coasted over her as his mouth searched hers, his strong, adept fingers sliding under the straps of her bra and finding the closure between her shoulder blades. Gamble took a second to look at her, his gaze hooded in a way that tempted her to lay waste to their clothes and let him take her quick and dirty after all. But he was doing what she'd told him she wanted—taking off her clothes to touch her—and while giving up control had never been her thing, the raw hunger on his face made Kennedy realize the truth.

Gamble might be making all the moves, but she still had just as much power as he did.

And it was the hottest thing she had ever seen or felt in her fucking life.

Purposefully, he skimmed his hands over her shoulders,

then her rib cage, before moving down to catch the edge of her already-open jeans. He paused while she toed out of her boots, then lowered her jeans to leave her in nothing but her thong. She reached out for the button on his jeans in return, a tiny pop of surprise pushing her heartbeat faster as he let her undo it and push the denim to the floor.

"Oh." Kennedy's belly squeezed as she took in the ridged expanse of Gamble's abs and the tightly corded muscles wrapped low around his hips. His cock stood, thick and fully erect, against the black cotton of his boxer briefs, and even though she knew she was staring, she couldn't force herself to tear her eyes from him.

Which he must have noticed, because his brows lifted slightly. "What?"

"I...you're really beautiful, too."

Her cheeks heated, the blush having nothing to do with either of them being nearly naked and fully aroused. She hadn't meant to blurt out *exactly* what she'd been thinking, but the words had vaulted out regardless. Gamble seemed just as stunned to hear them, and he shook his head.

"No one has ever said that to me before."

Kennedy stepped toward him, placing both palms flat over his chest. "Well, I'm glad to be the first, because it's true."

She kissed him, and all the seductive heat she'd felt a few minutes ago rebuilt quickly in her core. Curling his fingers around the low-slung satin at her hips, he lowered her panties, sliding a hand to the snug space between her legs.

She bucked into the touch, as light as it was, and a wicked smile formed on his mouth. "Greedy woman. You don't want to wait, do you?"

She tilted her hips again, desperate for the friction of his fingers in her aching, empty pussy. *Close. So close.* "Gamble—"

"Ian." He slipped his hand deeper, making Kennedy gasp.

"What?"

Tracing tight circles over her clit, he leaned in, putting his mouth to her ear. "Not to put too fine a point on it, but I'm about to fuck you senseless. A first-name basis seems kind of appropriate, don't you think?"

The promise made her bold—or crazy, maybe, but at this point, she wasn't about to argue semantics.

She dropped her hand and wrapped it around his cock, starting to pump. "Maybe, but Gamble suits you. And since I'm about to fuck you right back..."

"Gamble it is," he agreed. He broke from her body just long enough to grab a condom from the nightstand beside his bed. Returning quickly, he pulled off his boxer briefs and guided her back over the plain, dark blue comforter. Kennedy waited until he'd stretched out beside her before hooking a leg over his waist, using the leverage and his surprise to her advantage in order to reverse their positions and straddle his hips.

Even as Gamble's hands flew to her waist to hold her in place, he looked like he might protest. But she angled forward until her mouth was an inch away from his, kissing him with a brush of her lips before saying, "Everything you want to give to me, I want to give it back even more, remember? So, please. Lie back and let me."

He stared at her for a beat before nodding. She shifted back far enough to let him get the condom in place, reclaiming her spot in his lap the second he reached for her again. Kennedy parted her thighs wide over his lower belly, the blunt head of his cock nudging her ass. The sensation, and all the deliciously dirty thoughts that accompanied it, sent a dark thrill up her spine, and she bit back a moan as she slid lower, letting her already-slick folds ride back and forth over Gamble's length. He hissed out a breath at the contact, and she didn't wait. Canting her hips forward, she reached down to fit his cock against her opening. He filled her in slow degrees, pulling back a time or two to ease deeper inside and stretching her so completely, her breath caught in her lungs.

Oh. God.

His body was bowstring tight beneath hers, his cock buried deep. "Fuck, Kennedy," he grated, his hands turning to fists over the comforter on either side of his thighs. "Fuck, you're so tight."

She drew back, but only so she could slide right back home. Pleasure, want, tension—they all coursed through Kennedy in a demand for her attention. She took the slow rhythm of her hips faster as her body adjusted to the pressure of his cock between her legs, her inner muscles gripping and releasing with each thrust. Gamble's wide hands shaped her waist, his knees bending behind her to push her closer over his torso and drive his dick even deeper inside her pussy on the downward glide. Sparks lit behind her eyes, low in her belly, hot in her chest. The decadent push-pull of an orgasm gathered between her hips, and, hungry for it, Kennedy slipped her fingers to her clit to stroke herself.

"Let me see you, baby. That's it," Gamble said, rocking harder as she leaned back to let him watch her busy fingers slide over her sex. "Show me how you want it."

"Harder," she demanded, the need to feel him as deep as possible burning out from within her. "Please, Ian. *Please,* I want—"

He rolled her over so quickly, she was beneath him before she could even register the movement. Pressing one hand beneath the back of her right thigh, he scooped her leg up and away from her body to bury himself inside of her until no space remained between their bodies. The change in angle turned the sparks in her belly into wildfire, the thrust uncovering a wildly sensitive spot hidden deep in her pussy, and she came with a sharp cry. Reaching around to his ass, Kennedy held him in place, arching up to take him over and over again, and finally, his body stiffened under her hands.

"So good." Gamble's eyes were locked on the spot where they joined, his stare black and wild with intensity. "Christ, you're fucking me so goddamn good."

"Show me," Kennedy whispered, her heart pounding hard with the urge to make him come. "Show me how *you* want it."

He did. In an instant, he took back the lead, angling forward to press into her in a long, rough thrust. There were no pleasantries in his movements—not that Kennedy wanted any—and he pinned her into place, his hands pressed over her shoulders, his hips pistoning against hers. He fucked her hard and relentlessly, and oh God, she loved every thrust. She wrapped her legs around his waist, taking his cock as far and deep as she could, and only then did he start to shudder. Gamble called her name on a guttural grunt, his body shaking over hers. Even in release, he was careful not to drop all of his weight on her, shifting to his knees and forearms to cover her body without causing her pain.

They lay there together for a minute, trading breaths and heartbeats, until Gamble kissed her forehead and got up, heading through an adjacent door she assumed led to a bathroom. Sure enough, the sound of running water began a second later, dropping Kennedy the rest of the way back to reality. She was fully prepared to grab her clothes and go home—she hadn't come here with any expectations, and even though her orgasms had been good enough to have been measured by the fucking Richter scale, the last thing she wanted was for Gamble to think she had illusions of grandeur.

But then he opened the bathroom door, his big, beautiful body wrapped in nothing but a towel, and all her convictions disappeared like the steam starting to build behind him.

"You coming?" he asked, the unspoken *please* clear in his eyes as he hooked a thumb over his shoulder and smiled. "The water's warm."

Clothes forgotten, Kennedy nodded. Reality would find her soon enough.

Tonight, she wanted this. If only for a little while longer.

16

Rusty heard The Money far before he saw the glare of the space-age-looking xenon headlights cut through the darkness around him. The finely tuned sound of the guy's luxury sedan, too sophisticated to be a growl, yet too powerful to be classified as a regular old rumble, sounded off in a showy display of prestige as The Money pulled to a stop about twenty feet from where Rusty stood on the litter-choked sidewalk on the outskirts of Grant Park. The self-importance of a two hundred-thousand dollar Aston Martin was all sorts of ironic in this situation, considering Rusty was the only person who would see the pompous jackass driving it.

But that was Chaz Fucking McCory for you. Better to look good than feel good.

Or, God forbid, actually *be* good.

Scaling back on his eye roll, Rusty kicked his feet into motion and strolled toward Chaz's car. They knew better than to meet in a place that could remotely be considered public—Rusty for practical, cover-his-ass reasons, and McCory likely because he didn't want to be seen with the riff-raff. The fact that ol' Chaz had even dipped down low enough on the food chain to approach him for this job had been enough of a shocker to grab Rusty's attention from the get. Then again, greed knew no societal boundaries.

Guys like Chaz just called it ambition so they could sleep at night.

"Nice suit," Rusty said after Chaz got out of the Aston Martin, mentally picturing how much gasoline it would take to torch the thing right down to its fancy aluminum frame.

"Thank you." Chaz shot his cuffs, picking imaginary lint from one flawlessly tailored sleeve as if crossing the limits into North Point had made him dirty by default. "I'm headed to a gallery opening by the Plaza after this."

Rusty swallowed his snort. Art was just reaaaaalllll-lyyyyyy expensive kindling as far as he was concerned. "Of course you are. Saw you on the news the other day. You're quite the community activist."

"I didn't realize we were here for small talk." Chaz lifted a professionally groomed brow, and just like that, Rusty's indifference became irritation. Chaz might have enough money to be gunning for a spot on *Forbes* magazine's Top 500 Richest People one day, but he still ate and shit and bled, just like everybody else.

"Fine, your majesty," Rusty bit out. "Let's get down to it, then. The remote ignition device obviously works, just like I told you it would. All the loose ends in testing it have been taken care of"—a smile hooked over his mouth at the memory of watching the Camry burn, growing bigger as the mental image of Xander watching his own flesh scorch joined in—"so I'm ready for the next phase."

Chaz sniffed the air, looking at Rusty through the fluorescent glare of the streetlight a half a block away, on the corner. "Actually, I don't think you are."

"Excuse me?" Rusty's brows shot high over his forehead, but still, Chaz didn't change his tune.

"My source at the department tells me the arson investigation unit found enough of your device to rule the dumpster fire an arson. They've opened an active investigation into who set it, and that makes us both very vulnerable. Needless to say, I am not pleased. I told you we needed to act with the utmost discretion."

Rusty threw his head back and laughed, which, by the look of things, was dead last on the list of things Chaz expected he'd do. Good. Better to keep the fucker on the toes of those perfectly polished wing tips.

"Jesus, McCory. I thought you were going to come at me with a real problem."

"An active investigation by the RFD *is* a real problem," Chaz argued. "If they find out—"

"Do you know how many times a fire I've set has been investigated by the RFD?" Rusty interrupted, although he didn't wait for Chaz to formulate a decent guess. "Nine. Which is actually pretty low, considering how many others I've set that they *didn't* investigate. Or couldn't. Also, pretty impressive considering I've lived here for less than two years."

It was, in fact, the most annoying occupational hazard of being a serial arsonist. But even a busted watch was right twice a day, and on occasion, arson investigators grew smarter than they looked. The national arson database was woefully undermanaged and years behind the curve, so he didn't have to worry that anyone would trace the fires he'd set over half the Eastern seaboard back to him—which, quite frankly, pissed him off in a way, because *God*, they'd all been spectacular. Every once in a while, relocation was necessary to ensure that he stayed under the radar.

Still... "Out of nine tries—one of them including a disarmed bomb under a fire engine that made national fucking headlines, by the way—Remington's police force, arson investigation unit, and fire department haven't been able to touch me. They had an entire device, *intact*, to use to try and track me, yet here I am, still breathing the air of freedom."

"I pay a lot of money to be sure my information from the department is accurate. I've been assured that they've opened a case," Chaz started, and seriously, this guy was something else.

"Oh, I'm sure your pricey intel is legit. Those ignition devices are meant to disintegrate along with everything else, but every once in a while, one survives." With how quickly the RFD had arrived at the dumpster fire, Rusty had known this might be a possibility. "So, yes, if they got lucky enough to find one, the arson investigation unit probably opened a case. What I'm telling you is, neither one of us needs to worry about that. It's not going to become an issue, because they couldn't possibly connect the device to either of us."

Chaz slipped his hands into the pockets of his suit pants, measuring Rusty with a shrewd stare. "You're awfully certain of yourself, aren't you?"

"Uh, yeah. That's why you hired me," Rusty pointed out. For a guy who had probably gone to Harvard or Dartmouth or some Ivy League brat factory like that, Chaz was kind of a dolt.

"I hired you because you have a skill set I require," Chaz said. "What I *didn't* hire you for was to get us thrown in jail."

Jesus. Money made some people so fucking dramatic. "No one's going to jail. The ignition devices work exactly like they're supposed to, and when we use them for real, they'll burn hotter, longer. If anything is left behind to be found—

and that's a big-ass if, considering the size of the buildings you're paying me to burn down and how long it's going to take those idiots at the RFD to actually put them out—it'll look like part of the 'faulty' electrical work. So, relax and let me set some shit on fire for the world to see, would you, please?"

After a minute, Chaz let go of a slow exhale. "I've invested far too much time and money and effort into this plan to back out unless there's a very credible threat to its success."

"Right, I get it," Rusty said. "You couldn't buy those investment properties the good, old-fashioned way because you got outbid, or maybe outplayed when it came down to deal time last year. Who knows? But you wanted them so you could expand the Chaz McCory developing empire into a household name."

An ugly expression shaped Chaz's magazine-perfect face, and oh, if Twitter could see him now. "It's not my fault the original sellers lacked vision. But Remington is a city of culture and class. We need luxury accommodations if we're going to attract the right sort of people from bigger areas like Charlotte and Charleston and Atlanta. My condos would have provided the perfect upscale atmosphere for discerning residents...if those soft-hearted ingrates hadn't sold the buildings to developers who wanted a more 'community accessible' approach. Can you imagine? Recreational centers for after-school activities. An outpatient clinic offering affordable healthcare." Chaz paused to scoff. "One of them even wants to build a series of apartments that would serve as a safe haven for victims of domestic abuse. It's absurd. That space should be utilized by the people in the community who *matter*."

"Of course it should." Rusty stepped back and put his

hands in the air, framing imaginary marquee lights and trying not to throw up in his own mouth at the idea of luxury condos for Remington's one-percenters. "No need to get salty, Chaz. Once those buildings burn down from the shoddy work being done with the electrical renovations, the developers who bought them for all that feel-good crap will be faced with either waiting for the insurance settlements and starting construction from scratch, which is time consuming and costly as hell, or selling the properties to be rid of the hassle. Given the bad reputation that part of downtown has recently acquired, they're probably re-thinking plans for their community-accessible establish-ments, anyway. They'll be dying to offload those buildings at the first available opportunity, and cheaper than you'd have ever gotten them before. Then you can swoop in like the paragon of the community that you are"—ugh, there went that gagging thing again. Sure, it was a means to an end right now, and one that Rusty needed in order to get the spotlight he deserved, but placating the rich with what they wanted to hear was so fucking nauseating—"and buy them up. I'm telling you, the plan is a work of art."

"Hmmm. This is true," Chaz murmured, as if he'd been the one to come up with the plan in the first place. But what-ever. Pulling this off meant financial security to go with his spotlight. If that meant Rusty had to kiss some ass to get it, he wasn't above that. He'd certainly done worse for less, and anyway, vandalizing those storefronts to make the area look bad and old Chaz look good had been kinda fun, albeit anti-climactic without the fire.

Chaz continued, "Still, I'm concerned about the RFD. If there's even a small chance they could figure this out—"

An idea unfolded in Rusty's brain, and oh, *perfect*.

He held up one hand. "So, what you're saying is, you'd

be happier if the arson investigation unit was distracted. Say, by a bigger case than the dumpster fire."

"I'm listening," Chaz replied.

"We need to wait a little while for the electrical contractors to get on schedule before we can set these bigger fires anyway, right?" Rusty's heart pounded faster at the thoughts now racing through his mind.

"Yes." Chaz nodded, although not one hair on his head moved at the gesture, and yes, yes, yessssss, this was the best of both worlds.

"Okay. So let's give the fire department something to *really* keep them occupied. A warehouse fire ought to do the trick. Something nice and high-profile and dangerous, with tons of protocol and possibilities to run them into corner after corner."

Rusty paced the rough pavement beneath his work boots to offset the buzz in his veins, even though he knew it wouldn't be nearly enough to quell the excitement. So many choices, so many things he could set on fire, then kick back and watch as everyone *else* helplessly watched them burn...

"Are you sure that won't just bring the spotlight closer to us rather than farther away?"

McCory's question, and the condescending-as-shit tone he used to ask it, sent a bitter taste to Rusty's mouth, and he pivoted to face the guy, his hands turning to fists at his sides. "Are you implying that I do sloppy work, Chaz?"

"I'm *saying* I'm not going to jail just because you want to go off half-cocked and start some stupid fire that wasn't part of our original plan."

Rusty stepped in, close enough to smell the wave of fear beneath McCory's expensive cologne. "Let me remind you. You need me in order to get what you want."

"And let me remind you, there's no payday unless I do,"

the weasel replied. "Distract the fire department. Send the cops on a wild goose chase. Do...whatever it is that you're going to do. Just make sure your little side job doesn't produce any dead bodies or mess with the end game, and be damned sure it doesn't come back to me."

"You got it, Chaz."

Oh, this was going to be fun. Rusty could feel it in his fucking bones.

17

Gamble had woken up in a lot of places and just as many different situations. Foxholes. All-calls for a four-alarm fire. But the whole arms-full-of-ridiculously-sexy-brunette thing had been new.

How good it had felt on top of the fact that it had even happened in the first place? That had been fucking groundbreaking.

Clearing his throat, he looked around his now-empty apartment. While he'd made good on his promise to give Kennedy thigh-quaking orgasms all night long, she'd slipped into her clothes and past his front door at about oh-seven-hundred. She hadn't made much fanfare over her exit, not that Gamble had expected her to. Hell, he'd been shocked she'd stayed the night, and _definitely_ shocked when she'd rolled over and nestled between his arms just a little before sunrise. But something about the way she'd shown up on his threshold in the first place had made him glad she hadn't run. Kennedy had come to him because she'd needed something.

And giving it to her had felt startlingly right.

Gamble jammed a hand through his hair and found his feet, taking one last survey of his living room before grabbing his keys and getting the hell out of Dodge. Yes, spending time with Kennedy had felt better than he'd expected, and yes again, that wasn't just because they'd been naked and trading orgasms like baseball cards. But he had a case in front of him, and that case involved catching a dangerous, deadly serial arsonist who—oh, by the way—just happened to be hooked up tight with her brother. And after spending all day reviewing the files from arson investigation and his notes from the case report on the disarmed bomb, nailing Rusty before he set anything else on fire was going to take every ounce of Gamble's energy and concentration.

No fucking way was the guy going to walk this time. Not after nearly killing everyone Gamble counted as family.

Hitting the lobby of his apartment building, then the sunbaked sidewalk beyond, Gamble slid his Ray-Ban aviators over his face and scanned the street in front of him. August had dug in its heels, and even though it was creeping up on seventeen-hundred with the peak of the day's heat in the past tense, the air around him still made the early evening a poster child for hot and humid. Thankfully, the trip to the Thirty-Third was a straightforward one, and Gamble navigated the route with ease, parking his F-150 Raptor in the public lot next to the building and making his way past the desk sergeant's station and the metal detectors. He reviewed the facts of the case one more time to gear up, and by the time he got to the top of the steps, his brain was all-systems-go.

"Hey," came a quiet voice from a few steps down the main hallway. Xander pushed off the wall where he'd been standing, lifting his chin in greeting, and confusion sent Gamble's brows upward in reply.

"Hey. You been in yet?" he asked, gesturing to the doors leading to the intelligence office. Gamble made it a point to be painfully on time for pretty much everything—thank you, Uncle Sam—so he wasn't used to being the last person to arrive.

Xander shook his head. "Nah. Not yet. I was..." He trailed off, shoving his hands in the pockets of his well-worn jeans. "I guess I'm just still trying to get my head around all of this. Not in a second-thoughts kind of way," he added. "It's just all pretty hard to process."

"Makes sense," Gamble said. After all, not a lot of people were too used to the whole deadly-fires, life-in-danger, redlining-on-adrenaline thing. Guess he was just special in that regard. "If it helps, the intelligence team is the best in the city. And I can promise you, we all want this son of a bitch behind bars."

"Yeah," Xander said. "Well, I guess we should head in and get this over with, huh?"

"You got it."

Letting Xander lead the way, Gamble followed the guy through the doors leading into the main room of the intelligence office. Isabella, Hollister, Garza, and Capelli were already sitting around Capelli's multi-screened work station, with detectives Addison Hale and Shawn Maxwell at their desks nearby. Maxwell had always been his own brand of badass, a fact that his dark stare and bald-by-choice skull trim showcased. Hale might be the polar opposite of the guy, with her petite frame and heart-shaped face and blond ponytail that would make even a California cheerleader green with envy, but in her case, looks were deceiving. She held black belts in both Tae Kwon Do and Krav Maga, and

Gamble would no sooner fuck with her than shove his hand in a wood chipper.

"Oh, hey, you guys made it," Hollister said, looking up from his laptop screen. "I'll text Sarge and let him know."

While the detective pulled his phone from the back pocket of his jeans and tapped out a quick message, Xander sent a gaze over the group.

"Thanks for doing this in the evening so I could go to work this morning. It's, uh. Hard for me to miss more than a day. My landlady isn't exactly the understanding type."

"No worries," Hale said, her smile wide. "Crimes don't usually go down on a nine-to-five. We're used to off hours around here."

The concept of a traditional workweek was definitely not in Gamble's wheelhouse, either. "I'm not on shift at Seventeen until oh-seven-hundred tomorrow. I'm cool with being here tonight."

"Okay," Sinclair said, walking into the main room from the hallway that led to his office. "If we're all ready to go—"

"Sorry! Sorry I'm late."

Gamble's heart hit his sternum on a oner at the sound of Kennedy's voice, then again at the sight of her as she dashed into the office, looking rushed and worried and so damn beautiful, his fucking chest hurt.

"I had to make sure payroll was done and all the prep for the dinner rush was taken care of before I could leave The Crooked Angel," she said, her hair swinging over the shoulders of her dark gray tank top as she slid into the empty chair beside Isabella.

Unable to keep his mouth on lockdown, Gamble asked, "What are you doing here?"

It was the same question on everyone's mind except Xander's, judging by their shocked expressions. Kennedy, however, didn't skip a beat. "Xander's my brother and Rusty tried to burn down my bar. What do you think I'm doing here?"

"Impeding an investigation," Sinclair said. "You're a civilian."

"So is Gamble. God, for that matter, so is Xander," Kennedy pointed out, and Gamble had to admit, she had the sergeant on the technicality.

Not that the guy was going to give. "Lieutenant Gamble and your brother are both necessary to this investigation. An investigation, by the way, that you already lied to the police about once."

"I was trying to keep my brother safe!"

"Yet I could still bring you up on obstruction charges."

Kennedy's eyes flashed, dark green and deadly serious. "I'm not leaving my brother during this investigation. Not when his life is literally on the line. So you do what you've got to do, even if that means arresting me."

Gamble opened his mouth to launch the wait-just-a-minute that had hotly formed there, but Isabella beat him to the ol' one-two. "It *is* possible that Kennedy might be able to help us with this case."

The look on Sinclair's face suggested he felt otherwise, but Isabella had never really been one for backing down. "The Crooked Angel might've been a specific target for this dumpster fire," she said. "If there's a connection between her bar and the arsonist, she might be able to help."

"That's kind of thin," Maxwell murmured, lifting his hands in concession a second later as both Kennedy and Isabella served up death glares. "Not impossible, though."

Gamble's gut twisted at the thought of Kennedy being any closer to this case than she already was. "Rusty is dangerous."

"You're not *seriously* going to go all Cro-Magnon man on me, are you?" She threw her hands in the air. "I grew up in The Hill, for Chrissake."

"That doesn't mean you're made of Kevlar," Gamble argued. "This asshole planted enough C-4 in my fire house to put a crater in the entire block, and he wants to set fire to buildings across the city. Whatever's going on here is way bigger than the test-fire that went down outside The Crooked Angel." For fuck's sake, with how sophisticated that bomb had been, God alone knew how much collateral damage Rusty could do with a strategically planned building fire. Let alone a bunch of them.

"This whole thing *did* start at The Crooked Angel, though. It may not be a bad jumping off point," Hollister offered, and Xander nodded in agreement.

"Rusty had definitely scoped the place out. He never said why he picked it. Hell, I didn't even know where we'd be testing the ignition device until we got there. But he didn't choose The Crooked Angel randomly, that's for sure."

"Look," Isabella said, completely matter-of-fact. "No one is suggesting that if Kennedy helps, she'll be in danger, and yes"—she swung a don't-you-dare-argue stare in Kennedy's direction—"she screwed up by not coming directly to us from the start. But if we want to catch Rusty before he sets these fires, we're going to have to look at this case from every angle. All I'm saying is, she might be able to help, Sarge. And we could sure use all we can get."

Xander looked at Kennedy and shook his head. "You might as well let her stay. She's not going to take no for an answer. Unless you arrest her, but even then, she'll be back after she makes bail."

Funny, Gamble was certain the guy wasn't even close to kidding. A fact that Sinclair seemed to have come to terms

with, because he exhaled slowly before sending an uncom-
promising stare across the office at Kennedy.

"Fine. But you're strictly on the sidelines, no exceptions."
He didn't give Kennedy a chance to add a verbal agreement
to her nod before continuing with, "And if you fail to
disclose so much as a scrap of information directly to me as
soon as you uncover it again—"

"You don't have to say it."

"I'm going to anyway. You keep anything from this team
again, and I'll toss your ass in the cage on as many obstruction charges as I can make stick. Are we clear?" Sinclair
asked. Gamble knew—oh, how he *knew*—that Sinclair had
every right and reason to come at Kennedy with what he
had. Hell, Gamble had argued the same exact full-disclosure
point with her only days ago.

So it was definitely fucked up that his hands had
clenched into fists and his molars were cranked down nice
and tight as she said, "Crystal."

"Okay. Then let's proceed. Where are we?"

Capelli took the baton, pushing his glasses over the
bridge of his nose and gesturing to the keyboard in front of
him. "I ran the nickname Rusty through the system, then
cross-checked the possibles with the description of our guy,
but I came up empty."

"So, our boy has no record," Garza said, then tacked on,
"which means we have no leads on who he is."

Capelli shook his head and, surprisingly, laughed. "Oh,
ye of little faith. I didn't find anything in *our* system, so I hit
up hospital databases for white, male victims of facial burns
over the last seven years, and got a hit. Randall McGee,
twenty-eight, spent ten days in the burn unit at Cleveland
Med four and a half years ago. Look familiar?"

An image—a driver's license photo, from the look of it—

of a guy with dark red hair, a pair of flat, soulless eyes, and, yep, a nasty burn scar spanning from one cheekbone down to the corner of his mouth flashed over the center screen of the array, and Xander nodded immediately.

"That's him. That's Rusty," he said, and okay, yeah. Gamble had to admit it. McCullough's boyfriend had some skills.

"The Remington DMV has McGee's last known address on Berkshire Court in North Point—looks like an apartment building—but it's not clear if that's current, and he doesn't have a criminal record. At least, nothing that popped on our database. It looks like there was some stuff in a juvenile file in Lexington, Kentucky, that was expunged ten years ago when he turned eighteen," Capelli added with an apologetic frown. "Not even I can pull that up without a serious act of God, though. That stuff gets wiped pretty clean."

"Not sure it would help much," Sinclair said, and Gamble tended to agree. A profile would be nice, sure, but they had to catch Rusty in the here-and-now. "Garza, what's the word on Ice?"

At Kennedy and Xander's confused expressions, Garza explained, "Ice is the gang leader who hired Rusty to plant the bomb under Engine Seventeen last spring." He turned back to Sinclair, his own expression speaking of nothing good. "As you can imagine, he was less than cooperative when I went to pay him a visit earlier today to ask him about Rusty's involvement in the attempted bombing. I believe his exact quote was, 'unless you're offering full immunity on all my charges in exchange for my cooperation, fuck off and die, you worthless pig'."

"Sounds like he's still as charming as ever," Hale murmured.

"Yeah, I declined on reaching out to the DA with his

generous offer, although it would've been nice to get him to flip on Rusty."

"It would," Sinclair agreed. "But without concrete facts to back it up, anything Ice gives us is one criminal's word against another's, and Ice isn't exactly a shining star of credibility. I don't just want an arrest; I want a conviction, here. We need evidence if we're going to put Rusty away for good. Speaking of which"—the sergeant turned from the spot where he stood at the front of the office, looking at Gamble with his gray-blond brows lifted—"where are we with the device recovered from the dumpster?"

Gamble blew out a breath, because damn, he'd been dreading this question. "It's hard to say. The device was made with fairly standard materials, available in most hardware stores and on the Internet. They were all on the list of things Xander said he'd bought for Rusty over the past couple of weeks"—the kid had given up a surprisingly accurate inventory, to the point that Gamble had been impressed—"but they have such a wide range of practical uses that he could've just as easily been doing home improvement projects with most of them as making remote ignition devices. Delacourt is running tests for accelerant residue and the results are still pending, but I'd guess anything that pops there will be run-of-the-mill, too."

"So, what you're saying is, you have no way to link Rusty to the bomb from Seventeen," Kennedy said, and at least here, he had some decent news.

"Oh, no, I can definitely do that. The bomb squad disposed of the device after it had been completely neutralized." The polite phrasing used by the brass had always tempted Gamble to laugh. Those boys and girls from SWAT had blown that goddamned thing to kingdom come once they'd done their due diligence for the case. It wasn't as if you could keep a disarmed explosive device, especially one made with a bunch of C-4, in some evidence locker somewhere. "But we still have plenty of images to cross-check other devices against in addition to the information Kellan and I included in our report."

Not to mention all the details that were seared into Gamble's brain, but he wasn't about to go there in front of a room full of people. Or ever.

"Explosive and incendiary devices aren't one size fits all," he continued, smashing down on the twinge in his chest. "A pressure-triggered IED, for example, can be made one of at least a dozen ways, and even if you have five people make one using the same basic method, their technique, experience, preferences—all of that will make each device look a little different."

"Every person has his own signature moves, then," Isabella said, and Gamble nodded.

"Exactly. And even though the materials are pretty garden variety, the techniques used on both of these are a spot-on match. Whoever made that bomb"—Gamble pointed to the photo Capelli had displayed in the upper left-hand corner of the array—"definitely also made the device recovered from the dumpster. That, I know. What I don't have any proof of—yet—is that the person is Rusty."

"There were no prints on the bomb recovered from beneath Engine Seventeen," Capelli said. "Although, it's not unusual for someone working with volatile substances to wear gloves, not to mention that it would also cover his ass if he's doing something like planting a bomb for nefarious purposes. Fingerprints almost never survive the sort of heat that occurred in that dumpster fire—not that we didn't try, of course—but prints were a no-go on that device, as well."

"And you never actually saw him with the device from the dumpster?" Maxwell asked Xander.

"No," Xander said, and shit, so much for that. "I saw him make other, easier stuff, like those Molotov cocktails and fake bombs and all, but he made that ignition device somewhere else, then had it in a backpack when I picked him up at the pier the other night. I just bought the stuff, stole the car, then stood guard at the entryway to the alley while he planted it in the dumpster. Plus, I'm no expert. Even if I *had* seen the thing before he put it in that dumpster, no way would I be able to say it's the same as...that."

He gestured to the on-screen photo of the scorch-marked and heat-warped device that had been recovered by arson investigation.

Hollister tilted his head, his mind clearly going a mile and a half a minute, and he asked, "So, you don't have any locations or plans, or anything at all in writing? Not even texts?"

"No. Rusty did all the scouting for the test-run at The Crooked Angel himself." At the unspoken question on everyone's faces, and yeah, probably Gamble's, too, Xander continued, "He was way too familiar with the area outside bar and the locations of all the city cams not to have been there at least once, and I've never seen him work with anyone else, ever. The only other person I've heard him even talk about is The Money, and no way would the guy paying for the job do any dirty work. It had to be Rusty."

"Okay," Maxwell said, leaning forward to brace his forearms over the desk in front of him. "So we can't nail him for what he's done...yet. How about what's coming?"

Xander took his cue. "I wasn't trying to bullshit you guys when I said I don't know much. He told me the bare bones of the plan, which is everything I already told you about setting fire to some buildings while they're being renovated and screwing a bunch of developers out of some money, but I don't know which buildings, or exactly when. Most everything has just been prep so far, with me going out to buy materials and Rusty meeting with the money guy and working on those remote ignition devices. I *was* a little surprised when he said he wanted to set the fires remotely —I mean, he's not usually shy about torching shit. In fact, he kind of gets off on it. But for this, I guess he doesn't want to risk being right there at the scene and getting caught. Or hurt, although..."

Xander paused, his brows tugging downward in thought. "That burn scar, on his face? He seems kind of, I don't know...boastful of it sometimes. He never tries to hide it. Not even when people whisper and stare. It's like he *likes* to scare people with it."

"It's like a badge of honor," Isabella said slowly, and Gamble's gut iced over. He'd known guys like that in the Marines, who showed off their scars like trophies, or— worse yet—walked into harm's way sometimes specifically to get them. It was very different than being okay with injuries that had healed.

Guys like that? They were far from okay with anything.

"Yeah," Xander agreed. "I guess. Anyway, Rusty's been pretty secretive with the actual plans. He doesn't tell me much until things are about to go down. I really didn't even know the dumpster fire would be outside of The Crooked Angel until we got there the other night."

At this, Xander chanced a glance at Kennedy, who kept her eyes facing forward at the mention of her bar and the fact that her brother had, even unknowingly, been a party to the act that could've burned the place down if Gamble hadn't been there to call in the cavalry so fast the other night.

Xander got the message, loud and clear. "So, yeah." He shrugged, but the move seemed more resigned than noncommittal. "Until he calls me again, that's all I've got."

Sinclair looked at his detectives with a nod. "Okay, that's a start. Maxwell, you and Hale and Garza pull city cam footage from in front of The Crooked Angel for the three days prior to the fire, see if we can at least put Rusty there, poking around, and let's see if we can confirm that DMV address as current and try to get eyes on him there, too. Gamble, cross-check what you know with devices that have been recovered in other cases. And don't be shy about digging deep."

"Copy that," Gamble replied. It would be a hell of a task, and time consuming as hell, but he'd do it with a smile on his face if it meant getting a break in this case.

"Kennedy, come up with a list of anyone who might have a beef with your bar. Even a small one. Moreno, you and Hollister get a background on Rusty. I want to know where he was before he landed here, family background, anything we can use to figure him out. In fact, see if the department can spare anyone from their mental wellness staff to help us get a bead on what's going on in this psycho's head."

Another flurry of movement went down before Sinclair turned to Capelli and said, "Get Xander set up for surveillance. Everything you've got."

"Uh, no disrespect, Sarge," Capelli replied with care. "But I've got a *lot*."

"Well, good, because that's how badly I want to catch this son of a bitch. So let's make that happen before he strikes so much as one more match."

18

Kennedy stood behind the bar at The Crooked Angel and served up drinks that might as well have been made with dishwater. But after the meeting at the Thirty-Third and all the yo-yo emotions that had gone with it, she was pretty freaking distracted. The fact that her brother and Gamble had both relocated from the intelligence office to the bar right along with her?

Yeah. Make that *very* freaking distracted.

At least the Xander portion of the equation was fairly straightforward. After sticking around the precinct for a little while to make the list Sinclair had asked her to, and wait for Capelli to wire Xander up nine ways to Sunday (seriously, who knew you could put tracking devices in things like a simple stud earring?), Kennedy had asked Xander if he wanted to come with her to The Crooked Angel so he could grab a bite to eat, and he'd shocked the crap out of her by accepting. It was, she rationalized, a free, hot meal, and more than he'd get at home. But she'd been glad he'd said yes, not only so she could be sure he'd eat a decent meal, but also to ensure that he'd be safe and *not* in North Point. If only for a couple of hours.

The Gamble part of things was...not so uncomplicated. He'd been right there, walking out with her and Xander when she'd asked her brother if he wanted to come to the bar. Kennedy couldn't very well have not asked Gamble, too, nor could she deny the way her stomach had given an uncharacteristic and not-small flip when he'd said sure, he'd meet them there. Now, an hour later, he'd taken up residence at his spot at the end of the bar and started a non-conversation with Xander, by which the two of them sat next to each other and kept company in mostly silence, ate their burgers and fries, and watched baseball highlights flash over the big screen. January's boyfriend, Finn, had joined them not too long ago, but with the cops at the Thirty-Third working hard on the case against Rusty, and Seventeen's A-shift needing to be bright-eyed for their twenty-four-hour shift starting in less than twelve hours, the rest of the bar's regulars were absent.

And thank God for that, because Kennedy was having a hell of a time keeping her eyes off of Gamble, and her brain off the way she'd felt as she'd fallen apart beneath him last night.

Never mind that, as other-worldly as the sex had been, it had been nothing compared to how good she'd felt waking up in his arms.

"Yoo hooooo, earth to Kennedy."

Kennedy jumped six inches off the bar mats, her boots landing with a muted squeak and her heart climbing up the back of her throat as January waved pointedly from beside her.

"Sorry, what?" she asked, tacking a perfectly blank expression to her face and capping it with a polite smile.

"I said, I don't think that glass is going to get any cleaner." January pointed to the pint glass in Kennedy's hand, which was, in fact, sparkling under the bar lights. "You've been drying it for like, ten minutes."

Shit. "Ugh, sorry. Guess I just zoned out."

At least it was a truth she could tell. She didn't necessarily have a bad poker face—hello, she'd been raised in North Point, where 'do what you have to do' wasn't so much a last resort as a goddamned lifestyle—but still, she hated lying to her best friend.

Not that January wasn't onto her, anyway. "You just zoned out," she repeated, lifting an eyebrow over her skeptical, blue stare.

"Yeah," Kennedy said, because even though she'd never zoned out in her life, that was her story and she was sticking to it. "Just daydreaming. You know."

"Uh-huh." January sent her gaze down to the end of the bar where Finn, Xander, and Gamble all sat with the remnants of their burgers, shaking her head a second later. "Okay, I know I'm being nosy and I'm going to say it. I just don't care. What is going on with you and Lieutenant Gamble?"

"Nothing," came Kennedy's default, but January wasn't having it.

"'Nothing' does not make a man look at a woman the way *that* man has been looking at you all night. Nor does it make a woman daydream while absently looking back at said man, and it definitely doesn't make a woman's face turn the color of *your* face right now. So, please. Spare me the indignity of looking gullible enough to swallow that 'nothing' you just served up and try again."

Oh, God, Gamble had been looking at her? "Okay, okay.

Fine," Kennedy said, blowing out a breath. "It's...complicated."

January snorted. "What, are you a Facebook status now? Kennedy, please."

Tension scattered, at least for the moment, Kennedy chuffed out a soft laugh. "I just take my job here really seriously. I don't normally sleep with regulars."

"Oh, my God!" January's stare widened, her mouth parting in surprise that turned to a cat-in-cream grin a millisecond later. "You slept with him?"

Aaagh, she was seriously off her game when it came to anything having to do with the big, broody lieutenant. "Maybe?"

"Come on, girl." January at least had the grace to press her lips together to hide the smile that all but broadcast to the universe that they were talking about the fact that Kennedy had, in fact, recently been gifted multiple, earth-shattering orgasms by a guy who was sitting about a dozen feet away from them. "I mean this objectively, because I'm stupidly in love with my boyfriend, but Gamble is hot. I'm betting you remember sleeping with him in vivid detail."

"Oh, it was vivid, all right," Kennedy said, her cheeks heating. "But still complicated."

"What's complicated about it? Either you like the guy or you don't."

"I *do* like him." Whoa, where had that even come from? "I just...you know, probably shouldn't."

January measured her with a sidelong glance. "Unless I'm missing something, you're both single. Judging by the looks you're sending across the bar at each other, you're both interested, and you're obviously compatible." The last word arrived with a reprise of her grin. "So, honestly, why *shouldn't* you like him?"

Her friend's tone was so genuine that Kennedy actually paused. She'd sworn to follow protocol, which meant she couldn't exactly tell January about the case they were building against Rusty, or that she and Gamble and her brother were all working on it together. January might be tough, but she'd learned her hard-ass ways from her father, and Sinclair had made it wildly clear that Kennedy needed to follow every last rule in the book from here on in.

But to that end, there was certainly no rule that said she and Gamble *couldn't* tumble into bed together just because they were both working on the case that would keep Xander safe. Yeah, maybe Gamble saw through her a little more than she'd like, but he was also a decent guy, and he'd already proven they were definitely in sync in bed (and in his shower...sweet baby Jesus, the man had done things with his tongue that had made her shake like a busted washing machine). Neither of them wanted anything serious. Hell, he'd seemed just as fine with her falling asleep at his place last night as he'd been when she'd left this morning without any pleasantries like coffee or small talk.

Which meant Kennedy had exactly zero good answers to January's question.

~

"OH, my God, this has officially been the quietest shift *ever*."

A chorus of groans sounded off in the common room, and Gamble heaved a loaded, internal sigh. He considered schooling de Costa on the error of her ways—be careful what you wish for was a fucking *thing* when you worked a job like this—but since pretty much every other first responder in the room had just given the rookie an oh-no-you-did-not-just-say-that-out-loud stare, he figured he'd keep his yap shut and let the village raise the child.

"Don't go borrowin' trouble, now," Hawkins warned, looking at DC from the recliner where he always read the paper before hitting the bunks at night. "Fate's a finicky girl, and she's got damn good hearing."

"I'm not so sure she's not taking today off. We've been on exactly two calls in the last fifteen hours, and they were both false alarms," de Costa pointed out, her chin up and at 'em. "Ambo hasn't even treated anyone for so much as a paper cut!"

This time, Gamble's sigh made it past his lips, but Quinn beat him to the verbal punch. "Girlfriend." The paramedic looked up from whatever primetime reality show Faurier had conned them all into watching and shook her head. "Seriously, if I have to treat someone with a severed limb or a femoral bleed tonight because you said that..."

"Gah." Luke Slater, their other paramedic and Quinn's live-in boyfriend, winced from his spot beside her. "I'm all for doing my job and taking care of people who need it, but even I will pass on both of those scenarios, thanks."

"Come on," de Costa asked, her brown eyes brimming with the sort of ambitious restlessness that rookies tended to have in mass quantities before they'd seen enough to realize they had to either temper it or burn out. "Do you guys really want to just sit around all shift?"

Okay, yeah. It was definitely time for an intervention. "Everyone in this room has been on a shift they wished had been quiet," Gamble said, his voice low. "You'll have one soon enough. Until then, don't piss off your fellow firefighters. And for Chrissake, don't tempt fate."

de Costa bit her lip, taking in the nodded agreement from Faurier, Dempsey, and their squad-mate, Tyler Gates.

Those guys on rescue squad responded to not just every fire call in their district, but to search and rescue calls, water recovery at the pier, and pretty much every unthinkable disaster fielded by dispatch. They'd no doubt seen some of the worst cluster fucks the world had to offer.

And didn't Gamble know exactly what *that* could entail.

Pain twisted in his chest, and he promptly buried it, way down deep. "Anyway. I'm going to turn in," he said, pushing himself up from the couch he'd been sharing with Kellan and Shae and pivoting toward the hallway leading to the bunk room. At twenty-two thirty, it wasn't terribly late, but none of his fellow first responders so much as batted a lash as they offered up a round of goodnights. They had to get up and get out for every call that came in, even the faulty carbon monoxide detectors and people who had heartburn instead of heart attacks, and everyone in the house knew how exhausting the interrupted shuteye could be, even if there was no action to go with it.

Not that getting extra sleep was why Gamble had hightailed it out of the common room. But he wasn't about to 'fess up to the fact that decent rest hadn't been part of his nightly drill since before he'd become a firefighter, so hey. If a little misdirection was what it would take to get his ghosts back where they belonged, then he was cool with slanting the truth.

Heading through the bunk room, Gamble hit the locker room, brushing his teeth and going through his bedtime routine with efficient motions. He returned to the small office that doubled as his private bunk—one of the perks of being a lieutenant—and closed the blinds that covered the window overlooking the main bunks. Gamble dragged off his boots and uniform pants, swapping them out for a pair of sweats, but lined everything up on the chair beside his bed so it was within reach.

Truth was, de Costa hadn't been wrong. Today's shift had been one step up from watching paint dry. Most of the time, that wasn't a bad thing.

But every once in a while, it was the calm before the unholy shit-storm.

Gamble clicked off the lamp on his tiny bedside table and settled in beneath the blanket on his bed. Shadows danced over the ceiling, courtesy of the row of narrow windows set high along the far wall. Gamble watched them shift and change, unable to keep the tightness that had clung to his chest ever since the night of the fire at The Crooked Angel at bay.

Jesus, Gamble. Stop worrying. This mission's gonna be a cakewalk. We haven't seen any action for weeks, and anyway, it's a routine escort. Plus, if anyone can sniff out trouble before it goes down, it's you. So, really, we're money. Aren't we, Perez?

His pulse beat faster, his blood pounding in his eardrums in a rapid thump-THUMP, thump-THUMP, thump-THUMP, but his defenses weren't enough to dull the memories welling up from inside of him. He could still call up the smell of the air that night, dusty and cool, see the sand-packed path that had been beneath his boots with startling accuracy in his mind's eye. Feel the shockwave from the IED that had exploded with such force that he'd literally been thrown off his feet like a rag doll despite his size, and his ears had rung for days.

He'd still heard the screams, though. Flannery, Perez, Cho. Weaver had been the only one who hadn't screamed.

He'd never had the chance.

Gamble's phone buzzed softly, ripping him back to his bunk. His heart raced in a frenetic rhythm, his breath clogging his throat with short, sharp bursts that didn't make it to his lungs. Panic gripped every one of his muscles, insidious in the darkness of his room, as his phone buzzed again. He palmed the thing out of sheer habit, blinking through the shadows he'd learned to both fear and hate, and he forced himself to focus on the screen.

Kennedy's initials had popped up, with one lone word directly after them.

Hi.

Gamble grabbed onto the single syllable like it was a fucking lifeline, and Christ, it felt so goddamn good to have something to hold on to.

And so goddamn right that it was her.

Hey, he texted back, fear jabbing at his chest a split second later. Both Sinclair and Isabella had sworn to call him with a nine-one-one if anything went down with Rusty or Xander, but... **Are you okay?**

Kennedy texted back quickly. **Yes, I'm fine.**

A tiny smile snuck over his mouth, unbidden. She'd probably say that if her arm was hanging on by a couple of tendons. A fact she must've realized, because a beat later, she added, **I mean, nothing is going on. I know it's kind of late. Sorry if I woke you.**

Wake him? Fuck, she'd *saved* him.

Gamble cleared his throat and exhaled into the darkness of his room, which suddenly didn't seem quite as overwhelming as it had sixty seconds ago. **You didn't.**

Oh. Good.

For a second that turned into ten, then twenty, the screen remained unchanged, with nothing more from her and no little bubbles that said she was constructing a message. Gamble could picture her, though, with those slender, capable fingers hovering over her phone, her bottom lip caught between her teeth as she tried to think of the right words to say, and he typed out a message before he could stop himself.

I can hear the gears turning over there. What's on your mind?

For all the hesitation that had come before it, this time, Kennedy's reply came swiftly.

You.

The message had no sooner traveled from Gamble's eyes to his solar plexus than the piercing all-call of the station's overhead sound system shattered the silence around him.

Engine Seventeen, Squad Six, Ambulance Twenty-Two, Battalion Seventeen, structure fire, two hundred block of Camden Avenue. Possible entrapment. Multiple units responding to the scene. Requesting immediate response.

Ah, shit. Gamble flung the blanket off his legs, jamming his feet into his boots and thumb-typing as fast as possible. **Call just came in. Talk later?**

Sure, yes. Of course, Kennedy replied. Gamble's adrenal gland did its due diligence, pumping out all sorts of things that tempted him to give in to his pounding heart and the faster pace of his breathing.

But his fingers were perfectly steady as he typed out, **By the way? I think about you, too.**

He shoved his phone into his pocket without waiting for a reply, whipping his office door open and fast-tracking his ass to the engine bay.

Goodbye, calm. Hello, shit-storm.

19

F ive minutes after he'd climbed into the officer's seat in the front of Engine Seventeen, Gamble realized that shit-storm might be an understatement.

He squinted at the computer screen mounted to the dashboard, reading, then re-reading the update from dispatch before turning his mouth toward the mic on his headset.

"Okay, you guys. Listen up, because this is big shit. Dispatch has six nine-one-one callers reporting active flames all over a vacant commercial building in an industrial park."

McCullough's eyes widened, although they didn't budge from the windshield as she maneuvered the engine through the essentially empty city streets. "That's a ton of freaking call-ins for a vacant building in the middle of a part of town that should be dead quiet at this time of night," she said, her voice tinny over the headset. But between the sirens blaring full-bore over their heads and the boxy logistics of the engine's interior, they'd never be able to communicate without the damned things.

"You think this building is some sort of flophouse?" came Kellan's voice over the line, and even though Gamble would have to do some serious twisting around to put eyes on the guy all the way in the back step, he nodded.

"Entirely possible considering the location." A great part of the city, it wasn't. Then again, it wasn't as if a lot of people who slept in flophouses also had the cash for cell phones to be calling nine-one-one. "That, or a bunch of people broke into the place to party."

"Fucking popup parties," McCullough said. "A bunch of teenagers getting high and wasted and who knows what else in a creaky old warehouse with no heat and no power. Like nothing's going to go wrong there."

Gamble's gut knotted and dropped low beneath his turnout gear. They'd responded to enough of these calls for him to know Shae wasn't wrong.

All fires had the potential to be disastrous. But if there were people trapped inside this large, abandoned building, who might potentially be drunk or who knew what else, as the whole thing burned uncontrollably?

Yeah. This was the stuff of nightmares.

"Okay, so what do we do?" de Costa asked from her spot in the back step beside Kellan. They'd seen a handful of decent-sized fires since she'd come on board as Seventeen's rookie, and she'd even had her boots on the ground for a couple of them, going in with the rest of the crew to knock things down. But none of those fires had even come close to this in either magnitude or intensity, and Gamble had to hand it to her. For as much seriousness as de Costa's voice held, she didn't sound scared.

Even though she probably fucking should.

"Gear up. ETA is"—he swung a gaze at McCullough, who supplied "eight minutes" in answer before finishing with—"Bridges is behind us, and dispatch has two other units responding. Looks like we'll be first on-scene, which means Bridges will call the ball. Have your radios on, and do me a goddamn favor. Keep your eyes and ears wide, all of you, because it looks like we're gonna get toasty. You copy?"

"Copy," came the trio of replies through his headset. Gamble pulled on the gear he hadn't already gotten into place before climbing into the engine and kept an eye on the monitor for updates from dispatch, which only included more of the same; namely, that there was a fire, it wasn't small, and—*shit*—that two people reported having been inside when they'd smelled smoke and run outside, and they hadn't been in the building alone.

"Ho-ly..." Kellan's voice barely made it over the headset as McCullough pulled up in front of a huge four-story building and jerked the engine to a stop. Gamble didn't waste any time getting his boots on the concrete and his eyes on his surroundings, and ah, hell, Kellan's response had been accurate.

Adrenaline flooded Gamble's veins at the punch of heat and smoke already filling the nighttime air. Dark orange flames flickered upward from four—make that five—front-facing windows on the second floor, as well as from three more side-facing windows on the top level of the building. The smoke chugging past the gaps in the handful of windows that had been boarded up suggested there was plenty more fire inside that they couldn't see, and with just the feeble streetlights on either corner of the block for assistance, they had a hell of a job in front of them if there were people inside this building.

"Oh, God. Oh, *God*." de Costa stood on the sidewalk, gaping up at the building and looking terrified for the first time since Gamble had known her, and the emotion on her face snapped him to immediate attention.

"de Costa, look at me." He pushed himself into her line of vision to be sure to get the whole not-a-question thing across. "You're trained for this, and you're part of a team. We're all going to knock this fire down together, one command at a time. You copy?"

She nodded, her helmet wobbling. "Y-yes." At his arched brow, she shook her head, as if re-setting her resolve. "Yes, Lieutenant. I copy."

Relief filled his belly at her excellent timing as Captain Bridges's voice sounded off through their radios. "Listen up, Seventeen! We have reports of flames showing on Alpha, Bravo, and Delta sides of the building on floors one, two, and four. Multiple reports of entrapment. Apparently, some kind of after-hours party. Walker, you and de Costa prep the lines so they'll be good to go when everyone's out, and keep your eyes open from the outside. Gamble, McCullough, you're with squad for search and rescue, and I'll get Engine Forty-Two on venting the roof. Whatever's burning in there is doing it fast," he said, the implication not to take their time loud and clear in his tone. "I want all of you out of there faster. Copeland, Slater, set up triage and check everyone who's already gotten out for injuries. Let's move, people!"

Gamble buckled his helmet into place, sweat already forming on his brow beneath the rough, thick material of his hood. He regulated his breathing even though his nervous system was daring his heart to play full-contact dodge ball with his ribs, meticulously scanning not just the building, but the entire scene. Smoke funneled through the air, and Gamble knew from experience that he wouldn't get rid of the acrid stench in his nostrils or the taste of it in the back of his throat for days.

No time to think about that now. Block out the smell. Stuff everything down deep. Focus.

His boots slapped to a halt on the sidewalk in front of the building, McCullough on his six.

"Alright, y'all," came Hawk's drawl as he completed the same survey of the scene they'd all no doubt just done out of instinct. "We're gonna clear all the party people outta here, nice and easy, then get the hell outta Dodge so Walker and the rookie can get this place wet. McCullough, you and Gamble take floor two, Dempsey and Gates, floor three, and Faurier, me and you will head on up to four. We'll sweep from the top down and hit floor one last. Don't get shy on the radio if you need something, but let's get in so we can get out. Copy?"

Technically, as lieutenants, neither Hawk nor Gamble outranked the other. But not only did Hawkins have far more tenure when it came to both search and rescue and knocking down fires, but Gamble respected the shit out of both the man and his command. It didn't make it tough to follow his orders. "Copy that, Hawk."

The other firefighters all clipped out their agreement and hustled toward the front entrance of the building. Dempsey had the most experience breaching everything from standard-issue wood-framed doors to high-tech security gates to—in one very weird instance that had actually made the local news—the door to a bank vault, so he took the lead. Thankfully, he didn't end up needing to put his skills to use, though, as a young woman stumbled through the building's front door just as they arrived on the threshold.

"Ma'am? Are you hurt?" Gates asked, and even though

the teen was coughing heavily and covered in a film of ashes and grimy soot, she managed to shake her head.

"N-no," she coughed, her stare wild and panicked. "But my friend is still inside. There are *lots* of people inside. Oh, my God, it happened so fast."

"Okay. It's okay. You're safe now. Take a deep breath," Gates told her, and damn, the guy was good, because his even voice and calm expression did the trick. "Is your friend hurt?"

"No." The young woman coughed again and started to cry. "I don't know, maybe? He's t-t-trapped on the second floor, near the back of the building. We were trying to get down the hallway to get out, and a piece of the ceiling s-started to fall. He pushed me toward the door, but then he couldn't get past all the fire. It was *everywhere*. Please, you have to go help him. *Please!*"

Slater came running up, his jump bag firmly in place on his shoulder. "Come with me, ma'am. My name is Luke, and I'm going to check you for injuries, okay?"

Nodding in thanks, Gates passed the woman off to Slater. Hawkins looked at McCullough, then Gamble, but only for a split second before jutting his chin at the door.

"Find him quick, would you? And for fuck's sake, watch your asses in there."

Shae nodded, never hesitating. "You got it, Hawk," she said, swiveling toward Gamble. "You ready, boss?"

"Copy." His brain lasered in on the task in front of him, his focus straight-edge sharp. *Search and rescue. Nothing else.* "You're on my six until we hit floor two. Let's see what we're dealing with, here."

Gamble tugged his mask into place over his face and pushed past the front door, knowing Shae would be directly behind him because that's where he'd told her to be. A wall of heat and smoke did its level best to steamroll him as he stepped farther inside the building, and he tempered his pulse along with his breathing as he did a quick visual sweep of his surroundings. Visibility was dim, lit only by the glowing flames along the far wall, but the building looked like a warehouse of some kind, with wider, open spaces on the main floor. There were pieces of furniture scattered around and wooden pallets stacked up here and there, looking as if they'd been left behind from when the building had been in use. Flames were quickly consuming the walls on the Delta side of the building and the furniture close to it, but the floor looked thankfully clear of anyone trapped or trying to get out, despite the intensity of the fire.

"There," Gamble barked, pointing to a nearby door marked STAIRS. He cut a fast path to the stairwell, clicking on the flashlight attached to the front of his gear so he could see something other than the pitch black he'd been greeted with. Hoofing it up one flight, he palmed the door to the second level, his muscles coiling as he braced for whatever he'd find on the other side.

Fuck. He'd been right to buckle down. Pushing his way over the threshold, Gamble could quickly see that search and rescue was going to be a righteous pain in the ass. While the ground level had been fairly open, this floor held an L-shaped hallway with doors lining either side, as if they'd been offices of some sort, with at least five on either side of each corridor. And those were just the ones he could see.

Time to get moving. "Take Alpha. I'll take Bravo. Let's find this guy. Go," Gamble said, McCullough's "copy" hitting his back as he pivoted to his left. The radio on his shoulder crackled with byplay between Gates and command as the firefighter assisted someone out of the building, then again between Faurier and command for more of the same. Gamble checked the first two rooms, both of which were loaded with heavy, curling smoke, but thankfully free of flames. Shutting each door methodically after the room behind it had been cleared, he moved down the hall, trying to ignore the darkness just outside the reach of his flashlight.

Tell...tell my wife...tell her I love her...

He blanked the memory with a hard mental shove. He needed to find this guy who had allegedly been trapped, along with anyone else who might be stuck up here, and get gone.

Shadows be damned.

Gamble's SCBA tank hissed low in his ears, reminding him that air was at a premium. The news flash made his survival instinct override the thoughts trying to crowd his brain, and he pushed his way past another door. A wave of heat rushed forward in a rude-ass greeting, flames whooshing and crackling as they climbed the walls and stretched up toward the ceiling.

"Fire department! Call out!" Gamble bellowed, trying to get his voice to carry as far as possible past his mask. A quick check of the room—which was empty of furniture or other things that might block his view, thank fuck—turned up clear, and McCullough's voice grabbed his attention through the radio.

"McCullough to command, I've got a conscious female on floor two, Alpha side."

Gamble blinked. Hadn't the young woman outside said her friend was a guy?

"Copy that, McCullough," came Bridges's voice. "Is your exit path on floor two clear?"

Gamble allowed himself a brief exhale at Shae's affirmative reply, but his relief only lasted until she added that the rest of her search was all clear. It was possible the guy they'd believed to be trapped up here had been in some other room, or even on some other floor, and had already gotten out. But even with the heat and flames and smoke that seemed to be spreading through the building far faster than they should, Gamble couldn't take the risk.

There was one room left at the end of this hallway, and the guy might be trapped inside.

Gamble lasered his sights on the door at the end of the hallway. Pushing over the threshold, he immediately stumbled back at the surge of flames that rushed forward in the world's nastiest meet and greet. Fiery debris littered the room—Christ, half the ceiling had caved in, beams and all —and yeah, he needed to do his sweep and get the fuck out of here before the rest of the place decided to jump on the all-fall-down bandwagon.

"Fire department! Call—"

Gamble clapped eyes on the guy on the floor mid-holler, and his chest constricted as if someone had reached down his throat and grabbed the air right from his lungs. The guy —no, kid was more accurate, because he couldn't be any older than seventeen—was slumped lifelessly on his side. Both of his legs were trapped beneath one of the fallen ceiling beams, pinning him into place on the ash-strewn floor, and Gamble didn't stop to think, just shoved past the smoldering debris to get to the kid.

"Hey, buddy! Can you hear me?" Gamble's instincts took complete control, guiding his eyes in a lightning-fast sweep and regulating his nervous system to keep his breathing and heartbeat in check. The kid let out a low, weak groan—*yes, breathing*—and Gamble slapped the radio on his shoulder to life.

"Gamble to command. I've got a male victim in need of medical assistance on floor two, Bravo side."

He sent up a prayer that the primary exit was still clear, and for once, the powers that be did him a solid. "Command to Gamble, copy that. You're clear to fall out to the primary exit."

Gamble squinted past the sweat in his eyes and the smoke in front of his mask. Normally, he'd stabilize the kid first. Crush injuries were no fucking joke. But this place was burning faster by the second, the fire raging harder and hotter than even a minute ago, so Gamble's main priority was getting them both out of there as fast as possible. Reaching down low, he gripped the ceiling beam, along with the huge chunk of smoldering drywall that had fallen over the kid's body from the waist down, and lifted it high enough to shove it aside. His stomach bottomed out at the sight of the severe burns covering the kid's legs, but he had no time to waste with shit like feelings or fear.

Gamble pulled the kid into a fireman's carry across his shoulders, taking just a split second to recalibrate his muscles and his center of gravity to match the added weight before turning to move toward the door. Flames flickered, closer and faster, as the hallway became the junction to the stairs and the stairwell became the first floor. Gamble's lungs squalled and his muscles threatened to seize from the heat and exertion, but no. *No.*

He had to get this kid out of here in one piece. Alive. Breathing.

He powered his way past the front door, and for a split second, his senses overloaded in a jumble of sounds and lights and breathable air. But then Quinn was there with a gurney, Faurier helping to roll the kid safely from Gamble's back to the white fitted sheet covering the padded vinyl mattress, and he flung back his helmet and mask.

"Positive loss of consciousness. Breathing. Crush injuries with severe burns on his lower extremities." Gamble didn't so much speak as vomit out the words, but Quinn nodded.

"Got it." She turned to hustle the gurney away from the scene, presumably closer to the safety of the ambo. Even though it was August and not at all chilly, the nighttime air felt like an arctic blast on Gamble's face. He recalibrated, tweaking first to the shift in temperature, then the unrelentingly bright lights coming from the pair of media vans parked at odd angles nearby. He opened his mouth to say something—what numbnuts had let reporters this close to an active fire scene, he had no clue—but the sound of Hawkins's voice sounding off over the radio KO'd the words before they could form.

"Hawkins to command. Search on floor four is complete. This fire's haulin' ass. We've got a coupl'a minutes, tops, before it flashes over."

Shit. "Shit," McCullough echoed, and only then did Gamble fully register that she'd been standing next to him.

Bridges's voice cut through the static on the line. "I want you all out of there, right now. Hawkins, Dempsey, Gates, fall out immediately."

Hawkins burst through the primary exit a handful of heartbeats later, with Gates following fast on his heels. Flames engulfed more than half the building's windows now, actively rolling up toward the roof, and the back of Gamble's neck prickled in both warning and dread.

"Where's Dempsey?"

"He was on my six in the stairwell," Gates said, his chin whipping back toward the exit.

It was empty.

"Dempsey, report," Bridges said over the line, waiting only a second or two before barking, "Dempsey, *report*."

Gamble's chest compressed, his pulse tripping in his ears. No, no. Oh hell, no. He wasn't leaving anyone behind. Not ever again.

They'd all gone in together. He'd be goddamned if they wouldn't all come out that way.

Alive.

His legs began to move before he even knew they would, driven by raw instinct. Vaguely, he was aware of Captain Bridges's voice, swearing up a blue streak over the radio, just as he was aware of the epic ass-chewing he was going to receive for breaking both protocol and the chain of command.

Funny, it didn't slow him down a bit. Gamble rushed toward the front door, yanking his mask and helmet back into place as he barged through the front door. The fire had spread like, well, wildfire, and God damn, he'd never seen a blaze travel with such speed or intensity. It was almost strategic.

Gamble's radio crackled to life. "Dempsey to command," came the firefighter's voice, heavy with pain. "I fell on my way out. Pretty sure my leg is broken."

"Dempsey, this is Gamble," he replied, unable to keep his relief from spilling into his exhale at the sound of the guy's voice. "I'm on floor one. What's your location so I can get you out of here?"

"In the stairwell between floors one and two," came the reply. But Gamble was already in motion, his boots thundering toward the stairs, and seconds later, he had eyes on his fellow firefighter. Sure enough, Dempsey was sprawled over the landing, his left leg bent at an unnatural angle that looked like his self-diagnosis had been spot fucking on.

"Hey." Gratitude flashed past the pain in Dempsey's stare, and Gamble acknowledged it with a lift of his chin.

"This fire's bad. We've gotta go." The unspoken *I have to pick you up and it's going to hurt bad enough to shrivel your balls* must've carried in his tone, because Dempsey tensed with a nod.

"Do what you've got to do," he said, grabbing Gamble's coat sleeve at the last second to add, "Hey. Thanks for coming back."

Gamble's throat tightened, and he shook his head. "We don't leave our people behind, D. Now, come on. Let's get out of here, yeah?"

But before either of them could move, an explosion slammed through the building, knocking Gamble sideways and roaring against his eardrums as it shook everything right down to the bricks.

20

After ninety minutes of alternately staring at her ceiling and her cell phone, Kennedy gave up and got out of bed. Yeah, she was overdue to crash, and no, not a little bit, but her long, often odd hours at The Crooked Angel had made it so she and quality sleep hadn't been besties for quite some time. Add the stress over her brother and the stress *relief* she'd found with Gamble to the deep-thoughts mix?

Yeah. There was a zero percent chance she was catching any zzzs tonight, because her brain was on total freaking overload.

Tapping her phone to life, Kennedy read, then re-read the string of texts between her and Gamble as she padded down the hall toward her kitchen. She'd been inelegant, she knew, just hurling the fact that she'd been thinking about him right out there like that. But he'd asked what had been on her mind, and what's more, she hadn't wanted to lie or even change the subject to avoid the question.

She couldn't stop thinking about him. Or how good he'd made her feel.

And she'd wanted him to know it.

"Girl. You're losing your shit," Kennedy muttered to herself, placing her phone on the counter next to the sink before pulling a mug from the cupboard over the coffeepot. Since caffeine wouldn't help her current state of sleeplessness and she did hope to get at least a few hours of shuteye before the sun did its thing with the horizon, she skipped over the java on the counter, turning instead to grab the milk from the fridge and a packet of hot chocolate from her stash in the pantry. It didn't matter that it was August, nor did her meager attire of jersey shorts and a tank top factor into things. Hot chocolate wasn't about literal warmth. It was about comfort. Kennedy had made cup after cup of the stuff for Xander over the years, mixing it with water when they couldn't afford milk, pilfering packets from car repair shops and the middle school teachers' lounge when she got really desperate.

Her stomach panged, and she dropped her gaze to the mug in front of her. She hadn't heard from Xander today, but that, she supposed, was a good thing. The surveillance Capelli had put into place made state-of-the-art look like the stuff of fifth grade science fairs, and the intelligence detectives had no less than three sets of protocol in place in case of unexpected trouble. Anyway, Xander wasn't supposed to meet up with Rusty again until tomorrow night. She'd thought about calling to check in with her brother regardless, but with the exception of letting her feed him last night, he'd been dodging her like a land mine ever since he'd chosen working with the RPD over going into protective custody. At some point, they'd have to have a Come to Jesus talk about the rift that had grown between them, but since the topic paled in comparison to the whole serial-arsonist-slash-part-time-bomb-maker-on-the-loose thing, it would have to wait.

Kennedy pulled out a saucepan, going full-on old school to warm up her milk. She filled the mug first with the hot chocolate mix, then with the warm milk, her spoon clinking softly as she stirred. The smell of creamy cocoa and pure sugar made her taste buds spring to life, and she ditched the spoon in favor of a big handful of mini-marshmallows.

"That's more like it," she said, padding out of the kitchen and over to her couch in the living space beyond. Her place wasn't huge, nor was it the stuff of Pinterest boards (news flash: for as organized as she was at work, she'd never be in danger of anyone calling her a neat freak at home) but it was open and airy and decked out with modern amenities. When the landlord had first shown Kennedy the stainless steel appliances and granite countertops and gleaming hardwood floors, her first instinct had been to laugh. When he'd gotten to the master bathroom, with the shower big enough for two and the separate soaking tub beside it, and the bedroom that boasted a small but private third-story balcony with a view of downtown Remington, her instinct had been to cackle in disbelief.

Only when she'd signed the lease, filled that tub to the brim with hot water that had shown no signs of running out, and sunk in up to her chin, had she allowed herself to cry with happiness.

Placing her mug on the coffee table, Kennedy grabbed the throw blanket from the back of the couch and got good and comfy. Yes, she and her brother were going to need to talk, and more yes, she had feelings for Gamble that were starting to slide out of the nothing-to-see-here category. But she couldn't change either of those things tonight. She might as well channel surf her way to dreamland so she could figure out how to proceed with a level head in the morning.

Kennedy clicked the TV to life and hit the button for the electronic guide. The local news played in the background, sports scores and heat waves and, ugh, a spate of tire slashings three streets up from The Crooked Angel. She sipped her hot chocolate, focusing on the late-night/early-morning choices on the screen, when the thumbnail image from the newscast made her lower her half-empty mug to her lap in a rush.

"Oh, *God*."

Heart wedged in her windpipe, Kennedy reached out to trade her mug for the remote, her hand sticky—damn it, she'd spilled her hot chocolate on the hem of her tank top—as she turned up the volume.

"...more to add to this breaking story as Remington firefighters battle a huge blaze in the two hundred block of Camden Avenue, which you can see here behind me. The cause of the fire is unclear, but paramedics are treating people who appear to have been trapped inside."

The camera panned over to a blue and white ambulance with brightly flashing lights going full tilt, and Kennedy's gut knotted further at the sight of Quinn and Luke working in brisk, urgent movements. She clicked on the thumbnail to make the image full-screen, her pulse knocking faster as the camera focused on a firefighter running out of the building with someone on his back. Quinn rushed up with a gurney, and even though the firefighter's face wasn't visible past all of his protective gear, Kennedy would know that hulking frame anywhere.

Gamble.

The firefighter lifted his mask, and, sure enough, Ian's face flashed over the screen, turning frighteningly serious a few seconds later as he slung his mask back into place and retraced his strides toward the burning building to disappear inside.

The reporter continued, "A third fire house has just arrived on the scene, officially making this Remington's biggest, and presumably most dangerous, fire of the year. No word yet on any injuries, but, as you just saw in our exclusive report, firefighters have assisted several more victims out of the building, and we—"

A huge explosion rocked the building behind the reporter, tearing a cry from Kennedy's throat and making her drop the remote to the floor as she sprang toward the TV screen. The camera angle dropped sharply, showing a stilted view of glass shattering and flames bursting out from the windows on the upper floors before the image—no, no, *no!*—cut back to a shell-shocked news anchor in the studio.

"Well, we seem to have lost touch with Mike from the scene of that fire, but we'll continue to keep you updated with the very latest as..."

Kennedy's legs got the message to move on a three-second delay, her bare feet kicking into a sloppy run toward her kitchen. She scrabbled for her cell phone, tapping in her passcode with shaking fingers and pulling up the only number she could think of right now.

"Kennedy? What's the matter?" came Isabella's sleepy voice, and Kennedy plowed right in.

"Isabella! Isabella, turn on the news. There's a fire, some kind of building fire, and it's huge, and—"

"Okay, slow down," Isabella said, the sound of fabric rustling in the background. "A fire? Our surveillance has been completely quiet. Wait, is Xander in trouble?"

"No, it's not that." It couldn't be, right? Intelligence would've picked up anything tetchy on the surveillance monitors. "There's a fire in a big building, near North Point, I think, and Seventeen is there. I saw it on TV." Kennedy's stomach pitched, but she forced a breath into her lungs. "The building exploded, Isabella. It *exploded*, and I think Gamble was inside, and—"

"Where?" Gone was the soothing tone in her friend's voice, replaced by something calm and serious and made of titanium. "Did the news say exactly where?"

"I don't"—her mind raced, her thoughts tripping together, until, *ah!*—"Camden Avenue!"

"Okay, hang on."

Kennedy waited as Isabella's voice sounded off in the background, presumably on a landline and hopefully getting an update of some kind. Unable to sit still completely, Kennedy paced into her room, pulling off her shorts and shoving her legs into a pair of jeans, then her feet into her boots.

She couldn't just sit here. Not when Gamble could have been inside of that building. Not when he could be trapped or hurt or...

Yeah. She really *couldn't* just sit here.

"Kennedy?" Isabella asked after an unbearable couple of minutes, although she didn't wait for an answer—not that Kennedy wanted her to. "Dispatch is confirming reports that there was an explosion of some kind at the scene of that fire, but there's no word yet on what might have caused it. I called Sinclair, and given the nature of the case we've been putting together and Rusty's plans to torch those buildings downtown, he's reaching out to arson investigation and the bomb squad, just as a precaution. Hollister checked in with Xander, and he's fine. Surveillance monitors show him at home, safe and sound."

Kennedy loosened an exhale that had the world's

shortest life span as Isabella added, "EMS does have reports of multiple injured parties from the scene that are all en route to Remington Mem. Two of them are firefighters, but I don't know who."

Kennedy's blood turned to ice. "How bad?"

"I don't know that, either," Isabella said, the hitch in her tone becoming a promise with her next breath. "But we're going to find out. How quickly can you get to the hospital?"

Grabbing her keys and a hoodie from the hook by her front door, Kennedy's fear crystallized into purpose.

Go. Get there. Find him.

"I'm leaving right now. I'll meet you there in twenty minutes."

Kennedy slid her phone into her back pocket before continuing on a whisper, "Please, God, don't let me be too late."

GAMBLE'S HEAD felt like someone had used it to play a round of speed golf...with a rusty Halligan instead of a nine iron. But since admitting that out loud wouldn't win him any prizes—well, none that he wanted, anyway—from the doctors who had fast-tracked him into a private curtain area the second he and Dempsey had arrived in Forty-Two's ambo, he kept his thoughts to himself.

"Well, Lieutenant, I've got to be honest with you. I've never seen anyone with luck like yours."

The trauma doc, a young guy who looked more like an Armani model than an M.D., took one last look at the notes from the workup Gamble had tried to decline but had still totally received from the paramedic during transport.

"Does that mean I'm good to go?" Gamble asked, and the

guy—Dr. Jonah Sheridan, according to his fancy white coat
—laughed.

"I'll try not to take that personally. But since you appear
uninjured, you passed your rapid trauma assessment with
flying colors, and you didn't hit your head or lose consciousness at any point during the blast, I don't see any reason not
to clear you."

"What about the guy I was brought in with? Ryan
Dempsey."

Sheridan paused, his unnaturally blue eyes growing less
readable. "Officially, I can't give out any information on
another patient. Unofficially?" He stepped closer to the
gurney Gamble had just swung his legs over the side of and
dropped his voice a register. "His tibia looks like the day
after Mardi Gras, but other than that, he'll be fine. He's in
trauma two. Which I'm coincidentally about to walk right
past, in case you were to, oh, maybe follow me and just
happen to see him on your way out."

"Coincidentally," Gamble added. One corner of his
mouth lifted, just a degree, as Sheridan nodded and broke
into the sort of up-to-no-good smile that made Gamble
think the guy would fit in just fine if he ever decided to trade
in his white coat for a pair of bunker pants. Placing his boots
on the linoleum, Gamble followed the doc out of the curtain
area, and hey, what do you know, a couple dozen steps later,
they walked riiiiiiight past a trauma room with a wide-open
door and a gurney containing his fellow firefighter.

"Hey," Gamble said, relief spilling through him at the
sight of Dempsey awake and upright. The guy's gear had
been removed—with trauma shears, Gamble realized with a
wince—and he'd been gowned up, his injured leg splinted
nine ways to Sunday. But he looked otherwise okay, as
promised. In fact, he looked a little *too* okay.

"Heyyyy!" Dempsey said, a goofy, lopsided grin emerging on his soot-smudged face as he turned to look at the doctor quietly clacking away on the electronic chart in her hand. "Hey, it's my buddy. That's Gamble. He's a lieutenant."

Dempsey extended the word to *loooooooootenant*, and the doctor smiled. "Tess Michaelson." She extended her hand, revealing the slightest baby bump beneath her dark green scrubs. "I take it Mr. Dempsey here is one of yours?"

"We were brought in together," Gamble said, canceling out the sudden alarm on her face by tacking on, "Dr. Sheridan just cleared me."

"Ah. Well, I'm sure he also told you that the two of you are extremely lucky. Mr. Dempsey's broken tibia notwithstanding, of course."

Gamble thought of how much worse the whole thing could've been—Christ, it was why he'd run back into the damned building in the first place—and nodded. "Yes, ma'am."

"Isn't she nice?" Dempsey said, his head lolling back against the pillow as his gaze tracked slowly from the doctor's to Gamble's. "Dr. Michaelson is really *nice*."

Gamble's brows went up. "Morphine?"

"Oh, yeah," she agreed with a smile. "He'll be fine. Off his feet for a while," she added, giving Dempsey a look that read *don't get any crazy ideas*. "But after some healing and PT, he should make a full recovery. You want to sit with him while we wait for ortho to take him up for a cast?"

"You're gonna let me?" Talk about an offer Gamble hadn't quite expected.

Dr. Michaelson laughed, further fueling his surprise. "I know the drill, Lieutenant. If I tell you no, you're just going to do it anyway."

She did have a point. Still... "That obvious, huh?"

"I was in the Army for three years," Dr. Michaelson said, her smile sobering. "I get what a uniform does. Speaking of which, dispatch just got an update that that fire is under control, so the rest of the firefighters in your house are on their way here. I'll be sure to send along an update that the two of you are fine anyway, though, so they don't worry any longer than I'm sure they already have."

"Thanks." Gamble's thoughts of the flashover and the intensity of the fire itself tumbled as his adrenaline went into serious letdown, blurring everything together. "What about the people we pulled out of the building? There was a kid, burned pretty badly—"

Dr. Michaelson shook her head to cut him off. "I don't know details about anyone else, but I can tell you that if they were brought to this hospital, they're getting the very best care possible. Now, why don't you two just take it easy until your squad-mates get here? You've had a hell of a night."

"Thanks," Gamble said. He waited for her to quietly close the door behind her before turning to look at Dempsey. The guy's semi-focused, highly happy expression suggested he was well on his way to la-la land, but Gamble's gut still torqued at the thought of how easily he could be mourning the guy instead of sitting here beside him.

Five had gone out. One had come back.

And that kid Gamble had pulled from the fire? He might never go home.

"Maybe next time, you could skip the fucking theatrics, huh?" Gamble said, his voice rusty and gruff despite the levity he'd intended to stick to the words.

Dempsey made a sound that probably meant to be a laugh, but with the pain meds pumping into the IV in his right arm, it came out more like a grunt. "You're the dumbass who ran back into a burning building after Cap told everyone to get out," he reminded Gamble. "He's gonna be mad."

"Yeah." Gamble shrugged, his suspenders shushing over the T-shirt he'd had to strip down to in order to be declared injury free in the ambo, then again once they'd arrived in the ED. "Well, you needed a boost. I didn't want to leave you hanging, is all."

Dempsey pinned him with a bright green stare that was startlingly full of clarity, considering what his tox screen probably looked like. "Thanks for that. Not a lot of guys would risk getting their asses cooked in that situation. So, yeah." Dempsey dropped his gaze to his hospital gown and the light blue blanket bunched up over his unhurt leg. "Just...thanks."

Time to get this conversation back on the rails and these emotions out of his gut, ASAP. "Yeah, well, next time you want time off, just ask for it," Gamble said. "Now, close your eyes for a sec, would you? I'm going to go see if I can get an update on that kid before everyone from Seventeen gets here."

He saved the "and Bridges tears me a freshly minted asshole" part of the sentence all for himself, because there was no reason for Dempsey to worry about it, or—worse yet —feel bad that Gamble was almost certainly going to take a Jupiter-sized ration of shit for running back into that building when he'd clearly been told to fall out. Gamble had made that choice knowing the consequences. He'd take what he'd earned.

It was worth every syllable.

Dempsey nodded, his eyes drifting shut, and Gamble let out a breath of relief. Moving to the door, he swung it open to try and get his bearings and find the nurses' station.

But before he could get so much as one boot over the threshold, his arms were full of a very beautiful, very furious brunette.

21

G amble stood, cemented to his spot, and tried like hell to process what had just happened. He knew the woman who had launched herself into his dance space was Kennedy—after the other night, there was no way he would ever forget every nuance of the way her body felt jammed up against his. But what had him thoroughly confused was why on earth she would come down to Remington Mem in the middle of the night, anaconda her arms around his neck, and hold on for dear, sweet life.

"Oh my God, you scared me!" she said without letting go of him, so the words landed somewhere over his shoulder. "You scared the *shit* out of me! Are you hurt?"

Not waiting for an answer—not that Gamble was prepared to get past all the holy-shit shock ripping through his veins to offer one—Kennedy ran her hands over him hastily, her green eyes wild as she followed every touch with a frenzied stare.

Realization clicked in an instant, and his heart tackled his sternum.

She'd been worried. For him. For his safety.

Smart-mouthed, hard-edged Kennedy Matthews *cared* about him.

"I'm fine," Gamble said, his voice rough, as if it had come from way down deep inside of him. "Seriously, see?"

He took a step back to show her. Or at least, he tried to, but she wasn't having any full-bodied separation just yet.

"I saw the fire on the news, and they said it was the most dangerous fire of the year, and there was a shot of you carrying someone out to Quinn, but then you ran back inside and the building blew up, and then it took me and Isabella for-freaking-ever to get past the front desk just now —God, those intake nurses are *serious* freaking pit vipers— she showed them her badge and everything, but they weren't having it because you were being examined and they wouldn't tell us if you were okay, and then—"

"Kennedy. Hey. Kennedy." With his heart pumping hard against his rib cage, Gamble pulled back to press a finger over her mouth, because with how shaken she looked and felt in his arms, it was the only thing that was going to grab her attention right now.

Funny, she let him. "I'm all good," he said. "Not even a scratch." Okay, fine, so he'd collected a battery of bumps and bruises and probably a scrape or two when the building had flashed over and half the ceiling had become either dust or debris, but no fucking way was he going to split those hairs right now. "Really. I swear, I'm fine."

He let his index finger rest on her mouth for just a second longer while the words, and the reality that went with them, sank all the way in.

"But you were inside the building." Kennedy's black brows gathered together over the bridge of her nose. "I saw you. I saw you go back in just before..."

Gamble didn't let her finish. Also, he didn't lie to her. "I was inside. Dempsey fell and broke his leg, and he needed help getting out, so, yeah. I ran back into the building." Goddamned TV cameras. They were going to have to figure out how they'd slipped past the safety perimeter Gamble was certain Bridges had set up around the scene. "But we were in the stairwell when the fire flashed over, so we weren't hurt in the blast."

"Oh." Kennedy swung a look past him, her gaze landing on a now-snoring Dempsey in the room over his shoulder. "But you could've been. If you'd been in a different part of the building—"

"I wasn't," he promised. God, he knew all too well how fucked up those what-ifs were once they got into your gray matter. He didn't want to do that to her.

A thought winged into his brain, and he rushed to add, "Kellan wasn't in that building, either."

If Isabella had come to the hospital with Kennedy, that meant they both knew about the flashover. Which also probably meant that wherever Isabella was right now, she was out of her skull with worry.

Kennedy shook her head, quickly dispelling Gamble's concern. "I know. She's talking to him out by the nurses' station. He texted her from the engine to tell her he's fine, in case she saw the fire on the news, but at that point, we were already on our way here. Kellan said the fire is contained, and a battalion chief came in to oversee the rest of the call so Captain Bridges could head over here to check on you and Dempsey."

She'd no sooner gotten the words past her lips than a heavy set of footfalls sounded off from down the hallway. Captain Bridges rounded the corner, and Kennedy's muscles tensed against Gamble's chest, her weight shifting to the balls of her feet as if she was preparing to put a whole lot of space between them.

But rather than loosening his grasp to let her, Gamble held her even tighter to his side. "Captain Bridges," he said, capturing the man's attention from a dozen paces away.

"Lieutenant." Bridges's normally neat brown hair was sticking up in about twenty directions, as if he'd been pulling at it from every angle. "Good to see you upright."

Gamble's pulse kicked, nice and fucking hard. "Yes, sir. I'm fine. The trauma doc gave me the all-clear."

Relief traveled over Bridges's face, but it didn't last. "And Dempsey? Dispatch just put through an update about his leg definitely being broken?"

Ah, Dr. Michaelson had been a woman of her word. "He's going to be fine. His leg *is* broken, so he'll be out of commission for a while, but once he heals up, he'll be as good as new. He's crashed out on pain meds in the trauma room."

"I'll let him rest for now, then." Bridges looked at Kennedy, then the grip Gamble had around her waist. "I take it you're all set on getting home safely from here, then."

Confusion prickled a path up Gamble's spine. "Once I finish my shift at oh-seven-hundred, sure."

His reports on this fire would probably take him that long, alone. Add to it the conversation he needed to have with the arson unit, the investigation they had to get on top of now that the fire was on its way to being out, the follow-up with the witnesses to figure out what the hell had happened in that building...Christ, he probably wouldn't see the inside of his apartment for days. Not that it bothered him nearly as much as the oh-no-you-don't look covering Bridges's face right now.

"You're not going back to the house, or anywhere other

than *your* house," Bridges said slowly, but Gamble's reply followed the claim, hot and quick.

"What? Why not?" Dr. Sheridan had cleared him, for fuck's sake.

A fact that Bridges seemed to give not one shit about. "Several reasons, not the least of which is the stunt you pulled going back into that warehouse after being told to stand down."

Again, Kennedy stiffened against him, and again, Gamble held her close. "I know I broke protocol to go back and get Dempsey, but—"

"I don't think you want to go there with me right now," Bridges said, his tone implying that if Gamble did, the captain had no problem taking his pound of flesh in front of Kennedy. "At any rate, with Dempsey's injury and the nature of the call we just spent the last few hours on, dispatch has taken Seventeen off rotation until B-shift reports in at oh-seven-hundred. So you don't need to worry about the rest of your shift."

Gamble's heart lurched. "Okay, but arson investigation needs to get out to the scene of that fire as soon as possible so we can open an investigation, and we need to interview witnesses. With how fast that fire was traveling—"

Bridges went for round two in cutting him off, looking none too happy about having to repeat the gesture. "Delacourt knows how to do her job, Gamble, and the RPD knows how to do theirs." Bridges's expression reminded him in no uncertain terms that the captain was in the loop on the recent arson case at The Crooked Angel, and that he'd made the same logic leap that Gamble had.

If Rusty was diabolical enough to try to blow up a fire house and concoct a plan to burn down a bunch of buildings in the middle of the city, he was crazy enough to test his methods on something bigger than a dumpster.

"Detective Moreno already called Sinclair in on this," Bridges said quietly, waiting for a scrubs-clad nurse to pass by with an armload of electronic charts before finishing. "They're interviewing as many witnesses as they're able to right now, and both Delacourt and the fire marshal have been told to make this investigation their number-one priority. I know you've been tasked to assist the arson investigation team on another matter"—his expression warned Gamble not to argue in spite of that fact—"but we can't just jump in with both arms swinging and assume these cases are related. We have to let the RFD and arson do their jobs so we have solid leads to pursue. And until then, you are just going to have to wait. At *home*."

Gamble's mind stuttered and spun, but damn it, as much as he hated it, he knew Bridges was right.

And oh, he *really* fucking hated it.

He exhaled hard. "How's the kid I pulled from the second floor?"

"I don't know," Bridges said, but he'd paused too long for the answer to be the straight-up truth.

"Quinn and Luke brought him in, right? How was he when they got here?"

"Not good." At Gamble's unflinching stare, Bridges admitted, "He coded while they were en route. Luke was able to resuscitate him, and he was alive when they got here, but..."

Gamble's stomach dropped toward his knees, and fuck, he needed to shove these feelings way down deep where they belonged, before they rushed up to ruin him. "Right," he managed. "Not good. Are there any other serious injuries?"

"Three. Two burn victims, one smoke inhalation. Last I heard, they were all in critical condition."

"Are they..." Gamble's voice stuck to his throat, but he forced the words out. "Are they all teenagers?"

Bridges nodded, and Kennedy let out a soft gasp. "It looks that way."

Gamble's control slipped further, and damn it, he needed a lifeline. Something to focus on so his emotions wouldn't get the best of him. "I can help Delacourt with the investigation. Check out the scene, look for signs of arson. Cap, you know I'm good for it."

"What I know is that you recklessly ran into a burning building, against orders, even though *you* knew goddamn well that fire was going to flashover. So, no." A muscle hardened in Bridges's jawline. "Right now, you aren't good for anything other than taking a breather until you get your head on straight and I can count on you not to shoot first and ask questions later."

He shifted back on the linoleum, although he didn't lose the seriousness in his stare. Putting his hand into his pocket, he pulled out the keys and cell phone Gamble had left in Engine Seventeen's front storage compartment out of sheer habit and handed them over.

"Go home, Gamble. Get some rest. I know where to find you, and so do Delacourt and Sinclair. As soon as there's something to tell, you'll be the first to know. But until then..."

Bridges sent a pointed stare at the door. Gamble wanted to argue. Hell, he *wanted* to pivot on his boot heels and march his ass in a direct line back to that scene and comb it for clues until he dropped. But his pulse was thumping like the blades of a UH-60 Black Hawk, his lungs cranking down as if someone had suddenly trapped them in a vise, and he knew from experience that no amount of work—no amount of anything—would keep him from going mission critical if he lost control and these emotions took over.

So Gamble did the only thing he could.

He crammed his emotions all the way down and walked toward the door.

As FAR AS Kennedy saw it, she had two choices. She could either hustle to keep up with Gamble as he bolted for the door, or she could let go of him while he outpaced her.

On second thought, with the rattling thump-thump-thump of his heart against the side of her body and the spring-loaded tension coiling through every last one of his muscles as he moved, she had *no* choice.

She wasn't letting go of him for fucking anything.

Which made it sting all the more when he let go of her.

"Whoa, wait!" she said, scrambling to fall back in beside him, then scrambling faster to keep up with his ridiculously brisk strides. "Seriously. Gamble, hang on for a second."

Annnnnd, no joy. He kept moving as if this building was also on fire and his number-one priority was to get the hell out, away from everything and everyone inside. "I'm fine, Kennedy. I just want to be alone."

The words sailed into her solar plexus, and—damn it! Her untrustworthy legs hitched, making her falter. "Okay, tonight has been crazy and you need some space to decompress, I get it, but—"

"Believe me. You don't get it."

Salt, meet wound. Still, despite her aching, hammering heart, Kennedy didn't stand down. Gamble might not have been hurt in that fire, but the emotions churning in his nearly black stare told her he also wasn't okay, and she cared about him. Even if he was acting like a horse's ass right now.

"Okay, so explain it to me," she said. "I'm just trying to help you."

"No." Gamble headed toward the hospital's side exit without looking at her or breaking stride. The automatic doors whispered open, ushering them both out into the still, quiet darkness that marked the dead of night, and okay, Kennedy had officially had enough of this shit.

She jumped in front of Gamble, so he had no choice but to either stop short or mow her over. Thankfully, he was good on his feet.

He clapped to a halt, just shy of chest-on-chest contact. "I need you to move," he said, his voice low and carefully metered, his lips pressed into a flat, thin line as he loomed over her on the sidewalk.

"Oh, I don't think that's what you need," Kennedy countered, not intimidated in the least. The fact seemed to surprise Gamble, his brows edging up by the barest degree. His stare glittered in the ambient light spilling down from the hospital's exterior fixtures, emotion rolling out of him in waves.

"Really. And what is it you think I *do* need?"

Her hands found her hips. "A ride, for starters. And please don't tell me you'll walk," she added before he could interrupt. "Because I would hate to go back into that hospital and tell Captain Bridges you're planning a what? Eight, nine mile hike through the city in your bunker gear after you were just caught in a freaking building explosion? Especially since he just told you to go home and rest."

For a split second, Gamble looked as if he'd try his luck anyway. He must've realized she wasn't bluffing, though, because instead, he said, "You can't take care of this the way you try to take care of everything else."

Kennedy's chest constricted from the deep slice of the words. But rather than let them make her bleed, she unfolded her spine as tall as her frame would allow, looked him dead in the eye.

And volleyed.

"And you can't outrun your ghosts. So here we are, me and you, both fucked up together. Now, are you going to get in my car so I can take you home, or am I going to have to drag your ass?"

Wordlessly, he released an exhale, dropping his chin by a fraction. Kennedy realized it was all the concession she was going to get, so she spun on the heels of her black stack-heeled boots and cut a straight path to her car.

The nighttime air was temperate, not cool, but not quite warm, either, and Kennedy took a great, big breath of the stuff to try and settle the dual overdose of anger and hurt pumping through her veins. She allowed herself a small breath of relief when Gamble crammed himself into her passenger seat without argument, and it calmed her enough to let her drive with a (mostly) clear head. Having been there so recently, she made the trip to his place with ease, her pulse stuttering with a fresh round of dread when his hand closed over the door handle before she'd even pulled to a full stop in the visitor's parking lot next to his building.

"I don't need an escort," Gamble said when she caught up with him a handful of strides later. But between the ice-cold fear she'd felt earlier and the red-hot anger she was brimming with now, Kennedy had reached her limit. She'd never taken shit from anyone in her life. She wasn't about to start now.

"And I don't do anything halfway. I said I'd get you home, so that's what I'm going to do."

"Suit yourself," he huffed. His boots stabbed into the pavement, then the floor of the lobby, then the elevator, his long legs eating up the deserted stretch of hallway leading up to his front door. Gamble keyed his way over the threshold, but he only made it three steps into his apartment before turning back to pin her with a stare she felt in every part of her that would never see the light of day.

"I'm home, safe and sound. You can go now."

The calm she'd found on the drive over fractured, making her heart beat harder in her rib cage and her blood hum with a push of fresh adrenaline. "No, I really can't," she said.

"I mean it, Kennedy. You can't fix this. You can't fix me." Gamble's eyes flashed with barely banked emotion, and just like that, she snapped.

"I don't want to stay to fix you, you big fucking dolt! I want to stay because I *care* about you. I want to stay because even though you're doing your best to push me away for some reason that I don't get, I can't stand the thought of you hurting and I want you to be okay. So would you please just stop shutting me out and tell me what you need!"

Gamble stood there for a second, staring at her with an expression so intense, she could barely breathe under the weight of it. Kennedy's heartbeat pressed in a rapid tattoo against her ears, at her throat, and, oh God, deep between her legs as Gamble looked at her. Took a step forward. Then another.

"You. I need you. And right now, that scares the fuck out of me."

22

G amble had always thought a bullet would be the thing to end him, or maybe a bomb or a blade or any number of other bad-and-nasties he'd run into as a Marine.

The irony of the fact that it had been a woman—*this* woman—who had brought him to his goddamned knees?

Not lost on him.

"Is that why you're acting like a righteous asshat?" Kennedy asked slowly. "Because you're scared?"

Gamble stabbed a hand through his hair. Christ, he'd fucked this up so thoroughly, thinking he could keep her at arm's length and hide all this shit from her, just like he did with everyone else.

Kennedy wasn't like *anyone* else. What's more, he didn't want her at arm's length at all. Despite all the emotions slamming around inside of him like a Category 5 hurricane, Gamble wanted her close. He wanted to let her in. To show her all his fears and flaws in all their fucked-up glory.

So, yeah. Since that had never, ever gone down before, and up until tonight he'd been dead-certain it never, ever would, scared pretty much covered it. But even when his defenses had dug in and he'd tried to push her away, to cover up the emotions that were threatening to bare their teeth and swallow him whole, she'd refused to back down.

She gave a shit about him. Wanted him to be okay. Cared.

And right now, as crazy and mindless and impulsive as it was, Gamble didn't just want her or need her.

From the top of her head to the tips of her toes, he fucking *craved* her.

On second thought, scared might not touch this.

"Yes," he said, the admission sounding like RPG fire in the soft quiet of his foyer. Or maybe that was just the way it felt. "Most of the time, I've got nothing more than a head full of razor wire. So tonight...you...feeling like this...fuck, how much I want you..." His throat went tight. "Yeah. It scares me, okay?"

Kennedy tilted her head, one brow arched over her emerald-green stare as she closed all of the space between them, and sweet Jesus, Gamble had never seen anything so beautiful in his life.

"I'm scared, too. But I want you. I want *this*." Reaching up, she pressed her hand over the center of his chest. "If I'm what you need to be okay, then take me. Hold me, have me, fuck me. I'll give you whatever you need. Just don't shut me out."

His mouth was on hers in an instant, her lips parting readily beneath his, her body arching up at the same time he bent to pull her in close. The kiss was greedy and grace-less, but fuck, he didn't care. Every taste of her made him want the next one more, each slide of his tongue over hers daring him to go faster, hotter, deeper. Kennedy took it all, returning the kiss with equal intensity as she pushed past his lips to take from him in return. He opened just briefly to give her access, to let her lick her way into his mouth, to dominate the kiss once she was there. But as much as it turned him on to let Kennedy take the lead and have her way with him, Gamble had meant what he'd told her.

She was what he needed. And right now, he meant to have her, to strip her naked and do every dark and dirty thing he could think of to her tight, sweet pussy until the only word she knew was his goddamned name.

"Come with me," he said, grabbing her hand and turning roughly toward his bedroom. It took Kennedy about three steps to get over the surprise that had crossed her lips in a soft gasp, but she stuck right behind him as if she trusted him implicitly.

"Where are we going?" she asked as he crossed the threshold of his bedroom but bypassed the bed he'd made to military standards at oh-six-thirty this morning before leaving for his shift.

Gamble waited until they were both in his bathroom before dropping her hand to turn on the lights and pull back the shower curtain.

"You want to take a shower?" Kennedy's expression made it clear she wasn't done in the surprise department, and Christ, even this woman's shock was fucking sexy.

"Mmm hmm." He flipped the faucet lever, adjusting the water temperature to hot but not scalding, then stepping back toward the spot where she stood, wide-eyed, on the tile. He let his gaze drop to his soot-stained bunker pants and the T-shirt that had been plastered to his skin beneath the rest of his gear during the fire call. He might want to bend Kennedy over the nearest surface and sink balls-deep between her legs until they both lost their minds, but even he knew when to take a detour for the sake of decorum.

"While I plan to get filthy with you, literally being dirty isn't what I had in mind," Gamble said, shouldering out of his suspenders and yanking his T-shirt over his head to throw it in the corner.

"Oh," Kennedy breathed, her pupils dilating enough to turn her stare more black than green as it roamed over his bare chest. "Well, then, I guess a shower couldn't hurt. You do kind of smell like smoke."

He unzipped her hoodie and let it fall to the floor, a sweet, familiar scent drifting up through the mist starting to fill the bathroom. "And you smell like hot chocolate."

"I spilled it when I was watching the news," she said, her fingers making fast work of his bunker pants, then his sweatpants as he kicked out of his boots. "You're not off the hook, by the way." She ran her hand over the inside of his thigh, stopping just shy of his aching cock before going to work on her own jeans. "I am *really* mad at you for scaring me like that."

"I know." Unable to hold himself in check, Gamble gripped the denim she'd just finished unbuttoning and yanked it from her hips. "Now, are you going to take off those panties, or am I going to rip them off of you with my teeth?"

Mercifully, Kennedy obliged. Lowering the sheer black fabric from her hips, she slid out of both her jeans and her panties, leaving her in nothing but her thin white tank top. The moisture now permeating the air in the small bathroom made the cotton cling to her body, outlining her tight, dark pink nipples in a way that made Gamble's mouth water. She reached down, presumably to pull the thing over her head and get fully naked, but he captured her wrist in a quick, impulse-driven grab.

"Leave it."

He kicked his boxer briefs into the past tense with one tug, leading Kennedy toward the shower a second later. Pulling the curtain aside with one hand, he reached in to test the spray with the other, then stepped over the edge of the tub to guide her into the warmth of the shower.

"There," Gamble grated. The sight of her, with the water dampening her hair and spiraling over creamy skin and bright ink, made his cock jerk hard between his legs. He stood back, simultaneously wanting to take her in and just plain take her. But one look at the way the water had turned her tank top translucent, showcasing the firm curve of her belly and those gorgeous, upturned nipples just begging to be sucked, had him abandoning the sit-and-stare. His palms found her waist, pressing over the wet cotton to feel the heat of her body beneath, and she lifted her lashes until their stares met.

Wordlessly, Kennedy reached down for the bar of soap sitting on the ledge built into the shower wall. She worked up a quick lather, moving both her hands and the soap over his body in firm, efficient strokes. Shoulders, chest, rib cage, legs, she covered him in bubbles, letting the water wash away the reminder of all they'd been through tonight until the only thing that remained was the two of them. Here. Now.

"Better?" she whispered, putting the soap back in its cradle. Cupping her face with both palms, Gamble tilted her chin up, brushing his mouth over hers in the softest of motions before shaking his head to correct her.

"Perfect."

In less than a breath, the softness of the kiss became something else. Gamble's hands coasted from Kennedy's face to her shoulders, taking in every dip and flare and curve with growing urgency. He explored the landscape of her hot, shower-slick body, the friction of his fingers on the wet, see-through cotton sending sparks of dark, demanding want up his spine. He curled his palms beneath her tits, pushing the edge of her tank top aside with his chin to bare one tightly drawn nipple.

"Please. Please, please." Kennedy arched into his touch. But she was crazy if she thought he could deny her—Christ, he had a hard enough time not blowing his control when she was sassy and sharp. When she begged for his mouth in that velvet-covered, make-me-come voice?

Yeah, he wasn't saying no. *Ever.*

Gamble closed his mouth over her nipple. He skipped softer touches and swirls and flicks in favor of straight-up suction, and, ah, there it was. The cry that tore from Kennedy's throat was first pleasure, then want. His dick throbbed, the slide of his achingly sensitive skin over the flat of her bare lower belly tempting him to skip over anything that didn't involve him lifting her up to pin her to the shower wall so he could come deep inside of her right this goddamned second. But then she knotted her fingers in his hair, anchoring him just where she wanted him, and the silent demand for more of his mouth honed his purpose.

Alternating between both nipples—fuck, she tasted sweeter with every pass—he gave Kennedy exactly what she'd asked for. Each glide of his tongue made him hungrier, heat building in his blood to match her moans and sighs. She pressed up to the balls of her feet, her bowing spine proof of her greedy need for more, and something snapped, deep in Gamble's gut. Impulsively, he pulled back, but only far enough to lower his hands to her waist and turn her around. Swinging her so his back absorbed the spray of the shower, he slid his hands down her arms, circling her wrists with his fingers.

"Put your hands on the wall."

Kennedy looked at him over her shoulder, her eyes flashing with fire he knew the words would earn him. "What?"

But, oh, he had fire, too, and right now, he wasn't about to be denied.

"Put." Gamble dropped his mouth to her ear, his lips barely brushing her skin until she shuddered. "Your hands." He squeezed her wrists, enough to let her know he was there, but not enough—never enough—to hurt her. "On the wall, Kennedy."

Her exhale shook with desire as she lifted her arms and placed her palms flat against the shower tiles. He pressed against her from behind, his chest against her shoulder blades, his dick notched snugly against the curve of her lower back. Releasing his grip on her wrists, Gamble ran his hands over her arms, letting his touch shape the lean muscles across the back of her rib cage before reaching the hem of her tank top to push it up to bare her tight, flawless ass.

Gamble was on his knees before his brain even knew the rest of him would move.

"Open," he grated, a pulse of wicked lust moving through his blood when she did. Kennedy planted her feet wide over the porcelain floor, and Christ—*Christ*—he had never seen anything so hot or so simply beautiful in his entire life. Reaching up, he cupped her body with both hands, splaying his fingers over the spot where her thighs tapered into the swell of her ass and spreading her wide.

"*Ah.*" Kennedy's head fell back, her dark red fingernails turning inward against the tile, and Gamble felt his smile in no less than fifty places.

"I know you want it, baby." He stroked a thumb over her

folds, the wetness between her legs having nothing to do with the shower. "I won't make you wait."

He pushed forward to taste her with one long sweep of his tongue. A noise broke from her throat, her muscles clenching beneath his hands a split second later.

But hell if he was going to stop.

Fitting his shoulders against the backs of her thighs, Gamble increased their contact. Testing her out with slow glides of his tongue, he settled between her legs, using her moans as a guide. Kennedy was far from shy—not that he expected anything less—pumping her hips and widening her stance as far as the edges of the tub would allow. Gamble pushed his tongue farther inside, thrusting into the heat of her pussy until her motions and her breathing grew faster.

More. More. Fuck, he wanted *more* of her, hot and reckless and right goddamn now. Laying her bare with both hands, he dipped a thumb into her sex, sliding all the way in with ease. Kennedy tilted back into the touch, the move revealing the tight ring of muscle resting sweetly between her ass cheeks, and a shot of unrestrained want made Gamble slip his thumb out of her body to inch it higher.

"Yes," Kennedy murmured, consent and want mixing together in her honeyed tone. He didn't even think of not obliging. Circling the pad of his already-slick thumb around her hole, he leaned in to push back into her pussy with his tongue. He tasted and pressed and gave and took, pleasuring her in every way he could think of. His cock was hard as steel, jutting up between his legs and begging to be where his fingers and mouth were, working Kennedy's body in increasingly bolder strokes. She thrust against him, his tongue buried inside of her and his thumb gaining slow entrance into her tight, hot ass, until finally, he felt her muscles clamp down and begin to shudder.

"There you are. Right there." Gamble slid his thumb farther into her hole with firm yet shallow pressure, reaching his other hand over her hip to finger her swollen, needy clit.

"Please," Kennedy begged. "Oh, fuck, please don't stop."

"You want to give me what I need, baby? Then come for me. All I need is you."

The shudder between Kennedy's legs became a full-on quake, her inner muscles gripping and releasing as she came with a keening gasp. Gamble held steady, not wanting to lessen the pleasure of the touches that had gotten her there, but not wanting to short-circuit her senses, either. He slowed as she did, softening their contact breath by breath and finding his feet just in time to turn her around and pull her in close.

"I need you, too."

Her whisper was quiet, so much so that he nearly didn't catch it over the rush of the shower. But the words, and the emotion that went with them, were there in her eyes, and Gamble lowered his forehead to hers.

"Show me. Let me give you what you need, too."

Kennedy nodded. A quick pair of movements had the water, then her tank top off, and one more took them from the shower to the bathmat. Gamble didn't bother with a towel—nothing was more important than the woman leading him over to his bed right now—and his heart began to pound at the sight of Kennedy laid out in front of him, outlined in only the soft light from the bathroom. Her wet hair was slicked away from her face, all traces of the makeup she usually wore gone.

Yet she was more beautiful than ever. So beautiful, his chest actually hurt.

She parted her thighs, her stare holding no trace of shyness despite the fact that she couldn't be in a more vulnerable position, wide-open and completely bare. In that instant, Gamble realized Kennedy was doing what he'd asked her to, showing him exactly what she needed. Hesitating only long enough to take a condom from his bedside table drawer, he knelt between her legs, trying not to hiss out a breath as she took the condom from him and rolled it over his hypersensitive cock.

"I need you," she said again, the words arrowing way down deep. Reaching between them to wrap her fingers around his cock, she canted her hips up, and oh, holy hell, he was lost. Or maybe he was found, because all at once he was inside of her, and that was all that fucking mattered.

"This. Oh, God, this," Kennedy murmured. Gamble knew he should take a second to adjust to the sensations ripping through him—the warm, perfect squeeze of her pussy, the ease with which his dick had slid all the way home.

But he didn't. Instead, he gave her what she needed.

Gamble pulled back, but only so he could press back to fill her to the hilt, then repeat the wickedly sexy process again and again. He didn't go slow, and he sure as hell wasn't sweet. He gripped Kennedy's hips, a dark smile tugging at the corners of his mouth as she grabbed his wrists, turning her nails into his skin to ensure that he didn't stop. She lifted off the bed to meet him, their bodies slapping together with every thrust. Gamble sank into her over and over, his pulse racing faster and his need burning like a bright, uncontrollable fire. Kennedy opened her legs wider, hooking her thighs over his waist. She didn't knot her legs all the way around him, but held him just close enough to the cradle of her body to make his balls throb as he fucked her with hard, purposeful thrusts. The muscles deep inside of her clenched in promise, and oh yes. *Hell* yes. He wanted his name on her lips as she flew apart.

"Ian, please. I need *you.*"

Gamble buried his cock in her pussy, covering her body until there was no space at all between them from shoulders to thighs. He started to come just as she finished, his release rushing up from the base of his spine and barreling through him with enough intensity to steal his breath. Kennedy didn't hold back, not even in the haze of her own climax, her arms wrapped around his shoulders, her heartbeat a steady constant on his chest. Gamble let go of everything—the adrenaline that had gone with the fire call, the anger of having been benched, the fear of all the what-ifs that could've made tonight so much worse than it was—and focused on the one thing he could control.

But then he realized, as he looked down at the woman in his arms, that he couldn't control this at all.

Because he needed Kennedy. Craved the way she needed him in return.

And hell if that wasn't more dangerous than bullets, bombs, and blades combined.

23

Kennedy rolled over in a bed that wasn't hers, her heart squeezing in her chest. Funny how, all of a sudden, her heart didn't feel like it was hers, either. Guess that's what happened when your emotions blindsided you into realizing the truth that had been right there in front of you, as big and bold as a billboard, just waiting for you to have a lightbulb moment. Kennedy wasn't really sure what would happen now that her heart had—rather forcefully—informed the rest of her that she had all sorts of feelings for the sexy, tortured firefighter she'd fallen asleep next to, and who, despite his rough edges and sharp corners, seemed to have feelings for her in return.

Wait, she thought, rolling over in the tangle of bed sheets that smelled like laundry detergent with just a hint of something masculine that belonged uniquely to Gamble, and blinking her way fully into the reality of the soft, very-early morning light edging past the window blinds.

She might've fallen asleep next to him a few hours ago, but he wasn't here with her now. In fact, the opposite side of the bed was cool to the touch.

As if, even though she had drifted off for a few hours, Gamble hadn't slept at all.

With her pulse tapping her awareness and her instincts into gear, Kennedy reached for her cell phone, which she'd put on the bedside table just before closing her eyes, in case something went down with Xander. But she had no voice-mail messages and no new texts, the last exchange between her and her brother being the quick confirmation from last night that he was, in fact, unharmed and just as what-the-fuck about the fire as she had been. Kennedy knew the intelligence unit had his safety well in-hand, at least for the moment, so she slid the covers back and put her bare feet on the floor.

She realized belatedly that her feet matched the rest of her. Her clothes were still where they'd been hastily discarded on the bathroom floor last night, and she padded in to retrieve them. A wash of heat bloomed over her cheeks at the sight of her hoodie and jeans and panties folded neatly on the edge of the counter and her boots in a precise line at the foot of the vanity. Her tank top, which was still far more wet than not, had been draped carefully over the side of the bathtub, a clean, dry RFD T-shirt resting directly beside it, and her heartbeat conspired against her composure.

She cared about Gamble, which was crazy enough. But in his own quiet way, Gamble cared about her, too.

And Kennedy wanted nothing more than to let him.

Tugging the gray cotton over her head and her panties back into place for some semblance of propriety, she pilfered a swig of mouthwash from the medicine cabinet and pulled her hair into a knot on top of her head. She decided to forego her jeans for now—Gamble's T-shirt was big enough to hit her knees, and unlike the last time she'd crashed here, she wasn't in a hurry to motor out the door just yet—and tiptoed down the hallway leading into the main living space of his apartment.

"Hey," Kennedy whispered, even though the shift of Gamble's shoulders and the slight tilt of his bearded chin told her he'd seen her from the spot where he was sitting on the couch.

"Hey."

The room was half-shadowed, half-illuminated by the rising sun casting golden-pink light through the pair of oversized windows dominating the far wall. The TV opposite the couch was dark and quiet, and although his phone sat within reach on the coffee table, it too was untouched.

Kennedy walked over the floorboards to sit down beside Gamble, who was dressed in a pair of low-slung sweats and a hard, impenetrable stare aimed at the windows. "Any word from Bridges?" she asked softly.

"No." He shook his head, but didn't look at her. He didn't clam up or push her away, either, so right now, she'd take the win. "Have you heard from Xander?"

"No," she said, realizing she'd been too scared, then too angry, then too distracted to update Gamble on her brother last night. "I voice-texted him when I was on my way to the hospital, and he's okay. Isabella checked in with him, too, and of course, Capelli still has tabs on him, but..." She let the rest drift, and Gamble nodded as if he'd more than filled in the blanks. She and Xander might still have fences to mend, but she wasn't ever going to *not* worry about him. "Anyway. He was just as surprised about the fire as we were."

"Glad he's okay."

It was Kennedy's turn to nod. "Me, too."

They lapsed into silence, which, she supposed, was Gamble's default. But again, he didn't push her away, didn't get up to make coffee or go to take a shower, and screw it. She'd seen the emotions in his eyes when he'd ordered those shots of tequila at The Crooked Angel, then again last night when he'd told her he had a head full of razor wire.

And she didn't want him to face those ghosts alone anymore.

"You don't sleep much. Do you," Kennedy said quietly. Although her tone didn't label the words as a question, he answered her anyway.

"No. I don't."

Some feeling she had no name for twisted inside of her, but miraculously, her voice stayed level as she asked, "Do you want to talk about this yet? What keeps you up at night?"

"It's...complicated," Gamble said, more like a warning than a brush-off.

A warning she heard but didn't heed. "I'm okay with that if you are."

For a beat that became two, then twenty, he said nothing, and no less than a thousand questions swarmed Kennedy's brain, begging to be asked. But chances were, he'd been holding on to whatever this was for a long time, stuffing it down instead of letting it out. So she did the only thing she could think of to help him.

She turned off her brain, went with her heart, and gave him the space to find his voice.

"I joined the Marines on my eighteenth birthday," Gamble said finally. "My parents barely spoke to me after I got back from the recruiting center, or in the ten days before I left for Parris Island. I haven't spoken to them since."

Kennedy's tongue burned with the most malicious swear words she could think of, but she locked her molars together in an effort to keep them to herself. Not that she didn't want to launch every last syllable, because she *so* did. But this conversation wasn't about what she wanted. It was about what Gamble needed, so she nodded and waited for him to continue.

"At the time, I wanted the fastest route out of their house, and they were all too happy to have me take it. But it didn't take me too long to realize that not only was I pretty good at being a Marine, but I...liked it."

She tried to hold back her shock, but failed. "You *liked* basic training?"

One corner of Gamble's mouth lifted in irony rather than humor. "Don't get me wrong. There were parts of it that were pure hell, and that was on the good days. But I liked the order of it. The way the objectives were clear, the tactics precise. I've always been a physical guy, so the hard work didn't bother me as much as it does most people. And, yeah, I liked being part of a group whose job it was to watch my back, and that my job was to watch theirs."

God, of course. "You wanted the camaraderie."

"I guess. Yeah, I did," Gamble said. He paused for a minute, as if he was trying to get his bearing with the rest of his words. "I knew I wanted a career in the military pretty early on. I didn't want to just serve and be done, or use it as a stepping stone to something else. I wanted it to *be* my something else."

"I get that," Kennedy said, and she did. Even with that very first job in that shitty diner in North Point, she'd loved working in the restaurant industry. Callings came in all shapes and sizes.

Gamble nodded. "I wasn't really interested in becoming an officer—I didn't have a four-year degree, and I wanted my boots on the ground—so I set my sights on special operations. Specifically, Force Recon."

"Whoa." Kennedy's shoulders hit the back of the couch with a soft thump as her eyes went wide. His badassery had never been in question, but... "Force Recon is a really big deal in the Marines, isn't it?"

"It took a lot of time and training," he said by way of agreement, and it was just like him not to brag, or even make a fuss over a skill set that was probably so advanced and, well, downright fucking scary, that ninety-nine percent of people could never even dream of it, let alone survive whatever was necessary to qualify. "But the closer you get to making your way up those ranks, the more you find the people who want it just as bad as you do. There's not a whole lot of room for freelancing in Force Recon. You're either part of the unit or you're not."

Her chest squeezed in realization. He'd been looking for fellowship. Why not aim high? "So you completed the training and became a Force Recon Marine."

Kennedy let the *and then?* hang in her tone, and Gamble shook his head.

"I can't talk about a lot of it. Not because I don't want to," he added, "although most things, you probably wouldn't want to know even if I could. But nearly all of my missions were classified. Suffice it to say, I spent a lot of time deployed overseas."

"How much time?" Kennedy asked, her curiosity getting the better of her mouth. Gamble, however, didn't seem to mind the question.

"Four years—on and off, of course. I spent most of my leave traveling, though. Or with the guys in my unit."

At the mention of his unit, Gamble's expression changed, growing more shuttered and sharp. His shoulders crept higher around his spine, tension pulling his muscles tight like bowstrings.

Kennedy took a risk and slid her hand over one rock-solid forearm, her own heart beating in time with the pulse she could feel hammering away beneath his skin. "You must have been really close."

"We were," came the answer, low and quiet.

"So, what happened?"

Gamble said nothing, just stared out the windows with that closed-off look on his face, his dark eyes unreadable, and for a minute, Kennedy thought she might've pushed too hard. But then something inside of him seemed to break, emotion tearing over his face and taking over his stare as he turned to pin her with it, and oh, God, her heart broke at the sight.

But then it completely shattered when he said, "They were all killed right in front of me, and I couldn't do a damned thing to stop it."

∿

GAMBLE KNEW ALL the signs of physical duress. He'd had extensive first aid training and seen enough traumas to fill a dump truck with them. So he knew that his racing pulse, the lockdown in his chest, the clammy sweat between his shoulder blades, and the extreme dread crowding his brain right now were all classic signs of a panic attack. He just couldn't do a single thing to keep it from happening.

Second verse, same as the first.

"Oh, God. Gamble, I'm so sorry." Kennedy's voice pierced through the panic, and he focused on it, on the cadence of the sound, the rise and fall of the syllables.

He inhaled. Or at least, he tried to. "It was...bad."

Gamble waited for her to say he didn't have to talk about it, to backpedal or recoil or shove him away. But she didn't.

Christ, she didn't even come close. Instead, Kennedy pressed her hand against his forearm, her fingers warm and strong and so *there* that he opened his mouth and the words just started falling right out.

"There were five of us. Me, Flannery, Perez, Cho, and our captain, Weaver."

He saw each man in his mind's eye, as clearly as if they were right there in the room, Flannery with his bright red hair, Perez with that fucking perma-smile that always bordered on a smirk but somehow never managed to get the guy into trouble as often as it won people over.

"We'd just finished a long mission that had been kind of tedious, shitty conditions, not a lot of sleep, and we were on our way home. But then we got orders to divert."

Gamble knew he had to be careful here. Any mission where four Force Recon Marines had been killed in a cluster fuck of epic proportions on what was supposed to have been a goddamned cakewalk of a personal security detail was classified to the nines. He shouldn't even be acknowledging that there had *been* a mission, let alone that he'd been there and was the only survivor.

And yet, for the first time ever, the past was ripping a path out of him, whether he wanted it to or not.

"So, your unit was needed somewhere else for a different job?" Kennedy asked, seeming to understand his need to redact the details and stick to what had been in the state-ment made by the government after the fact, and Gamble nodded.

"Yeah. Usually, the military tries not to do that with a team that's been deployed for a while, but we were close, and the new detail was supposed to be quick." *In and out, just the way I like it*, Cho had said with a laugh, and even

Weaver, who had been the most stoic of the bunch, had laughed, too.

Gamble shook his head, more words spinning and churning from the spot where he'd shoved them, all the way down in his chest. "The conditions weren't ideal, but we'd seen way worse. Plus, we were there for personal security detail. It was supposed to be easy. Less than a day, then we'd all be throwing back beers on the beach, stateside."

"But that's not what happened," Kennedy whispered. She looked so pretty, sitting there in the growing sunlight of his apartment that was seven thousand miles away from the village in the desert where his entire life had changed, and he let out a shaky exhale.

"No. It's not."

Gamble couldn't give her the facts, not unless he wanted a big, fat court-martial sandwich. He couldn't say that they'd been ambushed, or that Weaver and the guy they'd gone to do PSD for had been killed instantly by an IED blast. That both of Cho's legs had been blown off in less time than it took most people to blink. That, despite his grave injuries and massive suffering, the guy still hadn't died for a full ten minutes afterward, and that every time Gamble closed his eyes long enough to dream, all he saw were those ten minutes, on a grisly, continuous loop in his head.

The ones where he'd tightened tourniquets, drawing unholy screams from the people he'd loved like brothers. Taken heavy fire, certain he would die at any second. Watched Flannery, with whom he'd been the closest, get shot in the head by a sniper as they'd ducked for cover less than six inches apart. Dragged Perez, whose femoral artery had been nicked hard by a chunk of shrapnel from the blast, to the most secure spot he could find so he could cover the guy with his own body while he radioed frantically for help.

Tell...my wife...tell her I love her, Perez had said, the coppery smell of blood clogging the air as Gamble had slid a tourniquet from his med pack around the guy's thigh and prayed for the first and only time in his entire fucking life.

You can tell her yourself when we get home, Gamble had replied.

He'd been a goddamned liar. Perez had bled to death just a few hours later on a field hospital operating table.

Five had gone out. One had come back.

But in a way, everyone had died.

"Ian."

The stability in Kennedy's voice brought Gamble back to the reality of his apartment, of the fact that he was sitting here when the other four members of his unit had been brought home in body bags. His lungs flattened, the shadows that haunted him in those rare, quiet moments he allowed himself closing in.

Kennedy's fingers were still there, though, warm on his forearm. Strong, like an anchor. Like a lifeline.

"Ian, look at me," she said. And funny, he was powerless not to.

She turned toward him as fully as possible, reaching up to cradle his face with reverence he was certain he didn't deserve, but Christ, it felt as vital and necessary as breath.

"I know you can't tell me exactly what happened. And I know that whatever it is, it haunts you. You might be able to hide it from everyone else, but I can see it in your eyes." She paused, and though her hands remained steady, the inhale she took wavered ever so slightly. "But I also know this. You're a good man. Don't blame yourself for surviving."

"But I do," he said. Although it was the raw truth, one Gamble had lived with for years, the admission still shocked him. Of course, he knew he wasn't to blame in the literal sense. The ambush had been well-planned, by a hateful and evil enemy, and he hadn't been negligent or remiss in his recon, nor had any member of his unit. The Marines had done a full investigation. Gamble had been quickly cleared, then commended for his bravery.

But he'd lived, and everyone else was dead, and for the first time ever, he'd admitted his guilt out loud. Those three tiny words had been like a cork, and now that they'd been released, everything they'd been holding back rushed up after them.

"I *do* blame myself. Every single one of us woke up that morning thinking we had our whole goddamn lives in front of us. We all had hopes and dreams and wants. We had each other. But I'm the only one who came home. Me. Not Perez, who had a wife and a kid on the way. Not Weaver, who had been within an inch of retirement, not Flannery or Cho, who had parents and siblings and people who loved them, too. But me. The guy who wouldn't have been mourned. The guy with nobody."

The shadows Gamble knew so well closed in on him then, crushing his rib cage and making it hard to breathe, but not even their presence could keep the rest from crashing past his lips.

"Everyone else *died*, Kennedy," he said in a voice so ragged, he barely recognized it as his own. "Who the hell else is there to blame?"

"No one, because it's not anyone's fault," Kennedy said. "Let me ask you this. Whose fault is it that Asher Gibson was killed when Seventeen responded to that house fire three years ago?"

The question threw Gamble so thoroughly that he answered it without thinking. "Nobody's. What happened on that call was a complete freak accident."

Asher had been Seventeen's newest member at the time, a great kid and a damn good firefighter. He'd gone in to do search and rescue, just as he'd done dozens of times before. Asher had done everything by the book, but the roof had collapsed without warning. Everyone on A-shift had been devastated by the loss, and although he'd never allowed himself to get nearly as close to his fellow firefighters as he'd been with his Recon unit-mates, the months after Asher's death had been hell on Gamble, too.

"Exactly," Kennedy said. "And whose fault is it that Dempsey fell in that stairwell and broke his leg? Or that the kid you pulled out of that warehouse last night ended up in critical condition in the ICU?"

Gamble paused. Processed what she was saying. Then shook his head. "Those things aren't the same as what happened to me and my unit." He'd been the *only* person to survive. No one else. Just him.

Kennedy surprised him by conceding. "No, they're not. They're all separate instances, with separate circumstances. But they do have one thing in common. As awful as they were, none of them are your fault."

"Kennedy—"

"No." She slid into his lap—not in a sexual way, but in that stubborn, won't-be-ignored, fierce sort of way that said she meant business. "I don't need to know what happened to know it wasn't your fault that you lived. But I do know that it's far past time for you to believe the truth. The fact that you survived isn't your fault."

Gamble's heart twisted, and oh, he was tempted to believe her. "I just...I miss them so much sometimes," he said, his voice nearly a whisper in the already quiet room. "And God, it fucking *hurts*. Not just knowing they're gone, but...it hurts to be alone again."

Kennedy's eyes filled with tears, and they spilled down her face unchecked as she looked at him with nothing but truth and said, "Don't you see? You're not alone anymore."

And in that moment, Gamble knew two things. One was that she was right.

The second was that he was falling in love with her.

24

Kennedy stood behind the bar at The Crooked Angel and tried like hell to focus on the inventory sheet stuck to the clipboard between her hands. But between the adrenaline overload of last night's fire and the emotional overload of this morning's conversation with Gamble, her brain was completely uncooperative.

Which was nothing, really, compared to her heart. Because that thing? Yeah, she might as well have signed over full custody the second Gamble had told her about his past.

The anatomy in question gave up an involuntary squeeze as Kennedy snuck a glance at the spot where he sat at the bar, just a handful of feet down the glossy wood. They hadn't spoken much after she'd promised him he wasn't alone anymore, but, then again, they hadn't really needed to. They'd simply wrapped their arms around each other and settled in on his couch, dozing for the few hours they had left until she'd had to get up to come in to work. Yes, she and Gamble had a lot in front of them with this arson case, and *hell* yes, some of those things scared her as much as the fact that she'd gone and impulsively fallen for the guy. But letting him in, and being there so he could let her in, too, didn't feel scary at all.

It felt right. *He* felt right.

Even if his expression was as serious as a triple bypass right now.

Kennedy put the clipboard in its designated space beneath the bar, her boots shushing over the thick rubber bar mats as she walked over to stand in front of him. "Hey," she said, and at least he'd eaten the omelet and home fries Marco had put together for him at her request. "You doing okay down here?"

"It was good to eat," he said, not a yes, but not quite a no. "Thanks."

"You're welcome." Kennedy reached out and put her hand over his on top of the bar. "Nothing from Bridges yet, I take it?"

"Not as far as the arson investigation is concerned," Gamble said, his shoulders easing slightly as he looked up at her, but only for a second before he continued. "The kid I pulled out of the warehouse is still unconscious. They're keeping him sedated. His injuries are...pretty bad."

Oh, God. "You got to him as fast as you could," she said with certainty. "And he's in great hands. You said yourself that the docs who took care of you and Dempsey are top-notch."

The look on Gamble's face remained serious, but at least he nodded. "Yeah. Speaking of Dempsey, he had a weird reaction to the pain meds, so they ended up keeping him at the hospital overnight. He's fine now," he added, probably because her expression had betrayed the worry his words had caused. "Just really out of it. Gates and Hawk and Faurier are with him at the hospital, in case he needs anything."

"Ugh, poor guy." Kennedy opened her mouth to offer to send some sandwiches to Remington Mem—their cafeteria food probably left a *lot* to be desired—but before she could get so much as a word out, a figure appeared in the doorway that made her jaw unhinge in shock.

"Xander?" she gasped, blinking a few times to be—yep —sure her eyes were functioning properly.

"Hey, Ken. Gamble." Her brother lifted his chin at the firefighter in greeting, then sent a suddenly wary glance around the empty dining room. "I thought the bar was open. Is it okay if I come in?"

"Of course," Kennedy said, shaking her head in an effort to anchor herself. "We just opened for lunch a few minutes ago, but you're always welcome here no matter what. Is everything alright?"

Xander nodded, walking all the way over to the space at the bar beside Gamble, who looked just as surprised as she felt, before continuing quietly even though they were the only three people in the front of the house.

"Yeah. I mean, everything with the case is cool, and I still haven't heard from Rusty about where or when he wants to use those remote ignition devices. In fact, he's been weirdly quiet for the last couple of days."

She exhaled in relief. "Good."

The farther away that lunatic stayed from her brother, the better. Just because Xander had made it clear that he didn't need or want her concern didn't mean she couldn't think it.

But wait... "If everything is okay with the case, then why are you here? Not that it's not okay for you to *be* here," Kennedy scrambled to tack on, and ugh, could she be any less articulate? "It's just that, you know. You mentioned your boss is kind of a stickler and, well, you live clear across town."

"Right," he said, sliding a look at Gamble, then skimming a palm over the back of his neck. "I told my boss I had a follow-up doctor's appointment for my burn."

"Do you?" she asked, her eyes immediately darting to the bandage on his forearm that his T-shirt didn't hide.

Xander shook his head. "No, my arm is fine. Healing up great, actually. But after last night's fire, I knew you'd be worried about things, so..."

Kennedy caged her shock, but only just. *That* was why he'd come out here? Because he'd known she'd be worried?

"You haven't heard from Rusty at all?" Gamble asked, and even though the doubt in his voice tempted Kennedy to bristle, Xander didn't even blink.

"No, but I know what you're thinking. That fire last night has his name written all over it."

Kennedy poured a cup of coffee for her brother, mostly so she could put her shaking hands to use. "It doesn't fit the mold, though. I thought he was supposed to be setting fires in empty buildings that are under construction. Why would he torch a warehouse with a bunch of teenagers inside?"

"I don't know," Gamble said, shaking his head. "But I *can* tell you this. With how fast that fire was traveling and how much damage it had already done when we got there, there's no way it wasn't arson. It was too strategic. And two arsonists in the same city at the same time? No way."

"Rusty doesn't need an excuse to set fire to things," Xander said. "Still, he's not stupid. With a big job so close, I'd be surprised if he didn't have a reason for setting fire to that warehouse. I just don't know what the hell it might be. He already knows the ignition devices work, and he definitely never said anything to me about a warehouse fire being part of this job." Xander paused for a second, his expression growing more shielded as he looked at Gamble. "You guys responded to the fire last night?"

"Yeah." Gamble nodded. Over the past couple of years, Xander had gotten good at keeping his emotions away from his face, but like it or not, Kennedy knew better. She could still see the traces of unease lurking beneath the toughness in his stare.

"Was, ah. Anybody hurt?"

Her gut panged. Gamble's shoulders tightened beneath his RFD T-shirt, but he answered the question without hesitation.

"I pulled a kid out of there who was hurt pretty badly. Some spinal cord damage and burns. Hollister texted me a few minutes ago with a brief update, and to let me know they're still interviewing everyone who was at the scene last night while arson investigation and the fire marshal go over the scene."

"I'm sure everyone who was inside the warehouse is probably pretty rattled," Kennedy said, her stomach knotting at the thought. Those teenagers might've been less than smart about breaking in to an abandoned warehouse to party, but they hadn't deserved to be hurt. "Did any of them see anything suspicious?"

Gamble shook his head. "It's hard to say. Hollister said most of the kids said the warehouse was dark, and of course, most of them had been drinking, so that complicates things a little. They're still waiting to talk to the kid I pulled out of there—his name is Zach, I think—and one or two others. The docs are hoping Zach will come around today."

Xander placed a hand on the bar, palm flat, as if he wanted to steady himself. "That's good, though, right? If they think he'll come around and be able to talk?"

"They're *hoping* he'll come around," Gamble corrected. Kennedy's fingers twitched with the urge to put her hand over Xander's in reassurance, but she dug them into her pocket instead. That Rusty might have done something as awful as put a couple of teenagers in the ICU was nauseating enough all by itself. That her brother was going to have to throw himself in the guy's crosshairs in order to put him away?

She wouldn't be able to live with herself if anything happened to Xander. Rift or not, whether he *wanted* it or not, she was still worried as hell for her brother's safety.

Gamble looked at her, and even though it felt more like he was looking through her, she let him. It wasn't like she could hide her feelings from the guy at this point, anyway, and yeah, the tension with her brother still smarted.

"I'm going to go try Hollister for more details, okay?" Gamble asked. "See if Zach woke up yet, or one of the last few kids they needed to talk to maybe saw something useful. I'll be at the end of the bar if you need anything."

Kennedy's heart jumped, although whether it was at the fact that he clearly wanted to give her and her brother space to talk or that he'd probably come barreling back over if she did need anything, however slight, she couldn't be sure. "Of course," she said. "Thanks."

His stare lingered on hers for just a beat longer before he slid off his bar stool and moved a few paces away to make his call. Xander, who missed nothing because she'd taught him to keep his eyes wide open before he'd even started middle school, raised one black brow at her, but didn't say anything.

"Are you hungry?" Kennedy asked, because even lame questions trumped the shit out of awkward silence. "I could have Marco make you a burger. Or maybe a Cuban sand-wich. They're freakishly good, and—"

"Ken," he said quietly, and oh, come *on*.

She knotted her arms over her chest. "I know you can take care of yourself." It was just a burger, for Chrissake! "You don't need me meddling or trying to help you. I just thought—"

"I'm sorry."

Annnnnnd cue up the old-fashioned needle-over-a-vinyl-album screech. "What?" she blurted, and oh my God, was that a smile poking at one corner of her brother's mouth?

"Thought that might get you," he said, shifting closer to sit down on the bar stool next to the one Gamble had vacated. "Look, I've been thinking about this all night, and an apology is kind of the least of what I owe you. Tensions have been pretty high with this case, and yeah, I am a decently capable adult. When I'm not caught up in stupid shit, anyway."

Xander blew out a breath and dropped his chin. "But you're still looking out for me even though I really fucked up, and that means a lot to me."

"Of course I'm still looking out for you," Kennedy said with surety even though the words emerged on a wobble. "You're my brother."

He let go of a sound that might've been laughter, except it was too loaded with irony to tell. "I'm sorry I shot my mouth off the other day about you being my perfect sister. I know it was a shitty thing to say. I was just trying to piss you off so you'd walk away from this whole arson thing."

Her brows shot up. "And you thought that would work?"

"Not really," Xander said with a shrug of his work-hard-ened shoulders, "but I had to try. Not because I was trying to cover anything up, but Rusty is...he's crazy, Ken. I didn't want you anywhere near that. If he knew what I was up to, or that you're my sister and you're working with the cops, too, he wouldn't hesitate to kill us both."

Nope. No way. Kennedy couldn't even allow herself to think it. "I know he's dangerous. But we're going to catch him before he can hurt anyone else. Including you and me."

"Yeah."

After a minute, Xander's gaze flicked across the dining room, landing directly on the spot where Gamble stood with his double-wide shoulders set tight around his spine and his brows knit together as he spoke quietly into his phone.

"Sooooo, you and the big guy are..." Her brother let the rest of his sentence hang, and Kennedy's face flushed with heat that had to be translating into one hell of a blush.

"I'm so not talking about that with you." She grabbed a bar towel from the stack by her elbow and started scrubbing at the counter even though it was already gleaming in the mid-day sunlight filtering in from the windows across the bar.

"I don't want *details*," Xander said, the horror on his face a very real thing. "I'm just saying. It looks like a thing. You two serious?"

"No. I don't know," Kennedy hedged, because the lie felt wrong in her mouth. "Maybe."

Now, a smile definitely kicked at the corners of Xander's mouth. "What, is this multiple choice now?"

"Shut up." She laughed, and oh God, after all the tension and stress of the past week, it felt really good. "Yeah, Gamble and I might be getting serious. How's your arm, for real?"

"Way to change the subject." At the hand she slid to her hip, he raised his palms and said, "Okay, okay. It hurts a little, but it is healing. Thanks for taking me to urgent care to have the doc look at it."

"Thanks for letting me."

"That offer for lunch still stand? Because I told my boss I wasn't coming back today, and that Cuban sandwich sounds pretty stellar."

Kennedy shook her head, but the hope in her chest refused to let her keep her smile at bay. "Yeah, it still stands."

She went to turn on her boot heels and head for the kitchen, but before she could make it halfway through the move, she was interrupted by the sound of a voice being cleared and a very haughty voice that followed from a few feet away.

"Ms. Matthews. So lovely to see you this morning."

The word *lovely* came out as a direct translation of "I'd rather be maimed in a car crash", and Kennedy's mouth filled with the sort of bitterness that usually accompanied the very last hour of a three-day tequila bender.

"Mr. McCory." There was a zero percent chance this douche truck had come here for anything other than personal gain. "What brings you out to The Crooked Angel today?"

Ol' Chaz sniffed and looked around the bar, his eyes skating over Xander the way a person might examine something they'd stepped in by unfortunate accident, and Kennedy inched closer to throwing the Armani-wearing POS out on the sidewalk just on principle.

"Community concern, of course. I wanted to check in personally to see how you're faring after last week's fire," McCory said, spinning his assessing gaze in a wider arc around the dining room and frowning slightly at the sight of Gamble, whose back was—thankfully—to them. "Such a shame this neighborhood is going downhill so fast, don't you think?"

Ugh, please. "The neighborhood is just fine. And the RFD has a handle on the fire investigation. I feel confident they'll make an arrest soon."

"Confident?" McCory repeated, his lips quirked up in an aren't-you-sweet smile Kennedy would bet her right arm he reserved only for people with breasts and XX chromosomes. "That seems a bit ambitious. Then again"—he arched a brow at the RFD logo on the back of Gamble's T-shirt—"you do *cater* to a certain kind of clientele, I suppose."

At the ugly innuendo in his tone, Xander stiffened, but Kennedy shook her head in just the tiniest movement. There were a lot of things worth getting in a tangle over. A guy like Chaz, who likely had a different attorney for every day of the week and all the money in the world to use them, wasn't one of them.

"Regardless of The Crooked Angel's clientele, I'm sure whoever is responsible for the fire will be caught," Kennedy said, smiling so sweetly that she could feel the cavities forming in her molars.

"Hmm. Well," Chaz said dismissively. "It's not too late for your boss to cut his losses and get out of this neighborhood while he still can. I've significantly upped the safety standards at all of my current properties, and I'm always looking for—"

Kennedy rolled her eyes and waited for the blah blah blah that always came next.

Only this time, it didn't.

"Mr. McCory?" she asked, peering at the guy closely in confusion, and whoa. His normally magazine-worthy face had gone the color of old ashes, his mouth gaping like a ten-pound trout. "Are you okay?"

"I..." McCory straightened, staring at the TV over the bar before taking a step back. "I'm sorry, I've got an urgent matter to attend to. If you'll excuse me," he said, his face pinched and his nod fist-tight as he turned to strike a path out of the dining room.

"Wow." Kennedy blinked in an effort to get past the truckload of WTF filling her head. "I wonder what the hell that was about."

Xander shrugged. "Can't say I'm broken up about him bolting out of here—that guy seems like a total jackoff—but yeah, that *was* a little strange. I mean, it's just the news." He nodded up at the TV, where some blond was starting to talk about the weather.

Kennedy's attempt to piece together anything that made sense for McCory's weird-ass behavior was cut short by Gamble's return to the bar, and oh, God. Oh, God. "What?" she asked, her pulse knocking hard against her throat as she tried to process all the emotions in his glittering black stare.

"I finally got through to Hollister. Zach is awake, and he just positively ID'd Rusty as the person who started the fire."

25

Gamble drove to Remington Memorial without breathing. Or at least, that's how it had felt. But between his shock and his fear and his anger and his hope, there hadn't really been room in his chest for air.

Zach was awake. He'd seen Rusty start the warehouse fire. Intelligence was going to make an arrest, and between this and Xander's testimony, it was only a matter of time before Sinclair and his unit uncovered Rusty's plan to set fire to the buildings downtown and linked him to the attempted bombing at Station Seventeen.

They had the little bastard by the shorthairs.

"Okay, so tell me what Hollister told you one more time," Kennedy said, her dark brows gathered over the bridge of her nose as she strode over the sidewalk between him and Xander, all three of them aimed at the main entrance to Remington Mem.

Gamble did a mental scan of the conversation for the fiftieth time since it had ended twenty minutes before. Shit, he could hardly process it all himself, and he'd been the one on the other end of the phone.

"Hollister didn't want to give up much over the phone. He said the kid"—Gamble broke off for a redirect, finally allowing himself enough emotion to put the name to the face—"Zach, regained consciousness about an hour ago. Garza and Maxwell were able to talk to him, and he put Rusty at the scene. Said he didn't hesitate with the ID when they showed him a photo array."

"And he said Zach definitely saw Rusty set the fire?" she asked, her voice bright with hope.

Gamble nodded, although, damn, he was almost scared to let himself believe it, let alone say the shit out loud. "Hollister said Zach witnessed 'suspicious activity' and they were working on an arrest warrant to bring Rusty in for arson."

"Son of a bitch," Xander muttered, his jaw cranked down tight. "I should've known he wouldn't wait until this other job was ready to go before he torched something."

"You didn't have any way of knowing that for sure," Kennedy said, rather firmly as a matter of fact, but somehow, Xander looked entirely unconvinced.

"He's obsessed with fire. It's like an addiction for him, worse than Molly or H or any of that shit, and I've seen it firsthand. So, yeah, I did."

Gamble stepped over the brightly painted curb, checking to make sure no bystanders were within earshot of their conversation before saying, "Okay, but Kennedy's right. You couldn't have known about this fire unless you'd been in his pocket twenty-four/seven. None of us saw it coming. Anyway, Zach ID'd him, and that's all that matters."

Yet still, the spot between Gamble's shoulder blades that always tingled when things weren't quite right had been pinging full bore ever since he'd hung up the phone. As ironclad as the news about Rusty was, getting a read on Hollister during the brief conversation had been tough. Not that Gamble hadn't asked a shitload of questions or tried like hell to gauge the guy's tone in order to take his temperature, but he'd gone sparse as hell on the details.

"I told Hollister I was with the two of you at the bar and he said it would be easier for us to update in person," Gamble said. "He's supposed to meet us in the lobby."

"Okay." Kennedy nodded, slipping her hand through his. The contact was simple and not at all sexual—hell, people clasped up in public thousands of times a day. Lovers. Friends. Parents with their kids. But despite its simplicity, the move said *I've got you.* This woman, who had to be just as chock-full of emotions right now as he was, recognized what he needed even before he did.

Fuck, he didn't want to let go of her. Ever.

"Here we go," Xander said, jutting his chin at the automatic doors outside the hospital's main entrance. Hollister stood just inside the spacious waiting area in the lobby, and holy shit, the guy had seen better days.

"Hey. Good, I'm glad you guys made it here fast," the detective said, running a hand through his already-messy auburn hair, leaving the strands to stick up in a bunch of different directions. "The hospital staff has given us a conference room for privacy. We should talk up there."

Gamble's heart started to bob and weave in his rib cage, but he knew better than to press until they were in a secure spot. They'd already had the media in their faces during the fire. There might not be any reporters in sight right now, but that didn't mean they couldn't show up at a moment's notice.

Squeezing Kennedy's fingers, he followed Hollister through the maze of hallways and into an elevator. They made it to a small conference room, where Moreno, Garza, Hale and Maxwell sat around a conference table littered with empty cardboard coffee cups, the first two murmuring into their cell phones while the other two pored over a stack of what looked like hand-written notes. Capelli and Sinclair were positioned at a much smaller table at the front of the room, the former clacking away on a laptop while the sergeant alternated between reading whatever had come up on the computer screen and frowning like it was his only purpose in life.

"Oh, good. You guys are here," Hale said, and even her normally bubbly demeanor had turned sledgehammer-serious as she lowered the piece of paper in her grasp to the stack of identical ones in front of her.

"What's going on? Hollister said you have a witness who saw Rusty start the fire last night?" Kennedy asked, and damn, Gamble had to admire her no-bullshit approach. After all, it matched his to a fucking T.

Hale and Maxwell exchanged a glance more loaded than a Howitzer, waiting for the door to close behind them before answering. "Yes and no," he said slowly.

"Okay," Gamble said, stretching the word out into a question, and what was *with* the grim look on the guy's face? "How can it be yes and no? Either we have a witness or we don't. Zach's awake, right?"

Hale hesitated, her Bahama-blue stare sliding over to Sinclair, whose expression looked more serious than all of his detectives' combined as he walked over to join the group.

"Zach regained consciousness long enough to tell us that, before he went up to the second floor of the ware-house, he saw a man he didn't know on the main level. Said the guy came in after everyone else had arrived, but stuck to the periphery. Zach noticed him because he kept playing with a lighter, and every time the flame caught, he could see the scar on the guy's face."

"Oh my God," Kennedy breathed, and Gamble's thoughts moved so fast they collided like a ten-car pileup on the goddamned freeway.

"So, Rusty was definitely there," he said.

Sinclair nodded. "Zach said Rusty didn't talk to anyone, but he bent down a few times to mess with something behind the old furniture the teenagers had brought into the place over the course of the summer and the wooden pallets that were left behind when the company that had been renting the space went out of business last year. He couldn't see exactly what, but then Rusty left, and the party continued."

The process lined up in Gamble's head all at once, his breath sticking to his lungs at the realization of what Rusty had done. He'd bet his left nut Delacourt would find remote ignition devices identical to the one they'd pulled from the dumpster outside of The Crooked Angel in all the places Zach had seen Rusty lurking. Good Christ, the guy was getting more brazen by the second. "But the party didn't continue for long, did it?"

"No," Sinclair agreed. "Zach went to the second floor after that, and said he smelled smoke and heard screaming about ten minutes later. The fire traveled extremely quickly. Zach's friend, Emily, was too scared to try to get down the hallway to get out and he didn't want to leave her. Finally, he convinced her they had to make a run for it." Here, the sergeant paused, a muscle in his clean-shaven jaw pulling tight. "Zach pushed Emily toward the door, but the ceiling collapsed before he could get out."

A low oath slid between Gamble's teeth, and Kennedy's expression echoed it. "Okay, but Zach positively ID'd Rusty, right? From a photo array?" Between what Zach had seen and what Xander could offer up about Rusty's future plans, obtaining an arrest warrant should be a slam dunk.

"He did," Maxwell said, his voice low and serious, and Gamble recognized the look in the detective's eyes a split second before the unease that went with it became a tidal wave of full-fledged denial and dread.

We did everything we could...Perez's injuries were too severe... I'm so sorry...

Gamble shook his head, his throat so tight, he could barely push out his words. "He's gone, isn't he?"

"Yes." Sinclair nodded. "Zach sustained third-degree burns over a large surface area of his body. Between that and the crush trauma from the beam...he succumbed to his injuries about ten minutes ago."

"What? No," Kennedy gasped, her eyes going as wide and round as dinner plates at the same time Xander let go of an audible exhale. "Zach *died*?"

"I'm afraid so," Sinclair said. "Dr. Sheridan, the trauma doc, said they did everything they possibly could, but Zach's injuries were too grave."

All of the fear and anger Gamble had felt on the way to the hospital radiated up from his gut, and fuck, it took every ounce of his willpower to keep his emotions in check. "Did anyone else see Rusty at the scene?"

Maxwell shook his head while Hale stepped in to put her hand on an obviously-shaken Kennedy's shoulder. "No. We're obviously still piecing everything together"—Maxwell gestured to Moreno, Garza, and Capelli, all of whom were backing up his claim a billion percent, either on their phones or hunched over laptops at the far end of the room —"but we've interviewed all of the other teens, and none of them have mentioned seeing anyone fitting Rusty's description."

Gamble filled in the blanks easily enough. "Which means, you don't have enough evidence to arrest him."

"Okay, wait," Kennedy said, her gaze growing frustrated as she moved it from Hale's to Hollister's to Sinclair's. "There's got to be another way we can catch him, right? There has to be *something* we can do to make sure he pays for this. He's a murderer, for God's sake!"

Sinclair nodded. "We're working a couple of angles right now, but I'm not going to lie. Without Zach's ID, everything else we have so far is circumstantial. It won't be enough for a warrant."

"What other evidence have you got?" Gamble asked. When the detectives swapped apprehensive looks with their boss, he didn't wait for the party line. He'd had enough of it from Bridges last night, fuck you very much, and anyway, if he didn't have something to focus on other than the fact that he hadn't been able to pull Zach out of that warehouse before the kid had been so badly injured, he'd lose what little was left of his goddamn sanity right now. "Look, I get that we're not cops, but the three of us are already in this up to our molars. No disrespect, but we all want to catch this bastard before he does any more damage, and you need all the help you can get."

For just a breath, Gamble thought Sinclair would give in to the *oh really* that had just flashed through his ice-blue stare and tell him not to let the door bang him too hard on the ass on his way out. But then—mercifully—the sergeant turned to lift his chin at Hollister and said, "Go ahead and run it from the top."

Hollister nodded and turned toward Gamble, Kennedy, and Xander. "All of the kids we interviewed have pretty similar stories. The warehouse was a known place to hang out, drink, hook up, so that's why they were all there. There's no electricity, so visibility wasn't great, but they used their phones and a couple of those battery-powered camping lights to get by."

"That means you can prove the fire wasn't an accident, right? It couldn't have started from faulty electrical work if there was no power," Kennedy said.

Hale nodded, offering up a nearby chair for Kennedy as she reclaimed the one she'd been sitting in when they'd arrived. "Delacourt is still working on it. Garza's on the phone with her right now. But yes, it does rule a few things out, which works in our favor."

"No one said they saw anything terribly out of the ordinary, like ignition devices, when they got there, although more than half of the teens reported a funny, chemical smell they didn't recognize, and a few noticed that the furniture and wood pallets that were usually on the main floor had been moved around since they'd snuck in a few days ago."

"So, Rusty altered the floor plan, too?" Gamble asked, his mind turning over the intel bit by bit since his only other alternative was to let his emotions have his way with the part of him that wanted to drive his fist through the nearest wall. Rusty had done everything possible to ensure maximum damage, even though he'd known there would be kids inside that warehouse when it ignited. Hell—Gamble scraped in a breath—maybe that had been the point.

"Looks that way," Hollister agreed. "There's not much left, but arson is mapping it out as best they can."

"I don't get it." Kennedy swung a confused stare around the table. "Why is the furniture even important?"

Xander, who had been unusually quiet since they'd gotten the news about Zach, blew out a shaky breath. "Because you can increase the likelihood for significant damage in a fire by creating a burn path that will spread quickly. The more kindling within reach of the heat source, the bigger and faster the fire can grow. With enough time, you don't even need accelerant to end up with a fire that causes a boatload of damage. It's the whole idea behind these ignition devices."

"So, Rusty snuck into this warehouse to move everything around, then used the remote ignition devices to test how they'd work in something bigger than a dumpster and splashed around some sort of accelerant to make sure the place burned all the way to the bricks?" Kennedy asked, her lips parting in surprise, and Gamble had to admit, the guy seemed to be stepping things up dangerously fast.

"Looks like that's a yes," Detective Garza said, pulling his cell phone from his ear and turning toward the group. "Delacourt's team found the remnants of what look like six remote ignition devices, all of them strategically placed around the warehouse's main level near items likely to burn. They also found residue and burn patterns that suggest some sort of accelerant was present. They're running tests to determine exactly what, but—"

"The damage is clearly done," Sinclair bit off. He turned toward Isabella, who had lowered her phone a minute before Garza. "Where are we with the ADA?"

Isabella's frown paved the way for her news. "Kingston said, and I quote, 'Come at me when you've got a confession, a statement from a witness, or a weapon dripping with fingerprints.' Other than that, no joy on an arrest warrant. In fact, she pointed out that we don't even have enough to bring Rusty in for questioning."

"That chick is a serious hard-ass," Hollister muttered, but Isabella lifted a hand before Kennedy could pop off with the hasty agreement her expression said she'd been constructing.

"Maybe, but before we all curse her up one side and down the other, let's not forget that she knows how to do her job. Kingston's as frustrated as we are. She's also not wrong. If we want to nail Rusty, we need the evidence to do it. Otherwise, the case falls apart in court and the charges get dismissed. Or worse, he gets acquitted."

Sinclair didn't disagree, but he also didn't look thrilled in the least. "This guy is getting bolder and we know he likes an audience. Capelli, what've you got on the news footage?"

"Not much," he said, pushing his black-framed glasses up the bridge of his nose as he shifted his focus from the laptop in front of him to the group in the room. "My source at the local news station said their reporter received an anonymous tip about the fire as it was breaking, directly to his home number. The reporter corroborated, and swears the guy never left a name, and his caller ID said the number was unknown. I traced the call anyway." Capelli's tone added an unspoken *of course* to the mix before he capped things off with, "It was placed before any of the nine-one-one calls came in, so the likelihood is high that it was Rusty, looking for some glory. But it dead-ended at a burner cell that hadn't been used before last night and hasn't been used since. I've scanned all the footage, and I don't see Rusty anywhere in the background."

The ensuing pause was packed with frustration, and yeah, Gamble could fucking relate. "So, we're right back where we started, only now we have a body count." *Damn* it, he should've gotten to Zach faster.

"For now, yes," Sinclair said. "We know this fire was arson, but we can't pin it on Rusty without more evidence. We'll continue to work this scene with arson investigation and see if it garners anything we can use. But until Rusty reaches out to Xander..."

"Wait." Kennedy's shoulders smacked into the back of her desk chair, her shock on full display. "You want to just sit around until he does this again?"

And here Gamble had thought they couldn't fit any more tension into the room. "Nobody wants that," Isabella finally said. "But without Zach's ID, we really have nothing else to go on."

"He was there," Gamble grated, his own patience stretching thin. "I get that you need evidence, I really do. But this should be game over. He fucking *did* this. He set that fire and he killed that kid. Who knows how many other people he might kill next time?"

Sinclair's expression hardened, the tiny lines around his eyes growing deeper with his frown. "I know he did this just as well as you do, but knowing isn't enough. We need proof. Proof we don't have."

"But we can get it. *I* can get it."

Xander's voice sliced through the tension in the room like a scalpel, clean and precise and right to the bone. The detectives exchanged a handful of expressions, ranging from brows arched to heads tilted, and oh hell, Kennedy wasn't going to like this one fucking bit.

As if a switch had kicked off in her brain, her spine snapped to attention. "Xander," she warned, but damn, her brother had come by that stubborn glint in his eyes honestly.

"I can get it," Xander told Sinclair. "The ADA said she wants a confession, a statement from a witness, or a weapon, right?"

"She did."

Xander's shoulders firmed up beneath his T-shirt. "What about catching Rusty in the act? Will that do it?"

"I'm listening," Sinclair said, much to Kennedy's very obvious displeasure. Without thinking, Gamble reached down for her hand, nearly losing the battle with his emotions as he realized how hard she was trembling.

He closed his fingers over hers, forcing himself to be steady. Right now, she needed him.

And so he would be here.

"Why wait until Rusty comes to me?" Xander asked. "I mean, before, it made sense. No one was getting hurt, and we were going to stop him before he actually triggered the ignition devices downtown. But now"—Xander paused long enough for his hands to become fists at his sides—"Rusty's getting out of control. People are dying, and more are in danger. If we need an airtight case, one that will put him away forever, then let's go get it."

"And how do you propose we do that?" Sinclair asked, echoing the question in Gamble's head.

"By playing his game instead of watching it. Look, Rusty is all ego, and he loves an audience. All I have to do is seek him out and tell him I want a bigger piece of the action. Hell, with how ballsy he's getting, he's probably dying to start these fires, and he already knows the devices work. If I can get him to trust me with more information on this job, we can figure out what he's up to sooner. I might even be able to get him to talk about the warehouse fire and the bomb he planted at the fire house. And if we could catch him in the act, with these remote ignition devices that match the ones found at these scenes—"

"We'd have him," Hollister breathed. "This *is* a solid idea, boss. If Xander can convince Rusty that he wants to step up his arson game, Rusty could give him—and us—everything we need to put him away."

"Or he might kill Xander where he stands," Sinclair replied, making Kennedy flinch and Gamble's pulse push faster in his veins.

Funny, Xander was the only person in the room who seemed a-okay with the risk. "It's possible that he'll try to kill me, but not until after this job is done. I might not know the particulars, but I do know that he needs me. If he didn't, he'd have done this whole thing himself from the get."

Gamble hated to admit it, but... "That's probably true."

"It's definitely true," Xander said. "So, if he needs me, let's go all-in and use it. Let me go after *him* instead of waiting for him to come around."

"Xander, this is really dangerous. You said it yourself. If Rusty suspects, even for a second, that you're working with the cops, he won't think twice about killing you. Don't you think he'll find your sudden enthusiasm for this job kind of suspicious?" Kennedy asked.

Xander shook his head, adamant. "I'll make sure he doesn't. Look"—he turned toward her, looking her fiercely in the eye although his voice remained full of certainty over confrontation—"That kid, Zach? His death is on me."

"You didn't kill anyone," Kennedy insisted, but Xander didn't back down.

"I might not have set that fire, no. But if I'd come forward sooner about Rusty, or if I'd tried harder to reach out to him over the last couple of days, maybe Zach would still be alive. It's past time for me to right my wrongs, Kennedy. I need to do this. It's the only way we're going to catch him."

Kennedy clutched Gamble's hand, but he held firm. Steady. Strong.

I've got you.

She nodded, then turned toward Sinclair, her stare as serious as it was stalwart.

"Okay, Sergeant. Just tell me what I need to do to help keep my brother safe and nail this son of a bitch, once and for all."

26

Rusty sat back in a corner booth at Houlihan's and watched the media footage of the fire with a smile on his face and an erection in his pants. No one in the place noticed his attention or his arousal, although honestly, even if that changed, it wasn't as if they'd be shocked. After all, worse things had gone down in this booth—probably in the last twenty-four hours—than him being glued to his cell phone and sporting wood. The fact that he was sitting here in public, with more than a dozen people in his direct line of sight and maybe a dozen more at various other locations in the dingy, dirty bar, while he watched the coverage that had been posted on the local TV station's website for anyone with Wi-Fi and two fingers to Google to see?

God, it was even more priceless than a fucking Michelangelo with Van Gogh sprinkles on top.

Rusty stared at the video clip splashed over the tiny, cracked cell phone screen even though he'd long since memorized it. Not the words—who gave a shit about the noob reporter who had bought every breath of his anonymous tip, hook, line, and of-course-you-can-get-as-close-as-you-want sinker. Shit, Rusty had muted the phone before he'd even hit *play*. No, he was focused on the background, on the rolling flames that reached up out of the windows, on the hypnotic way the fire danced and flickered and consumed every last bit of what it claimed before it moved on to the next thing to control it completely, too.

Fire was such a thing of beauty. Whether people were mesmerized or terrified, no one ever looked away from it. It never blended in or faded out. Everyone *watched* fire.

Rusty had watched. He'd stood outside that warehouse —way across the street, in the shadows, of course, because even though his audacity had felt addicting as shit, prison orange so wasn't his color—and he'd taken it all in. The heavy, bitter smell of smoke, not homey like a lazy campfire with a side of Kumbaya and s'mores, but the scent of real destruction. The rush and crackle of the flames as they'd spread out and wrapped around every inch of that warehouse, on the path that he'd predetermined. The terror and panic on the faces of the idiot teenagers who had been inside, so thorough that Rusty had been able to see the whites of their wide eyes, even from where he'd stood. The first responders had masked their emotions better—they usually did, although occasionally there was some dumb rookie, like the one with all that crazy curly hair who had been at the scene last night. She'd snapped out of her stupor quickly, but that didn't fool Rusty. She was as vulnerable as the rest of those fucking hose draggers.

Everyone was flammable.

Rusty shifted in the booth and continued to look at the screen, his attention snagging on the one firefighter, the huge guy, as he hauled some kid through the front door of the warehouse. *Lieutenant I. Gamble*, the back of his fire coat read in reflective letters that glowed against the camera lights. Excitement tripped through the lowest part of Rusty's gut at the seriousness on the guy's face as he looked back at the flames, and, oh, oh, oh, here was the best part. The guy turned on his boot heels and started hauling balls back into the warehouse, even though the place was fully engulfed in flames, and then...wait for it...*waaaaaaaaait* for it...

BOOM!

Rusty couldn't cage his giddiness at the sight of the flashover, grinning wildly through the dim light of the bar. The footage ended seconds later, and unfortunately, he only had a few minutes' worth of a mental reel to plug in to the dead air. After the idiot hero firefighter had come out with one of his idiot buddies on his back, all hell had broken loose with the cops and more ambulances and another fire truck arriving, so Rusty had reluctantly melted back into the shadows. It had meant not being able to hear the chaos or see the flames, but he'd still been able to smell the smoke for nearly a mile as he'd made his way back to his car and finally headed home.

"Well. There goes my theory that you'd gotten tired of North Point's good life and blazed on out of town."

Xander's voice captured Rusty's attention from the spot where the guy stood in front of the booth, his Converse planted on the questionably sticky floorboards. Normally, Rusty would be irritated at the interruption, but as it was, he was a little too surprised and a lot too intrigued to get his dick in a knot.

"What, and leave this paradise?" Rusty asked, the skin on his lip and cheek pulling uncomfortably tight as he flipped his phone face-down on the table and leveled Xander with a sardonic smile. With the competing odors of warm beer and stale piss filling the air, and the pair of worse-for-wear prostitutes sitting at the bar who would probably blow both him and Xander for the price of a McDonald's Value Meal, Houlihan's wasn't exactly the lap of luxury.

"Whatever," Xander muttered, sliding over the bench seat across from Rusty and taking a draw from his beer before putting the bottle on the table. "I'd take this place over The Plaza any day of the week and twice on Sunday. Downtown is full of pretentious pricks who think they're so much better than everyone else. Those assholes deserve what they get."

Ah, there it was. The chip on Xander's shoulder had been just the thread Rusty had needed to sew those puppet strings right into place. "Good to see your priorities are still straight. No hard feelings about the arm, then?"

Xander rolled his lips together in a flat line, and Rusty would give him this. The little punk was growing a backbone. Whether Rusty could use it to his advantage or he'd have to turn the guy into a live-action Roman candle for it remained to be seen.

"If you're asking whether I'm pissed at you for burning me, then the answer is yeah. It hurt like a motherfucker." He took another sip from his beer, and this one seemed to douse the heat of his irritation. "But I get why you did it, I guess. You needed to be sure I'm in."

"Mmm," Rusty said, his curiosity firing on all cylinders. "And are you?"

"Hell, yes."

Shock dominated Rusty's chest at the level of resolve in Xander's answer. "Bit of a change of heart, isn't it?"

For just a breath, Rusty sensed an odd sort of tension hidden in Xander's expression, some hint that he was...what was that? Restless? Shaky? Then a frown bracketed his mouth as if the tension had never existed, erasing all signs of anything other than his irritation.

"Funny how losing your apartment will do that to a guy," Xander said, and *huh*, talk about a plot twist.

"You got kicked out of your place?"

Xander shrugged, but his shoulders were too tight to pull off true nonchalance. "Some fancy rental company bought out my greedy-ass landlady—there's a frigging shock, I know—and they're 'revitalizing' the place."

He hung air quotes around the word, and Rusty couldn't help but laugh. "The best way to revitalize that place would be to take a fucking flame thrower to it and start from scratch." Ooooh, there was a thought.

One he'd have to put on hold until later, though, because Xander said, "Right? Like some spackle and a coat of paint is going to fix that shithole. But these *GQ* ass clowns are doubling the rent, so yeah. I'm out of a place to live after the first of the month. If this job you've got in the works will really screw over guys like that, then I'm so in. Just show me what to do."

The words arrowed through Rusty's gut and took root, making his pulse accelerate with an enticing whoosh. He'd never had a true apprentice before—that waste of space Billy Creed had been more of an errand boy-slash scapegoat than anything else. Xander had been filling the Billy-shaped hole in Rusty's world pretty well 'til now. But if Rusty could turn him into a protégé, someone who would not only watch everything he did, but wanted to *learn* from it...fuck, the possibilities would be endless.

"Okay, then," Rusty said, sweeping his phone from the scuffed tabletop and stuffing it into his back pocket. "Let's move you up in the world a little. I was just going to leave for a meeting with The Money. I'm assuming you want in."

McCory had called him in a panic just before lunch, insisting that it was "a matter of extreme urgency" that they meet. So, of course, Rusty had made the fucker wait until tonight. He was—oops—already a little late, but whatever. Listening to McCory whine about Christ-knew-what wasn't on his list of Ooooh, Sign Me Up.

"Yeah, I want in," Xander said with an emphatic nod. "Lead the way."

Oh, this was going to be even better than Rusty had hoped.

He'd agreed to meet Chaz not far from Houlihan's and the pier, so the drive took less than ten minutes. The nighttime air was humid and thick, the sort of thing you didn't breathe so much as wade through. They parked a couple of blocks away, hoofing it to the residential intersection where he'd told McCory to be, and yep, there was the Aston Martin, just like clockwork.

"What the fuck do you think you're doing?" McCory snapped as he burst from the driver's side of the car, immediately pulling up at the sight of Xander. Funny, both sets of eyes did the wide-and-round routine, with McCory breaking the standoff first. "Who's this?"

Rusty measured McCory with an assessing stare. "My associate. We're getting close to go time, so I figured we should all be on the same page."

"I know you," McCory said, his gaze narrowed over Xander, and ha, when had ol' Chaz grown a sense of humor?

Xander snorted at the same time Rusty barked out a laugh. "Yeah, because I totally frequent your country club," Xander said, rolling his eyes skyward. "Give me a fucking break."

"No, I do," McCory insisted, and wait. He looked serious. "Where have I seen you before?"

"Uh, nowhere." Xander trotted out his newfound attitude like a show pony, turning toward Rusty with both brows way up. "You trust this guy enough to do business with him? Seriously? Because he seems a little..."

Xander broke off to twirl an index finger in a tight circle near his temple. Rusty's temptation was to laugh it off and agree—after all, the vein in McCory's forehead made a fairly regular appearance over the dumbest shit. Levelheaded, he wasn't.

But Jesus, the guy was unshakable, looking at Xander with a metric ton of mistrust. "You and I have business to discuss," he said to Rusty, crossing his arms over the front of the custom-cut dress shirt he'd already sweat through. "*Privately.*"

Rusty's radar, the one that kept him from taking a dirt nap most of the time, started pinging, stirring the hairs on the back of his neck. "Xander, can you give us a second? Chaz here is a little twitchy when it comes to doing business with new friends."

"Paranoid is more like it," Xander said. "Come on, Rusty. I think I've proven my loyalty." His eyes darted to the bandage on his forearm. "Are you really going to put me at the kids' table, here?"

The tingle at the base of Rusty's neck settled in for an extended stay. "We'll just be a second."

For a heartbeat, he thought Xander would push—the look on his face certainly suggested he was heading there. But then he lifted a shoulder in a barely committal shrug. "Okay. You're the boss."

Xander took about ten paces in the opposite direction until he stood just outside of both earshot and the halo of fluorescent light being rudely cast down from the streetlight standing sentry at the intersection where Chaz had bolted out of his car.

Rusty turned toward Chaz. "So, what's got your panties in a knot?" he asked, even though he already knew what was coming.

"You're kidding me, right?"

When Rusty fixed him with a bored look that served as a nonverbal *nope* in reply, McCory hissed, "You were supposed to distract the arson investigators, not set fire to a warehouse full of teenagers. That blaze was all over the news. The place exploded, for fuck's sake!"

"The technical term is flashed over," Rusty told him. "And anyway, that fire did the job, didn't it?"

McCory snapped, "One of those kids died, you moron, and there are already reports that the fire was suspicious. How is that supposed to keep arson off our trail?"

Rusty's heart beat faster in irritation. McCory might have money, but seriously, cash couldn't buy brains. Or balls.

"Uh, because they'll be up to their asses in that case for days, if not weeks, and so will the cops. No one will see the real job coming until after it's too late."

McCory stopped mid-pace on the sidewalk and looked at Rusty, incredulous. "You're not suggesting we still go through with the plan?"

"Of course, we're still going through with the plan," Rusty bit off. "The devices clearly work, just like I told you they would. Everything has been set for weeks, and arson won't be able to prove a goddamn thing because there won't be anything left but ashes and a bunch of investors looking to cut their losses quickly. It's foolproof. Why *wouldn't* we go through with it?"

"Because of the warehouse fire, for one. Jesus, Rusty, you

killed a *kid*. Besides"—Chaz sent his gaze to the spot where Xander stood in the shadows—"I don't like that you've brought in another player. One who can connect me to this whole thing. That's not how I operate."

Okay, Rusty had pretty much had enough of this shit. "You don't get to pick it. You wanted the dirty work done, and I needed an assistant. Are you questioning my methods?"

McCory straightened, his haughtiness showing even in the shadows. "As a matter of fact, I am. I've been compromised, and I'm not going to jail. Not even for a gain like this. I'm pulling the plug."

Rusty had stepped in to wrap his hand around McCory's wrist and capture his pinky finger before the smug bastard had even stopped yammering, holding up his opposite hand to shush McCory's impending protest with a nasty glare.

"You will not scream, and you will not move." Rusty bent Chaz's pinky finger back just enough to feel the resistance that meant he was inflicting the severe discomfort that went with tendon strain.

"I—I—what are you doing?" Chaz yelped, trying to shuffle out of Rusty's grasp, and really, why did rich people *never* listen?

"I said no moving." Rusty applied a touch more pressure, and hey, what do you know, the struggling stopped. "Listen to me very carefully, McCory. You hired me to do this job, and that's exactly what I'm going to do."

"But...but that kid in the warehouse..."

Good Christ, with the whining! "Collateral damage is sometimes part of the deal. But make no mistake. You're not in charge here. You said you were in, and that means you're in. You don't get to back out. Do you know how easily I could plant a car bomb in that pretty little luxury sedan of yours? Hmmm? The electronics systems make it a breeze."

The thought of it made Rusty's pulse race in earnest, his blood humming in his veins. "Or maybe I could rig your mailbox to blow your head clean off. Or barricade you inside your penthouse while I paint the walls in gasoline and light just one match on my way out the door. I know literally dozens of ways to make it so they'd have to squeegee you up to get you into a body bag."

Chaz's mouth gaped open, just for a beat, before realization of the situation he was in settled over his features. "I still don't like the extra," he murmured, although all the fight had gone from his voice. "I'm telling you, I've seen him before...I just can't...wait!" McCory dropped his voice to barely a whisper. "At that bar, where you set the dumpster fire. The Crooked Angel. I saw him there. *Today*. He was talking to that bartender, the obnoxious one with all the trashy tattoos. They were talking like they knew each other."

"What?" The intel surprised Rusty enough that he dropped McCory's hand. "Xander knows somebody who works at The Crooked Angel?" How was that even possible? The guy hated downtown enough not to even go there on a dare, let alone by choice just for a burger and a beer. "Are you sure it was him?"

"I'm positive!" The sweat beading on McCory's forehead glimmered as he nodded hard. "And that's not all. A lot of firefighters hang out at that bar. *And* a lot of cops."

Anger pulsed through Rusty, replacing both his blood and his breath. No way. No. Way. Xander couldn't possibly have the stones to turn on him.

He inhaled slowly, flipping through all the odds and options in his head. It was possible that McCory was mistaken, or equally possible that Xander's new enthusiasm for this job meant he'd gone to The Crooked Angel because he thought it was one of the actual targets and he was casing the place. Rusty had never told him exactly what buildings they'd be using the devices in, and if Xander was as all-in as he claimed to be, the initiative made sense. Or perhaps he knew it was a cop hangout, and he'd been eavesdropping.

Or maybe he had grown a pair, and gone to the police, squealing like a little bitch.

There was only one way to find out.

Rusty exhaled, locking down on his resolve. "Okay, McCory, here's what we're going to do. You let me worry about Xander. If he's a problem, he won't be for long. But we can't fuck around anymore. This job has to go down soon." He did a quick mental calculation, then added, "The day after tomorrow. I'll let you know when everything is set and we'll proceed. Until then, for Chrissake, keep your mouth shut and act normal. *Especially* about the warehouse fire. Do you understand?"

McCory nodded dumbly. "Yes."

"Good."

Rusty turned back toward Xander and narrowed his eyes.

Time for some goddamned answers.

27

"I don't like this."

It wasn't the first—or, hey, even the tenth—time Kennedy had uttered the phrase over the course of the ninety minutes she, Gamble, and Xander had been sitting around her apartment, eating pizza and drinking beer. Her nerves had been at DEFCON Three ever since yesterday afternoon, when the intelligence unit had concocted the plan for Xander to actively seek Rusty out with the goal of getting all chummy while wearing a wire.

Last night, when Xander had actually found the bastard and they'd met up with Chaz McCory, of all people? Yeah, her nerves had pretty much skipped DEFCON-everything-else and gone straight to bright, brilliant, full-on detonation.

Xander sat back at the small table in Kennedy's kitchen, measuring her with a quiet gaze before forking over a nod of understanding. "I know. But honestly, it didn't shake out to be *all* bad."

Gamble, who had listened in on the intelligence unit's surveillance in case Rusty went into any sort of detail on the types of devices or methods he planned to enact, nodded as well. "He's right. I mean, yeah, it would've been ideal if Rusty had admitted to the warehouse fire in front of Xander and the RPD had been able to slap bracelets on him right then and there." It had been the goal, since they couldn't arrest Rusty on the spot otherwise, and as hard as Xander had apparently tried to make it happen, Rusty had been a great, big fan of covering his ass.

Gamble continued. "But we've still got the date *and* the location for the job, and we've got McCory's involvement on top of it. In two days' time, they'll both be behind bars, and the Rosemont Building will be safe."

That all sounded fantastic, in theory, but... "Chaz saw you at the bar yesterday, and Rusty totally called you out on it after he and Chaz had that little off-mic talk session," Kennedy said to Xander, dread claiming her gut at the thought. Sinclair had put the kibosh on her listening to the actual surveillance tapes, either during the conversation or after the fact, but both Xander and Gamble had filled in the blanks well enough after she'd made it clear she wasn't going to stop asking for details until they did.

"Yeah, but I totally worked around that," Xander reminded her, and she had to admit, he'd been fast as hell on his feet when he'd told Rusty that he'd been at The Crooked Angel because it was a known firefighter/cop hangout and he'd been trying to gather intel, especially since she'd gotten the impression Rusty hadn't exercised a ton of decorum in asking.

"And you're sure Rusty bought your cover story?"

Xander grabbed his beer bottle for a nice, long swig, and Kennedy recognized the nervous tell from a mile away. When in doubt, cover your unsteady hands with movement. Bonus points if you could buy a second or two to formulate a controlled response that matched.

"I told him a couple of things about the investigation that I knew wouldn't hurt our end of the case, but that also weren't disclosed to the press, so he knows I got some legitimate details. I mostly stroked his ego, telling him how he'd stumped the arson investigation unit and they couldn't trace the devices to anyone. Plus"—her brother dropped his eyes and finished his beer in one gulp—"Not to put too fine a point on it, but he didn't kill me right then and there and Capelli said no one's tried to tail me since I left the meeting last night, so yeah. I'm pretty sure he believed me."

Kennedy shuddered. "Ugh, please don't say things like that. I already *really* don't like this."

"Yeah, you might've mentioned that a time or two." Instead of accusation or heat, Xander's voice held a thread of teasing that chipped at the tension in the room. "Look, I get that you're worried. This is big shit. I'm a little worried, too. But this is also what I signed on for. I have to follow this case all the way through no matter the risk. It's the only way for us to catch Rusty."

Kennedy's brain knew he was right. Shit, part of her was proud as hell that Xander was doing everything within his power to right his past wrongs, and she knew the intelligence unit would do everything in their power (and they had a *lot* of power) to keep him as safe as they could.

Her heart, though? That thing was a lock, stock, and barrel realist, and it *so* wasn't on board with the idea of her brother anywhere near this psycho.

"Okay," she said, pushing the plate containing her mostly uneaten piece of pizza aside. "But this is all going down really fast. Tomorrow night?" Her gut pinched again.

This time, it was Gamble who went all voice-of-reason. "The intelligence unit has already come up with a really solid plan. Plus, the RPD's forensic accountant has already started poring over McCory's phone records and business transactions with a microscope. It's not as fast as it seems, and to be honest, the longer Rusty waits, the higher the chances he might get antsy and do something brash."

"He's already trying to burn down a building that takes up an entire block in one of the most densely populated parts of the city," Kennedy muttered. "He set a fire that killed a teenager. Hell, he planted a bomb in a fire house that could've killed *dozens* of people. If that's not brash, I don't know what is."

"Fair enough," Xander said with a nod. "But really, intelligence has this. *I* have this. I promise."

He looked so serious, so certain, that Kennedy had no choice but to trust him. "Fine. But I'll feel better when it's over." Changing tack, she tilted her head at her brother. "So, is what you said to Rusty about your landlady true? Did you really lose your apartment?"

Xander shot a nonverbal are-you-kidding-me glare at Gamble, which was pretty damned ballsy, considering Gamble's sheer size. "You told her about that?"

Gamble's nod came so fast, he couldn't have even considered saying anything other than, "Yup. Sure did."

"So?" Kennedy prompted. "Did you?"

After a minute, Xander said, "I'm not about to tell Rusty a lie about something he could easily verify as untrue. Yeah, I lost my apartment. I've got a week to pack up my stuff and go. But it's not a big deal. I'll figure something out."

It was hot on Kennedy's tongue to tell him he needed to come stay with her until he got on his feet, or, God, indefinitely. She had a second bedroom, with its own bathroom and everything—it made perfect sense. But Xander already knew she'd help him out if he needed her to. He was an adult.

As much as she might want to insist that he move in with her right this freaking second, she needed to let him take care of himself. No matter how badly she wanted to dive in for the assist.

"Okay," she said past the lump in her throat. "If I can help, just let me know."

Surprise paved the way for gratitude, both emotions flickering over Xander's face. "Thanks, I will." He looked at the nearly empty pizza box on the table, then the clock on the microwave across the kitchen. "Anyway, it's getting kind of late and I have to get across the city. I should probably go."

"Are you sure you don't want the last slice of pizza? I don't want you to be hungry," she said, immediately biting her lip, and okay, fine. So the not-taking-care-of-him thing was going to take some getting used to.

Xander smiled, pushing back from the table. "No, I'm good. Thanks for dinner." He looked at Gamble, who had been mostly quiet for a good chunk of the evening. "See you tomorrow."

"Copy that," Gamble said. Xander let Kennedy walk him to the door and hug him goodbye, promising her one last time that he'd be careful and call in if Rusty went off-book or anything seemed unusual between now and tomorrow night. The assurance made her feel at least a tiny bit better, and she re-locked the door and returned to the kitchen after he'd said his goodbyes for the night.

Gamble watched her go through the motions of wrapping up the last slice of pizza and tossing the empty box and trio of beer bottles into the recycling bin before finally breaking the silence.

"You know he'll be in great hands, right?" He stood, edging into her path in a way that still gave her enough space to move around him if that was what she wanted, giving her the chance to choose whether or not she'd let him stop her busywork to comfort her.

Oh, God, she didn't even think twice as she stepped toward him. "Keep talking so I'll feel better about it?"

"Hollister and Isabella will be undercover on the same block as the building, and Garza and Maxwell and Hale will be all over the perimeter. Half the RPD will be on standby. I'll even be close by with Capelli, too."

Kennedy's pulse skipped erratically at the reminder. "You're supposed to be reassuring me. What if Rusty tries to blow something up and *all* of you get hurt? Or worse?"

Gamble, not being stupid, maneuvered around the question. "You didn't eat," he said, gesturing to the lone plate on the table that still held the piece of pizza she'd taken half a bite from.

"I know." No use arguing with the evidence that was right there like a neon sign. "I couldn't."

"You should," he said, gently enough to make her heart lurch.

Kennedy edged closer to him, to the warmth of his body and the comfort of his touch. "I don't need food."

His pupils flared, turning his already dark stare nearly black. "Okay. What do you need?"

The answer formed immediately in her head, but it stuck in her mouth. She wasn't used to being vulnerable or asking for help, not even for small things. What she needed had always taken a backseat to what had to be done, and she'd always been tough enough to do it on her own. But then Gamble was right there, brushing his fingertips over the slope of her cheek and making her feel safe and warm and loved, and her heart pushed the words right past her lips.

"I need you."

"You have me," he said. Constant. Strong. Sure.

"But..."

"But what?" he asked, his expression so full of hard, intense edges that she knew he was prepared to argue anything she'd say.

"But what if I don't? You're going to be at that building tomorrow night when all of this goes down. I know you won't be right in the same room with Rusty, like Xander." *Don't think about it. Don't think about it.* "But you'll be close. That bomb Rusty planted at Seventeen was big enough to take out half the block. What if he plants another one? What if he does something else that hurts all of you?" She swallowed hard, her next words barely a whisper. "What if you and Xander both get killed?"

To his credit, Gamble didn't give her a there-there, don't-you-worry load of crap. Instead, he answered with nothing but pure honesty in his tone.

"I've lived with a lot of what-ifs in my life, Kennedy, and yeah, I'm not going to lie to you. There's a chance Rusty might do that. He's crazy, and he's clearly spiraling out of control. But the plan we have in place takes as much of that into account as it can, and every single one of us is going to do his or her damnedest to make sure it goes off to the letter. We have to take Rusty down. This is the best way to do that, even if it isn't risk-free."

"I know." God, as much as she hated it, she really did. "I'm scared for my brother. But I'm scared for you, too. I can't..." Tears formed, hot and insistent in her eyes, and wasn't that just an indicator of how big a deal this really was. She *never* fucking cried, and here she'd done it twice now.

But she also never hid the truth. Not about things like this.

"I don't want to lose you," she said.

"I'm right here."

Gamble took her hands, which were trembling despite her efforts to steady them, and placed them on his shoulders, reaching around her waist to pull her close. "I'm right here, right now, and I'm not going to leave you. If this is what you need"—he moved closer still, so their bodies were flush, his chest against hers, his heart on her heart—"then take it."

He dipped his head to kiss her, and her whole body pulsed with awareness and need. Kennedy wanted to screenshot the moment, to take hours to marvel at the way the kiss could feel so soft while Gamble's lips were so steady and firm. She wanted to memorize the press of his mouth on hers and the slide of his tongue as he parted her lips with ease to intensify their contact. Her breath rose in a honeyed exhale, and Gamble captured it fully, pushing into her mouth to kiss and swirl and stroke her lips and tongue until she felt nearly drunk with how much she wanted him.

But as consuming as it was, this kiss, this *need*, wasn't urgent. Its depth expanded in her belly on an endless rolling wave.

Kennedy wanted him slowly. Fully.

Forever.

Reaching up, she wrapped her arms around his shoulders. Gamble's muscles grew taut under her touch, the play of those strong lines and hard angles jumping beneath her fingertips. She explored each one as if she were touching him for the first time, biceps, shoulders, back. Her hands coasted higher to cup the back of his neck, as if she could hold them both right here in this moment, with him close and her anchored tightly to him, locked in the slow intensity of this kiss.

"Kennedy." Gamble pulled back, his eyes dark and glittering. He didn't say anything else, and she didn't answer. Not with words, anyway. But he seemed to hear her clearly enough—or maybe he read the desire in her eyes and saw the magnitude of her need—because then he was picking her up, his arms unyielding around her as he carried her to her room.

I'm right here. Right now. And I'm not going to leave you.

Gamble crossed the threshold into her bedroom, lowering her to her feet when he reached her bedside. Kennedy's room, which had never been anything fancier than cream-colored walls, a pair of black dressers with a darkly framed mirror to match, and a queen-sized bed that went unmade ninety-nine percent of the time, was illuminated only by the ambient city light filtering past the curtains from eight stories below and the light of the full moon, which hung low in the skyline. Without saying a word, Gamble's hands found her waist, grasping her solidly for just a moment before moving lower. He lowered his gaze, watching carefully as he hooked his fingers beneath the hem of her tank top and lifted it slowly over her head.

Kennedy's nipples hardened and peaked, but not from any sort of contact; in fact, Gamble wasn't even touching her now. But his eyes moved over her body, as tangible as a touch. Her heart pounded, filling her ears like the wild thump-thump-thump of an express train on a steep downhill grade, and catching in her throat when he reached out to free the button on her jeans. Kennedy let him undress her further, offering a small amount of assistance with her boots, then straightening to return the favor until the only thing between them was her bra and panties and his boxer briefs. She took a minute to simply look her fill, her breath catching at the sight of his massive, beautiful body backlit by the moon. The feelings of dread she'd been able to keep temporarily at bay resurfaced, reminding her how fleeting this might be even though it felt so steady and constant, and Gamble caught her chin with two fingers, guiding her up until their eyes met and held.

"I'm right here," he reminded her. "And I'm going to show you until you know it by heart."

Putting his hands on her shoulders, he walked her back to the bed until the edge of the mattress gently met the back of her legs. Kennedy grabbed the corded muscles at his waist to bring him down to the bed with her, opening her thighs to accommodate his frame, sliding back against the tangle of covers until they were both in the center of the bed. She arched up to kiss him, and even though the move started out sweet and slow like before, greedy need quickly pushed her for more.

"I'm here," Gamble grated against her mouth, the vibration of his voice humming across the sensitive skin of her lips. He proceeded to show her just how present he was, kissing and licking and taking her mouth so thoroughly, that by the time they finally came up for air, her exhales had turned into ragged gasps.

Gamble got the message. Sliding a string of kisses over her cheek and down her neck, he murmured into her shoulder, "I'm here, too."

"Ian," she pleaded, a ribbon of something both needful and proprietary uncurling between her hips at the way he tightened his grip on her in response.

"Don't stop," Kennedy said. "I need you everywhere."

As if a switch had flipped in some deep, dark place inside of him, Gamble's demeanor shifted. The seriousness he wore like a second skin grew so sharp, it was fierce, and his hands moved with clear intention to her breasts. He twisted the fabric nestled in the V of her cleavage to free the front clasp of her bra, sweeping the lacy halves aside and sending a rush of wetness between her thighs at the anticipation of being touched.

He did so much more than touch her. Skimming the straps from her shoulders, Gamble claimed her with his mouth. He kissed every inch of her, from the places Kennedy would've never thought erotic to her throbbing nipples. He cupped her firmly, each touch reminding her exactly where he was, as he worked her with his mouth.

"Oh, God. Wait, I—"

A wicked orgasm crashed into her with barely any warning, her achingly empty pussy clenching in intense pleasure. But Gamble didn't stop. He didn't even slow. He rode her through the climax, only to take off her panties and bury his tongue in her sex over and over until she had another one.

"I'm right here," he murmured, pushing back over her. But Kennedy wanted him, too. Not just in the heat of a sexy moment, but to really have him like he'd had her—deeply and completely—so she switched their positions on the bed and straddled his waist.

"I'm here with you, too," she whispered. Sliding down Gamble's body, she took his boxer briefs along for the ride, tugging them over his muscular thighs until he was fully naked. The arousal he'd just taken the edge off of rebuilt in her blood at the sight of his cock, thick and fully erect against his lower belly, and Kennedy didn't wait to prove her words. Wrapping her fingers around him, she parted her lips over his cock and began to move in a slow glide, up, then down, then again and again.

A sound came out of him that was half pleading, all dirty need. "Ah, *God*. Your mouth feels so fucking good, baby."

Not wanting to stop, she hummed her approval, which only made Gamble drop a hand to the back of her head and hiss. She sucked him in long, deep strokes, taking him as far into her mouth as she could before reversing each movement over and over. His breathing grew strained, his fingers knotting harder in the hair at the nape of her neck, and he switched his grip to lift her higher over his body in a rush that took her by surprise.

"Another time," he ground out, reaching quickly for the bedside table drawer where he knew from experience Kennedy kept a stash of condoms. "And believe me, I intend to collect. But tonight I want to come inside of you. I want to fuck you so sweet and so deep, you'll always feel me with you."

Gamble put on the condom and edged his way back between her legs. She opened without thinking, knowing she was wet and ready, proving it as he pressed forward to fill her with ease. His cock stretched her with provocative pleasure, her inner muscles squeezing until he was seated all the way inside her pussy. He angled his hips so the base of his dick was in direct contact with her clit, and the slight brush shot sparks across her vision.

"Ohhhhh." The moan tore from Kennedy's throat.

"I'm here."

Gamble cupped her shoulders with his huge palms, spreading his fingers wide to hold her into place on the bed as he started to move. He withdrew only far enough to push home again, changing the speed and depth of his ministrations, but not the angle of his body. The slight brush against her highly sensitized clit became a hot, slippery connection, his thrusts growing harder and faster.

"Kennedy." He bit down on his bottom lip. Kennedy

realized then that he was holding back, and she didn't think. Just opened her mouth.

"Ian, please. Be here. Be with me." His cock slid in deep, and oh God, oh God, oh God, oh God, there. *There.* "Come with me," she begged.

Gamble's body went utterly still at the same time hers shattered. Her orgasm rocked her so thoroughly that all she could do was arch up and take it, letting her body pulse in wave after wave as he clearly did the same. A few seconds later, Gamble shuddered, his grip on her shoulders slackening by just a degree. Then he folded over her, taking care not to crush her with his weight, but taking even more care to hold her close.

"I'm here. I promise," he whispered.

It was the moment she knew she couldn't live without him.

28

Gamble sat inside the stuffy confines of a utility van parked across from the Rosemont Building, trying to concentrate on the floor plan schematic in front of him even though his brain and his heart were a million miles away. He needed to get his shit together immediately, if not sooner, he knew. Only twenty minutes remained between now and midnight, when Rusty had told Xander they'd meet in North Point. After that, another thirty would pass while the two of them made the drive into the south side of the city to the second-biggest high rise under construction in Remington, where—oh, by the way—Gamble's ass and the van serving as their surveillance center were both currently parked. It sounded like ages, but Gamble knew all too well how the regular laws of time and motion didn't really apply to things like ops.

This is not *an op*, he reminded himself, cutting off any unnecessary adrenaline expenditure at the knees. He'd gone through this in the beginning with fire calls, too; hell, on occasion, a really bad one could still throw him for a rope-a-dope. True, Gamble couldn't deny that there was no small measure of danger here. Kennedy hadn't been wrong last night when she'd said Rusty could plant a bomb or do any number of other diabolically nasty things that proved he had a total lack of a conscience or a soul.

But when he'd left her at The Crooked Angel an hour ago, he'd reassured her again that he'd do everything in his power to come back to her safely, and to bring Xander with him. This wasn't an op. It wasn't going to end like that.

They were all going out.

And this time, they were all coming back home.

Trying to clear his mind, Gamble shifted back on the bench seat too narrow for his frame and reviewed the facts. After some digging and some more intel from Xander, the intelligence unit had come up with seventeen buildings that had fit the bill as possibilities for Rusty's hit list, all under various stages of construction or renovation. McCory already owned or had stake in eight of them, so they'd crossed those off the list. Then, three had popped up as buildings he'd recently bid on and lost, and—what do you know—the developers who had purchased them had all gone with the same electrical contractor for their renovations.

Bingo.

Gamble visualized the building Capelli had parked the van in front of, since the only windows the vehicle owned were in the front and the tech guru had blocked that off with a partition about four seconds after he'd cut the engine and he and Gamble had climbed into the back to set up coms. The Rosemont Building's seven-story stature didn't fool Gamble. What the place lacked in height, it made up for in sheer sprawl, marking it as a definite contender for all those other high rises dotted across downtown Remington. The Rosemont had been an aging beauty, for sure, but the future plans to turn it into a family-friendly apartment complex, complete with an on-site childcare facility, a market boasting fresh, affordable food along with a café for casual dining or quick takeout, and a fitness center with activities for all ages were pretty progressive, not to mention a pretty freaking cool option for people with families who wanted to remain in the city.

While Rusty hadn't gone into a huge amount of detail after Xander had reassured him he'd been at The Crooked Angel scoping out intel on the RPD, he *had* told Xander that his plan was to go in to the Rosemont Building and strategically plant remote ignition devices on each floor, then trigger them before moving on to the next building farther downtown. He hadn't specified exactly which building would follow the Rosemont—not that it mattered, because they'd have his ass behind a shit-ton of brick and steel before he could even think about setting the thing on fire—but they had enough of the plan to know they were going to nail him with the incendiary devices in-hand and his intent flying like a flag in the wind. All he had to do was set those devices up and try to kick them off, and bam.

They'd have him once and for fucking all.

"Okay," Capelli said from the seat in front of the bank of monitors that had been set up along the wall of the van opposite Gamble. "Let's get this show on the road."

Gamble refocused with a single blink. "Copy that."

Capelli handed him a wireless headset, then grabbed a matching one for himself and slipped it on, adjusting the piece that held the microphone around the arm of his glasses. "Test, test. Sarge, you want to call the ball?"

"Copy." Sinclair's sandpaper voice filtered over the wire from the unmarked Dodge Charger he'd parked in an alley at the opposite end of the block. "Moreno, you and Hollister in position?"

"Copy that," Isabella said in Gamble's ear. "We have a visual on the east entrance to the building."

Gamble re-visualized the street, adding Moreno and Hollister's position a half a block away from the van to his mental diagram. Garza, Maxwell, and Hale all checked in with their positions—Garza's in his own unmarked car a block away and Maxwell and Hale's on foot between him and the van—around the perimeter of the building. Gamble had to admit, Sinclair knew how to run a tight op. They had every base covered, every exit strategy planned for.

This is not an op.

"Okay, last up," Capelli said, completing the chess board of players in Gamble's head. "Xander, you there? Can you hear me?"

"Yeah, I can hear you," came Xander's voice from his waiting spot in North Point, and *damn* these coms were hi-test and a half. "This earpiece thing is weird, though."

"I know," Capelli replied, so matter-of-factly that Gamble had to wonder if the guy had any other settings. "But it's the most high-tech piece of equipment the department's got. If Rusty so much as burps within fifteen feet of you, I should be able to hear it. And trust me. That's a good thing."

"If you say so. Anyway"—Xander took the lead from all the intelligence detectives—"I'm all set. Sitting in my car at the meeting place, just waiting on Rusty to show at midnight, like his text said."

"Copy that," Capelli said, clacking away on the keyboard in front of him. "We have you on GPS via your phone and the device in the button on your jeans, and all audio is a go on coms. Now, all we've got to do is get cozy and wait for Rusty to show."

After a beat of silence that suggested everyone was going to spend that time contemplating deep thoughts, Gamble looked across the van at his partner for the night.

"Hey, Capelli, can you give me and Xander a minute?"

The tech's brows winged up toward his light brown hairline. "Ah," he said, only continuing after Sinclair had given a grunt of approval over the wire. "Sure. I can cut your coms over to a private channel for a minute. Whatever you guys say will still get recorded, though."

Gamble nodded. "Understood." He waited for Capelli to work his technological judo, then point at him in a nonverbal *you're a go* before continuing. "Xander?"

"Yeah?" he asked back suspiciously, and man, he and Kennedy were cut from the same fierce-ass cloth.

"Do me a favor," Gamble said, making sure his tone didn't leave any wiggle room for the guy to cough up a negative in reply. "If you think this is going to go tango uniform at any point tonight, just be sure you cover your ass, okay?"

Xander exhaled audibly, proving Capelli's point about how sensitive the coms were. "You promised her you'd keep me safe, didn't you?"

Shit. "Just be smart, would you?"

"Way to shoot straight from the hip, big man," Xander said with just the slightest hint of a smile layered over his sarcasm, and fuck it. The guy deserved the truth.

"All right, fine. I didn't promise her everything would be perfect and we'd all go skipping off into the sunset for ice cream and hugs." Gamble knew better than to swear on things he couldn't guarantee, and anyway, he'd rather strong-arm most people than even *think* about hugging them. "But I told her I'd do everything I possibly could to make sure we both come home safe. So, yeah. Don't go all yippe-ki-yay and make me a liar, or I'll be forced to make sure we all save your ass just so I can kick it. You got me?"

A second passed, then another, before Xander said, "Huh. Guess you're pretty straight-up, after all. But as much as I want to put Rusty away, I don't have a death wish. We're straight."

"Good." Gamble exhaled the breath that had been spackled to his lungs.

But then Xander added, "Look, if something happens to me in spite of that—"

"It won't," Gamble said, low and scalpel-sharp.

"*If* it does," Xander pushed, "you've got her back, right?"

In the same way Gamble had needed the promise that Xander wouldn't do anything unnecessary to put himself in harm's way, he knew Xander needed this in return. So he told Xander the truth.

"Yes. I'm always going to have her back."

"Okay, then." Another pause extended over the wire, this one sending the hairs on the back of Gamble's neck on end.

"What?" he asked, swinging toward Capelli. But the guy had already switched him and Xander back to the main channel on the coms and started clacking away rapidly at his keyboard, and Xander's barely there voice on the line clued everyone else in to the not-quite-right.

"Rusty's here, and he's early."

"Only by fifteen minutes," Sinclair said, his voice as steady as a metronome. "Hang tight and play it cool. You've got this, and we've got you."

Gamble looked at the sturdy black Luminox strapped to his wrist, reaffirming that it was twenty-three forty-five. *Damn it*, this didn't feel right. They were prepared, sure—it was why they'd set their own gears into motion early in the first place.

But why had Rusty done the same?

RUSTY PULLED up next to Xander's POS clunker of a car that was, in all likelihood, older than he was, and rolled down his window.

"Get in," he said, keeping his expression dialed down to the most bored setting he could manage. It wouldn't do to blow his load, so to speak, by getting too jacked up, too early. The night, after all, was an infant.

And he was juuuuuuust getting started.

Although Xander looked surprised, his black brows kicking up at Rusty's terse order, he didn't argue. Another twenty seconds had the guy buckled into the passenger seat of the nondescript, milk-toast-on-wheels sedan Rusty had stolen a few hours ago, and he pulled a U-turn to head toward the main road leading out of North Point.

Quiet filled the sedan's interior, punctuated only by the whoosh of the occasional passing car and the intermittent siren noise that signaled that all was status fucking quo in The Hill.

Rusty had to hand it to Xander. He wasn't all antsy or twitchy, like Billy Creed had been before the jobs they'd done together. And seriously, every single one of those had been finger paintings in comparison to the masterpiece that would go down tonight.

On second thought, Rusty grinned to himself, maybe he *would* get a little jacked up.

"You're early," Xander finally said, the way he might say,

"dude, pass the ketchup" if they were out grabbing a bite to eat, all no-big-deal.

Rusty's heart pumped faster, his adrenal gland picking a wicked fight with the rest of his central nervous system, which was trying to keep it cool. "No time like the present, right?" he asked, driving for another minute before pointing out the obvious. "Plus, you're early, too."

"Yeah. I couldn't help it. Guess I just want those fancy developers to get what's coming to them," Xander said on a shrug, and aw, social justice was just alive and kicking, wasn't it? "So, you got a new ride, huh?"

Xander gestured to the sedan, which had all the get-up-and-go of a goddamned go-kart and the sexy-factor of a turnip.

"Can't be too careful," Rusty replied, and oh, wasn't that the truth.

Xander nodded dutifully. "So, since we're on our way and everything, how do you want to play this, exactly? What's the plan?"

"That is an excellent question."

Without warning, Rusty wrenched the wheel to the right, screeching the stolen car to a halt on the shoulder of the dead-empty road and pulling out the Glock 19 he'd hidden between the console and his seat.

"First, I'd like to start by saying hi to the intelligence unit. That is who's listening in on the other end of your wire, right?"

At least Xander had the good graces to look shocked as fuck. Too bad for him, he replaced the expression with one of denial in less than a blink. "What the hell, Rusty? You're pulling a gun on me? I—"

File that under nope. "I *really* don't think you want to insult me by pretending not to know what I'm talking about right now, do you?" Rusty asked, jabbing the Glock in Xander's traitorous face. Admittedly, there were only a small number of things that would make Rusty forego his dead-bodies-are-a-messy-pain-in-the-ass rule of thumb enough to create one. Money was definitely on the list, and hey, as much as he hadn't specifically planned on any of those teenagers at that warehouse cashing in their chips, sometimes shit happened. But disloyalty? Enough to not only try to back out of a promise, but to go to the *cops*?

This was going to be worth the mess.

Rusty looked at Xander, who had thankfully abandoned his knee-jerk reaction to protest with a lie. "Take the earpiece out of your ear and hand it over," Rusty said. "Don't make me blow your head off to prove it's there," he added, because if he was sure of anything, it was that those fuck-tarts from the Thirty-Third had wired Xander up like a forty-foot Christmas tree.

Xander huffed out a breath and tilted his head to the side, plucking the earpiece from its resting spot and handing it over. Daaaaamn, those boys in blue must've had one hell of a budget increase. The department-issued listening devices Rusty had researched online yesterday to prepare for this little soiree—thank you, public library—had looked like brontosauruses compared to this baby. Nonetheless, he'd known Xander would be wired, so he'd needed to know how to proceed.

Oh, hey, segue. "Next, I'll be needing your cell phone and all your clothes and jewelry." Rusty eyed the pair of piercings in Xander's left ear. Really, you could never be too careful.

"You want me to get naked?" Xander asked in disbelief, and Rusty rolled his eyes.

"You're not *that* cute," he shot back. "But I'm sure you're wired in more places than this earpiece, so yep. Your stuff's gotta go. You can change into the clothes in that duffel." He flicked a nanosecond's worth of a gaze at the bag sitting on the floor at Xander's feet. "I'm not taking any chances. Now, hurry up."

The RPD's response time wasn't spectacular, but those patrol officers weren't complete sloths, either. He figured he had a few minutes, tops, before whatever GPS Xander had been tagged with would triangulate a location that the cops could close in on.

To Xander's credit, he didn't slow-roll things. "There," he said, looking down at the baggy sweatpants and the stained T-shirt with disdain. "Happy?"

"Very, thanks for asking. Into the bag they go," Rusty prompted, waiting for Xander to load everything up. "With your cell phone on top. Good! Now, we get to take a ride."

"You made your point," Xander snapped, and huh, backbone in the face of fear. How refreshing from a guy who had been such a hopeless pussy just a few weeks ago. Not that it would help him any now. "You figured out that I went to the cops. So, go ahead, shoot me. Get it over with."

Rusty's laugh echoed through the interior of the car. "No can do, my traitorous friend. See, you tried to back out of our deal, and then, when you realized that wasn't an option, you crossed me. People who do that don't just die. They *suffer*."

Then, he held the earpiece up to his mouth to add, "Have fun finding him, assholes", tossed the earpiece into the duffel, made Xander throw the whole thing out the window, and sped off toward the city.

29

For the first time ever, Kennedy was glad business at The Crooked Angel was dead. Granted, it was after midnight, so that wasn't a huge surprise considering how many folks were scheduled to do the wakey-wakey in just a handful of hours to be behind a desk or get their kids to school or punch a clock somewhere to make ends meet. Such normal things, she thought, dread dumping into her gut. Those same normal things had been her focus just a couple of weeks ago, too, and God, right now she'd give her left arm to worry about bar inventory and employee schedules and overhead costs.

Please. Please don't let Xander or Gamble die.

Swiping a hand through her hair, Kennedy looked around the empty dining room from her position behind the bar, and fuck it. She'd already sent January home hours ago—her best friend's eyes were all too keen, and Kennedy had run out of busywork that would keep her in the back of the house and away from scrutiny—and the kitchen had closed at ten, so Marco was also long gone.

The soles of Kennedy's boots clipped the hardwood

floors in a brisk riot of noise as she crossed to the front door
and locked up early. Repeating the process with the side
door by the pool table, she finally came face-to-face with the
giant pile of emotions she'd been trying to juggle ever since
Gamble and Xander had left to meet up with Sinclair at the
Thirty-Third a couple of hours ago. It was a true testament
to how far gone she was for the firefighter that she couldn't
decide which one of them she was more scared for. But
Gamble had promised her he'd do all that he could to keep
them both safe. It wasn't a guarantee, she knew—not that
there ever were any in life, especially hers—but it was close,
and she trusted him. She believed him. She loved him.

She had to believe they would both come home.

Her cell phone vibrated in the back pocket of her jeans,
scaring the ever-loving crap out of her and drawing an involuntary yelp past her lips. Xander and Gamble hadn't been
able to tell her any of the specifics for tonight's takedown,
and even though she'd hated it, she'd understood the need
for absolute discretion. Could they really be done already?
Was Rusty already behind bars?

Kennedy frowned down at the words *unknown caller*
flashing over her screen. "Hello?"

"Well, well. There she is. The infamous sister."

Her heart catapulted against her sternum, her knees
simultaneously threatening to go on strike. "Who is this?"

Sharply edged laughter filtered over the line in reply.
"Now I see where your brother gets that annoying habit of
insulting my intelligence from. Come on, sweet cheeks. You
know exactly who this is, don't you?"

Oh, God, she was going to vomit. "Rusty."

"Give the girl a gold star. Now that we're all on the same
page, I think a little meet and greet is in order. I'm already
with your brother, and we've ditched those pesky cops. I

know you're all ride-or-die with them and everything, but they'd only get in the way of what I have planned. So, what do you think? Do you want to save your brother's life tonight?"

Kennedy's pulse thundered in her ears. Think, think, she had to think. "I do," she said, forcing her brain to do something other than drown in panic. "I'll meet you right now if that's what you want, but I need to talk to my brother, first."

"You've got more brass than a marching band, don't you?" Rusty snorted.

She pressed the phone to her ear so hard, the contact was nearly painful. *Come on, come on, give me a clue. A sound, a sign. Anything.* "I need to know he's alive and okay." The words felt like razor wire between her teeth, and somehow, she managed to make her legs start moving to the back of the bar, where she'd stashed her jacket and keys in the office.

"Oh, Christ, fine. Say hello to your sister and tell her I haven't put a scratch on you, yet."

"Ken, don't do this. Don't meet him," came Xander's voice, tight and urgent. It sounded off over the line from a short distance, as if Rusty had held up the phone rather than handed it over, and Kennedy's exhale released in a huge rush.

"Hey, Xander." She would not let her voice waver. She. Would. Not. "I've got your back, okay?"

"Kennedy, *don't*—"

"Annnnd that's enough of that," Rusty said, returning to the line. "So, here are the ground rules, and you will follow them unless you want me to give your brother a Viking burial while he's very much alive. You will not call the cops. You will leave your cell phone in that shitty bar of yours and you will drive to Skyline Tower."

"Skyline Tower?" Kennedy asked, her thoughts sticking on the nearby high rise. "Isn't it under construction?"

"No *questions*," Rusty snapped. "You're a smart girl, you'll figure out how to get inside. Be there alone, in five minutes, or your brother dies. And if the cops show up instead of you, I'll make sure he doesn't go slowly. Are we clear?"

"Yes." Although Kennedy's hands shook at the knowledge of what she had to do to save Xander's life, she made certain her voice didn't betray her.

"I'll be there in five minutes."

THAT WHOLE TIME-WAS-RELATIVE-ON-AN-OP thing was coming back to bite Gamble on the ass in fucking spades. The last thirty minutes had both crawled and cracked like a lightning strike, the former in that it had felt like an eon for a patrol unit to find the duffel bag that had been discarded by the side of a semi-desolate road in North Point, the latter in that every member of the intelligence unit had rendezvoused at the surveillance van, all of them scrambling to locate Xander and Rusty on traffic cams, or at the very least, figure out where they might be headed in order to try to track them down.

So far, they'd come up with jack with a side of shit.

"Fuck," Gamble snapped, stabbing a hand through his hair for the hundredth time. "Tell me we have *something*."

Capelli, whose fingers had been a complete blur over the multiple keyboards in front of him ever since Rusty had pulled a gun on Xander and turned the night into a shit-show, shook his head. "We don't know what kind of car they're in, or at this point, if they're even still in transit.

Xander was smart to try to get Rusty to talk about the car, but..."

Gamble had been listening. He'd known, just as everyone did, that Xander's ploy hadn't worked. "Rusty's too far gone not to try to set *something* on fire tonight. Something big. Coming here to the Rosemont was obviously a ruse. So, what about the other buildings on the list?"

"There are eleven of them," Garza pointed out, and funny, Gamble wasn't deterred in the least. He opened his mouth to tell Garza as much, but he was cut off by the buzz of his cell phone.

"Wait," he said, hope shoving his shock aside as he flipped the thing into his palm. "This could be...shit, it's Kennedy."

Gamble knew he was going to have a hell of a time masking his dread, but he had to make sure she was safe. "Kennedy?"

"Gamble, listen to me," she said in a garbled rush. "Rusty has Xander."

It was on the tip of Gamble's tongue to tell her he knew, except... "How do *you* know that?"

"Because he called me. He knows Xander is my brother."

"Capelli," Gamble grated, his protective instincts slamming to life. "Get Kennedy's phone tapped up to your coms. *Now.*"

"There's no point," she said, although Capelli—smart guy that he was—did it anyway, and Gamble put her on speaker. "Rusty told me to leave my phone here, and I can't risk having it on me when I meet him."

The words *what?* and *oh fuck, no* collided in Gamble's brain. "Kennedy—"

"I don't have time to argue! He told me to meet him at Skyline Tower in five minutes, and it's going to take me that long to get there. He told me not to call the cops, either, but...I can't do this alone. I need help, and I don't know what else to do."

"Okay," Isabella said, leaning in from the bench seat in the van. "We can help you, but we're on the other side of downtown from Skyline Tower."

Gamble's chin whipped up in realization. Of *course* they were clear across downtown from where Rusty had gone. He'd baited the trap perfectly, hadn't he?

Hollister's nod said he was all-in on whatever plan Isabella was spinning up. "We can be there in—" He swung a look at Capelli, who shook his head and flashed both palms twice in rapid succession—"twenty minutes. Just sit tight."

"No," Kennedy argued. "Rusty said it has to be me, alone, in five minutes, otherwise he's going to kill Xander."

Before Gamble could launch the chain of *no, hell no,* and *over my cold, dead body, did I mention hell no* that had formed in the primitive part of his brain, Sinclair spoke.

"Kennedy, this is Sinclair. We can send patrol units to the building to keep Xander safe until we get there. But you cannot go into that building alone."

"I have to! Look, I'm wasting time. You know Rusty means what he says. Either I'm there in five, or Xander dies. You send patrol units to that building that Rusty can see, Xander dies. I'm not letting that happen. Not on my watch. I've got Xander's back. I need you to have mine. Please, Ian," she said, the words arrowing directly to the center of his chest. "I'll go stall him for as long as I can until you get there. But I'm going to get my brother."

In that moment, realization settled into Gamble's bones, turning him cold and numb. She wasn't backing down. She was going to walk into that building no matter what any of them did or said. And oh, the irony was enough to slide under his skin like a knife, slicing him deep and clean.

Kennedy had been so worried about losing either him or Xander that it had never occurred to Gamble that *she* might be the one who never came home.

30

Rusty stood in the open space of Skyline Tower's lobby-to-be and grinned from ear to ear as best his scar would allow. Actually, if he wanted to get technical about it, he and Xander were in the lobby that *wouldn't* be—or, at least, it wouldn't be what the current developers intended. Rusty didn't really know if McCory would follow through on trying to buy the place after all was said and done. After all, the building would have one hell of a stigma to overcome, and most rich folks kind of shied away from living at the scene of a brutal double murder. But he wasn't going to stick around to find out. He'd spent the day clearing out what little stuff he'd had in his apartment and all the various hidey holes where he'd stashed his chemicals and supplies, terminating his lease agreement and erasing all the connections he'd created over the past two years. After he watched this place burn tonight, he'd slip on out of the city just as quietly as he'd come, letting the cops sift through the ashes to try and find him.

They wouldn't. But they'd talk about him for a good, long time. Hell, he'd be the stuff of fucking legends in this city, and people would watch the footage for years. *Remember that guy who burned down Skyline Tower? Biggest blaze in the history of Remington. They never did catch him...*

God, he *loved* fire.

Re-routing his thoughts—he *did* have to stay on his toes for a few minutes longer—Rusty turned toward Xander. "Your sister sounds hot," he said, laughing at the protective sneer that moved over the guy's face in response. "I wish I had time to get to know her better before we all part ways. Too bad."

"How did you know?" Xander asked. Rusty kept the Glock trained right at center mass—they were well outside of earshot and eyesight of anyone who might be errantly passing by, and the building took up so much room that it was the only thing on the entire block, the businesses surrounding it all long-since closed for the night.

They had two minutes to wait for said hot sister to show up, all girl-power in shining armor, or whatever. Rusty supposed a little chit-chat couldn't hurt.

"What, that Kennedy is your sister? I almost missed it, to be honest. You two didn't make it easy, and I'll tell you, I actually believed you really were out at that bar doing recon, at first. It's the only reason I didn't kill you two nights ago."

He'd learned his lesson, for sure. He'd have to vet his people way better next time. "But then I did some digging, just to be sure," Rusty continued. "And I stumbled across an article about this hockey fundraiser held at The Crooked Angel last month. Imagine my surprise when I saw that the bar manager's last name is the same as yours, and that she has *so* many personal friends who work for the department. After that, I had McCory's source at the RPD take a look-see at the system—under the radar, of course—and what do you know? Your name was on the list of freshly-minted confidential informants."

Xander huffed out a sound Rusty supposed was meant to be a laugh, but there was no happiness in it.

"Fine," Xander said, although he'd gone noticeably paler in the glare of the ambient streetlight filtering in from beyond the construction barricades, a sheen of sweat dotting his forehead and giving away his fear. "I turned on you, and you caught me. But leave Kennedy out of this. She's not the one who made the choice to go to the cops. This doesn't have anything to do with her."

Anger pulsed through Rusty's gut. "It has everything to do with her. She's leverage. See, the best way to torture you before I kill you, is to torture her first. And honestly, I'm dying to know which one of you screams louder and smells sweeter when I douse you both with gasoline and set your double-crossing asses on fire."

Footsteps echoed at the building's front entryway, the one Rusty had cut the lock off of to ensure Kennedy would indeed find her way through. The owner of said footsteps didn't try to quiet them, just walked firmly yet carefully across the wooden planks of subfloor over concrete, and *yesssss*. "Looks like we can get this party started."

Rusty pointed the Glock at Xander with purpose, putting enough space between them that he'd see any movement coming, yet still close enough to ensure he had a kill shot if he needed it, waiting for Kennedy to get close enough to do the same with her.

"Xander, are you okay?" she asked, her stance defensive but her eyes wide, and Rusty cut off any answer Xander might offer up, taking quick control of the conversation. She wasn't in charge here, nor would she be at any time before he killed her.

Although, he'd bet Xander screamed louder than her when it came down to brass tacks.

"Hey, sweet cheeks. See you found the place. Do me a favor and shrug out of that jacket of yours, nice and slow. That's a good girl," he added as she glared and did what he said, dropping her jacket to the dusty floor. "Now, lift up that shirt and give us a spin. Don't be shy." He used the Glock to gesture for her to lift the hem of her T-shirt higher. The cotton was tight enough for Rusty to know she wasn't packing, but man, he was enjoying the show of her toned abs and firm, fit ass.

"I'm not carrying, you fuckwit," she said. "I just want to keep my brother safe."

"So touching," Rusty replied, making a gagging sound. "You two should make that into a Hallmark movie. Of course, it'll have to be posthumous, but hey. The sentiment is *so* there."

"Rusty," Xander started, but Rusty had had enough of this shit. It was time to set the wheels in motion. He missed his lover. His boss. His best friend.

He needed to set something on fire, and he needed to do it now.

"No more talking. Now, both of you, move." He pointed to the service elevator sitting at the bottom of the open framework of the building, the nighttime breeze filtering in just enough to make him smile at the knowledge that it would soon be filled with sweet, sweet smoke.

"We're headed up."

～

"Can't this fucking bucket of bolts go any faster?" Gamble growled at Isabella. He was dimly aware that he'd spoken with a complete lack of decorum, but at this stage in the game, pleasantries were the last thing on his mind.

Scratch that. If Kennedy had left when she'd ended their phone call, then she had, in all likelihood, reached Skyline Tower two minutes ago.

Gamble had already gone *out* of his mind, and everything else at this point was either instinct or insanity.

"I'm going to chalk that one up to your concern for your woman and let it slide," Isabella replied, not even hinting at moving her focus from the windshield of her Camaro, which she'd admittedly used to break at least a dozen traffic laws since she and Gamble had jumped in and aimed themselves at Skyline Tower, with the rest of the intelligence unit speeding along right behind them. "But to answer your question, if I could, I fucking would."

Gamble took a swing at an exhale and whiffed. "Sorry," he muttered.

"Don't be. I get it. I was a lunatic when that psycho DuPree had Kellan last year. But we had that, just like we have this. Speaking of which"—Isabella paused to make a hard left that made Gamble grateful he hadn't eaten a big dinner—"you're still carrying, right?"

"Of course I'm carrying," Gamble said. He'd told Sinclair as much when they'd all met up tonight. His Kimber Custom M1911 had been holstered just above his hip ever since he and Capelli had set up coms.

"Good. You might have to fight Sinclair on this, but I know better than to try to keep you out of that building when we get there."

"Sinclair's going to have to shoot me himself if he wants to keep me out of there," Gamble swore. "Even then, it might not do the trick."

Isabella nodded, her brows punching down at the sound of her radio beeping with an incoming call.

"Capelli to all intelligence units, be advised. The smoke detectors at Skyline Tower have just gone off on floors two and three. The RFD has been advised to standby before responding."

"Jesus," Isabella said. "He set the building on fire already?"

"Drive *faster*," Gamble told her.

But even then, the fear in his gut told him what his brain already knew.

No matter how fast they went, it wouldn't be enough.

THE SHARP TANG of smoke reached Kennedy's nose, filling her senses and tempting her to panic. But Rusty wouldn't set the place on fire and stick around if there wasn't time to get out, and—ugh—the asshole was totally still right there, standing a few feet away and pointing that gun at her and Xander, who stood side by side.

"Okay!" Rusty said with diabolical glee. The emergency lighting built into the steel beams overhead illuminated the open level of the building just enough for Kennedy to make out his creepy features. It wasn't the scar that freaked her out; on the contrary, she wouldn't have given it a second thought if it hadn't been flanked by Rusty's eerie smile and evil, soulless stare.

"So, here's the plan. We have about seven minutes before the RFD shows up, and, yeah, probably all your cop buddies, too, which means I have exactly six minutes to have a little fun with you two."

Stall. Stall. We have to stall. Kennedy tried to telegraph the message to Xander, wrapping her arms around her bare arms to try and ward off the wind whipping through the wall-less building. Thank God she wasn't scared of heights.

"I don't get it," Xander said, stepping in front of her, although whether it was to block the wind or put Rusty's focus on him rather than her, she couldn't be sure. "You don't want to get caught. You obviously don't want to go out in a blaze of glory if you're planning to get out of here before anyone else shows up, and you're smart enough to disable the fire alarms. Why *call* the fire department?"

Rusty cocked a brow, but still didn't move the gun. God, there was no way they'd be able to overpower him without at least one of them becoming Swiss cheese.

"You know, it's almost a shame that I have to kill you. You're turning out to be kind of smart. Anyway, to answer your question, I called them out here because I *want* them out here. See, I've spent the last three hours wiring the lower floors of this place with my ignition devices and the upper floors with enough C-4 to make it fly apart like it's made of Tinker Toys. C-4 and fire don't play nice, so I had to keep them far enough apart to give myself a bit of time, but once I hit the detonator, this building is going to burn all the way down to the bricks."

Rusty paused to let a smile twist over his face. "I won't be here when that happens, but I'll be close enough to watch your buddies shake and bake, and that'll be fun," he said as Kennedy's heart wedged itself in her throat and made breathing pretty much a no-go. Oh, God. Oh, God, Gamble was on his way here. There was no way he wouldn't come running into this building like fucking gangbusters, because that's *exactly* what she'd asked him to do.

"But you don't have to worry about it," Rusty tacked on, "because you'll be pretty crispy by then. Speaking of which,

I really don't have all night, so which one of you is going to go first?"

"I am," Xander said, and wait, *what*?

"No!" Kennedy half-gasped, half-shouted. "Are you fucking crazy? Nobody's *going*."

"Kennedy," Xander warned. "I'm not letting you do this." He turned back toward Rusty, planting his hands on the hips of his baggy sweatpants. "You want someone to torture? Let it be me."

"Okee dokee," Rusty said with a shrug.

And then he grabbed Kennedy's arm and pulled with a yank that rattled her from molars to marrow.

"Ah!" she cried out, stumbling along with Rusty, closer to the open edge of the building. He'd taken her by enough surprise that she'd had no time to react. Not that struggling against a gun would get her very far.

"What the fuck?" Xander yelled. "I told you *me* first."

"Right, but in order to torture *you*"—he pointed with the square nose of the Glock—"I have to burn *her* first. Here we go."

Reaching down, he pulled a red plastic container from behind a pile of drywall sheets, and fear formed an icy ball in Kennedy's stomach. Rusty held the gun steady on Xander, who looked as furious as Kennedy had ever seen him, and tipped the bright yellow nozzle until a cold stream of liquid poured out and onto her jeans, then the bottom of her T-shirt.

Kennedy coughed, her eyes burning and watering at the pungent scent of the fumes. Her lungs compressed, but she lifted her chin to draw in as much clean air as she could.

They were close. Gamble was close. He'd promised to help her.

Even if he couldn't save her, he could at least save Xander.

"Rusty," Xander growled, and whoa, when had he closed the distance between where they'd started and the spot where Rusty had dragged her, so much farther away from the safety of the middle of the building?

Rusty was so focused on his task that he hadn't seemed to notice Xander's change in position. Whatever her brother had in mind, she wanted to be ready—she wasn't going down without a cage match. Kennedy started to struggle, but *God*, Rusty was stronger than he looked, finally slipping his grasp up to yank her by the hair and haul her to his side.

She fought the tears forming in her eyes, her body beginning to tremble as Rusty pulled a pack of matches from his jacket pocket. "See, I told you, Xander. All it takes is a gas can and a match," he said with a laugh.

But Xander edged closer still. "Not today, motherfucker."

Then, three things happened in the span of a blink. Gamble and Hollister appeared in the shadows over Xander's shoulder, both of them with guns drawn and pure menace on their faces as Hollister yelled, "Remington PD, lower your weapon and get on the ground! Now!" Xander rushed toward Rusty, his feet leaving the floor in a full-body launch.

And Rusty let go of Kennedy long enough to turn his gun at her and pull the trigger.

31

As Gamble watched the scene unfold in front of him, once again, time proved exactly how not-in-charge he was. He saw Rusty's arm lift, recognized the instinct with which both his and Hollister's winged up in return.

But Rusty was faster.

The bullet from Rusty's gun knocked Kennedy back so hard, she spun halfway around before she crumpled to the ground, and no, no. No. For just a second—or maybe it was a year, for all it felt like—Gamble heard only nebulous clips of sound, muffled yells, shuffling. Someone was screaming, and he realized belatedly that the someone was him.

And then, time snapped back like a giant, vicious rubber band, thrusting him forward, and there he was, at her mercy. The primal part of him now dominating his thoughts and movements wanted nothing more than to go to Kennedy, but somehow, Gamble knew he had to ensure that the scene was secure, that the threat had been neutralized, first.

He swung toward the now-empty space where Rusty had

stood, his eyes telling his brain that Xander was still standing, that the room was swarming with detectives, each one of them with guns drawn.

Good enough, he thought, and not even the temptation (and, *oh*, it was strong) to murder Rusty with his bare hands was enough to keep Gamble from Kennedy. Six sloppy steps brought him to the spot where she had slammed down to the subfloor, dangerously close to the edge of the building. Reaching out to cradle her in his arms, he slid her to a safer spot out of sheer instinct. His brain knew the directives —*check airway, breathing, apply pressure to the wound*—but even as he performed them, he only had one true thought.

I will save her. She will come home.

"Kennedy?" Gamble asked, not giving one shit that his voice broke over her name. "Can you hear me, baby? I need you to talk to me."

Her eyes remained closed, her skin already frighteningly pale. Gamble forced himself to slap his fingers over her jugular, relief crashing through him at the presence of a pulse, fear skidding into it as he registered how thready and weak it was, and he ripped his T-shirt over his head, clapping it over the blood flowing freely from the bullet hole on the right side of her chest.

"Kennedy, listen to me. Xander's safe. Everyone's safe. But I need you to come back to me, okay? I need"—he broke off, and even with all the chaos and the smoke and the insanity around him right now, all he saw was her—"I need to you to come back. I love you, baby. I'm right here with you. Just come back."

"Gamble!" Hollister shouted, racing up to him and dropping to his knees on Kennedy's other side. "We have to get out of here, man. The second and third floors are on fire, and there's a fuckload of C-4 in this place. We can't wait for paramedics. We've gotta go *now*."

Adrenaline punched through Gamble's system in a fresh, cold burst. Kennedy wasn't stable. Christ, she was barely breathing. One wrong move and she could bleed out. She could die, and he'd be the only one of the two of them to survive.

And now her fate—whether or not she went home or went into the ground—was in his hands.

32

K ennedy...*I need you to come back...*
      Come on, baby...
      I love you...
Come back. Come back. Come back...

Kennedy's chest felt like someone had driven a freight train through it.

Her brain was hazy, like all of her thoughts were slow and full of wet cement, and wait, was she dreaming? No, her dreams never hurt like this, with so much pressure on her chest that she was sure it would cave in, and every last muscle in her body feeling like it had been used for batting practice by a whole team full of major league all-stars. Her head hurt, too, although in more of a thudding, far-too-much-tequila kind of way, and wait, was that why she felt so bad?

Why couldn't she remember? And why couldn't she see?

Trying not to panic, she searched her memory, calling up the last thing she could think of. Okay, yeah. She remembered seeing Gamble and Xander, remembered that they were supposed to do something important...a job, right?

Yeah, that was definitely it. Okay, good. She remembered being at The Crooked Angel, being worried, and then her cell phone had rung...smoke...something had been on fire...

Oh, *God*.

"Whoa! Whoa, whoa, whoa," a familiar voice ground out as white-hot pain careened through her rib cage like a wrecking ball on crack. "Take it easy. Don't try to sit up or the nurses will have a fit, babe."

Her eyes blinked open, and ugh, why was everything so freaking *hazy*? "X-Xander?" she croaked, slowly registering the salmon-colored walls and monitors and machines that all screamed *hospital room!* Damn, even her throat hurt like crazy, as if someone had spring cleaned the hell out of it with 40-grit sandpaper and industrial-strength bleach.

"Right here. Totally fine," came her brother's voice from her other side, and only then did she give up the I'm-getting-up ghost and lie back on...whatever it was she was lying on.

"W-w-where..." Yep. It was all she had.

Thankfully, Gamble translated well enough. "You're at Remington Memorial. You've kind of been through a lot, so do us a favor and try not to move right now, okay?"

She frowned—or at least tried to—and Xander laughed softly.

"I told you she'd be like this when she woke up. You might as well tell her what happened before she tries to get up and kick your ass."

Kennedy made a mental note to buy her brother a round of the best scotch they carried at The Crooked Angel as soon as she was well enough to get out of here. Her thoughts were growing less fragmented, although the pain in her chest was still as bright and intense as Broadway stage lights, and she turned her chin toward Gamble expectantly.

He exhaled, but didn't hesitate. "Do you remember being with Xander and Rusty in Skyline Tower?"

She nodded, because it was easier to conserve words. "He was...going to burn me."

"He was going to try," Gamble said, his dark eyes flashing even darker with anger. "Only, Xander took a run at him just as I got there with intelligence. Rusty"—Gamble paused. Breathed deeply. Then said, "He must have realized the place was swarming with cops, or seen Xander start to move and known he wasn't going to get the match lit in time. So he shot you."

Kennedy blinked twice, looking down at herself as if in slow motion. "Oh," she said, feeling as if she should've remembered that before she'd peered down and caught sight of the mass of snowy white bandages sticking out from beneath her pale blue hospital gown. Wait... "Must have realized?" she echoed, her brows tipping downward. "Didn't he tell you?"

"Ah." Gamble lasered a look at Xander, and for fuck's sake, she might've been shot, but she wasn't fragile.

A fact her brother must have taken to heart, because he said, "He didn't. Rusty's dead."

Okay, maybe Gamble was right to have wanted to give her a sec on this one. "He's dead?" Kennedy's heart beat faster, the monitor beside her bed calling her out in a series of upward spikes.

"Yeah," Xander said. "When I thought he was going to drop that match, I just snapped. I meant to tackle him to try and stop him, but he was really close to the edge of the building, and he went to step back to try and shoot me, too, but..."

Whoa. "He fell?"

"Twelve stories," Xander confirmed. "I didn't realize he'd

actually hit you until afterward." Xander's expression grew strained, and he scrubbed a hand over the dark stubble on his jaw. "Ken, I'm so sorry. If I hadn't fucked up, none of this would've happened, and—"

"Stop," she breathed. She must've looked pathetic—either that or she'd come closer to cashing in her ticket than she'd thought—because he actually did. "Not your fault. No arguing."

After a beat where Xander looked like he wanted to push his luck, Gamble said, "See? I told *you* she'd say that when she woke up, too."

Xander gave up a resigned nod. "I'm just really glad you're okay."

"Me, too," she said, and note to self: no laughing any time soon. That shit *hurt*.

"I'm going to go tell everyone you're awake." At Kennedy's questioning glance, he added, "January started a rotation. Everyone's been going back and forth between here and The Crooked Angel to help out. Except for the big guy, that is. His ass has been parked here the whole time."

Good Lord. "How long have I been out of it?"

"Twenty-nine hours, sixteen minutes, and"—Gamble checked his watch—"forty-two seconds. You were a bit of a mess when Quinn and Luke got you here, but your wound was closer to your shoulder than I'd originally thought. You had a nice, long surgery to remove bullet and repair the damage, which Dr. Sheridan assured me went incredibly well, then they kept you sedated in the ICU for a while. But the most important thing is that you're safe now."

Kennedy waited for Xander to squeeze her hand one last time and slip from the room before she returned her gaze to Gamble. "Thank you."

"For what?" he asked, brushing her hair away from her face with a gentle touch.

"Having my back so I could have his."

"You scared the fuck out of me, you know," Gamble said, and this time, Kennedy's heart lurched for a whole bunch of different reasons.

"Call it square for the flash-over?" she asked, and ah, there it was, her favorite tiny smile.

"Deal."

"And for the record, I love you, too," Kennedy whispered.

Gamble stiffened, his body stilling from the chair he'd dragged right up next to the side of her hospital bed. "What?"

"You said that, right?" Okay, so laughing might suck, but at least she could manage a smile without her chest threatening to implode. "I mean, I'm pretty sure I didn't dream it, but who knows what kind of pharmaceutical goodies are swimming around in my bloodstream right now."

Gamble huffed out a laugh. "Yeah, smartass. I said it. I love you. I am totally, completely, ridiculously in love with you."

"Oh, good." She reached for his hand, and there it was, immediately wrapping around hers, warm and constant and strong. "Because I'm totally, completely, ridiculously in love with you, too."

"Guess we're stuck with each other, then," Gamble said, his expression growing serious as he leaned in to brush a gentle kiss over her mouth. "I promise to always have your back, Kennedy."

Her smile grew bigger as tears filled her eyes, and all of a sudden, her chest didn't hurt at all.

"And I promise to always come home to you."